BY SUYI DAVIES OKUNGBOWA

Lost Ark Dreaming

THE NAMELESS REPUBLIC

Warrior of the Wind
Son of the Storm

David Mogo, Godhunter

MARVEL

BLACK PANTHER

THE INTERGALACTIC EMPIRE OF WAKANDA

△▽△▽

MARVEL

BLACK PANTHER

THE INTERGALACTIC EMPIRE OF WAKANDA

△▽△▽

SUYI DAVIES OKUNGBOWA

ADAPTED FROM THE GRAPHIC NOVEL
BY TA-NEHISI COATES

RANDOM HOUSE WORLDS

NEW YORK

Random House Worlds
An imprint of Random House
A division of Penguin Random House LLC
1745 Broadway, New York, NY 10019
randomhousebooks.com
penguinrandomhouse.com

LIBRARY OF CONGRESS CATALOGING-IN-PUBLICATION DATA
Names: Okungbowa, Suyi Davies, author. |
Coates, Ta-Nehisi. Black Panther.
Title: Marvel: Black Panther :
the intergalactic empire of Wakanda / Suyi Davies Okungbowa ;
adapted from the graphic novel by Ta-Nehisi Coates.
Other titles: Black Panther: the intergalactic empire of Wakanda
Description: First edition. | New York : Random House Worlds, 2025.
Identifiers: LCCN 2024052459 (print) | LCCN 2024052460 (ebook) |
ISBN 9780593723494 (hardcover) | ISBN 9780593723500 (ebook)
Subjects: LCSH: Black Panther (Fictitious character)—Fiction. |
Wakanda (Africa : Imaginary place))—Fiction. |
LCGFT: Science fiction. | Afrofuturist fiction. | Novels.
Classification: LCC PR9387.9.O394327 M37 2025 (print) |
LCC PR9387.9.O394327 (ebook) |
DDC 823/.92)—dc23/eng/20241115
LC record available at https://lccn.loc.gov/2024052459
LC ebook record available at https://lccn.loc.gov/2024052460

Jeff Youngquist, VP, Production and Special Projects
Sarah Singer, Editor, Special Projects
Jeremy West, Manager, Licensed Publishing
Sven Larsen, VP, Licensed Publishing
David Gabriel, VP of Print & Digital Publishing
C.B. Cebulski, Editor in Chief

Special thanks to Wil Moss

Printed in the United States of America on acid-free paper

2 4 6 8 9 7 5 3 1

First Edition

Book design by Edwin A. Vazquez

The authorized representative in the EU for product safety
and compliance is Penguin Random House Ireland,
Morrison Chambers, 32 Nassau Street,
Dublin D02 YH68, Ireland.
https://eu-contact.penguin.ie.

This one's for Chadwick.

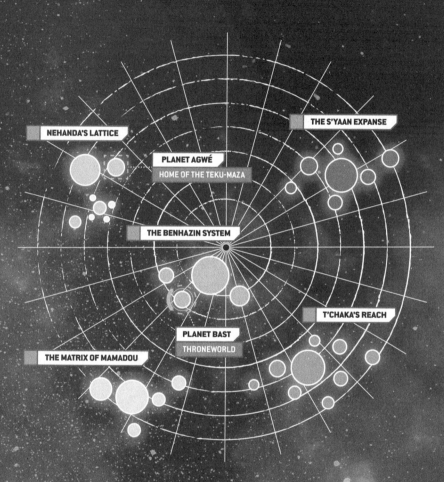

NEHANDA'S LATTICE

THE S'YAAN EXPANSE

PLANET AGWÉ
HOME OF THE TEKU-MAZA

THE BENHAZIN SYSTEM

T'CHAKA'S REACH

PLANET BAST
THRONEWORLD

THE MATRIX OF MAMADOU

MAP BY TA-NEHISI COATES AND ANTHONY GAMBINO.
ADAPTED BY EDWIN A. VAZQUEZ

MARVEL

BLACK PANTHER

THE INTERGALACTIC EMPIRE OF WAKANDA

△▽△▽

THE
PLANE OF WAKANDAN MEMORY

WELCOME, TRAVELER.

The story you're about to witness is a knotted string. It is a tale of galaxies, planets, and orbits, peoples wound one around the other, fates intertwined and inescapable. It is a tale of love and sorrows, of grace and retribution. It is a tale of heroes, each on their own path, each discovering that their path can never exist alone, but in community with others.

This is a tale of a truth that has always been known to us gods of the Orisha Gate, but continues to evade the human mind.

I, Bast, protector of Wakanda and giver of strength to my avatar, the Black Panther, have watched these journeys with interest. I was there, two thousand years ago, when a detachment from Wakanda Prime established a small, desolate colony on the outer edge of the cosmos. I watched these Wakandans, separated from their homeland and besieged by the whims of deep space, push their nation's traditional notion of self-defense to radical ends—investing in the conquest of all potential foes across the cosmos. I watched this small and starving colony, cut off from their parent nation, rise on the back of this bellicose ethic, transforming into an empire that now spans five galaxies.

This new spacefaring empire, upon conquering all within sight, now prepares to turn its acquisitive eyes on a fresh galaxy, one that contains something most precious—not just to me, but to the subdued peoples across the five galaxies, who wait upon me for anointing and restoration.

It is an unfortunate fate for a god to have, to safeguard both those who have done the conquering and those who have been conquered. It is unfortunate to be fated to anoint, to make avatars of men in whom I hold little belief. It is unfortunate to witness the subdued, with so little to believe in, continue to believe in me, holding on to legends and ancestral tales, hoping that I make a singular choice—a choice promised them in prophecy—to guarantee their restoration.

Therefore I, Bast, protector of Wakanda Prime and giver of strength to the Black Panther, have painstakingly risen to make that choice.

The tale that unfolds before you is that of three different men who will determine the future of this empire: a king who sought to be a hero; a hero who was reduced to a slave; and a slave who advanced into legend.

PART ONE

△▽△▽

CHAPTER 1

△▽△▽

GOREE

"COME BACK TO ME," the white-haired woman crooned.

The galaxy was inky black, all streaks and stars and nothingness. It was a cocoon that soothed and suffocated, that coddled and crushed. It was dread personified, a darkness that plagued and gave no assurances, save for the assurance of despair.

Anxiety brewed in the soul of the man, the dreamer, and panic bloomed in his sleep. He twisted and turned, sweat beading his forehead and dripping down his neck, face scrunched up in agony.

Yet, amid this consternation, the face of the white-haired woman was there, a balm. She lay next to him, shoulders bare, head in her hand, propped up by a crooked elbow. Concern was written all over her face, but that did not stop her from being beautiful. Her skin, smooth and dark and unblemished, reminded him of home, her shining eyes a guiding light, a way out of this hellhole and into the comforting arms of a warm place he struggled to remember.

"Come back home," the woman whispered, and he was filled with the desire to do exactly that. He reached out to touch her, gain hold of something real amid this etherealness. But he never got there because an eerie sound, loud and sharp, pierced the moment, and the woman was gone.

Rrrrooooo!

The man opened his eyes and sat up.

He was among people, like him and unlike him in many ways, all sitting on the floor of a cold, sterile room. Triangular windows brought little light in and opened up into nothingness: desolate land and planetary bodies round and large and far and near in the sky above the horizon. The vastness of space seeped from his sleep and stretched out before him, a dream he could not blink away. The stars offered no comfort, the constellations no familiarity; he could not shake the *wrongness* of his being among them.

Rrrrooooorrr!

Everyone in the room, though all different species, was dressed the same: a gray jumpsuit with snatches of blue, a label printed on their chests. He looked down and saw he was dressed no differently. They all wore the same tired, despondent expression, and no one spoke to anyone else. He mentally counted them in fives and realized they were about thirty, jam-packed into a room meant for half that number, which explained why he'd awoken to the sole of a boot resting an inch from his face.

Rrrroooorrrooo!

The man turned to the windows and peered closer.

Outside was a vortex. It was the only way to describe what he was seeing: a massive hole, surrounded by aircraft, groundcraft, and floating freighters, all hauling significant amounts of rock.

A mine, he realized.

Below, in the lower trenches of the hole—the *mine*—were beings all dressed like him. Some hacked at rocks with mechanized diggers, while others hauled large rock collections on their backs. There was something familiar about the rock itself, or about the mining, but the memory was too far to reach, buried somewhere too far back in time for him to place.

Rrrroooorrrooooo!

It took him a moment, but he began to piece it all together. The locked doors, the piercing sound that he now realized was an alarm, the room that increasingly looked like a cell, and beings that *increasingly* looked like fellow inmates.

But it wasn't just that this looked like a prison. It was the specific brand of imprisonment that dawned on him, that his bones recognized even though his mind's eye didn't. The complete absence of agency, a void where he ought to feel self-investment— a familiar song vibrating in his marrow. The walls here spoke a language his skin could understand: demanding, extracting, hard, hard labor.

Slave, he realized. *I'm enslaved.*

The hiss of a pressurized door caught his attention. He turned to see four guards dressed in combat suits, complete with helmets and red visors, fill the doorway. Their jaws, the only parts of their faces visible besides their eyes, were hard and set, teeth bared in disdain. They whipped out their stun batons, and the whirs of their windups echoed around the room. Electricity crackled at the baton tips.

"You heard the alarm!" the lead guard said. "Move, you dumb mules!"

The guard reached forward and stunned the first person before him. The prisoner, green of skin and eyes so large they occupied half their face, yelled in a language the dreamer couldn't understand and fell to the ground. The *bzzt!* of the shock did the job of jolting everyone else to their feet, some stopping to help their semi-stunned comrade up. The prisoner, on jelly legs, leaned against another.

"Let's go!" the lead guard screamed.

They began to file out of the room. The man, the dreamer, still not fully comprehending what was happening, remained seated on the floor. Consternation brewed within him. He wanted to remember more, to piece together this puzzle, but gaping holes opened whenever he tried, no glue to hold together increasingly disparate parts. Consternation turned into frustration, then anger, as he realized that these precious memories weren't simply *missing*.

They had been *taken* from him, from everyone in this room.

He was going to get them back.

"Hey!" The lead guard stepped up to him. "You."

The dreamer didn't look up. He felt his body tense, readying itself for the situation about to unfold. The memories of his mind might be far off, but the memories of his body had yet to forsake him. And how they bristled, stood at the ready, dared to be given a chance to demonstrate their prowess.

"You find my instruction confusing?" The guard was standing above the dreamer now. "Perhaps a clarification, then."

The guard swung his weapon, bringing electricity down on the dreamer. His arm and baton *whooshed* in a large arc, promising nothing but pain.

The dreamer's hand shot up and caught the guard's wrist mid-flight.

It was as if he were being controlled by a being from elsewhere—from else*when*—that understood him more than he understood himself. The memories of his body were swift, deadly, unparalleled. They responded without hesitation, his other arm swinging across and whacking the guard's jaw in an uppercut, sending him to the floor.

As the lead guard hit the ground, his comrades drew new weapons—firearms—and shot at the dreamer.

The dreamer's body moved, angled out of the way. The bullets whizzed past him, on one side and the other.

"Don't damage the emperor's property!" shouted the afflicted lead guard, still coming to his feet. "Stun! Stun!"

The guards' batons crackled. They advanced.

Property, thought the dreamer. *I am the emperor's property.*

This inflamed a new rage in his heart, rising up to his ears, filling his head. Now, he didn't even wait to be attacked. He moved first, tackling a nearby guard, grabbing his arm, and swinging the man over his shoulder. The man crashed into two others standing nearby. Another guard advanced too close, and the dreamer crouched low and swung his leg out, taking the man's feet out from under him. As the guard landed, the dreamer brought his knee down on his head, knocking him out.

Slowly, the dreamer picked out the fallen guard's baton. Electricity crackled.

"Don't you—" another guard started.

The dreamer didn't let him finish. Baton met chest, and the guard yelled. He squeezed his weapon, but the dreamer redirected his aim. The blast shattered the visor of another guard.

The dreamer picked up the firearm and looked at it. The weapon, so comfortable in his grip. It felt like power, a feeling he realized, now, was not at all alien to him. Sitting on that floor, clouded by doom, he realized how much had gone into ensuring that he and the others around him experienced nothing but paralysis. What he felt now was the opposite of that. As if he was *made for this*.

The face of the white-haired woman appeared to him again, her eyes unblinking, her gaze concerned, her unvoiced words pleading.

Come back home.

Indignation burned in his chest. His fellow inmates stared at him, confused, fascinated, enamored, their gazes asking the question their mouths dared not.

Surely, you would not?

Surely, I would, thought the dreamer. *And so should you.*

His grip tightened on the firearm. He turned, swiped one of the guards' keys, and jammed it against the sensor. The door hissed open. Then he was running in the hallway.

VOICES FOLLOWED HIM wherever he turned. *ATTENTION, ATTENTION! ASSET LOOSE IN THE SOUTHWEST QUADRANT! ASSETS ARE THE EXCLUSIVE PROPERTY OF EMPEROR N'JADAKA.*

That word again: *property.* It triggered something feral and violent in him, a desire for revenge of the most brutal sort. Whoever this N'Jadaka person was, just they wait until he found them.

He would make sure they paid for what they had done to him, for what they were doing to everyone here.

ASSET MUST BE RETRIEVED WHOLE AND ALIVE! FAIL TO ACT ACCORDING TO THIS DICTUM, AND ONE OF YOU WILL TAKE THE ASSET'S PLACE IN THE MINES!

Something about this announcement pricked him. Was this emperor so brutal that they were willing to sacrifice anything, their own people included, in service of this mine? No faces came to his mind, no names sprung to the tip of his tongue; *his* people were abstract but the dreamer could never imagine sacrificing them for something so trivial. What was so special about this place worth such a sacrifice? What was so precious about him, this *asset*, worth keeping intact?

Who *was* he?

A door ahead of him beeped. Someone was on the other side, trying to get into the hallway. He searched frantically for an escape route, and his eyes landed on a vent above.

The door opened. Guards piled into the hallway.

"I swear I saw him here a moment ago over the feeds," one of the guards said. "Where is he?"

Overhead, the dreamer crawled in the dark through musty vent corridors laced with delicate fibers that oozed an incandescent violet. He turned wherever he felt a stronger breeze, as in his head it meant an opening to the outside world might be close. He turned, turned again, and continued to follow this path for what felt like eons.

Then suddenly, one of the openings led downward. He slipped through and landed in a large space with one exit through a small grate that was sealed shut.

Flashing lights. Angry alarms. Aircraft whooshing by overhead, all in search of him. But he was not afraid. Rather he felt something else, like he had returned to a place he belonged. It took him a moment to realize what this familiar feeling was: freedom.

Whatever this place was, he was not meant to be here. Wherever he was headed—though he did not know where—had to be much, much better. There, he had to be someone useful, maybe even *important*. He could feel it in his bones, and the farther he got away from here, the more this feeling would grow and the sooner he would have all his questions answered.

This realization fed strength to his legs. He leaned forward and prepared to jump down when voices filtered up to him.

"One more year out here in Goree," the voice was saying, "and that's it for me."

Three guards, chitchatting. Another set of three on patrol. He wasn't worried about them. Something else registered with him.

Goree. That was the name of this place, wasn't it? He mentally shelved that for later. Once he was free of here, he would remember that name, find a way to return, and do for others what he had done for himself.

"No more mules," the guard continued. "No more mines. No more—"

Okay, that was enough. He yanked the vent grate off its hinges. He would not abide one more person being referred to as a *mule*.

The dreamer dropped the metal grate. It sailed down and smacked the guard before he could complete his sentence.

The dreamer slipped down, sailing more quickly than the grate, faster than the others could look up, and landed on the shoulder of a second guard, bringing him to the ground along with the third standing next to him. In the same falling motion, he trained his firearm and squeezed the trigger multiple times at the patrolling trio.

He got all three.

He ran.

The platform ahead was vast, stairs and hangars, takeoff and landing strips. All he needed to do was get his hands on one of those aircraft. He had confidence in the memory of his body that he could fly such vehicles. It felt like something he'd done before.

But ahead, the static aircraft suddenly blared to life. Lights snapped on and washed over him. Guards poured out of every nook, firearms raised.

They fired, fired, and fired. He dodged, somersaulted, jumped. His body wriggled and writhed in evasion, rounds missing him by inches, their danger signaled by the holes on nearby walls and scorch marks on the floor behind him.

Home. He was determined to get back there.

Alas, even he was human, and soon enough, one of the bullets found his back. A stun round, he realized, that merely numbed.

Home. He staggered forward, tried to regain his balance. More stun rounds rained around him. He turned and shot back in the general direction of his pursuers. The air felt thicker, harder to breathe. But the aircraft, the one that was going to take him *home,* it was oh so close.

Another round struck him in the calf.

He fell, firearm skittering across the platform. The ground smelled of dirt and oil and the soles of boots. Smoke from the singed fabric wafted up to him. Vision faded. He wanted to crawl forward, to reach the aircraft, to go home.

The white-haired woman was there, urging him on.

"Come home," she crooned.

Then everything went blank.

CHAPTER 2

△▽△▽

THE
MACKANDAL

SOMEWHERE IN DEEP SPACE, the engines of the *Mackandal* thrummed.

The cruiser, a spiderlike monstrosity with a sleek fore and wings it did not need to fly, drifted between systems, outside the reach of the Empire. Within the ship, officers of the Maroon Rebellion worked away in preparation for something impending, something big.

The command center, bathed in a dusk-like glow, lit up as a door zipped open and Taku, the chief intelligence officer of the starship, sailed in.

"Intelligence report from the colony, Captain," she said. Taku, one of the many Rigellans on board, spoke with an air of authority few of her species possessed. Minuscule as she was, merely a few feet tall, Taku stood at attention, her chin jutting out of her oval-domed panther helmet, amber eyes stern.

Captain N'Yami, commander of the starship and the most important Teku-Maza in the rebellion, sat in her armchair on the command center, one leg crossed over the other.

"Goree?" she said.

"Yes, Captain."

She sat forward. "What do you have?"

"Trouble for them," said Taku. "Opportunity for us." She tapped her handheld and projected a holo image to the captain. "Goree is a major Vibranium node for the Empire, but their complement of security is severely lacking."

N'Yami scoffed internally. This was the thing about empires: Anything so large was destined to become unmanageable and therefore filled with cracks. It irritated her to no end that the Empire seemed to project its might based on nothing but tales of conquest, conquests that it was only able to achieve by underhanded means, when victims were at their weakest or blindsided or betrayed. The Empire was vast, sure, but it was still a mouth, and every mouth could only bite off and chew so much before it became too full to do anything else.

"We knew they would one day overreach," said N'Yami. "The Shi'ar War seems to have done it." She glanced at the screen. "This may be our moment, Taku."

The projection showed an overhead video feed from a prison cell at the Goree mines, filled with inmates. Or *slaves,* if she was being honest. In one moment, they sat unbothered. In the next, there was an alarm, some disturbance. Shots were fired. Then the guards began to attack someone off camera. Yet, surprisingly, each guard was knocked back into the frame, unconscious.

"We're not alone in that conclusion, Captain," said Taku. "Just last week, we received another report of an uprising at Goree."

The feed switched to another. Three guards approached and encircled a man. Wielding a baton, the man took on all three, knocking them down with a combination of strength, skill, and angry confidence.

"How many men?" asked N'Yami.

Taku pointed to the screen. "One."

DEEP IN THE BELLY of the *Mackandal,* M'Baku and Nakia prepared for jetoff in the armory. They were already dressed in the Maroon panther armor, a simulacrum of the ancient Wakandan battle suit—panther helmet with embedded communications, black bodysuit with violet ballistic lining, tactical gloves sporting retractable claws. They were surrounded by assault firearms of all shapes and sizes, from which they selected their preferred gear.

"How do we know they'll even fight?" M'Baku asked. He was a big man with a gruff voice and the air of a battle-hardened general who didn't abide fall-behinds. A Maroon leader through and through.

"We don't," said Nakia. She, on the other hand, was the more agile of the pair, lithe and slick and assassin-like. She spoke differently, too, with a lilt to her intonations that betrayed the fact she didn't have the same origins as most of the Maroon Rebellion: She had never once been the property of the Empire.

"But if we're ever going to go beyond these ragtag hit-and-runs, we need more soldiers," she added. "And we've got intelligence that Goree is a factory for them."

They strapped in their chosen firearms, grabbed their panther helmets, and strutted down the hallway, headed for the hangar.

"I don't know, Nakia," said M'Baku. "It feels desperate."

"And when have we not been desperate, M'Baku?"

They got into the elevator and zipped down to the hangar. Below them, rows upon rows of zulu aircraft awaited. Beside each spacecraft was a squadron of Maroons, dressed similarly and waiting at the ready.

"Who knows if we'll truly find any soldiers down there worthy of the Maroons?" Nakia mused aloud. "But what we do know is this: We're not the only ones who are desperate."

The elevator stopped and the door opened. They stepped out.

"Hmm," said M'Baku as the Maroon soldiers stood to attention. "Let's hope you and Captain N'Yami are right."

CHAPTER 3

◬▽◬

GOREE

THE DREAMER EXISTED in a state of fitful consciousness. He remembered being carried, dumped unceremoniously on the floor. He remembered the white-haired woman staring at him, silent, then shaking her head, disappointed. He remembered being lifted again, roughly, and dragged down corridors. He remembered downward motion—an elevator. He remembered being dumped on harder, rougher ground. He inhaled dust, sneezed, and licked his lips. They tasted metallic.

A boot prodded his side, more gentle kick than nudge.

"Get up," someone was saying. "Start digging. They whip all of us if one of us is slacking."

Shuffling sounds surrounded him. He blinked, sat up. Everything was too far and too near at the same time. His calf and back where the stun rounds had hit him felt numb. He rubbed them and glanced around.

Jagged stone rose above him on all sides, going up forever. He was deep in the center of the mines. Fellow inmates—slaves— trudged around, lugging filled bags. A constant grinding sound came from the mechanized diggers operated by the others like him.

"You no hear him?" someone else was saying, less patient. "Get up!"

Something heavy clanked next to him, raising dust. A mechanized digger.

"That's your own," someone—large, brash, dressed like an inmate—said. "Start that corner, finish all that section, since you so strong." The inmate kissed his teeth and left.

The dreamer, still dazed, rose and followed instruction. He grabbed the digger, plunged it into the general vicinity of the corner, and pushed the button. The machine roared to life and dug into the crust, kicking up rock dust and sending vibrations down his body.

He welcomed the vibrations, passing through his arms to his shoulders, ribs, thighs, tingling his toes. It woke him up, the rush of adrenaline. It was the only thing that made him feel sane, alive, in control of his senses. When he was digging, the visions that plagued him—the bleak space, the white-haired woman, the place called home that he couldn't remember—they vanished, his mind filled with nothing but vibrations.

The dreamer tried to piece together what he knew. *Enslaved in a prison mine*: confirmed. *Home somewhere, not here*: confirmed. *Fighter in former life*: confirmed. Now, the hard part: What did the empty spaces between mean?

He pushed the digger harder, *chug chug chug,* as if to dig up the missing parts. The holes in his memory, in the dirt, grew even larger. He gritted his teeth. *Chug chug chug.* Who was he, then, if he only knew voids? A man of voids, in the belly of a rock, in the void of space. *Chug chug chug chug.* What was the point of trying, of escaping, if he couldn't remember? *Chug chug chug chug.* What was the point?

He didn't know how long he was there, covered in dust. Could've been hours or minutes. It was thirst, a patch of dryness in his throat, that brought him back down to his corner of the mines.

He shut off the digger's engines and looked up. It was dark—it was *always* dark down here, it seemed. Lights from the freighters twinkled above. The pit was still full of fellow inmates working, carting dirt and rock and sand. Sounds of diggers filled the air. The ground vibrated from their combined influence.

The dreamer put down his digger and headed for the water drum, where a fellow inmate poured out small helpings for thirsty workers. He grabbed a bowl and held it out. The inmate poured water. The dreamer drank.

It wasn't like the water he knew, even though he couldn't quite remember what that tasted like either. He just knew it tasted different, *wrong*, as if this water was *made* and not a natural resource.

Nevertheless, he held out the bowl again for another helping. He was really thirsty. But just as he put the bowl to his lips, a three-fingered hand appeared out of nowhere and slapped it away, spilling the water all over his chest. The bowl clattered to the ground.

"You new here, so Daoud tell you how this work," the owner of the hand said. The dreamer recognized this voice as the same person who'd handed him the digger earlier and given him a spot to work on.

"Daoud *king-mule*," said the man, who it turned out was named Daoud. "You need something? You ask Daoud first. Nothing—not even water—move without Daoud."

The man before him was a mountain, or something close to it. Unlike his fellow prisoners of the same species—red-eyed, narrow-faced, flatheaded, wide-jawed, and three-fingered—he was of the broader variety, with a head that seemed to rest solely on his shoulders and a demeanor that spelled danger.

The dreamer was of one mind. Here was someone clearly angling for a fight. *Just walk away.*

He turned. Daoud's eyes followed him as he took a few steps forward.

"Did you hear Daoud, mule?" The inmate's hand was already moving backward, preparing for assault. "Daoud say—"

Okay, that's enough, the dreamer thought. *Let's dance.*

He caught Daoud's punch midair and, without waiting for further assault, threw the man against the barrels of water. Daoud crashed into the barrels, knocking both over. He rose slowly, rubbing his neck, seething, anger coming off him in waves.

The dreamer by now had learned how to listen to the memories of his body. He settled into it now, leaned back, crouched, fists clenched, arms stretched out in a fighting pose.

Come if you must.

Daoud lunged for him, moving fast, a hefty mountain bent on brute force. The dreamer leaped, pushing off his haunches and flying over the advancing juggernaut.

But Daoud, it turned out, was just as skilled as he was fast. He caught the dreamer by his ankle as he flew and slammed him down to the ground.

For a moment, the dreamer expected impact to be fatal. His head, slamming into the hard ground. All the breath leaving his chest. His eyes swimming. Blood dripping down his temple. But it was more akin to a punch in the gut that knocked the wind out of him, leaving no other real wounds.

"Daoud try telling you nice-like, boy." Daoud grabbed his neck and lifted him off the ground. "Daoud be peaceable, but you push Daoud. And Daoud push back!"

The dreamer grabbed sand and threw it into his attacker's face. Just as Daoud was reeling, he slammed his elbow into the man's face, following through with a kick to his mouth.

Inmates had gathered around them both now, cheering and cajoling, a few expressing dissent as the dreamer pummeled his attacker. Blow after blow after blow on Daoud's face, which was now leaking blood. Daoud became too dazed to respond but that didn't stop the dreamer, who'd now given in to the memory of his body—the wrathful side that raged at the injustice, the oppression, the inability to find from within who he truly was.

Somewhere amid the blows, a voice interrupted.

"Are you so lost?"

The dreamer paused, fist hanging midair.

"Are you so lost," the voice repeated, "that you will let them reduce you to this?"

The speaker stepped forward. It was a fellow inmate, an elderly man with hair draped over his face. His gait was slow and measured, regal, though he looked strong enough to work down here in the pit.

"What do you hope to prove by killing him? That you truly are a beast?"

Even the man's tone was stately. He stood over the dreamer as he rose from Daoud, knuckles bloodied, patches of red staining his uniform.

"They have stolen your name, your culture, your god," the inmate said. "Do not let them steal your mind."

As he said this, a team of guards rushed into the pit in a storm of boots. They grabbed the dreamer and pinned his arms behind him. He didn't resist. He couldn't take his eyes off the old man who was like a statue, watching and unmoving. For a moment, he was unsure if the man was really in the mines or a product of his imagination, his subconscious filling in where his memory could not.

As they led the dreamer away, the elderly man watched.

"Do not let them," he kept saying. "Do not let them steal your mind."

THEY HAVE STOLEN your name, your culture, your god. Do not let them steal your mind.

Back in the cell, the dreamer started to realize something: He wasn't dreaming. This was real. The prison, the slave pit, the mining, the inmates, the guards. The fact that he was a mule, a *slave*, the property of an emperor.

Your name. The fact that he could not remember it.

Your culture. The fact that he could not remember home.

Your god. The fact that he could not even remember who he was to pray to for respite.

Despair began to wash over him, seeping in slowly until it took over his whole chest. He felt cold, colder than the cell afforded. His muscles tightened. An anxious fear grabbed hold of him and wouldn't let go.

What if he never made it out of here? What if he never remembered? What if this were to be his life—forever?

Promise you'll come back home.

Somewhere in the pit of this despair, the white-haired woman appeared again. She lay next to him, head resting on the back of her hand. Her face before his was soft, compassionate. She placed a hand on his crooked elbow.

"Promise you'll come back home . . ."

And he realized, now, that this wasn't a dream either, but something real. A memory. It was the one crack in the tightly shut fortress that was his missing memories, the one sliver of light spilling hope over the rest of this dark room.

So he grabbed this hope with both hands and held tight.

"I promise," he whispered.

Somewhere in the ether, the god he'd forgotten must have heard him, too, because as soon as he spoke, there came an ear-rending explosion that threw him to his back. Then a blinding flash of light filled the cell.

CHAPTER 4

△▽△

GOREE

"GO, GO, GO!" screamed Nakia.

Landing on this scraggly rock undetected had to be up there with one of the most tactically challenging tasks she'd ever had to accomplish. Sneaking a squadron of Maroons through the canyon and across the open rift that allowed them to access the mines unseen was yet another. But this part—confrontation, combat, decimation—this was the part that was always toughest. Her enemies, the guards she was surely about to face, served the Empire willingly, but was she snuffing out their chances at redemption?

And yet, the moment she, M'Baku, and the rest of their team blew open the doors of the first cell, as the despondent eyes of the enslaved inmates, stripped of all light and life and personhood, stared back at them through the hazy smoke, she had only one thought: *They deserve it.*

"Light them up!" she screamed.

The Maroons lifted their firearms and squeezed.

The Goree guards, easy targets who were thankfully separated from the inmates, were unable to draw their firearms before they were hit. All five, down in a matter of seconds. Smoke filled the cell.

At the other end of the cell, the door had opened. An alarm

blared and a much larger squadron of guards poured through, crowding the small holding unit.

"M'Baku, cover me!" screamed Nakia, and then she was off. She slid to the center of the room, right into the core of the prisoners. Then she pulled out her dome shield and slapped the device on the floor.

"Get low!" she yelled, pushing down the heads of as many inmates as she could. Then she slapped the device. It whirred, beamed a blue, transparent dome over her and the prisoners, and slammed shut with a soft *pop*.

Now, M'Baku, her eyes said, holding her comrade's, delivering the command she couldn't voice across the shield's sound barrier.

M'Baku lowered his firearm and reached behind him, retrieving a rocket launcher. He balanced the launcher on his shoulder, aimed it at the advancing guards behind the dome, and fired.

The explosion shook the ground. The heat, though milder within the shield barrier, washed over them in a wave, fire forming a clean curve as flames licked the edge of their half sphere of protection. Smoke filled the room once again.

When it cleared, not a single guard was left standing.

"Covered," said M'Baku.

Nakia scrambled to her feet and stood at the pulverized door. Weapon in hand, she turned to face the still dazed inmates.

"You're free!" she said to them. "Go! Fight!"

It took a while for the command to register. She could see the train of thought pass through them. How quickly their muscles twitched in response to her perceived authority. Their hesitation and suspicion were clear once the impossibility of the command sunk in: They were being asked to be . . . *free?* They were struggling to grasp the concept of freedom after being locked up for so long, battered, broken. They realized they were *free,* free. They could leave this pit, this hell of despondency, and never return.

Only then did they begin to rise more quickly, helping one another up, shuffling out of the cell as fast as their tired legs could carry them. Soon the cell was practically devoid of living people save for an inmate who stood above another sprawled on the floor.

"What are you . . . ?" Nakia began, and then realized who it was.

It was the man from the video feed, the one Taku had shared with them about the latest uprising. The man who'd single-handedly taken out multiple guards and almost made the greatest and only escape from Goree in the history of the five galaxies. He stood there, rock-solid, staring at his fellow inmate on the ground, a man almost twice his size who seemed to be only half alive. The floored prisoner was clearly injured, but she couldn't tell from what—the guards, the explosion, a previous altercation?

Without warning, the man bent low and pulled his fellow big inmate up, hoisting the man's arm over his shoulder. The big man groaned.

"Leave him," Nakia said. She had to clear this area and reconvene with M'Baku and his group, who'd likely congregated by their exit craft by now.

The man seemed not to be listening. He continued to drag his comrade, however slowly, past the blasted door, down the hallway.

"Maroon girl right," the big man said through a broken nose and bloodstained teeth. "Leave Daoud! Daoud want no help from you, mule. Daoud kill you!"

More guards were arriving. The inmate seemed unperturbed. Nakia turned and fired back at the guards, slowing their progress down the hallway.

Soon they were at the exit point, the zulu craft open and ready. More prisoners rushed out, embraced by the Maroons at the other zulus. Nakia pointed the inmate and his friend toward M'Baku's craft, its door open and inviting.

"Go, go, go!" One of M'Baku's Maroons urged them on. He balanced a rotary multiple-barrel cannon on his hip, aimed it at the hallway, and fired, stalling the guards' approach. M'Baku joined in and kept the advancing, increasing Goree squadron at bay.

Bullets and explosions and smoke and screams pierced their eyes and ears and hearts.

Once Nakia was sure the inmate had climbed into the zulu with his friend, she turned her attention to the others still coming out of the doors, including her fellow Maroons. Goree's defense aircraft had joined in the fight now, shooting from above, so they had to run for cover before they could reach the escape crafts. Even the freighters had been commandeered and turned into guard-carrying platforms from which Goree guards fired.

For the most part, the Maroons had yet to lose any important soldiers. A few inmates had already fallen, but there was little Nakia could do to help them—they were already gone. Now if they could just get everyone that remained alive out . . .

A Maroon ran from the farthest cover to M'Baku's zulu and was hit twice: once near the elbow, once on the thigh. He fell on his chest, his firearm skittering away. He tried his best to rise quickly, to take cover once again, but it was too late. A Goree guard was too close and the Maroons were too far.

Bast be with you, brother, Nakia thought.

But she thought too soon. Out of nowhere, from M'Baku's zulu, flew a double-headed ax. It struck the advancing guard in the face, and he crumpled to the ground with little else but a choking sound.

Someone was running from the zulu into the heat of the fire, heading for the fallen Maroon.

It was the inmate from before, the rebel who'd piqued Nakia's interest. His face was set in a way Nakia had never seen, as if he knew this fallen Maroon personally. Nakia wanted to scream at him, to yell, "Get back! What are you doing? Are you crazy?" But he was already standing before the Maroon.

He grabbed the fallen man's arm and yanked him up. The Maroon, clearly one of their better soldiers, looked weightless in the hands of the rebel inmate, who slung him over his back.

Nakia swallowed. *This man is strong!*

Then he was running.

Nakia cast a glance at the far side of the field where M'Baku was reloading. He, too, glanced at her. A silent message passed between them.

You know what we must do, his eyes said.

We protect our people, Nakia responded.

"Cover them!" M'Baku commanded.

All the might of the Maroons turned on the Goree squadron. They poured every piece of ammunition they had to provide cover for the running man. They rained fire and force on their adversaries, an umbrella over their comrade coming home.

"Come on!" everyone in the zulu cajoled, the door about to close. "COME ON!"

Nakia made her way backward to the zulu while emptying every clip in her firearm in the direction of the guards. *Come on, come on, come on!*

And then they were in the zulu and the door was finally shut, the bullets from the guards striking the metal outside in clinks that sounded like raindrops on a water surface.

Nakia tossed her firearm aside and hopped through the crowded zulu into the cockpit. She leaned onto the throttle, which sent the aircraft shooting forward and yanked everyone back, including herself. She regained her footing and flipped every switch she needed to, smashed every button that required smashing, and leaned even harder onto the throttle, sending the zulu off the ground and into airspace.

Sixteen Maroon zulus took to the darkness beyond the sky, thousands of Goree bullets following in their wake but never reaching them.

Nakia didn't know how long she stood there, breathing hard, contemplating how narrow their escape had been. She crumpled to the floor, exhausted. Only then did she notice the big prisoner from before, the one who referred to himself as Daoud. He also lay on the floor of the cockpit, opposite her, breathing heavily. He grinned, or maybe it was a wince. She grinned back.

Through the still open cockpit door, the groaning sounds of rescued inmates filtered in, interspersed with M'Baku and his crew offering reassurance and reprieve to the wounded. The injured Maroon, who she now recognized as a member of M'Baku's squad, sat still, weak, tired, but seemingly grateful just to be alive. He was looking up at someone, a bit of awe in his stare.

Nakia followed his gaze. The rebel inmate stood just as still as she'd seen him back in the cell on Goree: rock-solid, muscles taut, as if he was afraid to move, as if moving would cause everything around him to melt. He was staring out the window, watching the galaxy zip by, or at least whatever the darkness outside allowed them to see.

She had so many questions. For him, about him—who he was, where he came from, why he was here. She was sure he'd be unable to answer, seeing as how the memories of all inmates were stolen before they were put to work on Goree. She was more interested in how those answers, whether he had them or not, might serve a bigger purpose—for her, for the Maroons, maybe even for the galaxy.

Such matters would have to wait. First, they had to get home, to safety. And perhaps bring him to N'Yami on the *Mackandal*.

"Daoud no want help." The big inmate in front of her was speaking through bloodied teeth again. "Daoud kill—"

"Shut up, Daoud," she said.

CHAPTER 5

△▽△▽

THE
MACKANDAL

N'YAMI, COLD BEVERAGE in hand, stared out the window of her quarters on the *Mackandal*. It was something she liked to do in her downtime, lose herself in the endless nothingness of space, the occasional streak of light or flash of movement reminding her that there was life—*lives*—out there. In that way, space was like the viscous liquid in her cup, thick and murky, its secrets hidden away.

But truthfully, she liked to look upon the void because it reminded her so much of her home planet, Agwé. Parts of it, at least, the places where the lights of their aquatic abodes couldn't power through and reach. Teku-Maza elders—who, like many under imperial rule, passed on the lore, myth, and history of their lands via oral tales—told imaginative cautionary tales of how easy it was to get lost out there, how swiftly one could get swept up by unseen dark forces. *In the beforetimes,* they said, *the Ancient Jengu, our genetic forebears, protected us from such predators. They held our stories, our histories, and passed them down from generation to generation.* But eons had passed since then, and there were fewer Jengu now. Even more predators lurked in the shadows and waited for nonchalant stragglers to fall into their sharp-toothed jaws. It was wise, then, to remain in the light.

N'Yami blinked. All that was a long time ago, too, before the Empire had locked its teeth into the Teku-Maza homeland and never let go, before the Ancient Jengu were hunted into extinction by imperial forces. She herself had been born off-world, away from Agwé, her memories stripped, never to be recovered. It was the search for those memories that had forced her to return to her ancestral home. Those same oral tales from the elders led to her forming the Teku-Maza Revolutionary Guard, which in turn helped liberate the planet. Agwé might be free now, but the elders' tales were still cautionary. There were still predators waiting in the dark, jaws open.

This was why she had returned to the rebellion. Someone had to do the same work here: be their Ancient Jengu, pass on their oral tales and histories, hold on to belief. First, for the Maroons, then for the five galaxies. The Maroons were her family now, the rebellion her new home. *This* was why she was here, why she fought.

This was why it was worth risking what she was about to do.

The door to her quarters slid open.

"Yes?" she asked without looking.

"Captain N'Yami." It was M'Baku.

She turned. Standing alongside him was the rebel inmate, the man of legend that every Goree rescuee couldn't stop talking about, and now even her Maroons couldn't stop talking about. He'd showered and put on new clothes. His injuries had been patched up. Still, he possessed a dour expression, one that seemed lost and sad and angry and determined all at once.

"Thank you, M'Baku," she said. "You may leave us."

She sipped from her cup, waiting for M'Baku's back to disappear with the closing door. The rebel didn't even look up. She recognized it, this learned behavior. Everyone who'd ever become a slave of the Empire, including her and her people, had once been this person. Enslavement was like acid. The thing burned itself into the very skin and twisted whatever it found there, leaving a tangled mess of hurt and harm that could never be extricated without eviscerating the person who wore it.

"May I offer you anything?" she asked him. "Something to

make you more comfortable?" When she'd first made her escape, she remembered wanting nothing but a wet towel draped around her at all times. Despite being Teku-Maza, and therefore amphibious and cold-blooded, she'd found that she had yet to grow accustomed to living on land, especially the dryness of the mines. Being in the overprocessed air of spacecraft still made her pores feel clogged and parched.

The rebel didn't ask for anything. He continued to stare into despondency.

"No, of course not," she said. "You are Nameless. What need have you of comforts? This is what you're thinking, yes? I understand." She walked over to her control console and tapped a button. "I worked the mines once. But I tell you, comforts are not all bad, soldier. It's really a matter of source." She pointed to the holo image that had sprung up from her console. "*This,* for instance, gives me great comfort."

It was a visual recording of his endeavors at the Goree escape: flinging the ax, striking the guard, cutting through bullets to pick up the fallen Maroon. She observed his face as he watched, waiting for a response. It was a crumb, just like how she'd called him *soldier* was also a crumb—the layout of a path toward a lost memory. She was trying to see if any of these sparked something, a recognition of self that could only come from within.

The rebel remained as plain faced and unmoved as when he'd come in.

"One slaver killed, one Maroon saved," she said. "They say you carried one of your own under a hail of fire. Impressive."

He said nothing, and so she put down her cup and changed tack.

"I am told that you know who we are, that you are aware of what we do." She approached the wall that held her personal safe. "And that you are eager to join the battle against the Empire."

She punched her code into the wall. The safe appeared.

"Know that my Maroons have committed their lives to the Empire's destruction," she continued, entering the safe's code. "But also know that it is not enough for a man to declare what he would die fighting against. He must know also what he lives to fight *for*."

She retrieved the case containing a storage drive she had prepared just for him. Hand-selected recordings—holos, images, writings—from the Maroon Archival Project, or MAP. Only a selection, of course. The Maroon Archival Project itself—a compilation of all secret oral, visual, and written records passed down since the rebellion began—was too large to contain in one drive. It was an antithesis of the Empire's own vault, where they hoarded the stolen memories of the Nameless. Rather, MAP was maintained across a system of disconnected archival hardware and backed up in physical memories. There were Maroons dedicated to memorizing as much as possible. In no way, therefore, could the Empire ever steal their history or memories ever again.

In this drive, N'Yami had chosen all that the rebel ever needed to know about the Maroon Rebellion: not just *how* they were formed, but *why*, and why they continued to fight against the Empire even in the face of seemingly insurmountable odds.

"You know," she said, "M'Baku was adamant against bringing you in."

"You don't say," the rebel replied sarcastically. N'Yami chuckled.

"Indeed. He was once Nameless, an enslaved miner, just like you. He feels responsible, therefore, to buttress why he believes you to be impulsive, obstinate, and unable to accept authority. He believes these things make you a poor fit for a Maroon soldier, if any soldier at all."

The rebel grimaced, silent.

"Nakia, however," N'Yami continued, "now *she* is open to the idea of bringing you in. And yet even she remains hesitant. You know why?"

The rebel shrugged.

"Because even though they know that you can fight, they—like me—struggle to see what you fight *for*."

His body language acquiesced, which warmed her heart. She'd

noticed little qualities like this while watching his recordings and realized where she'd seen such traits before: in MAP, from tales of legends prior. There was something about the way that this man moved and fought and protected that required *blessing*, the kind of anointing only bestowed by gods. The Teku-Maza did not quite believe in the same kinds of gods as many others, but N'Yami had traveled far and heard many stories, some of which she'd come to claim for herself. This rebel, complicated as he may be, belonged in those stories. Who was she to stand in the way of the opportunity to put him there, in that rightful place?

"And so I ask, my son," she said. "What do *you* fight for?"

The rebel finally looked up. His eyes sparkled. In them, she could see recognition, even though this recognition had no surety of memory behind it. It was conviction, assurance that he knew what he was looking for, where he was going, *who* he was going to.

"Home," he said. "I fight to get back home."

And that was enough for N'Yami.

"Where is home?" she asked.

He lowered his gaze again. "I do not know. I feel it more than I can recall it. I cannot remember . . . anything." He paused. "I do not even know my own name."

N'Yami nodded. *Not to worry,* she thought. *I have just the right name for a man like you.*

"Of course." She placed the drive in his hands. "They took that from you, took it from us all, and left us with only scraps of some other life." She punched a button on her console and the stars and planets of five galaxies surrounded them. A swirling delight. "So at night you are left to wonder, *What was I before this? Who did I love? And what became of them?*"

N'Yami returned to the rebel. His eyes were shining now, brimming with tears. She was finally convinced that he possessed the possibility she hoped for: the correct balance of hardness and softness, a mollifiable obstinacy, a potential for leadership.

The panther god, Bast, may have anointed another man—the emperor who now sat on the panther throne—as her avatar, but there had to be someone better. She could imagine the goddess's inner turmoil, being forced to give credence to that poisonous man and his poisonous empire, her name and worship employed in service of erasure and colonization. But if Bast did indeed listen to her supplications every day, she would agree. Her avatars of yesteryear were proof that the ancient goddess had yet to forsake them. Their job was to present her with better, worthier options.

Before N'Jadaka, there had been such a man, an apple of Bast's eye whose actions did not bring her name into disrepute. One who worked to forge rather than destroy, a leader and protector who, much like this rebel, arose from humble beginnings.

So here she was, standing before a slave who could be king and legend. N'Yami knew just the name for someone such as this.

"We are the Nameless, my son," she said. "Orphans of the cosmos, the flotsam of the Empire. But now is the hour of our restoration." She tapped a finger on the drive in his hands. "The new names we bear are taken from the legends of our past. So that we, marooned in the Empire, are Nameless no more." She stepped up to him, face-to-face. "And so to you, I give the name of a man who was born a king and died a hero." She placed a hand on his shoulder.

"Arise, T'Challa."

CHAPTER 6

△▽△▽

MOONBASE CUDJOE

THE MAN NAMED T'Challa crouched in the darkness, awaiting a signal. Around him, swamp reeds swayed gently in the midnight breeze. A night animal cooed in the distance, and another brayed, and another cackled. He could neither see the animals nor tell from where the sounds originated. He couldn't even identify the species by sound. All he could perceive was what the dim light afforded—the offerings of a small moon overhead north, peeking through the canopy above and setting the forest awash with soft light. It was unclear if this would be the only moon to rise tonight or if there would be others.

He shifted his weight on his knees and tiptoes, angled his body this way and that, trying to get his ear in the right position to hear just that much farther, to gain a sense of the enemy and when they would make their move.

"Wait," came M'Baku's voice. "No movement until the signal."

He wanted to tell the lieutenant that he knew what he was doing, that he didn't need such direction. His body, it was obvious now, held memory, which his mind couldn't access. And in a way, he didn't really need his mind. His body was mind enough.

Movement. In the reeds.

"Steady, Goree." M'Baku's demanding voice.

T'Challa ground his teeth. He hated being called that, the name of his former prison. He could understand that the Maroons didn't yet know exactly how to address the newer rescuees. They had to find a way to differentiate them from the other Nameless rescued from other mines, who it turned out also couldn't remember their names. Addressing each rescuee by the name of the place from which they'd been saved seemed like useful shorthand, especially when the freed Nameless had yet to choose new names. But T'Challa found it distasteful. Yes, he'd yet to tell M'Baku about his meeting with N'Yami and her bestowal of a king's name upon him, and that he'd eventually accepted said name. Still, there was no good reason for M'Baku to keep calling him *Goree* like he called other Nameless. What difference was that from being called a mule?

T'Challa shifted on his feet, trying to quell his burning irritation. The swamp water at his feet twinkled. Ripples spread around him and disturbed the reeds.

"Stop. Moving," M'Baku hissed.

That did it. T'Challa reared on his haunches, yelled, and pounced.

In his annoyance, he hadn't quite heard the enemy approach. But his body knew danger, sensed it before his mind could, and suddenly there he was, in the midst of three, four attackers. Like the guards on Goree, they held weapons of various kinds, everything from stun batons to firearms to throwing spears. Unlike the guards at Goree, they were quick, flitting from one location to another, the grass no obstruction to their movement.

But the grass was no obstruction to him either, the swamp water no challenge. He flitted with them, caught them when they went left, right, attempting to find vantage points of attack. He did not need a weapon to strike, taking out the one with the firearm first, dodging the first thrown spear, and the second, before taking those enemies out as well. Bearers and weapons splashed into the understory. He went for the stun batons, blocking their swings with the combat shield deployed by his wristlet. He took them down one by one before they could each swing twice.

Once he was done, standing in the swamp forest, heaving and

sweating, darkness enveloped him completely and the simulation disappeared. Bright lights filled the room.

"You don't move until I give the command!" M'Baku stomped into the combat practice chamber, his footfalls and the weight of his boots straining the projection plates. They bent from the force of his anger. "You stay put until I say so! How many times must I repeat this lesson? How many times will you heed only your *own* plans?"

T'Challa stood firm, let the lieutenant come up to him until they were almost chest to chest, forehead to forehead.

"I don't need a command to know when to move," T'Challa said. "I cleaned them out, did I not?"

"Yes, you did," M'Baku replied sarcastically. "You cleaned out the enemy, and then you cleaned out your own people as well."

It took a moment for T'Challa to see the projected spear sticking out of M'Baku's back. He looked behind M'Baku, and true to word, the rest of the Maroon force he'd been training with—he'd forgotten completely about them, to be honest—stood behind M'Baku, all in various states of digital injury, projected blood seeping from various parts of their bodies where bullets had hit.

M'Baku waved an arm at the projected spear. It fell from his back and vanished into the simulation program from whence it came.

"You call yourself a great fighter, a great weapon," he said. "And maybe you are—who am I to deny your impact? But you wasted all that time and energy attacking the wrong unit. That was a dummy force, sent to distract. While you engaged them, the program sent us a real force. And now all your fellow Maroons are dead."

T'Challa grunted. Was it his fault if others couldn't look after themselves?

"I am one person," said T'Challa. "I cannot be everywhere at all times."

"No one is asking you to," M'Baku pressed. "All we ask is that you not just be a good fighter, but a good soldier, too. And a good soldier uses *this*." He tapped his temple. "Not *this*." He jammed a fist into his palm.

T'Challa grunted again. "Fine. Is that all?"

M'Baku growled, frustrated. "That's training for today. We pick up tomorrow."

T'Challa walked away without waiting to be dismissed. He knew M'Baku would call him back. He wanted an opportunity to let this man know what his name was *not*.

"Goree."

T'Challa turned, rebuttal at the ready.

"We're all angry," said M'Baku before T'Challa could get a word in. "There's not a single Maroon you'll meet who doesn't carry anger in their heart, like you do. But we do not let that anger cloud our judgment. We find a way to channel that rage into something useful for our people. Because if you do not, it will kill them, and then it will kill you."

M'Baku said things like this all the time. *Fight, Goree,* he'd say, *but not for yourself. Fight for more than just to go home,* he'd say. *Fight for us.* He'd begun saying these things from the very moment Nakia had brought T'Challa to join the new Maroon training program, with N'Yami's blessing. This was not their first clash as T'Challa chafed against new rules, new constraints. All three knew he didn't need combat training, but for some reason, they'd decided this. It made T'Challa's chest burn. He shouldn't have to endure being treated like a child—he was a great soldier!

But M'Baku's latest words struck him this time. *It will kill them, and then it will kill you.*

He couldn't remember what had happened in his past—how he'd gotten here, where his people were—and this forced him to wonder: *Did my rage kill them?* Was it this rage that sentenced him to death in the Goree mines? Was this rage the reason he'd ended up here? Will this rage kill these Maroons, too, the same people who'd risked so much to give him back his freedom?

These were good questions, and he would do well to ponder them. But that was for another time. In this moment, there wasn't much else he could offer in response to M'Baku's rebuke, so he offered an answer to a question unasked, the only question he had an answer for.

"My name is T'Challa," he said, an announcement, and then left the chamber.

THE WHITE-HAIRED WOMAN came and came and came.

Sometimes, she arrived at night, as he slept. Not much changed about how she showed up in his dreams. It was often the same scenario: Together they lay in bed and spoke intimately of things they'd been through and seen together. He told her of his dreams, of the things he wanted most in the world, and she smiled and affirmed his words and told him that his dreams were noble. He told her of how he needed to bring them to fruition, and she reached out, placed an affectionate hand on his cheek, and bid him to go while imploring him to return.

Come home, T'Challa. Come home.

He knew, now, each time he awoke, that this was no ordinary dream but a fragment of memory rearing its head. How much of it was true recollection and how much was his imagination filling in the blanks, he didn't know. Surely she couldn't have called him T'Challa, a name only bestowed upon him a few fortnights ago? Surely she'd have referred to him by his own given name? Perhaps his mind had done the good work of substituting a name he knew for one he didn't. He couldn't even remember the contents of what they talked about, only the feeling that they'd discussed things that mattered immensely to them both.

Who was she? Why did she have such a hold on his mind? Why was she so crucial to his recovery?

Why *this* memory? How did it connect to everything else?

He went back to bed and dreamed of her some more.

"DO THE NAMELESS ever get their memories back?"

Captain N'Yami looked up from the holo screen she was working on. "Hmm?"

"Nameless," T'Challa repeated. "Do we ever retrieve our memories?"

The captain was an unusual woman. T'Challa was unfamiliar with the Teku-Maza, the species from which she hailed. There weren't many Teku-Maza among the Maroons at the moment, save for one or two recent rescuees T'Challa himself hadn't gotten to know. The captain had the same pale greenish skin as them but wore her gray-white hair in a more elaborate updo decorated with various bands of metal, some the same as those piled high on her neck. The only thing he knew about her species was that they were amphibious, which was why the captain always seemed to have a gleam of sweat on her forehead. ("It's not quite sweat," Nakia told him once. "It's a type of bodily fluid that helps her pores adjust to surface dryness.")

T'Challa wondered if the ability to thrive underwater took the edge off the pressures of life. The captain never seemed stressed, even though he was sure that leading the Maroon Rebellion came with indescribable strain.

She regarded him now with an inordinate amount of calm. "T'Challa, that is not why I invited you here."

He nodded. "I know why you called me."

"Yes, you likely do." She was firm but not unkind. "Do you care to explain?"

"That I don't need the Maroon induction program because I already have the skills of some of your top fighters? No, I do not care to explain."

She nodded slowly. "But clearly M'Baku thinks you do, and I'm inclined to agree with him."

"Because?"

"Because though your fighting skills need minimal improvement, your *people* skills are sorely lacking. Apparently you're in the habit of not listening to your comrades and therefore getting them killed?"

"That happened *one* time."

"Once is enough."

T'Challa scoffed. "I can't be responsible for how others fare."

"Ah." N'Yami made a disapproving sound. "Now that's a contradiction if ever I heard one."

"How so?"

She leaned in. "How did you get here, T'Challa?"

He frowned. "I don't understand the question."

"How did you get rescued?" She angled her head. "Wasn't it by our Maroon force taking responsibility for your rescue? And wasn't it by you taking responsibility for your fellow inmate, and then later, for an injured Maroon?"

T'Challa said nothing.

"We are all responsible for each other." She relaxed in her chair, still regarding him. "And part of me is convinced that you used to be responsible for much more than just yourself. One doesn't learn to fight the way you do in defense of themselves alone."

She returned to her work on the holo desk. Her words made him think of the white-haired woman.

"We've agreed that you will continue with the program," she said. "And I've assured M'Baku that you will be more amenable to his teachings upon your return." She paused to look up at him. "And you will be, will you not?"

"What does Nakia think?"

The question seemed to strike her out of nowhere. "I'm sorry?"

"Nakia," he repeated. "Does she think I should continue the program, too?"

Among Maroon leadership, Nakia was the only one who'd so far shown a balanced approach to his predicament. While M'Baku was impatient with him, and N'Yami patient—perhaps to a fault, in a manner T'Challa found infantilizing—Nakia seemed to approach his situation evenhandedly. She'd once told him that she thought his skills were too important to go to waste training in simulations, that she'd rather have him with her at the strategy desk, discussing attack, defense, and infiltration approaches and formations. She'd even informed M'Baku and N'Yami that this might be a better way to curtail his impulses to go solo; if he had a hand in planning things, he'd be less inclined to make an ill-advised move.

T'Challa thought he would always make a move if he saw an opening to strike, his body's memory responding to a threat before it manifested. But he still preferred Nakia's approach.

"Nakia has informed me of her thoughts," N'Yami said. "I have taken them into consideration. But my decision remains the same. You will return to the program and stay there until I determine otherwise." She paused. "For your own safety."

T'Challa gritted his teeth. There it was again, that infantilization. But he nodded in acquiescence.

"Good." She returned to work. "Dismissed."

He was halfway out the room when she said, "And no, we do not remember."

He turned. "What?"

"You asked if the Nameless ever recover our memories." Her eyes were trained on him. "Not a single one of us has recovered our original memories since the Empire began its project of decimation and erasure. All we know right now of our galaxies, our technologies, our own selves—all that is our culture, tradition, legacy—is what we have been able to piece together through the hard work of those who came before us. In secret, and at great cost, they passed down oral tales, recordings, archival documents. The Empire destroyed all it could, our memories included, but some things survived, and therefore so have we."

She balled her fist and gently placed it on the table. "That is why memory remains at the center of everything we do here. Every fight, every raid, every mission—we get closer to retrieving our original memories, regaining something that leads us to a solution. In this way, our victory begins the moment the first of us remembers." She pointed to him. "Dwell on that in training." Then she went back to work.

CHAPTER 7

△▽△▽

MOONBASE
CUDJOE

IT TOOK WEEKS before Nakia came into the training chamber one
day and said, "All right, that's enough."

T'Challa was in the middle of a focus session with a few fellow
Maroon inductees from the Goree rescue, as well as other fresh
inductees. They were to infiltrate enemy territory, a fortress at the
top of a mountain, which involved them climbing what T'Challa
guessed was the wall of the chamber. As he moved from handhold
to handhold and foothold to foothold with ease, leaving most of
the team behind (but every now and then, remembering N'Yami's
and M'Baku's words and stopping to wait for his lagging colleagues), Nakia's voice cut through the program.

The simulation ended and the lights came back on. They had
indeed been climbing one of the chamber's walls.

"What is it, Nakia?" M'Baku emerged, impatient.

She jutted her chin toward T'Challa. "I need him for something."

"What?"

She eyed M'Baku. "Strategy."

Even from where he was still hanging off the wall, T'Challa
could see disagreement in M'Baku's posture.

"Is this for the mission I think it is?" the commander asked.

Nakia shrugged. "I guess so."

"You want *him* on that mission? Are you trying to get us all killed?"

"I said I need him for questions about *strategy*. Whether he will be on the actual mission is the captain's decision."

M'Baku held back a grunt, then shook his head. He spoke loudly, so T'Challa could hear. "All right, Maroon, you heard the general."

T'Challa descended with agility, slipping past his comrades as quickly as he'd left them behind. He landed on the floor with cat-like reflexes, lithe, silent, deadly. His comrades held back gasps. Nakia looked impressed. M'Baku pretended not to see.

"The rest of you, on with it," he said. Without looking at T'Challa, M'Baku turned off the lights and resumed the training sim.

Outside in the hallway, Nakia explained.

"They say you're killing it in the flying sims," she said. "Apparently you've surpassed the best scores of the best pilot we have here."

"Who's that?"

She lifted an eyebrow.

"Oh."

"Took me a few training rounds to get them that high. I hear you dusted them off after a few tries."

He shrugged.

"Oh, don't be humble now," she said. "It's the very reason I came to get you. I'm thinking of a plan of approach for our next major mission, and I need someone to bounce ideas off of." She leaned in. "Off the record, of course. Captain isn't really buying the narrative that you're getting better at working with us."

"I *am* getting better."

"I know." Nakia wore a soft smile. "So *prove it*."

The hallways were filled with various species of Maroons hailing from one or the other of the five galaxies conquered by the Empire. He'd learned all about it as part of his training—the induction program, in addition to combat, included history, geography, and spirituality.

There he'd learned that humans like him, Nakia, and M'Baku—descended from the first visitors from Wakanda Prime who later formed the Empire—dominated the Maroon population. When the Empire began mining the Benhazin System for Vibranium and extended their operations into the neighboring galaxy now known as T'Chaka's Reach, they encountered the Rigellans and conquered them. Taku was one of the survivors, though she'd never been a slave herself. She'd escaped and roamed the galaxies as a trader before joining the Maroons. It was from these lessons he'd also learned that once upon a time, Rigellans could control minds, but they'd lost that ability after their memories and knowledge were stolen by the Empire. For them, reclaiming their original memories—and in tandem, their history—was the key to recovering that ability.

It wasn't just the variety of species coming together to usurp a powerful force that warmed T'Challa's heart, though. Rather, it was the sight of various kinds of worker uniforms. He'd spent so much time with the soldiers and combat units that he often only thought of his new allies as a force, rather than simply . . . people. People who just wanted to survive. Most of these workers in the hallway didn't wear combat suits like he and Nakia did but were dressed for other duties: engineering, medical, cleaning, food prep, garbage collection. These were people who went home to families, who worked for the Maroon Rebellion because it helped them survive economically but also kept them alive in other ways. They weren't at the forefront of the war but were dedicated to the cause regardless.

They went up a transparent elevator to Nakia's strategy room. From this high up, Moonbase Cudjoe was a sight to behold. Orbiting the planet Oshun—a rogue planet in the Zanj Region of Nehanda's Lattice—it was the last place the Empire would look for the Maroons. Its surface was too scraggly and rocky for proper habitation, which was especially why it had been chosen. Most of the Maroon infrastructure was built into the rock formations themselves, mimicking the surface structure so much so that it was impossible to scan and find them with regular equipment. Besides, who would look on a small, throwaway moon when the planet itself was right there, looming over them all in the distance?

But the moon itself was beautiful as well. Little lights pockmarked the surface, each piece of Maroon infrastructure lighting the crevice into which it was built, reflecting colors all over the surface. Oshun cast a large and constant darkness over the moon, too, which made it a perfect hideout. Anyone approaching from the planet would take a while to orbit the moon to fully scope it out, by which point the Maroons would've found them out and prepared a defense.

They got out near the top of the building, and soon they reached the strategy den—Nakia's term for the chamber. Screens and holo projections filled the room, a full team already at work. The team was small, a handful of Maroons T'Challa didn't quite recognize except for one person.

"I hear they call you T'Challa now," said the young Maroon, smiling as he walked past the duo when they entered. He wore a protective brace that connected his shoulder and upper arm, and another from hip to foot. It took a while for T'Challa to realize where he'd seen him before.

"You're the one—"

"From the Goree rescue, yes," he said. "Can't go back into the field until I'm fully healed, so they put me here for the time being." He put out a hand, which T'Challa grasped. "My name is Anika, but they call me Nik." He leaned in slightly. "By the way, I never got the chance to thank you . . ."

T'Challa shook his head. "It's no problem." He eyed Nakia and said, "We do what we do to protect our own."

Nik looked to a smiling Nakia. "He's joining us, General?" When she nodded, Nik beamed and turned back to T'Challa. "Welcome to the strategy den!"

When he left, Nakia said, "Seems you're making an impact already."

T'Challa harrumphed. "He's young. He'll find out soon that war is no fun."

She stared at him, amused. "Sometimes you speak like a wise old sage. And then in the next moment, you act like a petulant little child." She chuckled. "It would be frustrating if it wasn't a bit endearing."

T'Challa found his chest warming up in a way he couldn't explain, so he said nothing in response.

"All right then," she said. "Time to show you what the adults do."

THE LAYOUT OF the imperial target was nothing like T'Challa had ever encountered, not that he could remember much from his former life. He'd resigned himself to going wherever his mind led, trusting the answers it could provide and relying on his instinct for all else. But deep down, he wanted more. Each time something hovered near the surface, almost within reach, he stretched with his mind, trying to grasp it, claw at it, only to feel it dissipate, a cloud of smoke floating through his fingers. The loss felt continuous, the emptiness larger and larger every day, the harm and hurt fresh.

But what was he to do? He was once a slave, and at least in one way, he'd been rescued from that imperial grip. But as long as his memories remained elusive—as long as his past remained smoke, slipping through his fingers—he was still in the Empire's control, still a slave.

In this strategy den, though, his mind offered no answers, no information beyond what Nakia was explaining. The layout of the imperial compound filled the screen before them. Nakia and T'Challa stood up front, staring at it, while the rest of the team worked behind them. To T'Challa, every angle seemed covered by defenses, every approach facing an obstacle.

"I have . . . nothing," he conceded.

"That's all? No suggestions?"

"It's . . . a good plan?"

Nakia laughed. "How is it that the one time I want some canny, recalcitrant braggadocio, I get the humble and acquiescent T'Challa?"

He chuckled. "Those are a lot of big words for saying you think me weak."

"No, I'm—"

"I'm not weak. I'm just . . . unsure?"

"Well," said Nakia. "That's even worse."

He turned away from the screen and led her aside.

"Can I tell you a secret?" he whispered.

Her expression became slightly guarded, like she didn't want to know what this secret was.

"I don't think I do all that well with this . . . strategy," he said. "I don't remember enough about myself to know if I'm actually good at it . . ." He paused. "Listen, everything I do, my body already knows how to. I don't think too hard, I just follow. It's all intuition. I need the heat of the moment to know what to do, how and where to move. Behind closed doors? Not so much." He sighed. "I know you brought me here to hear my opinions but, if I'm being honest, I already knew I wasn't going to be much help. But I really—desperately—needed a reason to get out of that training. And if possible, to stay out."

"Ah," she said. "So it's not nerves, then."

T'Challa frowned. "Nerves?"

"Yes. You know, the legion of tiny wires in your body . . ."

"I know what nerves are, Nakia."

She gave a small laugh. "*I know what nerves are, Nakia.* So serious all the time." She patted his upper arm. "You need to learn how to make jokes. Or at least take one. Otherwise this Maroon life won't be much fun for you."

"I know how to take jokes," he said, but she was already moving.

"Right!" she announced, addressing the strategy team. "Apparently we won't be getting new insight today, so we're sticking with our current plan of approach." She motioned toward T'Challa. "We'll also be sticking with the new team member as well." She eyed him. "Seeing as we have no choice."

The Maroons laughed. T'Challa didn't.

"Prepare the strategy holo for presentation to the captain and lieutenant," Nakia said. "Good work, team!"

They slapped one another's palms in loud handshakes. The atmosphere was joyous, even though T'Challa thought there was nothing to celebrate. But perhaps this was an opportunity to take Nakia's advice, to be lighthearted and invest in camaraderie.

So, when Nik invited T'Challa back to his quarters for celebratory drinks with a few others from the strategy den and a couple of other Maroons, he agreed. Once inside the cramped quarters, however, T'Challa realized that "a few friends" was actually a full-blown party. He suddenly found himself among boisterous Maroons he was meeting for the first time, some having spent quite a while on the moonbase, some new rescuees like him.

His body, it turned out, offered no instinctive memory here, forcing T'Challa to navigate this party alone. He stood by himself in a corner, clutching his drink tight but never taking a sip as a carousel of people swung by. It all went the same way: Nik, out of earshot due to the loud music—"Tunes inspired by Ancient Wakanda!" one nearly drunk Maroon screamed into his ear—would point toward him and say something. The listener's eyes would widen, and T'Challa would realize they'd just learned that he was the rescuee from Goree who'd saved Nik, that he was the one of whom grandiose tales were being spun. Then they would slink over and attempt to strike up a conversation.

Each interaction was its own thing to behold. Between the differences in species, language, gender, and temperament, T'Challa could never really decide how to proceed. One Maroon, a Rigellan, kept running fingers down his arms while asking about his time at Goree. Another—a human—after learning about his training, kept trying to teach him.

"Did you know that the S'Yaan Expanse was so rich and beautiful that they nicknamed it after a folktale from Ancient Wakanda?" The heat of the man's whispers clouded T'Challa's ear as he leaned in. "The Empire didn't even go there for Vibranium! It's why you don't find S'Yaans at the mines—the imperials finished them. They won't teach you that at training, though!"

"I'm going to get another drink," T'Challa said. "Want one?" He'd learned, through observation, that it was courteous to ask.

"Please," said the man, handing T'Challa his cup. T'Challa cursed under his breath as he went and got fresh beverages. The man was ready with another tale.

"After S'Yaan, they went for Matrix of Mamadou," he said. "You know them Kronans, the stone people? You won't see them up here—they like to work in the down-belows, like back in Mamadou."

"I'm going to go over there and be by myself," T'Challa said, and walked away.

It was like this for the most part. The only good conversation he had was with a new Teku-Maza rescuee, a woman finding the party just as challenging to navigate as he was. They shared little about themselves, but he learned from her that the Teku-Maza were the most recent additions from Nehanda's Lattice. The capture of their home planet, Agwé, had become one of the biggest sparks for rebellion against the Empire. Next to humans, she said, the Teku-Maza and the Revolutionary Guard N'Yami established there, had the biggest role to play in this fight.

"Makes sense that N'Yami's captain," she said, and T'Challa couldn't disagree.

Someone loud came into the party then, greeting everyone in a rambunctious manner.

"Ah, Daoud," said the Teku-Maza.

T'Challa turned to look. It was indeed his old enemy from Goree, now healed and surrounded by fellow Maroon inductees.

"You know him?" he asked the Teku-Maza woman.

"*Everyone* knows Daoud," she said, shaking her head and walking away.

T'Challa stayed out of eyeshot, learning from nearby whispers that Daoud had been invited by a friend of a friend of a friend of Nik's, and had come straight from his own training sessions. There were a few other familiar faces from Goree, though the names were new. Daoud was rare among the recruits, claiming a name for himself even before the rebellion. T'Challa had learned that Maroon leadership had specifically placed them in separate training groups to prevent a repeat of their skirmishes back on Goree. He didn't think they should've bothered. He had no use for this man, hadn't even thought about him since their liberation.

As soon as he thought this, Daoud turned and spotted him. A wide grin spread over the big man's wide face. T'Challa sighed.

Ah, well. Perhaps Maroon leadership had it right. Perhaps their paths were destined to always cross.

"Madman!" Daoud said, strutting over with a handful of fellow Maroon inductees. "They say they call you T'Challa now." He made a disapproving click at the back of his throat. "They give great name to man so tiny?"

His fellow Maroon inductees guffawed at the joke. T'Challa didn't see what was so funny, but then he remembered Nakia's petition: *Be more lighthearted about things, okay?*

Okay. He could try.

"Perhaps they should have named you 'grain,'" he said.

Daoud looked confused, as did his comrades.

"What is . . . grain?"

"The smallest piece of . . . you know . . . things."

"Hehn? And is to be my name because . . . ?"

"You know, because your brain is . . ." T'Challa pressed thumb and forefinger together and squinted through it. "*This* small."

Daoud punched T'Challa so hard in the cheekbone that T'Challa was sure he'd eaten his tongue. The drink in his hand spilled all over him as he fell. The big man and his comrades laughed and left

T'Challa sprawled on the floor, much to the amusement of the rest of the party.

T'Challa lay there, blinking at the ceiling. *Well deserved,* he thought. Jokes, it turned out, were not a part of his repertoire. This was what he got for listening to Nakia. Never again.

△▽△▽

CHAPTER 8

MOONBASE
CUDJOE

"THE SHANGO ARRAY holds something of great importance to the Empire," said Nakia. "A survey of the nature of the defenses around the array tells us so."

The day of mission strategy presentation to Maroon leadership had finally arrived. Nakia found T'Challa tucked in among the other faces and ranks that came to the briefing. He hadn't been much involved in preparations other than asking lots of questions about the mission itself, but she hoped that doing so had taught him far more about the history between the Intergalactic Empire and the Maroon Rebellion than he would have learned arguing with M'Baku in a training simulation.

"*Something of great importance* does not seem like a good reason to pursue a mission," said N'Yami. She leaned on a nearby table in the room that held M'Baku, the strategy team, and the most experienced Maroons among the field squadrons. They all gazed at the holo presentation, which showed a visual of the Shango Array's sprawling façade as well as an approximate floor plan.

"No, it does not," Nakia agreed.

"So you have more information?" asked M'Baku.

"We have suspicions," said Nakia. "But we think they're credible."

N'Yami nodded. "Walk us through it."

Nakia progressed the holo. Now it highlighted various points on the array's façade.

"For quite a while—we're talking many, many years—the Empire retained something of note on this base," she began. "They had anti-craft defense systems and fighter craft on standby. Then, one day, *poof,* all gone. The base was simply left with as skeletal a staff as possible. Practically unmanned."

"So they moved whatever was there," said M'Baku.

"It's what you would think," said Nakia. "Or perhaps it's what they *want* us to think."

N'Yami frowned. "You think otherwise?"

Nakia poked the holo so that it shimmered. "We *have* been hitting a lot of Empire assets for a while. Perhaps they're giving us something to hit that has no significance."

N'Yami seemed confused. "I fail to follow your reasoning, Nakia."

"As do I," said M'Baku. "Is this or is this not a location we should be targeting?"

Nakia looked exasperated.

"Listen," she said, "I think that with these many defenses, whatever was there had to be of great importance to their conquests across the galaxies. No doubt about that. But our research shows that they'd never had to move anything major from that array at any time in the past, even during some of their more embattled wars, like capturing the Matrix of Mamadou. This place suddenly being stripped of an entire imperial force and any large-scale weaponry can only mean that whatever is there doesn't need to be moved in order for it to be effective—it's useful over long distances—and maybe it's something that can fend for itself?" She pointed at the holo. "The Empire *never* leaves its assets undefended, no matter how unimportant. So either this is of the utmost least importance, or it's so great that any further protection would be an overconcentration of resources."

"I'm leaning toward unimportant," said M'Baku.

"Then why protect it so much all this time?" Nakia shook her head vigorously. "I'm of the belief that whatever was there is still there. We can answer the question of *why* they've left it once we get it. But I believe this is an easy mission that, best case, gains us something valuable and, worst case, will be another blow to the Empire."

"There's another likely option," said T'Challa.

He'd spoken so little throughout the meeting that everyone turned, surprised.

"*Now* you decide to contribute?" asked Nakia, an eyebrow raised.

"What's the option?" N'Yami asked, her words gentle.

"A trap."

M'Baku chuckled. "I typically don't agree with this one"—he motioned toward T'Challa—"but I have to say, he's not wrong."

"Maybe," said Nakia. "We've dealt with traps before. Worst case, we retreat."

N'Yami rose and paced the room, weighing the options. A beat later, she said: "Nakia, do you have *any* suspicions as to what's in there?"

She nodded. "I didn't want to say earlier, but . . ."

"Why not?"

Nakia angled her head. "Because . . . you might laugh?"

This did get a chuckle out of N'Yami and the rest of the room before the captain said, "Well, we've gotten the laughter out of the way. Nothing to lose now."

Nakia progressed the holo. Images of a war—craft, artillery, explosions—filled the room. She knew some, like T'Challa, might recognize the Empire's Askari, but not the winged species with which they were at war. But N'Yami did.

"The Shi'ar War," she said softly, almost a whisper.

A collective hush fell over the room. Nakia could understand the gravity of the images, the despondency that arrived with them. The Shi'ar War, the Intergalactic Empire's biggest triumph—

defeating the only other major expansionist power in the five galaxies—was a surfeit of chaos, doom, death.

At least that was how her imperial education had taught it. *Hard-fought, bone-aching battles against the most advanced force in the history of the cosmos,* the learning materials said, *and yet we prevailed.* It was there she'd first learned about her emperor: N'Jadaka, the Black Panther, Avatar of Bast. *As commander of the imperial army,* the materials said, *N'Jadaka led Wakanda in the fight against the fierce Shi'ar warriors. He forcefully dethroned the Shi'ar Majestor and destroyed the M'Kraan Crystal, that which gave the Shi'ar their conquering capabilities.*

"What has this got to do with the Shango Array?" N'Yami asked, bringing Nakia back to the present.

"Bear with me while I offer a theory," she said. "Now, our research shows that the earliest instance of the Empire improving its guard over this base—introducing defenses *three times* the functionality of other similar bases—was right after the Shi'ar War. My thesis is that, after defeating the Shi'ar, the Empire brought something back from their home planet of Chandilar and put it on this base."

"A weapon?"

"Not quite. More like . . . a jewel. Of unknown origins, older than history, and whose destruction could cause the annihilation of the whole universe."

M'Baku cocked his head. "That sounds like myth."

"That's because it is," said N'Yami, turning to Nakia. "You're talking about the M'Kraan Crystal."

Nakia progressed the holo. A large pink crystal, practically unremarkable in every way other than the fact that it emitted its own light, filled the space.

"The histories lied. It was never truly destroyed. The Shi'ar took it to their homeworld after destroying the M'Kraan people," Nakia continued. "It makes sense that the Wakandan Empire has it now after winning against the Shi'ar."

"While the Empire's records are undoubtedly inaccurate, there are other legends. And they share the same end result. The M'Kraan Crystal has been lost for eons, Nakia," said N'Yami. "Our records in MAP state that, according to Shi'ar legends, their god K'ythri gifted it to his wife, Sharra, and she lost it in the deep voids of their godworld."

"You of all people know how much legends are ridden with half-truths, Captain," Nakia pressed. "I'm convinced that the Wakandan Empire holds the crystal, because everything we've thought about this base makes sense if we think about it in terms of the crystal. Empire captures crystal, protects it while trying to siphon its power, fails to do so—if they'd succeeded, we'd know; we'd be the victims—and then abandons it afterward."

"But what *is* its power?" asked M'Baku.

Nakia shrugged. "We don't know."

"So it could be a useless artifact?"

"Absolutely not," said N'Yami and Nakia at the same time.

"It's the oldest artifact in the known universe," said Nakia, "surviving all of time's ravages. Legend says that it holds a galaxy of its own within its white-hot energy. We may not be able to siphon this power for use, but that's not to say the crystal is *powerless*. Even if we get ahold of it just for bargaining power, that could be a huge coup for what seems like a fairly straightforward mission."

"Either way," N'Yami said, "I remain doubtful that they have the crystal. That base is too small to hold such an artifact. Shi'ar history says it was *gigantic*."

"Then a small piece, perhaps?" said Nakia. "Whatever it is, the Empire has *something*."

N'Yami paced again, quiet. "Fine," she said finally. "Plan the heist. But we move only after we complete every other mission on hand. I don't want to risk our best resources on something so unsure."

△▽△

NAKIA TOOK T'CHALLA and the rest of her team to a local bar to celebrate their mission being approved. She did this often, and yet it still surprised the Maroons who worked with her. Maroon life didn't allow for much celebration beyond major conquests or key events. But she'd since learned—from her imperial education, surprisingly, one of the few good things to come out of it—that good camaraderie was just as crucial to working well as a team as skill.

The bar was a small, ramshackle affair put together by a Maroon who volunteered in the kitchens. Drinks flowed. Popular dance music from the imperial capital played—an Ancient Wakandan tune of praise and redemption bastardized by a young singer from Planet Bast. Nakia stood with T'Challa in a corner, laughing as Nik sung over the music, slightly off-key but with abandon.

"This is . . . good," said T'Challa out of nowhere.

Nakia looked up into his face. Stubble covered his jaw. Someone had to tell him to shave; scruffy wasn't the most flattering look on him. She wanted to, then decided that though she was the closest person to him on this base, she wasn't his lover.

But maybe, perhaps, some piece of her wanted to be.

"Oh yeah?" she teased. "Which part?"

He shrugged, unsure. "I remember some things about myself. I don't remember much fun, though. Much joy. But this . . ." He gestured toward the bar with his drink. "This is fun. This is joy. I'll now have a memory like this. I'm happy about that."

Nakia smiled, watching his face. He didn't look at her, but she knew he was aware of her attention. She watched his body language shift uncomfortably, struggling to process her gaze. She let out a small laugh.

Perhaps it was this that she found attractive about this man. Strange he was, even to himself; a mystery a part of her wished to solve. So despite his sometimes brash attitude and often stubborn countenance, a part of her wanted to grow closer to him, and she could tell that a part of him wanted that, too. Underneath all that hard exterior, there was still softness. He was still as human as anyone else, and his body still wanted affection.

But then she remembered why they were here, what was at stake. She remembered that if this succeeded, his memories would return, and he would remember someone else—somewhere else—that he loved just as much, if not more. He'd want to leave, to return to said person and place. And once again, that would leave her high and dry and alone.

She didn't want that for herself and she didn't want that for him. So, despite the flutter of warmth that gathered in her chest when her body touched his, rising to her neck as heat, she composed herself. There were things bigger than the two of them, and she would just have to stay focused on that.

She lifted her drink and clinked it against his.

"To fun," she said.

He looked at her and smiled, perhaps with understanding. "To fun."

CHAPTER 9

△▽△▽

MOONBASE CUDJOE

THE MAROON REBELLION took a long time getting to the Array mission.

First was the need to complete the most pressing mission: the raid and destruction of one of the Empire's most crucial Vibranium depots. The rebellion was running out of Vibranium for attack and defense weaponry and other types of equipment, and thus required a new batch of the ore. However, Nakia managed to bake a secondary reason into the mission: improve cloaking technology for the fighter craft to allow for a stealthier attack with the Array mission. (This was the *one* suggestion from T'Challa she'd taken on board so far.) Needing so much Vibranium to make new body plates for a whole squadron of zulu crafts meant they were forced to hit a bigger depot than initially planned.

The mission went successfully. So successfully, in fact, that the information gathered from the depot led Nakia to realize that there was a certain Ras politician they could track down who could give them some useful information on the Shango Array and what it held. So they raided the first place he was believed to be hiding—a throwaway house of amusement under imperial protection in the S'Yaan Expanse. They didn't find the politician but gained further intel about his ownership of a musa-class freighter.

Yet another raid was planned, this time of the freighter. The craft
was captured, but the politician wasn't on it. However, the crew,
after being captured, offered some useful intel which the Maroon
force used to track down the politician to a small planet in
T'Chaka's Reach. Unfortunately, as soon as he was discovered, he
was killed while attempting to fight back.

"There goes our intel," N'Yami said upon hearing a summary
of the case.

"Which we don't really need," Nakia pressed. "Captain, I
think we have enough information to proceed with the mission.
All we need is your approval."

N'Yami released a deep, long, tired sigh and said, "On one
condition."

"Yes?"

"T'Challa. Take him with you."

Nakia lifted an eyebrow. "*T'Challa,* Captain? Are you sure
about that?"

"No, I'm not," said N'Yami. "But if we're going to go in half
blind, we might as well take all our best flyers. M'Baku says he's
up there with you in aviation skills."

"He is."

N'Yami shrugged. "Well then, that settles it. Bring us something to celebrate."

NAKIA'S PLAN WAS SIMPLE: overwhelm the Shango Array, capture the M'Kraan Shard (or whatever it was the Empire was hiding
there), and escape with minimal casualties. Then, whatever the
shard was capable of, employ that capability against the Empire.

It seemed simple enough, easy enough to execute. But now she
had to do it with T'Challa.

She didn't disagree with her captain. T'Challa was indeed one
of the best fliers among the Maroons. However, she'd planned this
with a tight crew of a few fliers she could rely on not to go out of
their way to do something stupid. T'Challa was the wild card she

couldn't predict, and she worried about having such a presence on her mission.

And then there was that little thing budding between them. She didn't have a name for it yet—not the way she felt when she took her time to *look* at him, and not the way she saw him readjust his posture when he noticed what she was doing. There was no name for the energy that passed between them whenever they were in close proximity. Or perhaps there was, but she didn't want to call it that. She didn't want to call it anything. She simply wanted to be focused.

She recalled the moment he'd finally come around to understanding what the shard was. After the mission was approved, they'd taken time to study every myth around the shard they could lay their hands on. They came across a legion of tales about a crystal that could warp time or reshape bodies or destroy planets. It was impossible to know which was which, and the Shi'ar themselves didn't leave any documents about their crystal.

The tales were all they had, but eventually, they were enough, as all seemed to point to two distinct capabilities: destruction . . . or creation.

The first school of thought was that the shard, upon exploding, could take out a large area. Planet sized, city sized, it didn't matter; there would be mass casualties all the same, with a decimated infrastructure. This was an idea that excited many on the heist team, T'Challa included, but which Nakia didn't favor. She'd witnessed imperial destruction; she didn't wish to be an agent of such, even in the name of good. She didn't wish to have the blood of innocents on her hands.

So she favored the other school of thought, the one that suggested the shard could create shifts in reality. She hoped—and therefore believed, perhaps naively and with wanton abandon, an abandon she liked to think of as *hope* and *faith*—that it could be used to retrieve Nameless memories. What the Maroons would do after such a retrieval, she wasn't sure. But there could be no rebellion without some kind of recovery of said memories.

T'Challa had only heard the first theory and that had been enough for him. He didn't even wait to hear the other. And that was how Nakia knew that, though she cared for him, and though she saw that he bore some promise, there was no way she'd want him on the heist team.

Unfortunately, now she had no choice.

Nakia wasn't a spiritual person, but the night before the mission, she found herself praying.

Bast, she whispered. *Mother Bast. Help us see clearly what the shard may be. Help me see clearly and remain focused. But most of all, dear Bast, help* him *see clearly, tomorrow and for all the days to come.*

CHAPTER 10

△▽△▽

THE
SHANGO ARRAY

TWELVE ZULUS, CLOAKED, floated over imperial sky.

Two sets of squadrons, six each, in formation, zeroed in on the imperial site of interest. The Shango Array was much like every other base in Nehanda's Lattice or the Empire's throneworld: Its visage was menacing, its architecture modern and brutalist, and it spread out as far as the eye could see, like an infection crawling across the landscape.

None of this was enough to stop the Maroon Rebellion force from fulfilling their mission.

"Status check, General," said a tinny voice from the foremost zulu in one of the formations.

"Check," said Nakia, leading the first formation. "Check squadron?"

"Check" came voices from the pilots of the other zulus.

"Check mother nest?"

A slight delay, then a voice from the *Mackandal,* which lagged behind both formations. "Check, Nakia."

"Thank you, M'Baku. We're green to go on—"

Something flashed from afar, in the darkness below. A light, the kind that came from a beacon. Nakia peered through her panther helmet, but the array below was dark, cold, dead. It seemed abandoned, which didn't quite make sense based on the intel they'd received. It was supposed to have minimal defenses, not *none.*

"Hold that thought, Lieutenant," said Nakia, turning on her scanner. "Scanning for hostile cloak."

It took a moment. Voices on comms paused, breaths held in anticipation. Then . . .

Mother Bast! thought Nakia. *Is this real, what I'm seeing?*

"M'Baku," she said, pushing the image on her dashboard to the rest of the Maroon squad, "the Shango Array was said to be unmanned, but look!"

Ahead, as the full array came into view, the assemblage of defense assets popped up one by one on every screen. Fighter craft, anti-craft weaponry, defense force shield infrastructure. All hidden under the cover of darkness, behind imperial cloaking technology similar to their own.

No, no, no, thought Nakia. This was completely against all the intel fed back to them by their network of Maroons hidden among the Empire's soldiers—and their intel had been solid, had it not? Unless . . . something had changed. Had someone talked? Had something leaked? Was there a traitor in their midst?

What was the best play here? Engage or turn away? She made quick calculations, counting with her eyes.

"M'Baku," she said, "there are fifty masai fighters in the air and fifteen fully charged guns down there on that base."

"Copy," came the response, then a breath.

"Speak, Lieutenant."

"We should have known, Nakia," said M'Baku. "This last year of Zanj raiding has been too easy. It appears we now have the Empire's attention."

"Dammit!" Nakia didn't know when the swear spilled from her lips. "We're *so close* to all that the Empire stole, so close to redemption."

"I don't know, Nakia." M'Baku sounded unusually defeated. "Maybe some things are best forgotten."

Nakia heaved a sigh. She wasn't Nameless and didn't know what it felt like to not have a past to look back on. Harmful and painful as her own past was, at least she could dip into it, let it fuel her rage. Where did rage come from for Maroons unlike her, who only had the moment, who had to subsist on the promise of what would be returned to them? How could she fail them in said moment? How could she ask that they simply *forget*?

No, no. She couldn't do that.

They could regroup and return for a better planned mission. They could arrive with a bigger force next time, try to take on the imperial defenses. Perhaps they could stealthily slip in and steal what they needed to. But they sure were not simply going to give up and *forget*.

"Doesn't matter now," she said to M'Baku, trying to sound reasonable amid the heavy air of despondency settling across the crew. "Even though we're cloaked, we must still retreat. Flights one, two, four, and six, head back to the *Mackandal* and—"

Another flash of movement, this one from beside her, swift and sure.

"What's going on?" she screamed into the headpiece as a single craft broke formation and sped toward the array. "Who the hell is flying that zulu!?"

WE'RE SO CLOSE to all that the Empire stole, so close to redemption.

This was all T'Challa needed to hear.

He had a singular memory, one that plagued him just as much as he treasured it. He would do anything to banish dreams and waking visions of the white-haired woman from haunting him. But he'd do much more to find out who she was, what she wanted from him, and why he felt, deep within himself, that he would do anything to give her what she wanted.

He adjusted his panther helmet, breathed deeply, then toggled on the zulu's neural interface. He could do this. He could take them all out himself, or at least enough to give the rest of the Maroons time to catch up.

NEURAL INTERFACE ENGAGED.

A whine screamed through his head. He felt concussed, weightless, like his brain had been invaded by foreign mites. It took a moment to reorient himself. He'd always found the Maroon neuro-adaptive tech to be quite brutal in the initial pairing stage—no matter the amount of training sessions he'd undergone, he'd never gotten used to it. But this was different. His adrenaline had never been so high during trainings or any of the other missions leading up to this critical last juncture, and he'd never experienced these odds, with failure staring him in the face before the mission had even begun. His senses were on high alert, his nervous system running on full, and with it, the zulu's actions just as charged, vibrant, bristling with the desire to attack.

He narrowed his eyes and gave in.

The zulu shot forward, faster than he'd thought possible. It zigzagged between the buildings of the array as quickly as he could imagine, angling itself and sliding between slim spaces. He felt the craft like it was his body, like he could twist it any way he wished, as swiftly as he could rotate a wrist or flick a finger. The craft responded to his involuntary neural movements, a reflexive blink of the eye or a hand up to block an attack. It was fight *and* flight all in one package.

Behind him, the defenses of the array came alive to his presence. Lights and alarms blared, craft engines roared to life.

But T'Challa was faster, guns out and blazing, taking them down before they could even warm up.

In this haze of speed and smoke, a tinny voice came to him over comms.

"T'Challa," said Nakia. "Of course it's you." He could feel the disapproving shake of her head. "You want to die, fine, but leave my zulu out of it!"

She didn't sound like her typically placating self, which was . . .

good? But she also sounded angry in a way she hadn't been with him so far.

He wanted to listen. He truly did. But he was already far too deep. He and the zulu were one now, and he felt the danger all around it, all around *him*. He simply couldn't let go.

Three masai fighters. On his tail.

They fired without warning, but he had eyes in the back of his head. He swiveled this way, that way, and not a single piece of ammunition scraped his craft. He settled into a medium distance ahead and knew immediately the moment they locked guns on him.

Space fold, he thought.

SHORT-RANGE SPACE FOLD ENGAGED, the zulu announced, and then, in a blink, he was gone from their sights. He counted the seconds, imagining their befuddlement, their confusion about how it was possible for him to be so fast, so slippery, so—

SPACE FOLD COMPLETE.

—deadly.

He reappeared in just the exact position, the right distance in their rear, to get a lock on all three craft at once. From there on, it was easy.

One down.

Two down.

Three down.

"T'Challa!" Nakia's tinny voice was back in his head. "You've made your point! Get back here now!"

She was angrier. No matter.

"He's not turning around, Nakia." Another tinny voice, this one M'Baku's.

"Fine." Nakia sounded determined. "Prepare to jump."

More masai fighters on his tail.

He tucked, ducked, swerved behind a building, came up on the other side. The imperial crafts came with him. He swiveled midflight and took down the nearest two. Then he tucked behind the building again.

He took them all down by repeating the pattern twice more.

By now, the voices in his ear were a chatter.

"I'm not letting that madman get us killed!" Nakia was saying.

"He's *certainly* going to get someone killed," said M'Baku. "But I don't think it will be us."

The *Mackandal* was yet to drop from cloak, as were the other zulus, which were already breaking formation and rejoining the mother ship. Only one zulu remained, tracking his every move: Nakia.

Behind him. More masai fighters.

He led them as far as he could from the Maroon fleet, diving deeper into the array's infrastructure. He shot down one masai and led the other to crash into a nearby bridge.

"Are you watching this?" Nakia asked. "It's like the imperials are two steps behind and he's three steps ahead."

"Told you he was a liability," M'Baku replied. "But I have to say . . . the results of this action don't seem . . . bad?"

"T'Challa, please," said Nakia. "We can't back you up on this. And we can still—"

WARNING, the zulu announced. NEURAL NET APPROACHING MAXIMUM SENSORY PROTOCOLS.

More imperials. They were everywhere now—above, below, beside him. The anti-craft guns had come out, too, now that he was much closer to the array.

"Disengage protocols," said T'Challa.

The zulu disengaged. A large rush went through his head, as if an escape of wind. He felt like he'd been suddenly born into the world, into the seat of the plane, feeling the rough material of the controller in his hand, the tight pinch of the seat belt in his shoulder, the sweat gathering behind the panther mask on his face.

"They've got you surrounded, T'Challa," said Nakia, more criticism than warning.

T'Challa inhaled deeply, preparing his next move, and then he spoke.

"Nakia?"

"Yes?"

"I'm not the one that needs backup."

NEURAL INTERFACE RE-ENGAGED.

All imperial fighters were on him now. He could feel every single one of the remaining tens, readying guns, converging, as if he were prey.

But they were wrong. He was no one's prey.

He might be unable to tap into his mind's memories, but he sure was able to tap into his body's. And all along, his body had been trying to remind him of something he didn't know, wasn't sure was possible. But in this moment, surrounded, it was the only card he had left, and he would play it, going all in.

Cloak, he thought, succumbing.

"What the—?" came the voice in his ear. "Where did he go!?"

"T'Challa? T'Challa!?"

He could see the confusion spread, not just among his comrades but among the imperials as well. All of them, guns hanging out, stopped short, confused. Where had their prey gone?

T'Challa let the zulu float so that the imperials shot past him, unaware of his location.

He put a lock on as many as he could. And then he let them have it.

IMPERIAL CRAFT FELL. Bright explosions and smoke filled the array.

"M'Baku," Nakia called into her headpiece. "How is he doing this!?"

Scratches filled the other end of her comm. M'Baku was probably dealing with all the other zulus that had returned to the *Mackandal.* She and T'Challa were the only ones left out here now. Speaking of which . . .

Where is he?

More explosions. The sounds of more engines, none his.

Then suddenly, an explosion, and his zulu appeared amid the

smoke. A rail gun had caught the tail of his craft, and now it was spiraling, burning bright and fast, spewing and trailing black smoke.

It tumbled into a dark corner of the array, out of sight.

"Nakia!" M'Baku was back on comms. "He's hit! We've got to help him before they finish him off!"

She was already way ahead of him, descending, breaking cover and cloak to rain fire on the converging imperials. They were just as surprised with her presence as they'd been with T'Challa's, perhaps thinking him to be a lone fighter. Nakia scoffed. As if the Maroons would ever let one of their own go off on a self-sacrificial mission, no matter how stubborn said Maroon was.

"All flights on the Shango Array!" M'Baku announced over fleet-wide comms. "Now."

Ten more zulus dropped from the sky.

Nakia didn't know when they all broke cloak and emerged. Suddenly the number of explosions quadrupled, imperial fighters vanished from the sky, and rooftop guns were ineffective against them.

"Clean up and get those guns down," she ordered the fleet.

As the zulus faced off against the rest of the guns, now that the imperial fleet was pretty much destroyed, Nakia turned her attention to the one thing they'd come here for.

COME BACK TO ME, *T'Challa.*

A bright light appeared above him. First, it was her face, then her eyes. Then everything was too bright, so that it had to be neither.

Hands pulled him out of position, unlinked him from the zulu. He felt the rush of neural disconnection. Hands moved him. Then he felt weightless, lifted through air.

CHAPTER 11

△▽△▽

PLANET BAST

TWO COUNSELORS KNELT before the panther throne.

They were dressed similarly, in the flowing Wakandan courtly robes that signified their status as high-ranking political civilians and metal headwear carved specifically to mirror their skulls. Demba, red robed, was the more theatrical of the two, and his striking appearance (he wore blue beautifying facial markings) and rambunctious proclamations (he was always a shade louder than everyone else in the room) proved it.

In this moment, on his knees, he pleaded fervently, a performance in and of itself, as he regaled the emperor with the reasons why the imperial forces had been unable to hold back the rebellion forces at the Shango Array.

"Normally, such a matter would not rise to the level of his majesty," he said, "but this zulu fighter—this was a man possessed of unusual . . . ability."

Achebe, the other counselor, blue robed, was on the more muted end of the spectrum. He kept his head low, eyes trained to the ground. He was often happy to let Demba do the talking, especially in this case, coming off the back of a failure. This, he'd learned from childhood, was the way to thrive in this empire. Hold your tongue for as long as possible; speak only when required; enjoy loudly, endure silently. The golden rules of the Intergalactic Empire.

"Emperor," Demba said, "if it pleases you—"

"It does," said the emperor.

The panther throne sat a few steps up and ahead of the counselors. The throne room, often lit by strategically placed lamps and firepits, was bright. But today, for some reason, the emperor had chosen to keep the area surrounding the throne darkened so that only his silhouette could be seen. In this way, it felt to Demba like the darkness itself was speaking.

Demba rose tentatively. "Sire, this is not the first such report." He pushed the device embedded in his arm and light sprung from it, projecting a holo screen. "There was the recent destruction of the Vibranium depot, a raid on a house of amusement in the S'yaan Expanse, the taking of a musa-class freighter, and the assassination of a Ras politician."

He looked up at the emperor's silhouette. The ruler of the Wakandan Empire had risen, too. Whether in anger or perplexity, Demba couldn't tell.

He swallowed and continued.

"All of this, in Zanj space. All accompanied by reports of a rebel possessed of *unusual ability*."

The emperor tapped his armrest gently with his fingers. This was how he often signified that he was mulling something over.

"We have to consider the possibility, Lord N'Jadaka, that our efforts failed. That the heretic who claimed the mantle of T'Challa the Wise has returned."

The emperor flinched. Achebe knew, now, that Demba had made a mistake. He tried to pinpoint the exact moment of this overstep—was it by suggesting that the Empire's efforts had failed, or was it the mention of heresy, of someone claiming to be a reincarnation of *the* greatest Wakandan warrior of all time? Or perhaps it was the mention of this specific heretic, one whose name the emperor had worked hard toward squashing stirrings of for quite a while now?

It took Achebe a while to realize it was neither—it was a different thing, for now: Demba had addressed the emperor by the name he used to go by once, long before he ever wore the imperial robes and sat on the panther's throne.

The emperor had sat back down. Demba followed his cue and dropped back to the ground.

"No, no, Counselor Demba," said the emperor. "You may rise."

His voice was even but boomed, seemed to carry throughout the room. Demba rose jerkily. Even Achebe, kneeling beside him, shivered.

"Counselor," the emperor began, "you were tasked with dispatching the heretic. You were to do this quietly, obscuring the marks of the imperium."

The emperor had risen again. He descended the steps slowly, soundlessly, stepping away from darkness and into the light.

Demba looked up at him and gulped. Demba was over six feet tall, but the emperor was a tower, a floating darkness of sinew. The ink-black panther suit gripped his body tightly, stretched across the broadness of his muscled chest, shoulders, thighs. A spatter of yellow in his necklace and armlets, the flat and menacing ovals of his helmet. And his cape, a billowing monstrosity with a strikingly high collar that shrouded the emperor's head and gave his jaw and cheekbones a menacing visage.

The *Black Panther,* through and through.

"You have *not* dispatched the heretic," the emperor proclaimed. "And what should have been obscured may now well be made plain." He scratched his head, in performance of ridicule. "How, Counselor . . . how have you failed the Empire so profoundly?"

Demba sweated. The emperor, by now, was standing within touching distance. He didn't seem angry. Demba didn't feel any sense of indignation in his countenance. But experience had taught the counselor that to rely on such lazy external markers of the emperor's state of mind was, often, to be wrong. The emperor was a blank slate to those who didn't know what to look for. But for those who knew to pause and read between the lines, the emperor was always filled with writing. And to Demba, in this moment, the emperor's slate was covered in angry scribbles.

"Mercy, Emperor," said Demba. "Allow me to ferret out those who failed you—failed us."

Silence engulfed all three. Achebe, who had yet to speak, didn't look up. He kept his face down, away from Demba, as if he knew what was to come, as if he didn't want to see.

Then, as slowly and soundlessly as he'd descended from the throne, the emperor lifted off the ground.

Achebe had seen this before but each instance was different, the same conversation with new words. Yet some things were the same: the viscous blackness coming slowly into view, emerging from a corner of the emperor's body; the sound it made, a screech that felt like dread and laughter mingled into one; the symbiote—as this was what it was—lurched from the emperor's body into the air, gathering and garbling and distorting into tentacles of itself, so that it was now its own thing with arms and heat and *intent,* yet was all at once one with the emperor's state and his deepest wishes.

"There will be no ferreting," said the emperor, continuing to rise by the power of the symbiote. "Only purging."

His voice had become corrupted, a dissonant thunder, a chorus of booming overtones that didn't belong together.

"And as for mercy, Counselor," the earsplitting voice said, "every breath you take is mercy from me."

The symbiote lunged and planted itself into Demba's chest. It bound his arms and legs, ribs and chest. It wrapped around his eyes and ears and windpipe. It surged into his mouth and silenced his screams, seeped into his nose and blocked his airways. Then, when it had wound itself tightly enough, it squeezed.

A *crack* here, a *snap* there, an orchestra of syncopated percussion, as Demba's bones broke one by one. Blood spilled out of every orifice: eyes, ears, nose. His metal headwear, bent out of shape, dug into his skull. His wrists dangled, shuddered, waved, like leaves in a drizzle.

Then he became still.

The symbiote loosened, dropping the counselor's body to the

ground, headfirst. Every lick of viscous blackness then retreated, slowly, back to the emperor's body.

"Counselor Achebe." The emperor's voice was back to normal. His back was turned to the still kneeling, still quivering, still sweating counselor, as if hiding his face in shame, as if he didn't wish to be perceived in this way.

"Emperor." Achebe's throat was parched, voice cracked.

"Have everyone in Demba's unit interrogated," said the emperor. "Then executed."

Achebe didn't think twice. "Yes, my liege."

The emperor walked back into the darkness and eased onto the panther throne.

"I shall require all reports on these disturbances in the Zanj Region." He sounded fatigued, weary, like an old man. In many ways, he was one—he had lived for so long and seen *so* many things.

"Yes, my liege."

He made a small motion with his hand, which Achebe interpreted to mean he was dismissed. He rose to go, then realized something needed to be done with Demba's body. He headed for the throne room doors to get a guard or two to come clean up the mess.

"Achebe," the emperor called, just as he turned away.

"My liege?"

"What was it about the Shango Array base that so interested the rebels?"

Achebe gulped. This was the one question he'd been hoping the emperor wouldn't ask—at least not ask *him*. It was the one question he'd hoped would've died with Demba. Too late.

"An artifact, my liege," he said tentatively. "Captured during the Shi'ar War." He paused. "Something called . . . the M'Kraan Shard."

CHAPTER 12

△▽△▽

MOONBASE
CUDJOE

WHENEVER NAKIA RECEIVED an invitation to the captain's quarters, she believed it was never for good reason. Though she was as much an advisor and second-in-command as M'Baku, he was the one who often got all the good news while Captain N'Yami called upon her for matters of a more . . . complicated nature.

Nakia knew that the captain didn't think less of her for not having Nameless origins like most of the Maroons, for coming from somewhere more fraught: from the imperials, the enemy themselves. But she had proven herself well enough in both her rejection of the imperial ideals and her role as tactical leader of the Maroons to the point that the captain and the rest of the community trusted her just as much as one another. Regardless, this didn't stop anxiety from brewing in her chest whenever the captain asked for her. A part of her always remained acutely aware of who she was and where she came from, always wondered if she'd truly been fully accepted or if the other shoe would finally drop one day and she'd realize they'd been pretending all along.

She wondered if today was that day.

The doors to the captain's quarters opened. She stepped in. Captain N'Yami, busy putting together images on the holo, looked up as she came in and flashed a broad, earnest smile.

Well, thought Nakia, *I guess today is not that day.*

"You are no doubt familiar with the Chronicles of T'Challa, Nakia?"

N'Yami, not known for lengthy pleasantries, had already returned to the work at hand. Nakia looked up and saw that the image projecting from the holo was one from the Maroon Archival Project. This one was a holographic re-creation of the original oral tale of the great T'Challa of Ancient Wakanda—or Old Wakanda, or Wakanda Prime, depending on which version of the tale you learned and from whom. All were in agreement, though, that he was one of the greatest ancestral heroes from the long beforetimes. His panther suit—called a *habit* back then—had inspired the design of the very uniform every Maroon warrior wore.

"Of course, Captain N'Yami," said Nakia. "I was practically raised on them."

If there was one thing the imperials and the Maroons agreed on, it was this very thing: that Ancient Wakanda was just as great, if not greater, than the Intergalactic Empire of Wakanda. The difference was in specifically what they'd been taught. Growing up an imperial, Nakia had been educated in the feats of the greatest heroes and legends of Ancient Wakanda as the precursor to the current empire. Only after she'd left that life behind and committed herself to the revolution of the Maroons did she learn the reverse side of that tale: that the people born of these very heroes had then formed the brutal, merciless Intergalactic Empire of Wakanda.

A hard lesson to learn that both tales were true.

"T'Challa the Avenger, who banished the usurper, Ulysses Klaw," she said to N'Yami now, recapping what she'd learned. "T'Challa the Ultimate, who thrashed the demon Mephisto. T'Challa, Consort of the Goddess Bast. T'Challa, whose name in old Wakandan translates to *He Who Put the Knife Where It Belonged*."

As Nakia spoke, N'Yami nodded and moved through the holo images she'd arranged, showing still representations of these events as they'd been re-created to mirror the oral tales. T'Challa, clad in his all-black panther habit, in each case was warrior, savior, deliverer, priest, prophet. Ancient Wakanda personified.

Except the Wakanda of yore had never been invested in the brutal wiping away, enslavement, and subjugation of peoples. While they'd also had access to Vibranium, they never believed, like today's Wakandans did, that it made them masters of the world and everything the darkness of space touched. They never thought that the Wakandan gods had blessed them with the wherewithal to conquer and rule over every galaxy their ships could reach. They didn't believe that they were superior to every other being and species through the simple task of existing. All of that was the belief of today's imperials, which Nakia had learned from the Maroon Archival Project.

She found it dissonant, then, that N'Yami's images presented no lies and yet were the *exact* same kind of images imperial education employed. It was in the lips, through which words were spoken, where the lies lay.

"Now," said N'Yami, "what if I told you that this T'Challa of legend walks among us?"

Nakia felt her bodily senses recoil. Her vision slowed, as if everything was moving faster than her eyes could perceive. Sounds dulled and became distant. Her skin, suddenly extra-sensitive, so she could feel every woven thread in the cloth of her garment. And her heart, a loud and heavy hammer thumping against her chest bone, reverberating in her ears.

She stared at the last image above them both, one where the legendary T'Challa had implanted a blade in an enemy's chest. *Impossible. Just . . . impossible.*

She cleared her throat. "I would say that T'Challa is the most common name in the Empire. And it's often adopted by those wishing to be a reincarnation of the ancient one."

N'Yami, silent and ponderous, nodded. "Quite so." She moved to another image. Above them towered the Black Panther, tall and proud.

"And yet, years ago, a man appeared claiming to be the true T'Challa. This man was mocked at first, much as you mock me now. He was subjected to trials of strength and courage and outlasted them all. We know that on Planet Bast, this man was hailed as the second coming, that he journeyed out to Nehanda's Lattice, that he fought the Shi'ar War on behalf of the Empire and there met an untimely end."

Nakia watched as N'Yami put forward her own images of the war. From the Maroon Archival Project, Nakia had learned of a man, one completely absent from the imperial records of the Shi'ar War. A man from nowhere who'd suddenly appeared on Planet Bast and found his way among the imperials. Not much was known of him, until suddenly, the name "T'Challa" was being passed from lip to lip. The man—who'd announced himself as *the* T'Challa of Ancient Wakanda, returned—was quickly besmirched as a heretic.

Many such men had come and gone since the Empire's formation, claiming to be similar reincarnates, and were often swiftly disappeared by imperial forces. This one was no different. So, even though records of these occurrences existed in MAP, such men and their heretical proclamations were also long forgotten by the average Maroon.

Yet here N'Yami was, yanking them back into these muddy waters. Couldn't she see? Bast had anointed N'Jadaka avatar, and that was that. Some said that the goddess's hands were tied, that N'Jadaka had proven himself in multiple undeniable ways, and therefore she had no choice but to crown him avatar and king. Others said that the goddess had changed, that she'd abandoned them, that she'd chosen the Empire over them. They believed that Bast now fed upon their suffering, grew fat on the agony that wrung from them more supplication, which kept her thriving, flourishing.

Some people didn't believe in gods, period.

Nakia was a skeptic. There were gods, sure, but she didn't think they were infallible beings, and thought that Bast—if she *was* out there, and if she did possess the power her believers claimed she did—was simply stupid, then. Anointing a tyrant as avatar? Hands tied? What a joke.

All of them, including these heretics N'Yami was talking about, and this rebel as well. He was no different than the others that had come before him. He simply had the advantage of being alive . . . for now.

To N'Yami, choosing her words carefully, she said: "You do not believe he—the heretic—met such an end."

N'Yami had a set, convinced expression. "No, I do not." She turned from the holo to face her second-in-command.

"Nakia," she began, "I know that I can be a dreamer. Dreaming is what saved me from the mines. Dreaming brought me to the Maroons. But this is no dream. T'Challa—*our* T'Challa—is the Ultimate, the Avenger, He Who Put the Knife Where It Belonged."

Nakia's senses were receding again, but N'Yami continued on.

"How many times has he charged an enemy column alone and left splinters in his wake? What other theory can you offer?"

Nakia inhaled deeply. This woman could *not* be serious, could she? How could that prisoner from Goree, that brash, obstinate, most un-Wakandan-like man be the same wise, gentle T'Challa of yore? How could the savior and protector of Ancient Wakanda be here, today, learning their ways? How could he be struggling so hard to adapt if this was his home? She even had a hard time accepting that he could be that same heretic believed to have perished in the Shi'ar War, a fallen soldier returned to life; and yet N'Yami wanted her to believe he was the *avatar of Bast*?

"Respectfully, Captain," Nakia said, "the absence of my own theory is not proof of yours."

N'Yami, ever patient, nodded. "Indeed. Which is why I share this only with you." She leaned in more closely. "If my theory were known and wrong, it might spread false hope. And if it were known and right, N'Jadaka would never stop hunting us."

It was truly a conundrum. Nakia could see, now, that the woman had been grappling with this, and had been burning to discuss it with someone since they'd returned from the Shango Array heist. Nakia felt a little glad that N'Yami had chosen her for this intimate secret, then realized that it wasn't quite a blessing. Keeping this secret was now her burden as much as it was N'Yami's.

But she couldn't abide this kind of discourse. The rescued prisoner from Goree being both an ancient legend *and* a recent heretic? Blasphemy.

"Where are you getting your evidence from?" she asked.

N'Yami walked over to the M'Kraan Shard, now enclosed and safely stored where the captain could keep a close eye on it. Didn't Nakia already stake so much hope and faith on such a delicate sliver of space rock? The captain shook her head. "I don't want to involve you deeper than you already need to be, Nakia. I only want to share what you need to know. But suffice it to say, I have it on good authority that what I share is correct."

If N'Yami was still unclear, Nakia realized, it was because she was waiting for confirmation of her theory. The only way to do so would be for the prisoner himself to remember his origins. And since he was Nameless, and his memories had been stolen, they had to be stored in the one place where the Empire kept the memories of every person they'd enslaved.

"You want us to attack the Imperial Archive," said Nakia.

N'Yami shrugged, neither confirming nor denying it, which Nakia assumed to mean that she was pretty much confirming it.

"Is this why you agreed to us getting the M'Kraan Shard?" she pressed. "Is there something it can do? To their—*your*—memories?"

N'Yami smiled again, warmth and earnestness reaching her eyes. Then she turned off the holo.

"Dismissed, Nakia."

At the door, hand on the panel, Nakia stopped just short of opening it. Without looking at N'Yami, she said, "You know I'm going to ask him, right?"

Silence. Nakia pushed the panel and the door opened. By the time it swooshed shut behind her, she'd already made up her mind.

CHAPTER 13

△▽△▽

MOONBASE CUDJOE

THE FORMATIONS ON Moonbase Cudjoe were often of the harsher, rockier kind. Why the Maroons had chosen this specific planet to set up their hideout was a mystery to Nakia. There were much better planets out there with better weather, landscapes, and natural vegetation. She could do with the pleasures of a natural hot spring right about now. Somehow, they'd chosen one of the most desolate places to plant their roots.

Luckily, desolate rocky planets were good for one thing: climbing. Apparently it was this rock climbing that T'Challa seemed to enjoy the most, the activity that took him away from the other Maroons as much as possible. When she'd asked to join him on his routine climb from the base of the mountain that housed the observatory deck to the top, from where they could watch the activities of larger fleets, she'd expected him to say no. To her surprise, he agreed, and even seemed quite effusive about it.

Now she understood why. There was climbing, and there was *climbing,* and the one T'Challa was fond of—and exceptionally gifted at, seeing as he was now many paces ahead of her midway through their climb—was closer to the latter than the former.

"Hurry, Nakia," he even dared to say. His voice was tinny through the comms mic, though that didn't make it sound any more annoying—she wished to reach up and pinch him. But instead, she gritted her teeth and dreamed of soaking her bruised and sore palms in healing ointment. For now, her mind was occupied by a concern far greater than reaching the terrace at the top: She had something T'Challa needed to know, and his awareness might just be the key to unlocking the Maroons' next step, resulting in the greatest victory against the Empire they'd had in years.

T'Challa, oblivious to all this, was still prattling on. He stopped, turned, looked down at her through his protective glasses, and said, "At this pace we'll miss the chaga's landing."

She scoffed. "It's just another shipment, T'Challa. Is that really why you think I invited you out here?"

"No," he said, and he seemed to mean it. "I thought it was for my lively banter and renowned sense of humor."

Okay, still bad at jokes, she realized, though she made a clear effort not to respond to his attempt at lightheartedness. He noticed.

"It was a joke, Nakia," he pressed.

"Ah, of course," she said dryly. "That *renowned* sense of humor." She shook her head. If this man was truly the same T'Challa of legend, she was sure he'd be able to tell a proper joke. That T'Challa was wise and funny, the tales said. This one was the equivalent of a stone licked by a child—rough-edged and sharp, but upon taste, holding nothing juicier at its core than the bland exterior signified.

If he truly was the T'Challa of legend, perhaps all the juice had been sucked out of him.

"So, you didn't invite me here for the jokes," said T'Challa. "Why, then?"

Nakia paused her climbing, holding on to a rock. *Breathe, Nakia. Breathe.*

"I have information," she said, easing the words out slowly. "About your memories."

T'Challa paused his climbing. They had reached the top of the formation, where it transitioned from roughly hewn rock into the smooth concrete of the building that crested it. T'Challa hung on to the narrow slits that marked the side of the building, little hand-holds, or peepholes, depending on how one saw them, that held nothing but darkness within, giving sight to the unpolished innards of the concrete exterior. Head lowered into his chest, the Maroon soldier looked like his eyes were shut, though Nakia couldn't tell from this far below. He seemed to be weighing the choice he had to make—whether he wanted to venture into this minefield of new information, or whether it was best to stay uninformed, unplagued.

Finally, he lifted his head. "I'm listening." Then he resumed climbing.

Nakia followed.

"When the Askari steal memories," she began, "they store them in the Imperial Archive. Every bit of that archive is then mined and researched."

This part was mostly common knowledge among the Maroons. She wanted to begin here, to ease into the stuff that was *not* common knowledge, the stuff that N'Yami, after their uneasy alliance in her quarters, had finally, reluctantly, revealed to Nakia. This wasn't the kind of information she could take to M'Baku or the general Maroon population.

"Mmm-hmm." T'Challa grunted his acknowledgment. "Researched for what?"

"Anything unknown to them—anything. Thoughts, ideas, emotions, stories, methods, half-formed notions. All of it, appropriated for their interests. Do you think they really invented the stellar engine?"

They had reached the top of the building. They climbed over the parapet and jumped down to the rooftop terrace, startling the guards posted there, who then relaxed once they realized who the two were. Giant rooftop guns lined the terrace, casting long shadows over everyone. It seemed they had landed on the wrong side of the building and would have to go around to see the platform where the chaga would land.

T'Challa had yet to speak another word.

"Do you understand what I'm saying?" Nakia pressed, trying to drive home the message. "Your memories are *knowledge*. All our memories are. And the Empire doesn't destroy knowledge, they plunder it."

They rounded a corner. More guards and giant anti-craft guns. T'Challa kept musing.

"So, my memories," he finally said, "whoever I was before this, it's all in the hands of the imperials to use as they wish?"

He sounded so earnest. Looked it, too. But Nakia didn't have time for earnestness. The Maroon Rebellion didn't have time for earnestness. They needed something big, and this man could be the catalyst that triggered it all. She had to be firm.

"Yes." She didn't mean to sound so blunt. "It's sickening. The Empire speaks of the grandeur of its civilization. And it *is* grand. But it is also *stolen*."

He turned to look at her now, eyes blazing with a warrior's intensity. "This is where you tell me about the plan to get those memories back," he said.

Wonderful, thought Nakia. *He's catching on.*

Above them, the sound of incoming aircraft filled the air. The chaga landing had to be soon now. She needed to get her message across clearly before his attention drifted and he became disinterested in discussing the Empire, as he often was.

"There *is* a plan," she said quickly. "The M'Kraan Shard we recovered from the Shango Array base? We believe it can—"

He wasn't listening to her. He was staring past her, behind her, up into the sky, where the chaga was landing. His gaze wasn't one of wonder or interest but of concern and anger.

"T'Challa?" she asked. "What's wrong?"

"I would like very much to hear this plan," he said, calmly taking off his protective eyewear and comm, his voice no longer tinny in her ear but full-blooded, filled with purpose. "But perhaps now isn't the time."

Nakia turned. In the clouds above, the outline of a few craft took shape. She couldn't see much and took off her own eyewear, counting five or six craft. The outlines became sharper, and she breathed a sigh of relief. The chagas were here.

"It seems, Nakia," said T'Challa, chillingly, "that we are under attack."

WITHOUT FURTHER WARNING, T'Challa leaped for the nearest anti-craft gun, yanked it around, set it in the direction of the advancing ships, and fired.

The terrace shook with the blast of the anti-craft gun, heavy pellets thundering in the sky, explosions rocking the terrace in mini-vibrations. The first chaga was hit. It exploded in the sky in a bright flash of orange, yellow, and red. The others maneuvered out of the way.

Nakia was aghast.

"T'Challa!" she cried. "What are you doing? Are you crazy? Those are *our* ships!"

"No, they aren't!" he screamed back. "Look!"

The five remaining chagas had stopped advancing. They opened their maws and released a flurry of buzzing humanoid shapes, scores and scores of them, all of which descended in a buzzing black cloud with fierce alacrity and determinedness, headed straight for the terrace.

Oh no, thought Nakia, and then as loud as she could, screamed: "Askari Raiders!"

She turned to the Maroons standing guard on the terrace, all of whom had become frozen, discombobulated by T'Challa shooting down one of their ships. The sight of the advancing Askari was equally confusing, causing them to stay stuck, unsure of what this all meant, what action to take. But Nakia knew it meant that the imperium's brutal force, the Askari, had intercepted the chagas on their way in and caught a ride to their hideout. It was her job to pass this message to the Maroons on the roof. But there was no time for lengthy stories. There was only time for one command.

"Maroons!" she yelled. "Shoot them down!"

That did the trick. They moved as one, each planting themselves behind a nearby rooftop gun, aiming for the advancing imperial force and the distant ships both, unleashing hell.

Chug chug chug. The thunder of ammunition filled the roof. The terrace shook with overlapping vibrations. The air was sharp, filled with smoke and the smell of burned metal. The shells caught most of the Askari in the front rows, sending their rocket packs into double explosions so that they each spun down in a trail of smoke, like a bee that'd lost its wings.

But the cloud of Askari was a harder target to hit than the chagas above, and so in a few short heartbeats, a flurry of imperial soldiers had landed on the terrace, pulled out their firearms, and opened fire on the Maroons.

It didn't take long before the first rooftop gun exploded.

"T'Challa, look out!" Nakia called as she dove out of the way of flying debris.

T'Challa was already ahead of her, slipping away from the gun before it exploded, charging headlong into the advancing crowd of Askari who'd landed.

Nakia followed.

She pulled out one of her throwing daggers and in the same sweeping motion, flung the blade at the nearest Askari. The armor-piercing blade caught the soldier in the neck. As the Askari fell, sharp, bloody teeth gnashing in agony, Nakia swept up its fallen weapon, turned to the remaining oncoming Askari, and opened fire.

The imperial force fell.

"T'Challa!" she called over the roar of gunfire and explosions.

"I'm fine!" T'Challa's voice shuddered from the vibrations of the rooftop gun he was firing. "But something's wrong!"

Nakia shot down another Askari. "What!?"

"Why would the imperials send so large a force against us?"

"I don't know! But I don't think we've seen the half of it yet!"

Above them, more chagas appeared, raining down an angry cloud of Askari so many in number that, for a moment, they blocked out the light from the sky.

ON THE OPPOSITE, southern side of the roof where Nakia and T'Challa held back an Askari force, a fresh dispatch landed on the terrace and attempted to breach the building through a narrow corridor. But as they proceeded, a hail of bullets fell on them as a fresh squadron of Maroons suddenly emerged and blocked off the entryway, led by none other than the commander of the revolutionary force, M'Baku.

"Hold them back, Maroons!" M'Baku screamed as bullets flew between both parties. "Stay strong!"

Hefting his favorite rotary gun, M'Baku thundered hell and fury upon the advancing Askari. His fellow Maroons followed his lead. The squadron, which included the recent rescues from Goree—among them the big man, Daoud—pushed the Askari back with a fierceness.

But many of this squadron were new recruits, yet to learn the finer intricacies of battle in such close quarters. Fear clouded their eyes, and a few hesitated a moment too long, just enough time for an Askari bullet or two to gun them down.

As many Maroons fell as Askari.

"So, this is it, then!" said M'Baku, watching his comrades' lifeless bodies hit the ground. "We die here!" He pulled back his reloading lever, switching to a new belt of full ammunition. "Let's make it count, Maroons!"

"M'Baku no die today!" Daoud appeared in the front row, M'Baku's rocket launcher balanced easily on his shoulder. "Only imperial." He aimed the weapon at the advancing force. "So say king-mule Daoud!"

Thunder boomed. Fire and debris rained. More Askari fell.

Then Daoud was flying into the dazed Askari survivors, swinging fist and firearm, catching two, three, four Askari in each attack. For a big man, he moved fast, and as much as M'Baku didn't appreciate soldiers who moved without first awaiting commands, he was grateful for the opportunity of having someone like Daoud fighting for their side.

It was all for naught, though, because as he looked up, a new set of Askari were already descending to replace the ones they had just defeated.

Time to call for backup.

"Hello!" he screamed into his comm. "Can anyone read me? We need backup here!"

Static, a crackle, and then—

"M'Baku? M'Baku, it's N'Yami—"

Thank Bast, he thought with relief. The captain was aware of the attack and had probably moved to the *Mackandal* already, a safer place from which to strategize and conduct resistance to the attack. If they were lucky, Taku, their chief intelligence officer, was already there with her.

"I'm sending reinforcements to the hangar bay!" N'Yami said. "But you've got to get the ships going now! We're almost overrun!"

"Yes, Captain!" M'Baku turned to the Maroons behind him. "Squad Five, with me!"

Soon they were retreating, moving from the entryway and running down the corridor, headed for the hangar bay as Captain N'Yami had directed. A new set of Askari had landed, though surprisingly they didn't pursue with any degree of alacrity. M'Baku thought it odd, but not completely out of turn—their comrades had been swiftly and decisively defeated, after all. But a part of him wondered if they were up to something.

He received his answer soon enough. Before they could make significant headway down the corridor, everything went black.

"Dammit," said M'Baku. "They've hit the power supply."

"Don't worry, Lieutenant," a nearby Maroon said. "I've got it."

Green light suddenly filled the hallway. It was a glow tube, brought to life by the Maroon who stepped in front now to light the pack's way. M'Baku whispered another prayer of thanks and was about to give another order when the Maroon before him paused, becoming still as stone.

"Wait," the man said, firearm in one hand, glow tube held high above his head. "I think I see—"

He never got to complete the sentence as blinding orange light manifested before them. Out of it sprung something . . . someone. An arm, a leg, a *weapon*—whatever it was, long and strong— struck the Maroon and sent him flying into the darkness.

Then the orange light disappeared as quickly as it had arrived, and in its place was a shadow, a mountainous silhouette of a man.

The fallen glow tube illuminated the outlines of the figure before them. He was as broad as he was tall, and towered above even M'Baku, one of the biggest men among the Maroons. Light clung to the defined muscles of his arms, and he stood there without fear, ready and willing to take on them all.

"Let him have it!" screamed M'Baku, and all the Maroons emptied their clips.

Ga-ta-ta-ta-ta!

Gunfire flashes lit up the corridor. M'Baku could see the enemy wore a great, heavy helmet that shielded his face and similar armor that covered his body. But he stood unmoved as they fired. And then, faster than the human eye could track—faster, even, than their bullets maybe—he lifted his hand.

A shield made wholly from light appeared out of nowhere. But it was no ordinary shield. It was a *repellent* shield, because every single bullet that touched it bounced and returned to whence it came.

"No!" screamed M'Baku, but it was too late. The bullets struck down the Maroons on either side of him.

And then he felt a hot, searing pain in his shoulder. He touched it, felt heat and blood.

"Take him!" he screamed anyway at the remaining Maroons.

"He's just one man!" Then he was running toward their adversary.

But the man wasn't stopping. That orange light had filled the hallway again, and suddenly there was a hole, a portal, and out of it flew a fellow Maroon who had, only seconds ago, been behind him.

What's happening!? M'Baku found himself asking, and as if answering the question, his brain put together the puzzle of everything he'd just witnessed: the imperial attacker's sudden appearance; his ability to move so quickly, unexplainably appearing in different places.

He's teleporting! M'Baku realized.

And just as he thought it, one such hole manifested in front of him in a blinding flash of orange light. Out of the hole stepped the attacker, big and loud and truly frightening. M'Baku tried to slow his approach, but even he knew it was too late.

The imperial attacker slammed his fist into M'Baku's chest. All the breath left his body, and he felt light and suddenly weightless, a balloon quickly deflated. He reeled, his legs giving way, and he expected his back to hit the ground harder than he'd ever remembered in his time as a combatant.

He fell for much longer than anticipated, his back yet to touch the ground. Then he looked up and realized he'd been slammed *through a portal,* and that only meant one thing: This fall was going to hurt.

Oh Bast, he thought, and then he hit the ground.

For what felt like a long time, he couldn't remember where he was. Then his senses slowly came back: first, the smells, of blood and sweat and burning; then the sounds of agony from his fellow Maroons; then the aching pains in his tailbone, elbows, the back of his neck; and finally, the fact that he couldn't see anything— even the greenish glow light had gone out.

Who in Bast's name was this imperial?

As if in response to his question, boots made of heavy

Vibranium—he could tell from the clunk it made with each step—appeared before him. He looked up, and over him towered the imperial, his bodysuit covered by orange lights, as was his helmet, which contained three slits on each side but no eyes or breathing apparatus in view. This close, he was even bigger and more fearsome. Behind him, the portal which he'd just walked through closed softly without sound.

M'Baku wasn't a coward but a brave, experienced soldier who also realized one thing: Anyone who didn't fear this imperial was a fool and would be quick to die.

"You are wrong, mule." The imperial's voice was whiny, mechanical. Inhuman.

M'Baku gritted his teeth. *Call me mule one more time* . . . But at the moment, he was more interested in another concern: *What am I wrong about?*

"You are wrong," the imperial repeated. "I am no man. I am . . . the Manifold."

CHAPTER 14

△▽△

MOONBASE CUDJOE

M'BAKU BLINKED. *The Manifold?* What was that—a nickname? Was he supposed to know what that meant?

Before he could raise these queries, the Manifold lifted one of his heavy, armored boots and stomped it on M'Baku's chest. Air whooshed out of every orifice. Blood filled his mouth. He swore he felt a rib give way.

"So it ends," the Manifold said. "The slave is returned to his natural state."

Now *that,* M'Baku could not abide. His squad had been single-handedly defeated, sure. The Manifold was a worthy opponent, sure. But he'd called him a *mule* once, and now he'd called him a *slave.* That, in M'Baku's book, was worthy of punishment.

"No different than your own," M'Baku replied through blood-stained teeth, buying time. All he needed now was to get the imperial sucked into conversation, distracted. And when he saw an opening, he would make his move.

"And what makes you think I am anything like you, mule?"

Good. He's buying it. "You don't get it. Under N'Jadaka, we're all mules."

And then, a blast of fire and light and retaliation struck the Manifold in the back.

He didn't scream, didn't give any signs of agony. Like a machine, he simply crumpled, slowly and grudgingly, and clattered to the ground with a heavy thunk.

"M'Baku! Are you okay?"

From the darkness, multiple figures ran carrying firearms. There was just enough light to make out the panther helmets. The person in the lead came into view—the thick white hair and sleek skin of a Teku-Maza.

Captain N'Yami. M'Baku collapsed with relief. The Maroons quickly picked him up.

"What *was* that thing?" N'Yami stared at the Manifold, who lay motionless a few paces away.

"He called himself *the Manifold*," M'Baku replied through gritted teeth. "Whatever that means."

N'Yami didn't seem ruffled by this revelation. "I have some ideas," she said. "But what I don't have is time. We need to get everyone to the shuttles."

M'Baku grunted his agreement before a thought landed upon him.

"N'Yami," he asked, "where is Nakia? Where is T'Challa?"

BACK ON THE TERRACE, more and more Askari soldiers dropped from the sky.

The Maroons were overrun. Noting the danger of the rooftop guns, the Askari had altered their angle of approach and now descended upon a portion of the terrace where there were no anticraft guns. Even fewer Maroons occupied the area, and T'Challa and Nakia had to turn their focus toward providing aid there.

Gunfire thundered. The air smelled of burning metal. Everything was on fire.

"I won't lie to you," T'Challa said to Nakia through his comm as soon as they arrived, returning fire. "This doesn't look good."

Nakia counted with her eyes. "We're outnumbered three to one." She pulled out two short spears and flung them to T'Challa. He caught them with ease.

"N'Yami's ordered a retreat," she said. "Good for her, bad for us. There are no reinforcements. We've got to get to the shuttles on our own." She angled her head, poised for the attack. "Not ideal. But we're Maroons."

"Yes," said T'Challa, equally poised. "We've cut our way out of worse. It should be easy to cut our way *through*."

And then he flew.

It was always a beauty to watch him fight, Nakia thought. The way he put up a shield to deflect bullets, dropped the shield just long enough to strike down one, two, three Askari soldiers, then put it back up again before another could fire at him. Rinse, repeat, rinse, repeat. Even those far from him weren't safe—he threw the spear whenever he could, catching a distant shooter through the front of his helmet. Then he picked up the fallen soldier's firearm and rained destruction on the advancing force.

Not a single Askari was spared.

After T'Challa had moved through the Askari battalion, all lay fallen in a sea of fire and smoke and blood, enough to cloud the senses and suffocate whoever breathed within the vicinity. But out of this vestige of destruction emerged T'Challa, unscathed, unfazed.

"See, Maroons?" said Nakia to those around her. "Like the man said, *easy*."

"I thought he was being ironic, General Nakia," a nearby Maroon said.

"Soldier, our T'Challa is a man of many virtues. Irony is not one of them."

She couldn't believe the words out of her mouth. Here she was, showering this man with praise. Perhaps N'Yami and her story about the second coming had rubbed off on her more than she cared to admit.

There was no time to consider this as a new Askari battalion arrived.

She dashed forward, striking the incoming soldiers with her charged spears. One got too close, hooked her in a choke hold. She stabbed his hand and the blade went through. But surprisingly, the Askari didn't flinch.

"Nice try, mule," he said in her ear above the thundering gunfire. She could smell the wetness of his teeth, sense their sharpness. He squeezed even harder, tightening his hold on her neck. "Now *bow*."

Nakia gritted her teeth, extended the spear in her free hand, and aimed downward.

"You . . . first." She stabbed him behind the knee.

He growled, loosened his hold, just enough for her to turn around and swing the second spear, finishing him off. A second Askari nearby, seeing the tussle, fired. Nakia dodged and threw the spear, catching him in the jaw. As he writhed on his knees, she retrieved his firearm.

"I said *bow,* jambazi." Then she fired, first into him, and then into his comrade.

"T'Challa!" she said into her comm. "We've got to start falling back! I don't know how much longer the shuttles can wait!"

T'Challa, shells clinking around him from all the gunfire, turned to her in acknowledgment.

"Not long at all, Nakia," came a voice through her comm. It was Taku, from the *Mackandal.*

"Go ahead!" she screamed into the comm.

"You've got to get back to the *Mackandal* now!" Taku *always* sounded urgent—it was her job—but this was different. "Our situation is deteriorating rapidly!"

"TAKU," SAID N'YAMI into her comm.

"Captain," Taku replied.

"The first shuttle is headed your way. What's going on up there?"

They had successfully completed the rescue of M'Baku and his squad and were making their way back to one of the nearest shuttles.

"The second wave is here, Captain," said Taku. "A flight of masai fighters."

As if on cue, a fresh wave of Askari fighters appeared in front of N'Yami's rescue group. Both sides camped behind barriers and exchanged fire.

"We can hold them off for a bit," Taku was still saying over comms, "but I don't know how long."

"Taku," M'Baku interjected, "if you have to leave, then do so." He activated a flash grenade and threw it. "Remember, the M'Kraan Shard is aboard. It's more important than any of us."

The grenade exploded in the midst of the Askari. In their moment of disorientation, the Maroons opened fire.

"Go, go, go!" N'Yami screamed.

And just as she said so, orange light spilled all over them, coming from the Askari.

"Wait," said M'Baku. "He's back!"

The Manifold stepped out from the portal that had just opened and onto the terrace. He looked every bit as hale and strong as he'd been when M'Baku first encountered him, as if he hadn't been recently defeated.

"Remember me, mule?" asked the Manifold, and then swung back his arms and threw a discharge of energy their way.

"N'Yami, watch out!" M'Baku, now familiar with the Manifold's attacks, shoved his captain out of the way and ducked to evade the energy blast.

"It's okay, Lieutenant," said a nearby Maroon. "We've got him."

"You have nothing," said the Manifold. "Least of all your own lives."

Then came blinding flashes of orange. He was everywhere, appearing before and behind and beside, using every weapon in his arsenal: fists, firearms, portals. He smashed a Maroon's head so that brain mush swam in his panther helmet. He crushed a few upon landing from a portal above them. He shot others with their own firearms. He sliced a group of Maroons in half by shutting a portal across their waists.

He was a feral killing machine, unstoppable, only satiated by more blood, more guts, more murder.

N'Yami stood frozen, unsure what to do. M'Baku had no solutions, either, other than firing even more bullets that simply bounced off the Manifold's suit. Maroons fell left and right. N'Yami's heart sank. All these years of building up a resistance, and they were simply going to lose to a single imperial machine of death?

But then, as if from nowhere, a fresh hail of bullets descended upon the Manifold, not enough to harm him, but enough to get his attention.

"We're here, N'Yami!"

Nakia. N'Yami had never been so relieved to hear her general's voice.

Beside her, T'Challa, running and firing, said, "Analyzing our enemy . . ."

Then, for some reason, he slowed.

N'Yami had never seen T'Challa slow down in battle once. Not as the ancient T'Challa, and not as this man he was now. But there was something about the way he slowed when he scanned the Manifold, as if he suddenly recognized or remembered something.

And that moment of hesitation was all the Manifold needed.

The imperial machine of death, spotting T'Challa, spun and flung something in his direction, heading straight for the Maroon's chest.

But the spirit of the panther god was alive in T'Challa, because as swiftly as the Manifold had flung his weapon, T'Challa lifted an arm—

—and caught it midair.

It was a spear. Vibranium, ancient-looking yet sturdy. New Vibranium didn't hold up like this, seeing as the Empire liked to dilute its properties during mass production of weaponry and equipment for warfare. This had to be the old kind of Vibranium, the kind once employed in times before N'Yami herself, before her forebears, even before the Empire.

It had to be from Wakanda Prime. And that could only mean one thing.

"Is that—" said Nakia.

"The Spear of Bashenga," N'Yami finished.

It was impossible. Relics of Wakanda Prime were forbidden in the Empire. Somehow the Manifold had gotten hold of this relic of the old panther king, or his imperial masters had given it to him. Worse, by the way he'd reacted to T'Challa, N'Yami surmised that he'd been instructed to use it specifically for him. To kill the heretic with the spear of the king . . . just in case he was *actually* the king.

And then T'Challa had caught it.

As if responding to N'Yami's train of thought, T'Challa, frowning at the spear in his hand, growled. With the same spinning motion the Manifold had used, he swiveled, aimed, and threw the spear back at his enemy.

No one expected it, not even the Manifold himself. The imperial was equally as surprised as N'Yami was when the spear struck him, went *through* his armor, and exited at the back.

By Bast! thought N'Yami, and she could see everyone thought the same. *He truly is him!*

"Captain!" Taku was screaming, jolting them back as the Manifold staggered, ever so slowly, and fell. "We have to go!"

TO ALL SHUTTLES: THIS IS SHUTTLE 43. WE HAVE N'YAMI AND HER SQUADRON. HEADED TO RENDEZVOUS WITH THE MACKANDAL NOW.

"Go N'Yami! Go M'Baku!" Nakia shouted. "We'll take the last shuttle and be right behind you."

N'Yami stared out the window as the ground fell away and the shuttle rose into the air. She breathed a sigh of relief as she watched the first shuttle dock, knowing M'Baku and his squad made it safely to the ship. True to their word, Nakia, T'Challa, and the rest of their team had quickly boarded the sole remaining shuttle and were virtually beside her own. They had all made it out. In her heart, despondency and hope battled for command. Below her, on the grounds of what was meant to be a refuge for all who'd escaped the iron clutches of the Empire, were the very bodies of those she'd sworn to protect. It didn't help that scattered among them were their fallen enemies, two to every Maroon. She knew that though they were retreating from this battle, fighting their way through the enemy chagas with an eye on space folding the *Mackandal,* they were winning the overall war. But that did not dull her sadness.

Yet, a ray of light: the image that was now forever imprinted on her mind—T'Challa catching the Spear of Bashenga. Hurling it back at the Manifold, wounding the imperial death machine for the first time. *He Who Put the Knife Where It Belonged.* It made sense now.

This man was truly T'Challa the Ultimate, the Avenger, the long-forgotten king of Wakanda Prime. And she could not wait to shout this joyous news to the rest of the resistance, light the fire of new hope, and ride the blaze to victory.

She stared at the fallen body of the Manifold. Just imagine how many more enemies were going to be defeated like this, the Empire's best super-soldiers thrown against the Maroons, each falling by the wayside upon meeting the immovable object that was the original king of Wakanda. A great pride filled her chest and rose to her throat, and she had to swallow her joy to prevent herself from screaming.

The Manifold moved.

The shuttle had barely cleared the atmosphere, but N'Yami could still see the bodies below. She cupped her hands against the glass and peered down. *Surely . . . not?*

But there it was—the twitch of an arm, of something clinging to life by any means. And then, as if to answer her question, the orange lights of the Manifold's suit lit up and the imperial death machine clambered to his knees.

She should've opened her mouth. She should've screamed for the shuttle to turn around, fire at the monstrosity, make him stay down for good. But she was too shocked by the turn of events, the swiftness with which the Manifold moved, grabbing the weapon nearest to him—a rocket launcher, it looked like—and mounting it on his shoulder.

She felt crushed by the burgeoning promise of retribution, so quickly splattered before her. Every belief she'd so carefully cultivated, swiftly squashed by the fact that the Vibranium spear had not, in fact, hurt the Manifold—it had simply damaged his armor. Weighed down by the possible truth that the spear was not, in fact, the Spear of Bashenga. That it was perhaps just another imperial spear, not made of old Vibranium, but perhaps simply old, and therefore easy for a reflexive soldier to catch.

And perhaps this man whom she called T'Challa was simply an ordinary man, not the Ultimate, not the Avenger, not *He Who Put the Knife Where It Belonged.*

The Manifold manifested a portal above himself then leaped into it, disappearing from sight. Another portal appeared level with the rising shuttle. From it popped the Manifold, rocket launcher still balanced on his shoulder. In that split moment, he leveled the cannon and fired.

Fire blazed toward N'Yami and the shuttle, assuring her of the death she'd always welcomed and never feared. Her only pain was that it had to happen this way; that she had believed in something—someone—and it had turned out to be false hope.

But no, she would not go out like this, despondent and resigned. She would hold on to hope in the rebellion. She prayed that, if anything, the same hope would be transmitted to all the Maroons, across the galaxies, even though she wouldn't be there to see to it. And she would hope that maybe, just maybe, she wasn't wrong about T'Challa.

"Prove me right, dear Bast," she whispered, her final words. Then she shut her eyes.

T'CHALLA HEARD THE EXPLOSION before he saw it.

TAKU TO ALL SHUTTLES, the comm said. *THE DOCK-*

ING BAY IS OPEN AND WE'RE TAKING HEAVY FIRE. YOU MUST DOCK IMMEDIATELY.

T'Challa wasn't listening. When he jumped down from the escape shuttle and sprinted across the docking bay of the *Mackandal*, for what felt like the first time, it wasn't to grab fresh weaponry to hit back at the attacking imperial craft. He and Nakia ran for the elevators, through the hallways. He tossed his panther helmet aside as he muttered one word over and over and over.

No no no no no no no. No no no no no no!

The doors to the command center swooshed open.

Everyone was there—Taku, M'Baku, and the rest of the command staff. Everyone but the one person he knew had been on the shuttle that had just exploded—shuttle 43.

"No . . ." he said. "No . . ."

"Lieutenant M'Baku." Taku was gentle but firm as she turned to the somber general. "We can grieve later. You have the command. I suggest a space fold immediately." Her tone was brisk but not unkind. She truly was a product of N'Yami's leadership, as they all were.

And now that leadership was gone forever.

"How can . . ." M'Baku started, but his throat couldn't make the words.

It can't be. She can't be gone.

"Lieutenant?" Taku pressed. "I need your authorization for a space fold. We're getting battered out there."

M'Baku swallowed, clearly struggling to compose himself.

"Na . . . kia," he said.

"What?"

"Nakia." He turned to the former imperial, who, in truth, was higher in rank than he was. "It should be you."

Nakia, whose body language had so far been stiff, holding back the rage and sadness that threatened to burst from her, finally gave in.

"No!" Tears clouded her eyes. "No, I—I can't. She would never have wanted that. She respected me, cared for me, but she would never let me break Maroon law." She looked into M'Baku's face, tears pooling, falling down her cheeks. "It has to be one of the Nameless."

M'Baku stepped forward and wrapped his arms around her. She held him back, tightly, and together they bore each other's sorrows.

"Lieutenant!" Taku interjected. "There's no time. Can we execute the fold?"

M'Baku let go of Nakia and looked around the command center. Every eye was on him. But T'Challa couldn't help but focus on Nakia's rare outburst of vulnerability. Everyone else just wanted to get out of there.

"Okay," said M'Baku, his chest filled with resolve. "Execute the fold."

CHAPTER 15

△▽△▽

PLANET BAST

THE EMPEROR WAS QUIET. He was always quiet, regardless of the situation, reserving his actions—small or mighty—for moments after he'd deeply pondered the information he'd received. Achebe sometimes wondered if he'd always been this way, this melancholic, if his silences had always carried this weight.

He hadn't known the emperor well in the beforetimes, back when he was still Commander N'Jadaka, the most formidable and popular mercenary in the service of the Intergalactic Empire of Wakanda. The emperor had been young when his path began— barely a teenager, Achebe remembered. That didn't stop him spearheading some of the Empire's key campaigns in the five galaxies, capturing planets from the S'Yaan Expanse to the Matrix of Mamadou.

The songs sung about him now were the same as those composed back then, praising his prowess and conquests, only now *commander* was replaced with *emperor.* He was every bit as popular now as he'd been back then, and it was evident in the emperor's interactions as they crossed an open courtyard in the palace.

The emperor was barely seen in public, but his visage and likeness were everywhere. Statues, holos, paintings—every opportunity to impress the image of him as the Black Panther on the residents of the throneworld, as well as other worlds once they were conquered. Here, on Planet Bast, it was easier than in other places. Everyone already loved him, having seen him rise from nothing. He was one of their own.

As they crossed the courtyard, many bowed to greet him with alacrity and a grin. A few even dared to offer the Ancient Wakandan salute, crossing their arms over their chests. *Our liege lord!* some whispered silently. *Wakanda forever!* When the imperial spacecraft flew over the city, many citizens would place one hand to their chest and lift the other up, as if in worship. *Bless us, oh Avatar of Bast. Take our supplications to the goddess!*

The emperor knew these parasocial displays were all part of imperial strategy—the people needed something to believe in, and though he barely acknowledged these things, Achebe knew he understood they were necessary, especially for those here in the palace for whom the emperor's reticence didn't matter. They had *seen* him. Now they would have stories to tell when they returned to the city, in the bars and pleasure houses, in the marketplaces and trading hubs, in the shrines of worship. *Did you know the emperor is seven feet tall?* they would say, exaggerating. *Did you know he can disappear on the spot? Did you know he can kill you with a blink? Did you know he shuts his eyes and convenes with Bast whenever he desires?* It didn't matter if these words were true or not. Their mere utterance was enough.

So, what did someone so venerated by his people, so blessed and protected by the gods that he had the nine lives of a panther, have to be so melancholy about?

"The Manifold performed wonderfully, my liege," Achebe said, hoping to lift the dour mood. They'd just logged their first major victory against the rebellious heretics in a while. Reports had even come in that their captain had been killed in the battle as they fled their hideout base. All the work of their research and development teams had finally paid off—in one fell swoop, imperial forces had located and invaded the rebellion hideout, taken out their leader, chased them into the annals of space, and razed all they left behind to the ground, reducing the rebellion to nothing but rubble and smoke and a handful of spacecraft in the wind. A comprehensive defeat in anyone's eyes.

Not in Emperor N'Jadaka's, though.

"Hmmm," he said. They were now walking across the tunnel that led to a chamber the emperor often went into whenever he wished to consult the Wakandan gods. The emperor had decided he was going to pay a visit to the goddess Bast.

"The terrorists are in flight," Achebe added. Perhaps the emperor didn't hear the first time? The Empire had won! The rebellion was scattered to the wind! No more stealth attacks!

"Hmmm." N'Jadaka remained unimpressed. "But the heretic lives."

Ah, there it is, thought Achebe. Now he understood why they were here, why the emperor was going to convene with Bast. Ever since the name *T'Challa* had made its way back into this court, the emperor had become unsettled, more unsettled than Achebe had ever seen him.

It was obvious why the emperor had such a rich vein of disdain for this particular man. The stories that wagged most from rebellious tongues spoke this name often: *T'Challa*. Not in the same manner as the imperials spoke it—as the revered name of the warrior-king from Ancient Wakanda who'd founded them, who brought this very empire to being. So revered was this name, in fact, that it was forbidden, blasphemous, for anyone under imperial rule to bear it.

The emperor's ire, therefore, made sense, as the heretic—and now the rebellion he'd joined—spoke this name differently. They spoke of a warrior from Ancient Wakanda reawakened, reincarnated, returned to topple the Intergalactic Empire. They buttressed their tales with snippets from the original legends, passed down for generations, right from the Wakandan ancestors who first arrived in these stars and made their home here. Lies and half-truths commingled, particularly those that included mentions of the N'Jadaka of Ancient Wakanda, who'd also been an adversary of the real T'Challa.

Was the emperor concerned that this was his fate? Did he believe that he was doomed to have this heretic as an adversary due to the weight of history and legend?

"He does live," Achebe acceded. At this point, there wasn't much left to add. If the emperor had already decided that he'd never be satisfied until this singular man was brought to heel, then there was little else Achebe could do to convince him otherwise.

"How much longer, Counselor?" They'd stopped by the door at the end of the tunnel now. Behind this door was a black, cold, and empty room no one but N'Jadaka was allowed to enter. The emperor went inside whenever he wished to seek the goddess Bast's counsel. Achebe had often wondered what happened in there, if the emperor truly traveled to the chamber of the Wakandan gods as rumored. But today, he didn't have time to wonder. He was simply happy for the emperor to turn his attentions away from him.

"We're closing in on him, Sire," said Achebe, which wasn't quite the truth. "His death is assured." Also a lie.

The emperor didn't seem to care. He placed a hand on the door panel.

"See that it is, Achebe," he said. "For in the end, there can only be one avatar of Bast."

Then he went into the darkness.

CHAPTER 16

△▽△

THE
ORISHA GATE

THE ORISHA GATE was alive.

Moving from the corporeal world of the galaxies into the realm of the Wakandan gods was always a rush of the senses for N'Jadaka. The wind through the portal wafted against his skin, soft like the velvety fur of a panther. The gate tasted like salty metal whenever he walked through it, as if all his blood was being drained away, and all that was left behind was the husk of his skeleton and spirit. A whine like a thousand bees played in his ears. Everything around him was pitch-dark, with the odd swirl of color in rainbows: magenta, cyan, indigo, white, gray, yellow. The smell was sharp, like freshly ground ginger.

Then all of it vanished as suddenly as it had arrived, and only his sixth sense was left alive, the only sense he needed in this realm: the ability to see and converse with the gods.

Before him, thrice his height and just as wide, stood Bast. She was in her panther form, black fur harboring a sheen, eyes yellow, gaze piercing. Her panther ears flapped absentmindedly as she registered his presence, and her neck curved forward ever so slightly in acknowledgment.

He got down on one knee and bowed his head.

"Blessed Bast, protector of Wakanda, in this life and in the next," he announced. "I humbly come before you in reverence and supplication."

The big panther blinked. Her godly form barely betrayed expression, face prone to less discernible, tiny movements.

"So," she said, her voice big and booming. "You have returned, my emperor."

N'Jadaka nodded, looking around. They were at the top of a bare platform, the shimmering gate closing behind them. Stairs led below to the lower platform where the next tier of gods in the Wakandan pantheon resided. He could see the gods who shared that tier in their animal-human hybrid forms, each with their staff of command: Ptah the Shaper, the metalworking god; the war god, Kokou; Thoth, god of intelligence; and Mujaji, god of agriculture. They watched Bast's tier above them but did not speak.

"My champion, my son," said Bast, and slowly, she morphed.

Her human form, when it arrived, was no less fierce than her panther's but was far more beautiful. Her hair, cut short to the scalp, was adorned with a flowing headdress bearing tassels in the same burst of colors that he'd experienced while crossing the gate. Her jewelry was equally as exquisite, stacked neck rings of gold bottomed out by a shawl. She wore a warrior's bodice designed to look more ceremonial than practical, and her calflets carried the same colors as her tunic. She was barefoot, pattering softly as she settled into her new form and came head-to-head, face-to-face with N'Jadaka.

"Speak, child," she said, even though her human form was much younger than N'Jadaka. "Long have you fled my regard. What now brings you to the chamber of the Wakandan gods?"

Without waiting for a response, she began to descend the stairs, proceeding to converge with the lower gods. Movement in the Wakandan pantheon, N'Jadaka had learned, only went in one direction: Those above could descend but those below couldn't ascend except by special circumstance, say, in the event that a god above was displaced and a replacement was needed. Not that gods in this pantheon were easily displaced or otherwise removed from existence. They were much too powerful for that.

N'Jadaka rose and followed.

"Regrets, my lady Bast," he said. "The gravest of regrets brings me."

"Regrets? This is not like you, N'Jadaka."

She stepped into the lower tier, ignoring the other gods and walking onto what appeared to be clouds. N'Jadaka tested them with a foot. They were soft but firm. He followed her.

"I have had my share of champions through the years," said Bast. "Mamadou Fall was the most fearsome. Nehanda was the wisest. But none were more certain."

She waved an arm, and images of her champions of legend materialized before them. Mamadou Fall, the fearsome warrior from the Jabari lands of yore, the first panther to emerge from that tribe. Iya Nehanda, his daughter, also a panther, so skilled that she earned her title at one of the youngest ages ever—a mere twenty human years. And there was the third, a handsome imperial warrior with fire in his eyes and an impeccable sense of Wakandan fashion.

It took N'Jadaka a while to recognize himself when he was much younger. He'd grown older and wearier since then, lines digging deeper into his face. It was why he preferred to keep his panther mask on in the presence of his subjects. They didn't need to see what managing the affairs of five galaxies did to a person.

"Time has had its way with me, Goddess," he said to Bast as the image of his younger self dissolved. "Time has humbled me."

Bast glided up to him, placed a hand on his cheek. "But what is time to mighty N'Jadaka, master of the five galaxies? What does the decimator of the Teku-Maza, scourge of the Rigellans, need with humility?"

There was something in her tone that made her words teeter between praise and mockery. Bast was like this often, and it made him wonder if she was the same way with other panthers from before, or if she reserved this sliver of contempt just for him? Many times, he'd wanted to confront her about it, to ask if she hated the

atypical way in which he'd become her avatar; if she'd have preferred one reincarnated from the lineage of her previous avatars,
like the heretics often claimed. But Bast never discussed her previous avatars in detail. As long as he was in front of her, she gave all
her attention to him, and him alone.

Except, of course, when it came to that *one* heretic, the man
from nowhere.

Perhaps this was her reason for being snide? That despite these
titles she showered upon him, there was another name spoken by
inhabitants of the five galaxies with much more reverence than his
would ever be?

"I have seen him, mistress," he said. "Your chosen avatar." He
squinted. "Your redeemer has come."

If Bast understood that he was talking about the man who'd
once called himself T'Challa, the man he'd been forced to
disappear—and then who had *actually* disappeared—she didn't
show it. Her face remained expressionless in the same way her
panther likeness typically did. She blinked and resumed walking
away.

He didn't follow.

"N'Jadaka," she said, stopping to look back at him. "Do you
know what drew me here? What pulled the orishas away from
Wakanda Prime?"

He, like many of his generation, knew only of Wakanda Prime
through the stories of legend. As a graduate of the military academy, he'd been educated on every important aspect of the Empire's
history, from the tales the first explorers had brought with them
and left, passed down through centuries and generations, to those
fashioned more recently to firm up the Wakandan concepts every
imperial subject should ideally embody. But of the gods and their
choice to travel from that faraway place, over time and space, to
cater to the Intergalactic Empire, he knew even less. He could only
guess in the same way his own teachers at the academy had.

"Faith," he said. "The abiding faith of your subjects must have
pulled you toward us."

"Yes," said Bast. "But this understates things."

She began another slow wave of her arms. A new batch of clouds swallowed them, and within it were born new images, steeped in a golden hue yet sharper and clearer than the last. Before them stood a mountainous bust of the panther likeness in statue form, worshipped by a gathering of Wakandans who looked nothing like the subjects of the Empire. In a parallel image, they seemed to be going to war. Their weapons and dress belonged to another time, one far, far removed from the present.

"True enough, the faith of your ancestors freed me from mortal shackles," Bast continued. "For millennia, I guarded Wakanda alongside my fellow orishas from threats mystic and pedestrian. But I was not the only one seeking to escape the coil."

Another image: space, its vastness. A tiny shuttle whistled through the blackness, a thin streak. Then suddenly, that thin streak became a large system of lights, first across one planet, then across various planets, and then—this part he recognized—across various galactic systems. These lights were stars, ships, peoples.

"Across the vastness of space, I saw the very name of Wakanda expand. And what I found in this expansion was not merely the faithful, but the fanatic. And who was more fanatical than the young N'Jadaka?"

Wars, conquests, expansions. Spears, panther helmets, blood. Legions and legions of imperial warriors hoisting the flag of Wakanda in faraway places. And he, the young, handsome N'Jadaka, leading them all.

This part, he remembered clearly. It had taken a special kind of toughness for him to rise from his humble and lowly beginnings, crawl his way through the imperial academy and emerge as the most popular mercenary—and later, captain—in the imperial army. He had become the old emperor's prized asset by sheer force of will. All, of course, with the blessings of the gods.

"Yes, I was your chosen," he said to Bast. "I razed whole star systems, imposed order where there was none, brought the purifying light of your gospel."

But parts of their history he chose to no longer remember now that he was emperor. Parts that made rageful anger burn within him; emotions too strong to reveal, lest they cause him to act in a manner unbecoming of a leader.

"They called me a *monster*." The words, which he'd never spoken to anyone else, came out of him forcefully, vulnerably, to the only person who could understand the state of his spirit.

Bast held his gaze, nodded. She understood.

"But I knew that the weak crumble, while the strong endure," he pressed on. "Only among the strong can a durable peace be made. My methods were not civil, but they were necessary."

Bast nodded again. "Of course they were. Besides, how can they know what was done to you? What do they know of betrayals? Of losses?"

Sometimes Bast spoke like the mother he never had. Her words had a calming effect that doused whatever flame blazed in his heart. It was why he used to visit. She was the only one whose words could bring him peace.

"Perhaps I should have listened to you," he said. "I should have known."

"Yes," she said. "But your faith was ultimately in men, not in gods."

She waved her arms. A new image. One of him, his younger self, returning from battle, his name chanted by the people.

He turned away from the image. He didn't need her to show him because he remembered well enough what had happened.

"The people chanted your name," said Bast. "Bathed in your triumphs. They all *loved* you."

"*Almost* all of them, Goddess," he said. *And not long before they thought me monstrous,* he thought, remembering being summoned to the very throne room he now occupied. There, the emperor's two advisors at the time had already been present, making their case against him.

The people chant the name N'Jadaka louder than your own, Sire, they'd said. *His impudence grows with each victory. How*

long before this mercenary feels himself to have no need of his bet-
ters? For the sake of the Empire, he must be neutralized. The time
is now, Sire—put the blade where it belongs.

When he'd knelt before the emperor, the man had already made
up his mind. He had a special mission for the young commander
N'Jadaka.

"Did I not warn you, my child?" Bast's words brought him out
of his reverie. "Trust not in mortal men—"

"—glory only in the orishas," he finished. "Yes, but that was
not *all* you said. *The day would come,* you told me, *when a legend-*
ary avatar would return." He gulped. "When I would be discarded
and replaced." He narrowed his gaze at the panther god. "How
was I to have faith in you? How was I to believe, knowing you
would someday discard me like all your other 'champions'? What
choice had I then but to put my trust in mortal men?"

Bast watched him quietly for a moment, then waved her hands
again. Yet another image appeared, this one from the very mission
the emperor had sent him on. He and his squadron were to visit an
obscure planet in the Matrix of Mamadou, where the Between—
Vibranium machines hosting the consciousnesses of a breakaway
sect of imperials who sought longevity and immortality—were
holed up. They were to destroy this group completely in order to
finalize the Empire's claim on the system.

It was a simple mission on paper, yet it soon became clear that
it was anything but, something specifically engineered to alter the
direction of his life forever.

And alter the direction it did.

"The choice, my son," Bast said, "was to see yourself as the
steward of great power instead of its sole claimant." She still
sounded like a mother, only this time the chastising kind, the kind
N'Jadaka didn't quite appreciate.

"Only with power could I safeguard the Empire," he retorted.
How else did she think he maintained the Wakandan tradition of
expanding imperial reach? Because it was exactly that, wasn't it?
Conquest was as Wakandan as anything else. He was simply main-

taining a tradition Bast herself had overseen for centuries before this Intergalactic Empire. Why was she suddenly acting as if it was wrong only when *he* did it? How else was he supposed to hold on to the Empire for this long, amid all the opposition?

"So you believed." Bast sounded disappointed. "And so you trusted." Her gaze on him was acute. "And so you were betrayed."

The image she had spurred up was of the moment of failure in the mission, wherein the army of Between he'd been sent to conquer had turned up with fighters that outnumbered his own warriors three to one. This forced him to stage a retreat. He and his squadron fled into a cave, staving off the attack and taking time to regroup.

"You swore yourself to man," said Bast, "and man answered with treachery. Your loyalty was *weakness*. And because the weak would be destroyed, washed away, you swore to never again be among the weak."

She was right. It wasn't just the fact that his very own emperor had betrayed him that stung. It was the manner in which he had opted to do it, forcing him into a position of weakness, into retreat and hiding. That wasn't the Wakandan way. What message would it send to the rest of the galaxy to know Wakanda's foremost commander cowered in a cave on a foreign planet, shivering at the might of an otherwise banal army?

These were the questions seething under his skin when his second-in-command at the time had come up to him and said, "Captain, we were told this was merely a small outpost for the Between. Why would the imperium send us into a death trap?"

Why indeed, he'd thought, realizing that perhaps the imperium had other tricks up its sleeve. So into the cave he went, scouting, searching to see if there was something more dangerous than the horde of Between that awaited them outside.

That was how he'd found it.

Over the years, he'd wondered if this had been the aim of the imperium after all, even though he was sure such ideas were unlikely, since his discovery ended up not working in their favor.

He'd wondered, too, if it had been the work of the gods, Bast looking over her chosen warrior and providing him with a gift in a time of need. But listening to her now, he realized it had not been her hand either. Perhaps it was simply the hand of chance, of luck, of good fate, forces outside their control, that had led him to the discovery that would change his life forever.

The Klyntar symbiote.

The symbiote had simply lain there, as if waiting to be found. He'd known very little about symbiotes at the time, their interconnectedness, and the fact that it was the Empire's own activities that had driven them into separation and near extinction. (In a way, it was ironic, and perhaps a bit of poetic justice, that the very symbiote they'd almost destroyed became their savior in a time of need.) He had known little about their ability to communicate, to convince without words. But in that moment, when he raised his lamp in that cave and discovered that amorphous blob of black, he could swear he heard its voice, calling to the desire in him.

"What is it, Captain?" his second-in-command had asked.

"Salvation," he'd replied. "Power."

And he'd believed his words. He still did.

It was in that moment he gave himself over, let it take him. Symbiosis, he realized—as the amorphous blob had reached for him and became one with his very flesh—truly meant becoming one with something beyond oneself. It meant agreeing to be taken, to sacrifice something, like the searing pain that nearly crippled him when the symbiote conjoined with his body, his mind, his very being. But it also meant receiving a gift in return, one so enormous that it allowed him to rise, walk out of that cave, face the hundreds-strong army of Between all on his own, and destroy every last one of them with a single command of the symbiote.

He looked at Bast now. She spoke of placing his trust in gods? Well, what symbiosis did she have with him, with any of her champions? Did they not all die? What symbiosis did the gods have with their people if they could never protect them from the forces that sought to destroy them?

What kind of symbiosis was it that she was willing to anoint another avatar while he was still here, still alive?

Bast was still speaking. "The Klyntar were nearly driven to extinction by the Empire. In you, they found a host. In them, you found strength."

Indeed he had. He'd taken his shuttle back home and, without a second thought, walked into the throne room and, in front of the emperor, made the two advisors pay with their lives. After making the emperor watch as he employed significant power in crushing his guards to bits—thereby breaking the ruler's spirit completely—only then did he allow him the gift of death.

That became his first day on the panther throne.

"Yes," he said to Bast. "When I pledged myself to the Klyntar, I pledged to something that needed me, something that *was* me, and thus could never betray me. I knew then the folly of my ancestors who sought to avoid war through defense. *Conquest* was the only defense. And on that ethic, I became mightier than anything I could have imagined."

"A soldier no more," said Bast. "An *emperor*. No mere avatar, but one who seeks *godhood* himself." She turned toward him, gaze acute. "That is why you are here, is it not, N'Jadaka?"

He was surprised it had taken her this long to come to this understanding. But it was out now. There was no hiding his ambitions any longer.

"It is the only way," he said. "A legend moves against me. To defeat him, I need more than the Klyntar." *And,* he didn't say, *I will not find it in the promises of a god who already betrays me.*

Bast looked sad, like a mother lost. She seemed to have read his mind and realized that it was made up. This was inevitable.

"I have the faith," said N'Jadaka, his turn to speak with authority. "My people now believe in *me*. They are fanatics *for me*." The symbiote within him churned, flowed up to his neck, and rippled out of his skin, standing on end.

"The time of my ascension," said N'Jadaka, "is at hand."

"Is it, now?" In the split moment of his transformation, Bast had also made one of her own. Her sad demeanor was gone and her headdress reappeared. Her fingers grew longer, thicker, curvier, and claws began to emerge. Slowly, surely, she was returning to her panther form.

"You should have listened more closely, N'Jadaka." Her voice was a growl, a roar. "There is more to this life than eternal power."

N'Jadaka put on his panther helmet, adjusted it so it was snug. Then he let himself sink, let the symbiote spring forth and take over his entire self.

"Enough talk, witch," he growled back to Bast, now fully returned to her panther likeness. Then he leaped.

Bast leaped, too.

They crashed into each other, tossing in heavenly skies, tumbling along the platform. Bast thumped a foot into his chest, threw him like a light sack. Her attacks were fast, ferocious, and every hit she threw landed. He wasn't fazed, but he wasn't winning. He came back at her, flung a few attacks her way, none of which made impact. She was everywhere and nowhere, all too quickly. This was her domain and she made use of it quite shrewdly, appearing and disappearing at will, using every trick available to frustrate and eventually weaken him.

And weaken him she did until the symbiote became frustrated and retreated. His mortal body let the weight of his exertions hit him all at once, and when Bast arrived with her latest attack, he couldn't ward her off. She crashed into him, bringing him to the ground and pinning him there, baring teeth.

Then she went for the killing blow, biting into the flesh of his neck.

For a moment, he truly believed himself dead. He could feel her teeth deep in his shoulder, where it touched bone. An attack such as this on his mortal body in the godly plane was sure to do enough damage to ensure he never returned to the material world the same.

But then he realized there was no blood. There was no pain.

Bast, too, realized it at the same time. She sank her teeth deeper, taking a larger chunk of his skin in her mouth. No change.

And then something happened. Bast shut her eyes, and when she reopened them, the Klyntar symbiote was suddenly there.

She jerked away from N'Jadaka and stepped back, staggering, confused. "What—what is this?"

N'Jadaka rose, equally as confused, but understanding dawned on him as the symbiote flowed slowly from him and into Bast, the connection now fully established. He chuckled. He shouldn't have underestimated the symbiote.

"It is you who should have listened, Goddess," he said, pride creeping back into his voice, his demeanor. It was no longer him speaking alone but the voice of the Klyntar joined with his, individual thoughts shared as one.

"We could not force ourselves upon you," said the N'Jadaka-Klyntar. "You had to drink willingly."

Bast sank to one knee, then two. "No. No." Her panther likeness began to fade as slowly and surely as it had arrived, her fingers regressing to their humanoid shape, claws retracting, headdress peeling back to show her shaved, bald head.

The Klyntar seeped deeper into her, sunk its claws into her soul. "You . . . are . . . no . . . god."

She was speaking directly to N'Jadaka, but there wasn't much of the man alone left to speak to.

"Perhaps not," the man-symbiote voice said. "But now, neither are you."

The last of the symbiote seeped into the panther goddess. On her knees, she shuddered, once, twice, and then, with a final loud cry, screamed into the heavens.

The symbiote burst out of her and shot back into N'Jadaka. Along with it, as if wrapped tightly in its tentacles, was the panther spirit. It settled into N'Jadaka just as easily as the symbiote settled back into its host and covered him in the sheen that was specific to divinity, the light and power and affect of a god.

N'Jadaka turned to the four lower Orishas, who'd watched all this unfold before them in unbridled horror.

"The master and the servant are now one," he announced. "This is my word. This is my redemption."

Then he ascended the stairs to the platform above, where he stood and looked down on them. The lower gods hesitated for a moment, unsure of what to do. But the light of the panther spirit was with him, and that was all that mattered. Anyone who carried the panther spirit was worthy of this faith, this worship, this reverence.

Slowly, tentatively, they clenched their fists and crossed their arms over their chests, sharing their salutes of respect and recognition.

On the lower platform, obscured by clouds of her own making, the Wakandan goddess Bast lay motionless.

PART TWO

△▽△▽

CHAPTER 17

△▽△▽

NEW MAROON HIDEOUT,
NEHANDA'S LATTICE

THE HALL OF ASSEMBLY was packed to the brim. Since moving Maroon headquarters to this ice planet, M'Baku had never seen this much attendance at the seasonal function. Seasonal in the sense that they held it every month, counting time in the same manner they did back in Moonbase Cudjoe, and not seasonal according to the weather, since the weather on this tiny, undisclosed rock was always the same—deathly freezing and worsening.

Maroons filled the chamber, which wasn't a hall as the name suggested but a small room they'd set aside for meeting with larger audiences. Space was in short supply on this small, cold outpost. The infrastructure on the planet had been initially set up as a safe place for small Maroon squads to hide out for long periods of time, especially if the imperial search for them was hot. It was one of the last places the Empire would go looking for them because it was so uninhabitable, and staying here for too long was ill-advised. Unfortunately, it was also the only place the Empire hadn't tracked them after abandoning Moonbase Cudjoe.

Everyone huddled together, shoulder to shoulder, not only because the room was too small to fit them all but because the heating was simply insufficient. Everyone wore the warmest clothing they could find. Most of the soldiers wore panther suits, putting their thermal calibration capability to full use. Civilian Maroons were in more mundane clothing—several layers topped with heavy overcoats, headwear, gloves, and boots. Some of them were still thawing out, water pooling at their feet after they'd walked across the slippery ice to get here instead of using vehicles.

M'Baku glanced from person to person and his heart fell. They looked every inch like the cold, hungry, and suffering population they were. Sure, this was a far cry from the state of the mines in which they'd all been imprisoned as Nameless, but this was also a far cry from the promises they'd been offered when they joined the Maroon Rebellion, whether as civilians or as part of the fighting force. Promises that were made by the ones who came before him, but which M'Baku now had to fight hard to keep.

And I will, he told himself often, as he told himself now. But those were thoughts for later. Today was reserved for something much more solemn.

Once they were all settled, he rose and stood on the dais.

"Today marks the anniversary since our great and fearless leader, Captain N'Yami, was taken from us and delivered to the Plane of Wakandan Memory," he announced. "Let us begin this assembly by paying our respects. Elder Asare will lead us in the ritual of remembrance." He nodded at the wiry shaman, one of the Maroons tasked with holding physical memory, dedicating his own brain as storage for his people's history. "You have the floor, elder."

The small man shuffled up the ramp to the dais, found a spot, shifted his weight, cleared his throat, and began a song of solemnity. It was a slow and languid call-and-response chant, and the elder swayed gently from side to side, telling the story of N'Yami in song, while the assembly chanted back their acknowledgment, praise, sorrow, and hope.

The tale told of her humble beginnings laboring in the mines among other Nameless, before her eventual escape. It told of the relentless drive that led her to become one of the fiercest combatants in the Maroon Rebellion, the same drive that led her to return to her ancestral home of Agwé, founding the Teku-Maza Revolutionary Guard that fought the imperial occupation of their planet and won. And though her home had been decimated and her people and their evolutionary ancestors, the aquatic Jengu, neared extinction, she returned to the Maroon Rebellion because she believed the future of freedom in the five galaxies lay here. She gave every bodily offering to this cause, rising to the top, becoming a venerable leader, and ending her time as one of the most inspiring commanders of all time.

M'Baku watched fellow Maroons in the crowd, especially those with Nameless pasts, weep silently. He didn't have tears for this moment, but his chest felt dense, filled to the brim with the same despondency that hung in the air, thick and filmy. And yet there remained a strong sense of pride in the woman, in what she stood for. There was hope, even in her absence, because her very existence—the way she'd lived—had been a testament to a brighter, just future.

Scanning the crowd, M'Baku's eyes landed on Nakia's. Beside her stood T'Challa. They'd been inseparable since N'Yami's death, and somewhat more inconsolable than most in the Maroon force. M'Baku chalked it up to the fact that they'd spent the most time with N'Yami right before her death and had perhaps been privy to much of her last few mutterings about what and who she thought was the future of the rebellion. In his own engagements with her, he'd witnessed her seeking something big, a large and possibly final blow to be struck on the Empire. She had a few ideas, some rooted in the rebellion's alliance with the Teku-Maza Revolutionary Guard on her home planet and some rooted here, in the emergence of one whom she thought to be a hero—*the* hero—destined to lead them to victory if only he could find himself in time.

M'Baku's eyes met T'Challa's. They were as distraught as everyone else's. T'Challa didn't blink but acknowledged his superior with a small, perceptive nod. M'Baku, without responding, tore his gaze away and focused on the crowd.

Since N'Yami's death, rumors centering around T'Challa had grown among the Maroons. Little stirrings, born of whispers about the slain captain's beliefs. Nakia never uttered a word of what N'Yami told her in confidence, yet somehow other Maroons had learned she'd been the one who named this former Nameless rebel T'Challa. From that discovery, they came to their own conclusions about her beliefs: He was destined for greatness. It was believed that she paid ear to the words of prophecies deemed false by many—among Maroons and imperials both—of a man from Ancient Wakanda, a king, rising from the ashes to deliver the five galaxies from the iron grip of Emperor N'Jadaka. It was even whispered that she believed this T'Challa rebel might be such a man!

M'Baku, fortunately for them, had neither the time nor patience for rumors and whispers, especially for those of this nature. As far as he was concerned, prophecies were useless. He respected the shamans, and he respected N'Yami and her beliefs, but he refused to abide baseless would-be myths.

Could they not hear themselves? An ancient warrior reincarnated, resurrected, reappeared—or whatever it was the various heretics who'd appeared preached. How had he survived all this time? And how was he meant to become the Avatar of Bast when N'Jadaka himself had already been anointed by the gods? Was Bast to have two avatars, who would then proceed to kill each other? How could the same gods who anointed an avatar also offer a prophecy signaling his demise?

This was his struggle with believing any of it—in the goddess, in her supposed prophecies, and in any future for the Maroons dependent on perceived fate and blind luck. He would rather spend his time working on their current reality. What purpose did a promise based outside of fact hold? False hope, he decided, was *worse* than no hope at all.

The elder's song and story lifted, reached a crescendo. The room swelled. M'Baku felt even more just how much he loved N'Yami regardless of how he disagreed with her beliefs.

There would be no hero. There was no *one* final solution. There was only this small, ragtag group of survivors, and the massive

Empire against whom they were pitted. There was only one way to get out of this—sting as quickly and often as possible, as many times as they could, until the behemoth went down. Until then, he had one job: Keep the Maroons alive long enough to fight.

AFTER THE ASSEMBLY was over, M'Baku stood at the entrance to the hall, offering commiseration and goodwill to each Maroon as they left. It was the kind of thing N'Yami would've done, and if there was any day for him to do this, it was today.

People went by him in a blur, complaints rushing through him. *No hot water for days. When are the new rations coming? When will upgraded heating tech be installed?* He couldn't retain the specifics, only absorbing their depleting energies and depleting hope. He offered as much assurance of his devotion to their survival as he could, and then he let them go.

Soon T'Challa and Nakia, along with his immediate command team, were the only people left in the hall.

"A word, Captain?" asked T'Challa.

M'Baku sighed. No way this could be good news.

Back in the captain's quarters via elevator ride, M'Baku made a drink for himself and for his comrades, then sank heavily into a chair.

"To the memory of our fearless leader," he said, tilting his cup and pouring a few drops on the ground.

"To her memory," Nakia and T'Challa said, doing the same. Then they drank.

"Okay," said M'Baku. "What's this about?"

"You know what it's about," said T'Challa.

He sighed. "I don't have time for this, T'Challa."

"It's the only thing we should have time for, M'Baku," said Nakia. "It's been five years now."

"Yes, it has." M'Baku was getting impatient. "And in that time, I've worked myself to the bone to ensure that every Maroon that left Moonbase Cudjoe alive remains so. I've put myself on the line, going as far as to pilot a zulu alone—*alone*—to far reaches of this galaxy to barter for food on the black market, just to ensure that *we* have something to eat on this frozen rock." He slammed his cup on the table. "So don't tell me about what we should have time for. Keeping us alive is the *only thing* I've been doing."

Nakia nodded, solemn. "Yes. And as honorable as that is, it's not sustainable, is it?"

He had so many things to say about that, but none would come out of his lips. The Maroon Rebellion wasn't built for *sustainability*. That's how empires thought, and that was how they formed, and that was how they devolved into bellicose thinking, seeking more and more to conquer to satiate their ravenous desire to be *sustainable*. No. N'Yami didn't lead this force with an investment in sustainability—her investment was in whatever would best strike the Intergalactic Empire in a way it would never recover from. This was the mantle he would carry.

"An investment in sustainability is what led us to become complacent," he said to his comrades. "Complacency is what got us here. We cannot repeat the same mistake."

T'Challa, who it turned out had not taken a single sip of his drink, set it down rather abruptly.

"*Captain*," he said with as much respect as one would address a peer, "I'm sure the burden of leading the rebellion at this time must be a great one, but it does us no favors to keep digging ourselves into this place. You were at the memorial, you saw our people. There's no way they can survive another year here. This planet is no place for us. We *must* get off this rock, no matter what we believe."

M'Baku rose, poured himself another drink, drank it on the spot, then poured another and returned to his seat.

"How long have you been a Maroon, T'Challa?"

"Come on now, Captain," said Nakia. "There's no need for that."

"No, no," said M'Baku, putting up a hand. "It's important."

With his cup, he motioned toward T'Challa. "Answer the question."

"I don't think that's relevant," said T'Challa.

"And yet your captain thinks it is," M'Baku pressed. "Answer."

A tense beat passed between them. M'Baku held his gaze, letting T'Challa stew.

M'Baku motioned with his cup and clicked his tongue. "I'll answer for you. Not even enough time for a child to start speaking full sentences. But here you are, speaking full sentences on something of which you know little about."

"M'Baku," said Nakia. "That's a bit much."

"And you," said M'Baku, turning his attention to her. "I expect better from you. You were the closest to our leader, having her ear even in things she wouldn't disclose to me. Since we lost her, I expected you to become my closest ally and advisor, passing down the wealth of knowledge you have to us all. Instead all you've done since is crawl into this Maroon's chest and curl up there."

Nakia stepped forward, fist clenched. "Repeat that, Captain. Repeat it."

M'Baku laughed dryly. "Is that it? You will attack your own captain, your own brother in arms, for a little ribbing?"

She clenched her fist tighter, then released it, wriggling her fingers.

"You know," she said, pensive, "I expect better from you, too. I *am* your closest ally and advisor, even if you refuse to see that. I've tried my best to get you to have this conversation in good faith, to no avail. So, *this* is me giving you some advice: Insisting we remain on this rock will lead us into extinction quicker than the Empire will, and it will be your fault. *That* is the truth."

"Then where do we go, hmmm?" M'Baku rose again. "Tell me, then, since both of you are so intelligent—*where do we go?*"

Silence filled the room. The truth was M'Baku, Nakia, and T'Challa each had their own answer to this question, steps they thought the Maroons ought to take. But the one thing they agreed on, an obstacle they could not yet circumvent: There was nowhere else to go.

"I'm done with this conversation," M'Baku said. "We've spent years rebuilding our forces, technology, and resources. We've grieved and taken the time to purge ourselves of all despondency. We're continuing to research the M'Kraan Shard. It might not have produced results, but *you* convinced N'Yami of its importance and we cannot simply abandon our path. Now we're fully equipped to resume operations, to return to what we know how best to be: Maroons, soldiers, resistance, *without* sacrificing the sanctuary we've carved out for ourselves here. We cannot survive another assault like that on Moonbase Cudjoe."

The finality in his words carried through, and his comrades received it as such. T'Challa was the first to go.

"I know that I've already caused people pain by insisting on my own course of action. You've issued that guidance more times than I can count, M'Baku. But I cannot commit to making the same mistake through choices you insist on. I do not want to feel that way again."

"No, T'Challa, no," said Nakia. This seemed to surprise her even more than it did M'Baku, who didn't find it surprising at all. He'd never quite understood what all the fuss was about T'Challa. Sure, he respected that N'Yami had held him in high regard for some reason he had yet to understand, and he was well aware of the man's raw skill and prowess, but he didn't think either of those things made him the kind of Maroon he needed at this time. Good riddance, if anything.

"I can't, Nakia." Gently, T'Challa set down his panther helmet on a nearby table, and that was that.

"Where will you go?" asked M'Baku.

T'Challa shrugged. "There's nowhere to go, as you rightly said. Perhaps I'll make my own way otherwise."

"Perhaps."

T'Challa left the room. It was just M'Baku and Nakia now.

"Will you leave me, too?" asked M'Baku. "After all we've been through together?"

She took a long time answering.

"N'Yami would've wanted something different," she said, then left.

M'Baku sank back into his chair, picked up his drink, and sipped again. *Indeed. N'Yami would have truly wanted something different.*

CHAPTER 18

⟁⟁⟁

NEW MAROON HIDEOUT,
NEHANDA'S LATTICE

ONE MORNING, many months after the memorial, Nakia awoke with resolve. She dressed in her panther suit, packed up all that she had left on this ice rock, and headed for her shuttle.

She was leaving the Maroon Rebellion.

Making the decision to leave had been tough, but in retrospect, she realized it shouldn't have been. She wasn't *leaving* leaving. She was only going on a journey, and Bast willing, she would return with something the Maroons on this rock needed more than the food and water and air they so craved: a reason to fight again.

This early in the morning, the hallways were emptier. The few who saw her were all junior staff and offered nothing more than pleasantries. She answered them as good-naturedly as she could, trying not to raise any eyebrows. She wasn't deserting the Rebellion—not really—and she wasn't trying to keep her leaving a secret—not really. But she was aware of how it would look, how it would fall on the ears of the Maroons. The most senior officer, next only to their valorized late captain, abandoning them on this forsaken planet for who knew where.

But there was no good way to explain her choice. Especially when it would finally come to bear that she'd made said choice after the last time she'd seen T'Challa, while leaving M'Baku's quarters.

T'Challa himself had only then just made the decision to abandon the Maroon Rebellion. Somewhere between N'Yami's death and her memorial, T'Challa's spearpoint sense of purpose had slowly flattened, seeping out of him. It surely was hard losing the woman who gave you your own name. They all felt the loss of N'Yami in different ways, after all. But it wasn't just that. It was the weight of it all: the growing rumors about his possible past—*Is he really T'Challa of Ancient Wakanda returned?*—questions about his future—*Is he really the promised one? Will he lead us to victory?*—and the dissonance of those who couldn't understand how the goddess Bast could anoint an evil emperor as avatar, then be coy about whether she would anoint a liberator or not. (Here, Nakia shared their frustration. Did this almighty Bast care about the oppressed or not? Was she going to save them or not? She, too, had to bear the burden of choice. Everyone did.)

T'Challa had left because the noise became overwhelming. He'd become caught in the space between who he wanted to be and who the Maroons wanted him to be. *I fight to go home,* he'd told her once, to which she'd replied: *What is home?* The defeated look he'd given her was pretty much all the answer she needed. He didn't know anymore. He could not commit to fighting for this home; but without it, he could not fight for the one he'd lost. So he'd left the Maroons, choosing to fight for neither.

Nakia knew she couldn't begrudge him for that. But her leaving in his wake meant that she would be the second of the slain captain's close circle gone since the memorial. Hard for the Maroons to recover from that. Which was why she'd opted to tell no one . . . well, for now at least. Once she was out of the planet's airspace, she would send M'Baku a private message.

She took an elevator to the hangar, remembering that fateful day she and M'Baku had taken a similar elevator to go lead the Goree mission. Long before T'Challa had entered her life, long before N'Yami had revealed her hopes and dreams, long before she herself had dared to dream of a future without the Empire and therefore set herself on a road filled with doubt and disappointment. That felt like an eternity ago now, and all three of those people had left her in one way or another. She was alone again, as she'd once been when she'd first joined the rebellion.

And then, there was T'Challa forsaking all they'd worked toward—as Maroons, but also as budding lovers. M'Baku had been right to intuit that, since N'Yami's death, they'd grown closer, leaning on each other for comfort, finally giving in to the slow attraction that had built up between them since their first time working together on the Shango Array mission. Slowly, carefully, they'd worked together to answer the pressing questions—*What happens if we succeed? What happens to us when our histories are restored? What do we become?* The answers were neither neat nor obviously feasible—she had toyed with the thought of following him back to his home, if he'd let her; he had once mentioned possibly staying, even if his memories returned.

But then, on that day in that meeting with M'Baku, all of that was stripped away. It was why she'd chased after him in these very same hallways and grabbed his arm, pulling him to a stop.

"You can't mean what you said in there," she said. "You can't mean it."

His tense silence was louder than any *I absolutely meant it* that he could've said.

"N'Yami *trusted* you," said Nakia. "She *believed* in you."

He twitched with every word she emphasized but remained steadfast.

"She should not have," he said, then ever so slightly, leaned away so that his arm slipped out of her grip. It was gentle, but so *deliberate,* so *sure,* that it hurt worse than if he'd been more forceful. His gesture, so efficient in delivering his true message: *You should not have believed in me.*

She watched him walk away, defeat in his gait, and that was when she knew.

But no, she wasn't going to sink into despair. This disappointment would be her fuel. She would use it to jet herself toward a solution that would reinvigorate her, reinvigorate the Maroons, and most important, reinvigorate T'Challa.

She located her shuttle and keyed in. The hangar officer on duty received the ping on their workstation and strutted over.

"Good day, General." She was a young woman, probably just exiting her teenage years, dressed in the night-duty uniform of coveralls and boots, over which she'd draped up to three pieces of thick outerwear. It dawned on Nakia that it had to be deathly cold in here among all this metal, something she'd never quite had to contend with because her panther suit offered all the thermal comfort needed. She regarded the officer with a bit of guilt, although this only strengthened her resolve. *Even more reason to do this, right?*

"Quite early for a mission kickoff, isn't it?" the officer added. Nakia recognized the woman's bright disposition to be that of one who'd just been inducted into the Maroon workforce, whose pride in serving the rebellion had not yet been filed away by adversity. Perhaps, if this went well, she would never have to become that kind of Maroon.

"Indeed," Nakia replied, offering no further explanation. "Can you get someone to tune me up, please?"

The officer left and an engineer returned in her place, another young woman who opened up and prodded at the craft's engines without much talk. Nakia was grateful for the silence, taking the time to double- and triple-check the resources she'd put together for the trip.

How did you plan for a trip whose length one didn't know? It was the question that had plagued her since the conversation she'd had in the hallway with T'Challa, when she'd known that he would never return on his own, and that she might just be the only person left who could bring him back. And she had an obligation to do so because, well, whether M'Baku liked it or not (and knew it or not), N'Yami had believed, fervently so, that T'Challa was simply the key—or at least one of the keys—to defeating the Empire. Nakia didn't know for sure what was true and what wasn't—she wasn't a big believer in matters of faith and prophecy; they lay too close to dishonesty and conjecture. She *wanted* to believe in the rumors of T'Challa as savior, but for now, all her mind could allow space for was T'Challa as a person she should help. Because the only thing she was sure of was this: N'Yami had entrusted her with the task of keeping T'Challa honest, and by Bast, she was going to see it through.

The engineer soon completed the tune-up. Nakia got into the cockpit and tested the engines, satisfied they worked fine. This would get her quite a bit into the Zanj Region, which was pretty much all she needed. It was a straight shot from there to Moon-base Cudjoe.

She was going back.

She started the engines and gave a thumbs-up to the officer at the workstation, who opened the hangar doors. Beyond the horizon, the black inkiness of space stared back at her.

"Nakia," N'Yami said once, during one of those little meetings in her quarters, "I entrust these stories to you because someone needs to dream when I'm not here."

"Don't say that," Nakia replied. "You'll always be here."

"Maybe," she said. "But whether I am or am not, I'm bequeathing this to you all the same."

"And what is it you bequeath?"

She leaned forward. "That you will hold him to his duty and purpose, Nakia. Keep him on this path, no matter how far he wishes to stray. Stay focused—if not for him, then for us, for the five galaxies, for the cosmos. Give us hope, Nakia. Keep T'Challa honest."

N'Yami had said a great many things—the Teku-Maza woman with her little laughs and her grand tales, many of them about feats of Ancient Wakanda, and how she dreamed that the Maroon Rebellion could repeat them, defeating the Empire along the way. She firmly believed that the feats of T'Challa, Ancient Wakanda protector, *He Who Put the Knife Where It Belonged,* could become the feats of T'Challa, the Maroon Rebel, once Nameless, now nameless no longer. All it needed, in her opinion, was a little nurturing, a little softness, a little belief. And though N'Yami, like Nakia, disagreed with Bast's continuous support of the emperor— they thought of the goddess as trapped, in a similar way the five galaxies were, captured in the orbit of the overwhelming force that was N'Jadaka—it was the Maroon Rebellion's job to reinstate the Black Panther and help make Bast's decision easier.

Of all the stories and words of advice N'Yami had offered Nakia, it was this one that had most stuck, the one to which N'Yami continued to hold on tightly, even in death. So, Nakia held on to it, too, even when no one else would. And today, she would begin the journey to finding that hope. Even though she had to go back to the old Maroon hideout—the place of the rebellion's defeat, now overtaken by the Empire—to get it.

She eased the zulu forward toward the hangar's doors.

The attack on Moonbase Cudjoe played again in her mind, but only one particular moment: when the Manifold produced a spear, flung it at T'Challa, and he caught it. Something had come alight in him then, a self-recognition, a reanimation.

A *memory*.

He'd *remembered* something, even though his mind hadn't known what it was in that moment, adrenaline and all. But his body had remembered. Perhaps he should have held on to that spear a bit longer and not immediately thrown it back. Perhaps if he'd had the chance to cradle it, shut his eyes, and listen to his secrets—perhaps, then, some part of his memory could return, and with it, hope.

The shuttle dropped out of the bay and began to ascend into orbit. Nakia pushed the throttle forward, shooting the craft into space.

She was going to get the Spear of Bashenga.

CHAPTER 19

△▽△▽

UNIDENTIFIED LOCATION

ONCE T'CHALLA LEARNED of Nakia's departure, it became much easier to withstand the crashing waves of guilt that plagued him since he made the decision to leave the Maroons.

He'd begun to doubt himself, to be sure. But he'd already made his move well before Nakia left, packing up the few things he owned from his quarters and shuttling them out of the barracks. He first stowed away at a vacant dormitory not too far beyond the base. It was abandoned and run down over the years as the conditions of their new home took their toll, but it was shelter enough to tide him over while he plotted out his next steps. Despite the risk of being reprimanded for aiding a deserter, Nik helped smuggle the rest of T'Challa's belongings and essential supplies out of the base and was the one to deliver the news of Nakia's departure.

After she had left without telling anyone, T'Challa knew he couldn't leave the planet until she returned, until he knew she was okay and nothing had happened to her out there. This meant he would have to find something more permanent, something more private on some other cold and bitter corner of this dead planet to live on until Nakia returned.

Luckily, he'd already planned for this.

△▽△▽

ONE OF THE FIRST things he'd done when the Maroons arrived here was to find a safe place to store all the information N'Yami had handed him, to keep it safe in the event that the Empire happened upon the rebellion again. The Maroon Archival Project, when N'Yami had first handed him a part of the drive, looked like only a sliver of information, handpicked for him alone. But after N'Yami's death, he'd pored deeper into the drive and found that she'd been seeding even more information, linking his drive to various other sources, many now lost after the Cudjoe attack but some retained due to N'Yami's foresight and vision.

Here he was, sitting on an endless trove of oral, visual, and written information: history, art, culture, systems, schematics, instructions—all kinds of knowledge possible. He could simply have handed this to Nakia or M'Baku, but something had told him then that a day like this would come, when the relationship between them would fracture, and he would need to turn somewhere else.

So he built a cave.

Not a *cave* in the true sense of the word. A hideaway, a small base of his own.

He'd done it piece by piece, flying as many parts as he could carry on his glider over to a scraggly corner of the planet where no one could venture on foot or by vehicle, and where no zulu could land. There, he set autonomous drones to work, returning to replenish their resource base. Once the main structure was finished, he set them to weatherproofing it, which took a while, and then to security-proofing it, which took even longer. In fact, the job was yet to be completed; it had taken up so many resources, and the trips had weathered him so much, that he'd decided to stop.

But on the day T'Challa learned about Nakia, he knew he had to finish the job. So, his copy of MAP in hand, he got on his glider and shot across the planet.

The hideaway was not in as bad shape as he remembered. The weatherproofing was excellent—inside remained sensibly warm with minimal active heating. The security wasn't up to par, but he didn't have to worry yet. Very few people could find him, and the few who would look hard enough—Nakia, for instance—were no longer here.

He set about security-proofing, which took him the larger part of two days. Cameras, detectors, the like. Now that the autonomous drones had done their work, he was able to strip them for parts.

Once he thought the place was secure enough, he left MAP there and went to collect his things.

THE FIRST FEW days living alone were the worst.

T'Challa couldn't sleep. Images from MAP—which he spent all day consuming—swirled in his mind, choked his dreams. He woke up to the empty and silent place, and when he dared look out the window, there was nothing but ice for ages.

For the first time since he came to recognize himself at Goree, he was truly *alone*.

Loneliness wasn't something he'd had to deal with so far. He'd felt a yearning for a home he didn't know and for a woman he couldn't remember, but that was it. Now he realized how much the Maroon community had done for him, how much they meant to him. And he'd just *abandoned* them like that?

Suddenly, the weight of grief descended upon him, a weight that not even further forays into the pleasures of MAP could lift. T'Challa descended farther into the dark, realizing now that learning this information wouldn't help him get his memories back. If Nakia never returned, and M'Baku never allowed him to rejoin the Maroons, he would never regain his memories from the Empire.

He was farther from home, in more ways than one, than he'd ever been.

MOST OF THE INFORMATION in MAP was a cultivated history of the rebellion from the Maroons themselves, created by a bevy of eyes, hands, ears, lips. Once, though, he randomly happened upon a rare note left by N'Yami herself.

To anyone who is listening, it had said, an audio recording. *Believe. Believe. Believe.*

Was she talking to Nakia, or to him? (Was she talking *about* him? Was she telling the Maroons to believe in *him*?) He couldn't be sure. But there was a familiarity in N'Yami's tone, hard-edged yet utilitarian, the same soothing with a side of burn effect she'd always had on him when she was alive.

Stop, it was telling him. *Stop and believe.*

Despite these dark times, he would need to keep hope alive somehow. To begin, he would have to stop wallowing. Until Nakia returned, he would find a way to keep busy, go outside, feel the wind in his face, the world in his ears. Until Nakia found whatever she sought out there, he would wait; he would stay alive and believe.

CHAPTER 20

△▽△▽

ZANJ REGION,
UNIDENTIFIED LOCATION

SOMEWHERE IN THE DEEP SPACE of Nehanda's Lattice, Nakia's zulu floated.

The visit to Cudjoe had been a bust. Not only had the moon been commandeered by imperial forces, the planet Oshun itself was now also occupied by the Empire, which meant its orbit had become imperial airspace. It had been impossible to get within proximity of the moon's surface.

However, knowing all the angles of the planet's orbit, all the pockets of darkness with which she was familiar, just out of the reach of detection, allowed her to get close enough for what she'd needed to do. Scan.

The Maroon infrastructure had been completely destroyed. The pockmarks of light and color that once lit up the moon were gone, replaced by a gloomy, gray darkness that truly signaled a defeat in more ways than one. Nothing that was any kind of useful had been spared, so she didn't even need to scan for long to know that looking within her own old infrastructure was moot.

Now the imperial infrastructure? Whole other story.

The Empire hadn't quite integrated any of its own resources on Cudjoe. Made sense that they wouldn't, too—it was truly just a piece of scraggly rock, uninhabited, with nothing of use other than to ensure that no Maroon returned here and no one else used it as a hideout. They'd pretty much plopped down a couple of auto-defense mechanisms, a few personnel on watch, and left it at that.

None of those personnel was the Manifold, thank Bast.

She'd gleaned the signature of the Manifold's suit from the data N'Yami had gathered when she'd scanned the man once he'd been taken down during that first wave of the Moonbase Cudjoe attack. When N'Yami's belongings were being cleaned out from the captain's quarters so M'Baku could move in as new captain, much of her gathered recordings of personal interest had passed to Nakia, as stated in N'Yami's recorded trust. It didn't often include information about Maroon Rebellion missions of any sort—only personal quirks and interests, which Nakia found quite endearing. (N'Yami had a much softer soul than her leadership position allowed most Maroons to see.) However, for some reason, the final few pieces of data from her wearable console had somehow passed to this more personal collection Nakia had ended up with. It was a jumble of information: notes and imagery of strange flora and fauna N'Yami had encountered on her travels, an accounting of the very day N'Yami had died . . . and the signature of the Manifold's suit.

Perhaps this was N'Yami, from the Plane of Wakandan Memory, prodding, saying: *Do something with this.*

Nakia was obliging.

The Manifold's signature was a unique, low-vibrational frequency that the suit emitted whenever he was present, low enough to be missed by any poorly designed proximity sensor built into body armor, but strong enough to be read by a craft's sensor as far away as outside orbit. She'd found a shadow in the planet's orbit, as close to Cudjoe as she could, and she scanned.

Nothing, which was good.

But that was the problem, wasn't it? In N'Yami's same pool of data, she'd *also* received the signature of the Spear of Bashenga, which, it turned out, carried the same low-vibrational frequency of the Manifold's suit for some reason. Much lower energy readings, but there anyway, still locatable by her craft's sensors from orbit.

So being unable to find any trace of the Manifold on Cudjoe meant only one thing.

The Spear of Bashenga wasn't there either.

AS THE ZULU floated around the galaxy, cloaked and silent, Nakia pored over all the information she'd retrieved from MAP that concerned the spear. She wanted to remind herself of what made it special, why it was so important for T'Challa to wield it, and what chances it offered to prove whether this man was truly the T'Challa of Ancient Wakanda.

Idouah, the recording began, *is the Spear of Bashenga, first king of Wakanda and founder of the Panther Tribe. A centuries-old sacred totem born of Vibranium, wielded only by the chieftain of the Panther Clan—the Black Panther, Avatar of Bast. Passed down from Black Panther to Black Panther, only the Avatar of Bast may wield the Spear of Bashenga to its full power. For any other, it is simply an ordinary spear; but in the hands of the Black Panther, it is a formidable weapon that promises near invincibility.*

Nakia sighed, yawned, rubbed her eyes. She hadn't slept in a long time, and her body was beginning to ask sterner questions. But she had no time to sleep. Every second counted toward the search.

She moved on to a map of every planetary object dotting Nehanda's Lattice. There were simply too many planets to cover, and there was no way she could visit them all and scan for the spear's signature. Worse yet, the spear might not be on any planet at all, but instead on a ship, being conveyed somewhere the Empire wanted it. Possibly outside Nehanda's Lattice, which would make her mission next to impossible—leaving this galaxy increased the probability of her getting caught.

It had been years. Maybe the spear was lost for good.

She considered putting out a blast from her ship, casting a sensory net that would scan much, much farther out from her location and pick up any such signature of the spear. But that was ill-advised—it would give away her position, as any other ship or on-planet sensor scanning at the same time would be able to see where she was. No, bad option.

So, after she brought her zulu to rest in the shadow of a small planet, and before her droopy eyelids closed, she made a shorter blast, one limited to the immediate quadrant of the Zanj Region where she was. The planets here were mostly small, largely uninhabited, and saw minimal to no imperial activity. (It was why they'd chosen Cudjoe for a base.) The risk was small.

She sent out the blast, then drifted into long sleep.

A PIERCING ALARM woke Nakia up.

She jumped in her chair, grabbing the throttle, ready to fire herself out of danger. But it was just her scan coming back with a result.

A signature match.

Nakia rubbed her eyes. How long had she been asleep? She creaked the bones in her neck, shoulders, arms, then leaned forward and peered into the screen.

The planet didn't even have a name on the mapping system. Just a nondescript rock somewhere in the armpit end of the Zanj Region, not far from her current position. Baffling, seeing as it was likely to be sparsely inhabited. What did this mean?

No time to think. She rubbed her eyes and set course.

GETTING THERE WAS the easy part. Setting down the zulu on the rock—much harder. It was one of those planets whose proximity to its star made most of its surface dry and flaky and therefore difficult to assess if it would hold this much weight. She searched for a mountainous location on which to set down the craft, but most of it was flatland, no place to hide.

Eventually, she found an area that was semiarid with sparse but thriving flora, and managed to land the zulu amid grassland that, upon further examination, seemed to tower above her. Good news: It hid the zulu well. Bad news: She'd have to wade through a field filled with what looked like reeds, everything unsighted.

She jumped down from her ship, into the mud of the reedy grassland. It was ill-advised to walk through an unsighted landscape on an alien planet, but according to the terrain map her computer was generating in real time, this location gave her the shortest walking distance to where the signature was showing up: the only built area within scope. The grassland marked a winding green ribbon that cut through the rest of a landscape that looked desolate. Jagged rocks and hard, packed earth. A far cry from the lush and glittering cities of her homeland. But the place still bore an eerie kind of beauty. Pale greens and deep browns in stark contrast, the sky's green tint like an omen. A light mist hovered over the grassland, and Nakia knew those faint sounds she could hear in the stillness were creatures of stealth.

One hand hovering near the weapon at her hip, she emerged from the reeds. There was movement on the edges of her vision. She spun around to see two people, humanoid, standing there.

Frail, eyes large and set into slender faces. Bodies draped in green tunics, feet bare and caked with dust. They stood stock-still, surprised to see her. Most important, she assessed, they were unarmed—or seemed to be.

One of them lifted a long-fingered hand in a gesture of greeting or peace. They made a sound, something vaguely musical. She pushed the translation panel on her panther suit and waited for it to scan the sounds until they returned to her earpiece with a broad translation.

"Off-worlder?" came the translation.

"Yes," Nakia said into her mouthpiece, and the suit broadcasted back the translation.

The two looked at each other, excited both by the possibility of meeting an off-worlder and at being understood. The one who spoke earlier stepped forward.

"I am Sirigu," they said, "and we are Eri Kurao. This is my

partner, Donzea." The other person bowed. Sirigu lifted their arm again. "Forgive our surprise. We have never met an off-worlder. We mean no harm."

"Sirigu, Donzea, Eri Kurao." Nakia, practicing the new names on her tongue, slowly took off her helmet. "This seems far away from the nearest built areas. What are you doing out here?"

"Collecting traps." Sirigu pointed toward the grassland. "We are hunter-gatherers." Donzea lifted a metal and plant contraption to confirm. Trapped in what seemed like manufactured jaws was an animal Nakia couldn't recognize: a rodent-like snout, but with more than four legs, a large yellow belly, and no tail. If it still had eyes, she couldn't tell. It was dead, and the lids were shut.

"Who are you?" Sirigu asked.

"I am Nakia, of . . ." Here, she paused. These two seemed friendly so far, but experience had taught her that one could never be sure how sold someone was on the Empire's promises. It was natural, these days, to introduce herself as a Maroon regardless and deal with the consequences later. But what if she could harken back to another identity, one that she'd left behind but might be more useful to wear in a situation such as this, where wielding authority could go a long way?

"I am Nakia," she said, "Askari raider of the Intergalactic Empire of Wakanda. Take me to your leader."

NAKIA STOOD ALONE at the gates of the Morosi stronghold.

The two hunter-gatherers had refused to come with her. The ride over the vast plains had been a lengthy affair, despite all three being conveyed in a light carriage drawn by two rapid, six-legged beasts with formidable snouts that Sirigu referred to as rennas. Other than offering that word, Sirigu opted for silence throughout the trip, and Donzea—who it turned out didn't speak at all, for whatever reason—followed suit. Nakia was used to this, the fear and deference the imperial name struck in its subjects, even those quite far from its reach. Only these two did not quite seem deferential—once she'd introduced herself, a chasm had opened between them, and they'd immediately closed themselves up, their inquisitiveness and earnest curiosity gone out the window, replaced by a steely edginess she didn't realize they possessed. She decided she would apologize to them later, tell them the truth when she'd gotten what she wanted. For now, it was best that they continue to think of her as an imperial envoy; even if they shared the same beliefs as a Maroon, fear made hearts unreliable.

Sirigu had pulled the carriage to a stop once they'd reached the edge of the place where the spear's signature was strongest and pointed at the looming, gargantuan edifice looming before them.

"There," they said. "Morosi's stronghold."

"Morosi?"

"You asked for our leader." Sirigu pointed again. "There. But you will have to walk the rest of the way."

"Why?"

Both Eri Kurao looked at each other.

"We do not go there," said Sirigu, and turned the rennas away.

Now that Nakia had walked the rest of the way and was standing in front of the edifice, she understood their trepidation. It was less building and more anomaly, a devastated thumb sticking out of the flatland. It sat atop a small crest and was carved into what might have once been a hill. The edifice itself bore vestiges of being a cave. Crystal stalactites hung from the mouth that served as an opening, a row of large doors its teeth. Approaching them was akin to walking into a monster's rib cage. The ground was soft, breaking under her footsteps. The air had a harsh, minty burn.

Most important, the place was unguarded.

If Nakia knew anything about unguarded places, it was this: They were unguarded because nothing of substance remained, because they were in fact guarded but by forces unseen, or, worst of all, because everyone knew to attempt entering such places was to risk death and nobody stupid enough to try had lived to tell the tale.

She trudged up to the large doors, hoping it was more of the former than the latter. Sure enough, before she'd even raised an arm to knock, a drone appeared out of nowhere, zipping around the corner at alarming speed, and planted itself between her and the door. Behind it followed two larger, scarier drones, which remained a distance away, poised. She didn't see any nozzles but she was convinced that they were capable of firing *something* at her.

"Identification," said the drone before her, speaking the same language the hunter-gatherers had used, but with a tone so flat she was unsure if the voice was a person or software.

"I am Nakia, Askari raider of the imperial forces and envoy of the Intergalactic Empire of Wakanda," she announced. "I have come here from Planet Bast for an audience with Morosi of Eri Kurao."

The drone whizzed once, twice, as if confused, and said: "Kurao."

"Pardon?"

"Kurao," it repeated in a monotone. "*Eri Kurao* means *people of Kurao*. This planet is called Kurao."

Nakia's body tensed. She'd made a mistake. She should've spoken longer to Sirigu and Donzea, gotten a sense of this place before donning a disguise. No matter now—she was close to being found out. Her hand reflexively itched to reach for her weapon, to deal with the situation the best way she knew how. But another part of her brain tugged, urged her to reach deep into herself, her far past, and try something a bit more daring.

"I am Nakia Cabral, House of Tafari, tasked by the emperor himself to come here on his behalf," she said. "I do not care what your planet is named, and I take offense in your implication of doubt about my credibility. However, I understand the healthy skepticism of a foreigner, and therefore I will grant you this opportunity just once: You may look in your records, if you have them, and confirm that I am indeed of House Tafari. But if you wish, instead, for me to turn around here and return to our Panther Lord of Wakanda without seeing to his task, so be it. Invoke his ire upon yourself if you so wish."

Another squeak, another whiz, this one for a lengthy moment. Then:

"Lord Morosi of Kurao will see you now," said the drone.

A heavy clank, a large creak. The massive door before her began to open. The drone turned around and flew inside. Nakia followed.

THE SPACE WAS distinctly ornate, a mix between eclectic and rundown. Verdant tendrils snaked over ancient stone; lighting lodged between crevices cast a glow over the corridors, bathing them in a soft glow that was misleadingly ethereal. The whole interior was a surprisingly harmonious blend of organic curves and geometric patterns, as if sculpted by nature itself. Somewhere within the heart of this, though, there was the unmistakable hum of more advanced technological infrastructure, which thrummed like a heartbeat through the bones of the structure. That aside, there seemed to be a constant breeze that passed through these corridors, every now and then causing a stir, a fuss, like a never-ending sigh.

In this lighting, the drones looked poorly built, cobbled together from mismatched materials with differing strengths and properties. If she had to guess, Nakia would say this was a colony of scavengers, gathering material from various places in the galaxy and keeping the best scraps for personal use. Such a theory would explain why the Spear of Bashenga—which was *definitely* here, according to her computer's signal tracker—had fallen into these hands from the rubble of the battle at Moonbase Cudjoe. Morosi must have scavenged the site, found the spear, and kept it.

Nakia wondered why Morosi hadn't opted to turn it in to the Empire. This surely didn't look like the stronghold of one who was anti-Empire—for starters, it wasn't hidden. Unless, she surmised, Morosi wasn't sure about what they had and wanted to hold on to the spear until their suspicions were confirmed. Perhaps, in a way, they'd even been anticipating this visit.

It dawned on her then, that Morosi's scavenging venture definitely had the support of the Empire, and possibly its backing. It would be the only way they could be allowed to trawl the Moonbase Cudjoe rubble and possibly lots of other disaster sites across the galaxy without interruption. Perhaps they paid a share of their proceeds to the Empire. Perhaps the Empire employed them for other purposes. Either way, it was clear Morosi wasn't afraid of the Empire because they were allies, and perhaps this allyship didn't quite extend to the rest of the people who lived on the planet. A good explanation for why the hunter-gatherers had reacted the way they did when she'd introduced herself.

The drones led her into a vestibule that doubled as some sort of throne room. There were steps, and atop them sat the person she was here to see.

Even seated in an ornate throne, Morosi was twice the height of Sirigu and Donzea, and though their face and eyes were similar, their skin had a more purplish coloring. There was something artificial about their presentation—how shiny and *unnatural* their dermis appeared compared to the others, how clear the fluid of their eyes, how clean and cared for they looked. Nakia could always smell an augmented person from a distance away, and with Morosi, the stench of augmentation was overwhelming. She wondered what it was that they'd improved. Extended hearing? Mind reading? Intelligence? Whatever it was, she had to be *very* careful with this person.

"Welcome, off-worlder." Mosori's voice was soft, silky, charismatic.

"You will address me by my imperial title," she said.

A pause. Morosi scanned her, deciding if they wanted to be deferential or oppressive. They opted for both.

"Very well," they said. "Askari raider, imperial envoy. I have not received a physical imperial representative in a long time, not to talk of an unannounced one. To what do I owe the pleasure of a visit from the emperor's messenger?"

She looked around at the ornate pillars, the bejeweled furnishings, the sudden sweet fragrance of thriving flora that the land-scape outside lacked. No way this "Lord" wasn't in the employ of the empire.

"The emperor has received information that suggests you have an ancient artifact of the Empire in your possession." She paused. "A spear."

Morosi watched her for a while, then said, "I do not know of what you speak."

Nakia shook her head, tut-tutted. "I have been an imperial Askari for many Wakandan years, Lord Morosi of Kurao. Do not insult me and test my patience." She straightened her back. "The Empire *knows* you have it. We have confirmation that it is here, in your very stronghold. And I am here to retrieve it."

"We are scavengers. We have a great many things of various origins here." Morosi's manner was languid, unperturbed, but be-neath that façade lurked a bubbling darkness. "We do not always know what we return home with after a scavenging mission. Much of it is rubbish, and we treat it as such. Perhaps this spear is one of such things?"

Nakia chuckled. "Any Wakandan artifact will always be of value. And if you are a true ally of our Lord Panther as you claim to be, then you will recognize a Wakandan artifact when you come upon one. Our Vibranium does not hide itself."

"That is true. The Empire's mineral and technological resources remain imperious and unmatched. Perhaps I will ask my workers to dig into storage, see if they can come up with any of the Em-pire's artifacts we may have picked up in error. I will see to it my-self."

"That will be appreciated."

Morosi smiled back. They seemed unfamiliar with the human action and to be politely mimicking Nakia's wan smile. Only theirs did not do the job of hiding their intentions, which was that they did not intend to rise from their chair anytime soon.

"Where are these storage units?"

Morosi waved a hand. "Far."

"So this will take . . . all day?"

"Days. Many days."

Nakia looked around. Not a drone or Eri Kurao had moved to action.

"I see," she said. "You want me to come back."

Morosi smiled again. "If you wish for us both to please our Lord Panther."

Nakia nodded solemnly. The tide was changing. Morosi was up to something.

"I have no place to stay," she said, changing tack. "I cannot fly all the way to Planet Bast and back."

"There are many locations in the settlements." Another lazy wave of that hand. "You will find comfortable accommodations there. One befitting of a person of your . . . standing."

She could tell now that Morosi had made up their mind about her, and the conclusion they had come to was not a pleasant one. They hadn't yet figured out who she truly was, but they now harbored enough doubt that it was only a matter of time. She was sure they wouldn't make a single move to retrieve the Spear of Bashenga from wherever they'd hidden it. If anything, they were going to fortify the artifact even more while pretending to search for it under heaps of scrap and rubbish.

"I will be back." She turned away, accepting defeat of her plan.

Just as the doors opened and the drone guided her out of the chamber, Morosi said in a near whisper, "I hope to see you soon."

Outside, Nakia was sure of one thing: Morosi had finally figured out that the spear was of great importance to someone, imperial or not, and they were going to find a way to make the greatest profit from it. What they were going to do to her, she didn't know, but she was sure that if she ever returned to this place, she was a dead woman.

That left her with only one choice: infiltrate this stronghold and steal the Spear of Bashenga. For that, she was going to need help.

CHAPTER 21

△▽△▽

PLANET BAST

LONG AFTER HE had put Zenzi to bed, and the rest of the throne-world was quite asleep, N'Jadaka descended the palace, heading for the part of the royal barracks that formed the chief technologist's development laboratory. As usual, devoid of guards and wearing only his panther suit, he took the private elevator that went straight from the palace to the underground location. In his hand was a small box, a gift, roughly wrapped by Zenzi's child fingers.

The doors opened into the lab, and N'Jadaka walked into a flurry of Ancient Wakandan salutes, hands crossed over their chests. He nodded his acceptance. Most of the technologists on this special project were military trainees—the salute, a force of habit. They were well disciplined. The man who led them, who was now missing, not so much. N'Jadaka would deal with that later, once he was done with what he was here for.

"Same as always, my liege lord?" asked a young woman, whom N'Jadaka understood to be standing in the chief technologist's stead. Her disposition, to him, revealed her to be one of the military types. *Good.* Perhaps if this Kofi man returned, he'd find that the job was no longer his.

"Same," said N'Jadaka, and she led him to where they kept the Manifold.

△▽△▽

THE MAN, NOT THE SUIT.

He was a boy, really—N'Jadaka sometimes almost thought of him as a son. Strong, focused, dedicated. A true Wakandan soldier and worthy fighter, even without the suit and supplements. When he came into the room where they always met—*his* room, in *his* quarters, N'Jadaka always insisted upon it—the boy looked every bit like the scared young man N'Jadaka had stood over and watched awaken after he'd crashed on this planet, unsure of himself, knowing little else but his own name. N'Jadaka had seen to it, personally, that the young man did not become lost but grew into something—*someone*—useful.

"Hello, Eden," said N'Jadaka.

The young man named Eden, dressed in his sleeping clothes, regarded the emperor sitting on his bed. He still carried the bruises from the morning's training session, but they were already fading, soon to be gone. Other than increased strength, speed of thought and movement, and an acuity for combat, the supplements also offered healing and anti-vertigo properties that allowed his teleportations to occur without dire effects. Unfortunately, they also closed the distance between the man and the suit, so that N'Jadaka was never sure whether he was talking to the boy or the Manifold. But that was the point of these visits, wasn't it? For him to interface with another human? The technologists themselves agreed; they'd initially assigned a psychologist to the role. N'Jadaka thought he could do just as good a job.

Eden's eyes shifted to the box in the emperor's hand.

"From Zenzi," N'Jadaka clarified, shaking the box. Something rattled inside. "Would you like to guess what it is this time?"

The young man tilted his head, eyes only slightly shifting to regard a nearby shelf filled with small glass figurines. Every single one was the same: a machine-carved bust of the goddess Bast, featuring her panther likeness and headdress.

"Ah, well," said N'Jadaka. "You're right. It's the same thing."

He tore the wrapper apart and opened the box. Sure enough, it was another identical glass bust. He gently retrieved it and held it out to Eden. Tentatively, the young man came forward, took the figurine, and placed it on the shelf among the others.

It was their little secret, his and Zenzi's. Only she and the technologists knew of N'Jadaka's private visits to Eden, which, if he thought about it, was all kinds of sensible. Caring for and nurturing his daughter was the strongest tether to his humanity, keeping the symbiote—and now, the power of godhood—from overwhelming him, from crowding out the part of him that could still feel. These visits to Eden—helping the young man navigate the same challenge, where he held on to his humanity despite the pressures of being the Manifold, the omnipresence of the suit and supplements—helped N'Jadaka hold on to *his* humanity. Zenzi feeling connected to Eden was a sign from the gods that he was doing the right thing.

"How are you feeling?" N'Jadaka asked. "They tell me your readings were out of sorts this morning."

Eden offered a near imperceptible shrug. He barely spoke, not since the supplements began. They had only been meant to make him pliable, to give in to the demands of the suit. But the side effects were varied and unpredictable. A swollen tongue was one, memory loss another. There could be more the technologists were yet to discover: depression, for instance, or reticence. N'Jadaka thought Eden always seemed so. (Although, he did not find that too unusual. N'Jadaka considered himself the most blessed and powerful being in the five galaxies, and *he* was always depressed.)

"How are you liking the new modifications?" N'Jadaka changed tack once he saw Eden's discomfort with the previous question. "I know you complained about the suit weight last time. I spoke to them"—he tilted his head, referring to the technologists in the lab outside—"but you know how they are. *Vibranium is a heavy metal, we don't want to lose shield integrity* . . . you know, things like that. I apologize."

Eden offered nothing in response. So N'Jadaka did what he

usually did when the young man didn't want to talk: He talked about himself.

"You know," he said, sitting back in the bed, resting against the wall, "when I was your age, all I wanted was to be powerful. You know, like the gods. And now, well . . ." He put out an arm and shot a tendril of the symbiote at one of the glass busts, plucking it cleanly from the shelf and into his hand. He caressed the fine details with his thumb.

"Now look at me. I *am* powerful. But I don't feel powerful, you know? I feel . . . insatiable. A bottomless well. Nothing fills me, not the conquering of each new planet or the discovery of new technology or the crushing of the rebellion. Not even the power of the gods fills me." He gently placed the bust on a nearby stand. "I wonder, sometimes, if I enjoy the existence of resistance. Perhaps this is why I find myself thinking of this heretic. He's still out there, I know, but what end will pursuing him achieve? I am more powerful, more beloved, more praised, than he can ever be. So why do I find myself thinking about him, about another rebellion gathering around him?"

Eden shuffled slowly to the bedside and perched on the edge. His mouth worked, slowly, before he said: "I . . . think, too. About . . . him."

N'Jadaka lifted an eyebrow. "The heretic?" Eden nodded. "What do you think about?"

Eden tilted his head. "In the beginning, I wondered: *Why does he ask me not to kill this one?*"

N'Jadaka understood *this one* to mean the heretic they called T'Challa, and *he* to mean him, the emperor. Eden often referred to him in third person.

"And then," Eden continued, "in that raid, he caught that spear and threw it back at me."

"The spear?"

"There was . . ." Eden worked his mouth again. "There is *something* in it."

"Vibranium?"

"No. Something . . . else. The Manifold hates it. But the Manifold also likes it. And in my head—"

"Yes?"

"I think: *Maybe I know something.*"

Ah, thought N'Jadaka. "Like what?"

Eden shrugged. "Or I *think* I know something, maybe? I see the man, and I know it's not the first time I see him this way. I think . . ."

"What?"

Eden's eyes shifted to the glass busts of Bast on his shelf. "I think: *Maybe the emperor is right. Perhaps I should not harm this one.*"

N'Jadaka was unsure how much of this was the supplements talking or the aftereffects of training with the suit. Or worse, vestiges of the old Eden—the person he was before he crash-landed on this planet—resurfacing. Might be the reason for his strange readings. Best to up the supplement dosage, then. Keep him on track.

"You are right," N'Jadaka replied. "Perhaps I like the idea of always having the heretic around, of always having something, *someone,* to fight. A reason to have this power, you know? Else, what am I without that?" He sighed, rose, and patted the bed. "Get some rest, young one. Another training day tomorrow."

Eden's eyes flicked and took in the emperor. Then he turned away, his gaze fixed on the glass busts.

"Give my thanks to Zenzi," he said. "Tell her I appreciate the gifts."

"Always," said N'Jadaka. "She will be by the arena tomorrow to watch you fight."

Eden, eyes never leaving the busts, nodded. "I look forward to it."

CHAPTER 22

△▽△▽

PLANET KURAO

THE SETTLEMENTS IN question were at the base of the sole hill that housed Morosi's stronghold amid mostly flat terrain. The desolation seemed to shift, too, as she neared the settlements. Dry, flaky earth gave way to moss covered rock, a shiny carpet welcoming her in. The air here was thicker, filled with the scent of soil rather than dust. A fresh wound amid desolation, just like the grassland had been. Wind rustled through whatever jagged rocks were left, worn smooth by eons of harsh weather.

When Nakia entered the nearest settlement, the pale sun had just begun turning on its side. She wasn't sure how long days lasted here, and the setting star seemed to have no impact on the people, who carried on in full swing even as darkness slowly encroached on the land. The Eri Kurao all seemed to be of a singular species, similar to what Sirigu and Donzea looked like—the same large eyes and slender faces, lack of hair or fur, long digits (she'd counted earlier; they all had four each)—and without much phenotypical differences other than height (very tall to very short), tint of dermis (ranging from orange to purple), and a vast range of facial features. There were no obvious gender differences, and in fact, now that she thought about it, no augmentations other than Morosi themself, who might just be the sole augmented person among all of the Eri Kurao.

The settlement before her was all simple architecture, done with low-tech methods and with a clear focus on shelter rather than aesthetics. Critters, little and large both, ran around in the shadows but didn't seem to be bothering the people, and the people didn't bother them in return. Though this sector looked like its purpose was dedicated to both residential and commercial concerns, the bustle around her seemed to be mostly work-focused—some of it looked like trading, and others looked like the staples of a working community: construction, food, health care. Not much of the lodging Morosi seemed to speak of.

The Eri Kurao surveyed Nakia as she did them. As she walked past what seemed to be the busiest area of this settlement itself, everything paused around her. All sounds dropped to a hushed whisper, movement slowed to a standstill. It helped, of course, that she was dressed head to toe in her black armor, and after hiding her mask away, all they saw before them was what she wanted them to see: a representative of the Intergalactic Empire. It was the fastest way to get what she wanted.

That hope was dashed when she approached a nearby building, in front of which stood a small elderly Eri Kurao, half her height, drinking a steaming beverage from a stone bowl. She towered over them and spoke with as much authority as she could muster:

"In the name of the Intergalactic Empire of Wakanda and your Lord Morosi of Kurao, I, Nakia, Imperial Askari and envoy of the imperial forces, request your assistance."

The Eri Kurao looked up at her. They made a sound from their throat, which Nakia interpreted to be a chuckle. Slowly, they brought up a hand and placed it gently on their forehead. Then they returned to their drinking.

Nakia didn't know what to make of that, so she repeated her request, louder this time. The Eri Kurao made the exact same gesture in response: hand to forehead.

Her translator had nothing for that gesture.

Great.

She walked away, hoping to find another being who would act more decisively. She soon settled upon a slightly younger fellow who looked like they were tending to a trading stall.

Nakia repeated her request. This Eri Kurao repeated the same gesture, a bit more panicky than the elder, but with just as much conviction. Nakia grunted, turned to a third nearby person. Before she could even spit out the request—hand to forehead.

In fact, all around her, she realized, everyone had their hand to forehead, giving her a wide berth.

"They will not help you, off-worlder."

She turned to the source of the voice. It was a scrawny Eri Kurao, fresh-faced and wide-eyed, a child or at least a pre-adult.

"That is what this means." The child placed the hand on their forehead. "It is *I do not commit myself.*"

Nakia went down on a knee to meet the child's gaze, nodding slowly. "They do not commit to helping the Empire?"

The child, tentatively, mirrored her nodding.

"And what if the Empire insists?"

The child blinked. They had no eyelashes.

"Nothing," they said. "We tell our brains: *no commit.* Even when our body will."

"You people can turn off your brains?"

The child seemed to struggle to understand the expression "turn off," so they just blinked some more.

"Will you help me?" asked Nakia. She pointed to the child's relaxed hand. "You have not refused to commit."

The child blinked, then said, "For the right trade."

Ah, right. A child who was willing to do business. Nakia chuckled at how unprecedented that was.

"What do you want?"

Hesitantly, the child reached out and touched her panther helmet, grazing its smooth curve with their long fingers.

"Hmmm." Nakia rose. "Unfortunately, I cannot give this to you now. But—" She lifted a finger. "You take me to those I wish to find, and after I have concluded my business here on this planet, I give you my word. I will make sure you have this helmet before I leave."

The child blinked. "You are asking me to trust an imperial."

This was the first time anyone had mentioned the Empire directly in this way. She realized this lack of tact was due to them being a child. Funny how children, no matter where in the galaxy, were all the same: earnest, tactless, honest.

"No," she said, deciding on some honesty of her own. "Never trust an imperial." She squatted, met their gaze. "But I swear on my word, I will do everything to ensure you receive this helmet as soon as I am done with my quest here."

The child seemed convinced. They took their time to simulate a nod.

"Tell me what you are looking for," they said.

"Two hunter-gatherers named Sirigu and Donzea," said Nakia. "I met them earlier, at the grasslands in the outskirts."

"I do not know anybody named Sirigu or Donzea," said the child. "But I know where most of the hunter-gatherers live."

THE CHILD DIDN'T introduce themself, not while they navigated narrow and wide walkways both. As they moved farther away from the settlement's entrance, darkness fell and Nakia was less visible to passersby. The child offered her a large blanket to wrap around herself, which aided in their secrecy. The architecture of the settlement began to change, became sparser. From here, she could see lights in the distance under the inky green of the sky. Other settlements. Her computer's real-time mapping suggested that there were many like this, scattered all around the planet, but most were congregated here, around Morosi's stronghold. She had a mind to ask Sirigu about this once they met again.

The child stopped every now and then to ask an adult Eri Kurao about the hunter-gatherers and the names Nakia had mentioned. They received gentle responses, suddenly measured once Nakia was spotted. But soon enough, the child seemed to have gathered sufficient information. Their movements and navigation became surer.

Soon they came to a stop in front of a bare abode.

"The ones you are looking for are here," they said, then pointed at Nakia's face. "I will return for that."

And then, just as they had materialized from the ether, they were gone.

Nakia took a deep breath and knocked on the door. A pause, a shuffle, a light. The door clicked, and the face of a tired-looking Donzea poked out.

"I need your help," Nakia said.

Donzea scowled and shut the door, but not before Nakia wedged her foot in the gap between door and frame.

"Listen, listen. I beg of you, give me a moment of your time. I will explain everything. I am not who you think I am."

The words *I beg of you* seemed to have an effect on Donzea. Perhaps they'd never witnessed an imperial actor make a plea.

Donzea studied her for a long moment, then edged the door a bit wider before leaving it open and disappearing into the home. Nakia stepped inside.

The abode bore the hallmarks of a place inhabited by humble workers. Small, old appliances and weathered furniture. Each item handmade, the craftmanship raging from adept to could be better. Everything had the feeling of being lived in, used to the extent of its potential. Nothing existed simply for decoration. Utility first, aesthetics second.

Donzea moved with practiced ease and grace around the or-dered disorder of the home, returning to what looked like the kitchen to continue what they'd been doing before. They didn't once turn back to look at Nakia, not even a glance over her shoulder to see if she was making a move. When she perched on the edge of a seating cushion, she could see Donzea stiffen briefly, as if, without looking, they'd realized she had decided to make herself comfortable without asking her hosts for permission. Nakia wondered how much of this was a Kurao cultural thing and how much was particular to Donzea.

Sirigu walked through the doorway and froze. Without acknowledging Nakia's presence, they turned to Donzea and said something, a language that didn't register on Nakia's translator. Based on the tone, Nakia interpreted it to be something to the tune of: *What are you doing letting her in here?* Donzea continued to work, saying nothing, occasionally lifting their eyes to gaze meaningfully at Sirigu. Sirigu, firing more queries, began to shift tone, becoming more relaxed. It was a conversation between two people who'd lived with each other for a long time to the point where their communication exceeded singular language. It dawned on Nakia, now, that she'd never asked about their relationship. Were they family? Siblings? Parent and child? Partners? Lovers? It was unclear.

Sirigu finally turned to register Nakia's presence.

"I am not an imperial," she said hastily.

Sirigu gave a nod. "Donzea says so. Why did you lie?"

Nakia shrugged. "You can't tell who's a friend or enemy in the dark."

"I could say the same." They regarded Nakia up and down. "You look every measure like an imperial."

And I feel so, too, sometimes, thought Nakia, but she said, "I am of the Maroon Rebellion, and I need your help."

"And why should we help you?" They spread their hands. "Look at us. We are simple hunter-gatherers."

"Sometimes, the simplest of people have the greatest to offer." Something N'Yami used to say. A pang burrowed into Nakia's heart. How dearly she missed the woman.

Donzea had slowed their work. They seemed increasingly interested in what Nakia had to say, so she capitalized on that and turned to face them.

"I intend to infiltrate Morosi's stronghold," she said. "They possess an ancient Wakandan spear in there, one that's of great importance to the Maroon Rebellion. We stand for everyone who lives beneath the Empire's iron fist, and we wish to gain freedom for all. That spear is crucial to our plans, to help the only person who can challenge the emperor and defeat the Empire."

Donzea had stopped working altogether and stared at her. Sirigu was similarly captivated. Nakia pressed home her advantage.

"We need that spear," she said, "or none of us will ever be free."

That did it. The two Eri Kurao looked at each other, and another conversation passed wordlessly between them.

"Okay," said Sirigu finally. "Tell us how we can help."

TWO DAYS LATER, Nakia stepped into another abode.

This one was in a different settlement, arrived at by riding across the empty plains for a whole day in Sirigu and Donzea's renna carriage. The two Eri Kurao rode with her, barely speaking throughout the trip. They only informed her that they had sent word ahead to the person they were meeting, whose identity they could not divulge because it was a security risk. Morosi's drones were everywhere and could pick up all kinds of chatter, even whispered words.

"How did you send the message, then?"

It turned out that there was more to this planet than met the eye. Apparently, beneath its surface, every piece of flora Nakia saw—the reeds, the moss, the isolated clumps of blue vegetation in the plains—had an intraspecies connection via an intricate underground network of roots. Affecting one plant in a species affected every single one elsewhere on the planet. The flora transferred messages to one another through unique pulse patterns. Therefore, if one knew how to, one could *say* something by affecting a particular species in a specific way on one side of the planet, sending a unique pulse to someone who was listening to the exact same species on the opposite side of the planet. These patterns of pulses, translated, could become prose.

Morse code, Nakia thought, *but with plants.*

Donzea, it turned out, was quite skilled at this—it was how they "spoke" to Sirigu sometimes. They had contacts in various settlements that acted as conduits and secret messengers of sorts—it was another way they made a living beyond hunting and gathering. For this trip, they'd sent coded pulse messages to a specific species of shrub and received an invitation not long after.

And now Nakia stood with them both in a dimly lit room, eyes adjusting to the darkness. The green sky was slowly giving way to dawn outside, and it cast a glow over the two other people standing with them, both older and taller than her allies. One had dermis on the vibrant side of orange while the other was a deep purple.

"Nakia of the Maroon Rebellion," said Sirigu, "I want you to meet Gangwe, the most renowned landspeaker on Kurao."

The purple Eri Kurao stepped forward and gently rested their forehead on Nakia's chest. Nakia, slowly, returned the welcome, lowering her head as well.

"And this is Vhomafhlot, one of the few of us to have entered Morosi's stronghold and returned alive. You may call them Vhoma as we all do."

The orange Eri Kurao had a sterner demeanor. Their greeting was a bit more harried. Nakia repeated the gesture.

"Thank you for agreeing to speak with me," she said, addressing the two. "I know it must take a lot to trust a stranger like me, especially one who looks so akin to the Empire's forces."

The two looked at each other.

"You speak our tongue well," said Vhoma. "How do you do that?"

Nakia pointed to her suit. "Interspecies translator."

"Yes." They pointed a long finger. "Imperial technology."

Nakia nodded. "True. Correct. But I am no imperial." Half the truth, but sufficient.

"Donzea says you are of a resistance that wants to overthrow the Empire." This was Gangwe, who had a softer tone, almost nurturing. "I could not believe it. I had to see for myself this person crazy enough to go up against Morosi's drones."

Nakia shrugged. "Morosi has taken something very important to my people. If I do not get it back, our capacity to go up against the Empire will be significantly diminished."

Gangwe waved for them to sit. Vhoma—whose abode this was, as Gangwe had made the trip from a nearby settlement just as they had—left to prepare a beverage.

"Where are you from?" asked Gangwe. "Tell me everything."

Nakia revealed as much as she could, sipping on the salty-sour but soothingly warm broth she'd been served. She told them of the great Maroon leaders, of N'Yami and M'Baku and even T'Challa; of the suffering of those at Goree, the rescues, the losses at Cudjoe and the suffering at the new hideout. She told them of the promise held by the Spear of Bashenga and why she had to recover it.

It was late into the night when she finished speaking, all their broth bowls empty. All four Eri Kurao were now completely sympathetic to her plight and to that of the Maroons. They would help her. But they still had one request.

"If we help you get in there," said Vhoma, "you cannot just steal what you need and go. You must destroy it. All of it."

Nakia angled her head. "The stronghold looks quite . . . impervious."

"It is," said Vhoma. "Many have tried and failed to make a dent in Morosi's power. They get resources from the Empire that no one else ever receives, including new technology like what they use to make those drones. All attacks have failed before they even made it past the gates, and those dragged into Morosi's lair after being arrested—for one perceived crime or another—have never returned. The reason I'm the only one to make it out is because I was called there once. To fix something no one could fix." Vhoma rose. "And perhaps that was their mistake."

"How so?"

"Because I saw it. The heart of the stronghold."

"What is it?"

"A vault at the center. And in it lies the engine that runs that place, that gives power to everything Morosi owns—defense drones, scavenging freighters, augmentation machinery. It is in that vault where everything of value is held, and perhaps your spear may be there, too. If you can get inside and destroy the power core, we can shut off Morosi's choke hold on this planet once and for all."

"About that," said Nakia. "How does Morosi hold this planet hostage?"

Everyone turned to Gangwe. They looked wistful, crestfallen.

"You have witnessed, through the message that brought you here, how everything that springs from this land is interconnected," Gangwe said. "The first thing Morosi did after becoming one of the Empire's anointed scavengers was to forge something that could cause the land to stop giving as it should. Little by little, with the Empire's help, they scorched and scraped the surface of this planet until no plant dared return to the surface. Now only a few spaces are left for us—these are the spaces around which our settlements congregate. But they do not produce enough to cater to us. Morosi, who now owns the largest seedling bank of all the flora on this planet, also being held in that vault of theirs, has taken away our ability to make our own food. They sell us back our own seedlings, and we have limited space in which to grow them."

Gangwe stopped speaking, rose, and walked to a window to look out.

"What's wrong with them?" Nakia whispered to Sirigu.

"To a landspeaker," said Sirigu, "the flora are like friends. Gangwe can hear what they say, how they feel—it is how they hear Donzea's messages. Right now, Gangwe can feel the vestiges of their ancestries beneath the soil, unwilling to return until new seeds can coax them out." Sirigu made a sound of disappointment. "For us, defeating Morosi is not just about surviving. It's about the survival of this very land."

You and us both, thought Nakia.

"One of the seedlings from the bank—a tenacious vine—had somehow found fertile space and embedded itself inside a piece of the power core, rendering it inoperable," Vhoma said. "This is why I was called in. They needed someone with local expertise in both land and technology to deal with this encroachment, especially because the vine was, shall we say, aggressive."

All of this, Nakia found fascinating. She would've loved to stay longer and soak in this place, spend time with these endearing people. But she didn't have that luxury. Her own people back home needed her.

"Okay," she said. "The power core goes. I get my spear, you get your land back, and we both stick it to the Empire." She rose. "Now tell me about how you're going to get me in."

CHAPTER 23

△▽△▽

PLANET KURAO

A BLADE OF GRASS. That was how she was getting in.

"Not just any blade or any grass," Gangwe explained. "A rare species of blue brush, one which sprouts once every hundred or so seasons and dies without warning within a few days of its sprouting. We have been able to capture a couple of these blades in the last few seasons and preserve them, with the hope that a small group can use them for this very purpose. But we have never had enough for a sizable number of people to use. For one important and powerful enough person, though . . ."

As much as Nakia didn't come here to be some sort of savior, she realized, in a way, that she might just be, for these people, what T'Challa might be for the Maroon Rebellion.

"What does it do?" she asked.

Gangwe had learned from Nakia how to smile, and they did so now, a wry mimicry of an upturned slit.

"Let me show you."

They were still in Vhoma's home, where they'd stayed to complete their plans, as it was farther away from Morosi than Sirigu and Donzea's community. Here she had been educated on everything she needed to know about Morosi's stronghold, everything from a map of its choke points and points of security fallibility ("Where the fewest drones fly," said Vhoma) and the nearly impenetrable alloy the walls were constructed from. ("Do not let the flimsy look of those fortifications fool you," Vhoma insisted. "They do not come down easy.") Nakia drank in everything as quickly as she drank in Maroon intelligence (and if she was being honest, as quickly as she'd learned to drink imperial intelligence, which was where she'd honed this skill in the first place).

Gangwe returned with what looked like a handily crafted safe box and beckoned Nakia outside. Under a small canopy, she opened the box with a voice activated whisper, then took out what looked like a small, thin wafer.

"This is the *brepf* grass," they said, then put it to their tongue and swallowed.

It took a while, but suddenly, slowly and surely, the Eri Kurao before her faded into thin air.

Faded, as in, *disappeared,* but more like *became invisible.* Nakia could still feel their presence, the warmth of their breath and body heat, but it was like they were gone, like nothing existed in the space where they'd just stood. When they shifted, Nakia could feel their energy, their warmth, shift with them. But when she put out her hand into that space to touch them, she felt nothing. There was *nothing* there.

She was still waving into said space when Gangwe shimmered back into existence. Suddenly she realized her hands were *inside* the Eri Kurao's body, passing through as if no one were there. Nakia recoiled, horrified.

"Nothing to be afraid of," said Gangwe, smiling once they'd fully rematerialized. "It does not hurt, and one cannot solidify if there is any kind of organic or inorganic matter blocking their way. We have worked to graft the brepf grass with other components to make it so." They chuckled. "Imagine the disastrous effects if we hadn't."

Imagine indeed, thought Nakia. She'd almost dismembered this person who was so willing to help her. She shook off the horror, composed herself.

"So, I'm guessing this allows me to pass through Morosi's walls and navigate into the vault unseen."

"Precisely." Gangwe shut the box softly and handed it to Nakia. "It takes some practicing to get used to, though, especially for the amount of time you will be in there." They gestured toward the small chest. "That is all the brepf we have, and all we can hope to have for a while to come. You will need most of it to stay fluid during the mission. Which means you only have, give or take, one or two blades in there for practice." They patted Nakia on the shoulder. "Try practicing as soon as you can."

BY THE MORNING of the heist, Nakia and all four Eri Kurao were back at Donzea and Sirigu's, from where she would launch her offensive. They each gave her parting instructions, warnings, and slices of motivation: Sirigu, a simple nod; Donzea, wordless warm encouragement; Vhoma, even more instructions for navigating the stronghold's byzantine corridors; and Gangwe, offering the blessings and appreciation of the flora all over the planet, who'd been informed of this sacrifice in their name. Then she was off, ferried to a safe dropoff location by Sirigu and their rennas.

Once there, after Sirigu had wished her good luck and disappeared, Nakia gazed upon the distant citadel, its pillars piercing the sky like jagged teeth. The wind whipped dust around her as she checked her supplies. She'd returned to her zulu to stock up on everything she believed she'd need—from weaponry and ammunition to mobile instant medikits—and check in with her computer. As it stood, she was more prepared for this mission than any other imperial or Maroon mission she'd ever undertaken.

And yet shivers marched down her spine as she gripped her weapons and crawled up to the stronghold. This mission, unlike the others, carried with it the weight and future of a people she'd come to know intimately. And unlike other missions, it was up to her, singularly, to make this happen. It helped her appreciate, now, what she was asking of T'Challa, what all five galaxies were asking of him. *Save us,* they were saying, without asking if he was ready or had what it takes—if *she* was ready, or had what it takes.

Muscles as tense as the panther suit could allow, she crawled as close to the entry as possible without being sighted by the drones, and then she took out the brepf grass, inhaled deeply, exhaled, and put them in her mouth.

The sensation still took her by surprise, even after a few practice sessions. The gentle tingling in her fingertips; shadows taking on a new, heightened atmosphere; a swift untetheredness, the feeling that everything around her was suddenly so very far away, like she was floating alone in space. What a zulu or a planet must feel like: disoriented but buoyant, slipping through nothing but light and air.

She ran.

Straight ahead, toward the entryway that Vhoma had marked. Gliding, feeling as light as dust motes. Her feet left no prints, and the drones in the far area didn't turn toward her, completely oblivious to her movements and likely diminished heat signature.

Brepf. She said the name of the wonder grass under her breath. How she would have loved to take this back with her, help the Maroon Rebellion break into imperial strongholds just like this. Save all five galaxies and all planets, this one included. Too bad it only grew in small bits every now and then.

She was now at the entryway, which was only . . . a wall? She sighed. This was the worst part of the process, the one she absolutely detested, but there was no time to waste. She gritted her teeth and stuck her body, shoulder first, through the wall.

The disorientation intensified, worsened by the fact that her brain struggled to process the lack of resistance when her body pierced the barrier. Worse, the wall was thicker than she'd expected, so that when she put her head through, all visibility went away, spatial cues suddenly nowhere to be found. It also abruptly became much colder, the temperature shift contributing to the disorientation. Luckily her panther suit adjusted to counter this. All sound and light disappeared, and the tingling in her extremities extended to other parts of her body, a persistent warning.

Soon, after a few steps of drudgery, she emerged from the wall into a narrow corridor, currently empty, often unused, according to Vhoma. Her computer's signal tracker pointed her in a new direction with no signs of nearby drones. She was just a few corridors down from the so-called heart of this stronghold, where her prize—and the people's freedom—lay.

She moved quickly, wondering about a great many things. How was it that this place was so empty with no other person in sight? Did Morosi live here all alone with nothing else but their drones? Did they even *live* here, or did they only maintain this place as a symbol of conquest of the Empire's nearby hand? Absentee rule, in a sense. Perhaps they had gone on a scavenging trip? Or maybe on a visit to a *real* imperial envoy, to confirm whether the Empire had truly sent someone to speak on the emperor's behalf.

Whatever the case, it had to be an incredibly lonely life, didn't it? This was just like the Empire to offer, in exchange for its own gain, a miserable existence. An existence that Morosi surely deserved.

The corridors remained empty, with nothing more than a drone proximity alert registering in her helmet every now and then. She slipped through walls whenever she could, staying only as long as the strange sensation of being invisible, transparent, and porous would allow. And then she was on her way again, creeping and crawling, until finally, she emerged in the heart of the stronghold.

It was shockingly unspectacular.

It was a large but simple bay, stocked with tons upon tons of equipment. Imperial, from the looks of it, but not otherwise notable. No masses of guard drones as reported. Nothing to say that this was the singular place that held a whole planet hostage. The only notable thing was that the bay's ceiling reached to the top of the tower, with a roof that opened up to the Kurao sky, which was currently shut. Ahead was a docking station that, Nakia surmised, housed a craft that was currently not there. A small freighter, from the look of things. Morosi must have taken the freighter out on a trip. No wonder the place was so quiet.

All this talk about a stronghold, and its heart is a simple . . . garage? Nakia found herself more enraged than surprised. She scouted the place, noting even more security systems—rooftop guns, for example—and a couple of control nodes for sending commands to the drones. She worked a little to gain access to the governor modules that ran the drones, then paired her panther helmet with the stronghold's broadcast system, instantly achieving the same pairing she had with her zulu's computer. This would allow her to broadcast commands from here all the way to her craft.

Now, for the spear.

The safe was easy to find, and its wall thicker than she'd envisioned. After what seemed like eternity dragging herself through a metal and sand barrier, she emerged into darkness, engaging night vision immediately.

The safe, too, was unremarkable. It held artifacts of various manner, many of which she couldn't recognize, other than the seed bank Gangwe had mentioned, as well as the power core that Vhoma had described. She didn't see the spear at first, looking around, trying to pinpoint the location indicated by the tracker. And then she found it, hiding between stacked boxes of loot. She shoved them aside and grabbed the spear, the cool steel feeling at home in her palm.

Nakia let out a long breath. All this traveling, all this heartache, and finally, she had the Spear of Bashenga in her hands.

Now, to free the Eri Kurao.

The power core was really just a large module with a stack of cells. She could blow it up, but she'd likely be trapped here if everything got turned off. The seed bank might also be trapped in here. She also realized, now, as she moved toward the door, that the spear had not been in her hands when she took the brepf grass, and therefore wasn't part of the inorganic matter attached to her body. It *couldn't* become immaterial and invisible.

She had to find a way to open the door, *then* destroy the power core.

She put the spear close to the door where she could easily retrieve it, then went through the barrier again. But this time was different. The wall around her shimmered in and out of existence—far, near, far, near—and suddenly, as soon as she was on the other side, the feeling of disorientation disappeared. Everything that was far away suddenly drew close in a rush, like a yelling crowd running toward her. Sounds, smells, lights, cold air—all of it was suddenly there: in her nose, in her lungs, on her skin, in her eyes.

Oh no. The brepf grass was done. She was material again.

Her helmet went crazy, blinking incessant warnings as shadows descended upon her.

The bay was no longer empty. In the little time she'd spent in the safe, it had completely filled with drones, which now finally clocked her heat signature and rushed toward her, assembling as if preparing to execute a firing squad. They whirred together like a mass of winged insects, and though they didn't draw weapons yet, they scanned and scanned her and agreed that she was an alien entity.

Before she could consider a course of action, the aircraft roof overhead opened, and sailing down into the bay was . . .

. . . her *zulu*?

Then it dawned on her. Why the drones were assembling but not firing. Why the zulu had come to the very location where she was standing.

She'd *called* them.

While pairing with the broadcast system, she must have broadcast her location and primed them to assemble to her, which they were now doing. This was likely confusing the drones, which had yet to understand that their governing modules had been overridden by the very same entity they considered a threat.

Nakia almost laughed, appreciating how ridiculous this all was. But there was more to do yet, and she realized the unusual situation in which she'd found herself suddenly made it all easier.

Slowly, she sidled up to her landing zulu, avoiding sudden movements that would spook the drones, which had now gathered en masse. She climbed into the cockpit, and once she was settled in, finger on the trigger of the craft's guns, she gave the command.

The drones assembled at the front of the safe's door as ordered, packing themselves tightly onto the panel. She ensured that every single one of them was there, not a single drone left idling in the stronghold.

Then she squeezed the trigger and let them have it.

NAKIA SAT BESIDE her zulu atop the hill, a ways from the stronghold, and watched the Eri Kurao race into the giant structure still spilling smoke into the sky.

Most didn't even look in her direction. They ran with sole focus, mostly unarmed, into the place that had taken all that was theirs. They ran to reclaim all they had lost, the ecstasy of freedom written across their faces. It was a beautiful sight, and Nakia wished, so dearly, that one day, all in the five galaxies would wear such an expression.

Nakia's crew of Vhoma, Gangwe, Sirigu, and Donzea were the only ones to stop by after being awash with congratulations from their fellow Eri Kurao. They offered her congrats of their own, each thanking her in their own way—Vhoma with questions, Gangwe with blessing from the flora, Sirigu with *I knew you could do it,* and Donzea, as usual, with a silent gaze that needed no words.

"The guns," she told Vhoma. "They still work. You should make sure someone sits there behind them, pointed skyward, night and day. The moment Morosi's freighter appears—" She clicked her fingers. "Keep someone there at all times. Make sure that imperial stooge never returns to this planet."

Before she got into her zulu, she took off the helmet and handed it to Sirigu.

"There's a child in your settlement who will seek you out and ask about me," she said. "I promised them this helmet. Tell them I say: Keep it safe and close. Let it be a symbol of the good thing we've done here today, and a reminder that not all who seem like imperials—in body, mind, or in spirit—are."

She got into the zulu and took it to the sky, casting a glance at the Spear of Bashenga safely nestled in nearby storage. She set course for a return to the ice rock.

Now, for the next and possibly even harder task: Find T'Challa, return the spear.

CHAPTER 24

△▽△▽

NEW MAROON HIDEOUT, NEHANDA'S LATTICE

IT TOOK NAKIA a long time to find him.

Much hadn't changed on the ice rock when she returned from her months-long voyage. M'Baku was still leader. The Maroons were still cold, starving, and suffering. T'Challa was still gone, and no one had seen or heard from him.

M'Baku's welcome upon her return wasn't cold, but it wasn't warm either. He still felt hurt by her allegiance to T'Challa, compounded by her choice to abandon the rebellion without informing him, and then refusing to explain where she'd gone when asked. But she had good reason for keeping M'Baku and the other Maroons in the dark. She shared nothing of her travels, and especially nothing of the spear she'd just recovered. If her journey to Kurao had taught her anything, it was that hope was a thing of timing: Release the wrong information at the wrong time, and it could have a devastating effect. But information released at just the right time was enough to turn a dwindling flame into a blazing torch.

The Spear of Bashenga in T'Challa's hand, that would be a blazing torch for the rebellion. But until she could find T'Challa and put the spear in his hand—*the knife where it belonged*—that flame would have to wait a little bit longer.

And so her search for T'Challa began, combing every nook and cranny of the ice rock for months and months after her return, to no avail, while the Maroon Rebellion withered and shrunk.

Until one day, a bullet shot across the sky.

IT WAS NO BULLET. It was him.

Nakia was scoping out the northern edge of the planet, one of the coldest, scraggiest areas of the ice rock, when something silent and supersonic shot across her view. She knew, immediately, that it was no planetary life-form—nothing natural could move that fast. No, that was technology. And definitely not the rebellion's, as she'd have recognized it. No, this was something else.

She returned to the same spot the next day and waited, binoculars in hand. Sure enough, at some point during this day, she heard it, the silent whoosh of something soaring through the wind, slipping between streams. She put her binoculars to her eyes and zoomed in.

A wing-shaped glider. A man, suited. Shooting across the skies, fast. Too fast. Unsafe.

She tried to track the trajectory, but he soon disappeared behind rock formations and was gone.

EVERY DAY AFTERWARD, Nakia took the Spear of Bashenga, got on her powered cycle, rode out to the rock formations, and waited for T'Challa to fly across. Every day, he took a different trajectory, streaking past just quickly enough to disappear behind clouds and mountain both. Every day, Nakia went and watched, spending her waiting time wondering how much of him had changed during their time apart and how much had remained the same. She wondered if, now that she'd turned her sights further toward her role as kingmaker, it meant she was giving up on their romance. She wondered if his body was still warm, if his touch on her arm would still make her nervous, if the stubble on his chin was still there, and if he'd forgotten to shave because she wasn't there to remind him.

BLACK PANTHER: THE INTERGALACTIC EMPIRE OF WAKANDA 183

Each day, she returned home with nothing but was undeterred. Someone had to watch out for the Maroons, and someone had to watch out for T'Challa. If he was out here daredeviling across the sky each day, something was bound to go wrong at some point, and someone—*she*—had to be there when it did.

ONE DAY, the flying man fell from the sky.

It was a day like any other. Nakia was waiting in her usual position with her binoculars, Spear of Bashenga strapped to her back. Sometime around noon, T'Challa appeared in his glider suit, coming around the bend of a tall mountain. Nakia watched closely through her binoculars.

But today, something was different. He was moving faster. Much faster.

Worse, he was making turns at top speed, slipping between ice formations at a pace that no one should. And now he was headed for a narrow passageway between two slim formations.

"T'Challa, what are you doing?" Nakia found herself saying.

All this time, she had opted to hang back and simply watch. She believed that, by now, T'Challa must have seen her and known she was watching. Her decision was to approach him only once he showed any willingness to be approached. Flying all around was probably his own way of dealing with the grief that had stricken them all. She wanted him to be ready to receive her before she went. They'd been apart a long time, too.

But the moment she saw him headed for that narrow passageway, she knew what was coming. Caution thrown to the wind, she jumped on her cycle and zoomed across the frosty landscape in hot pursuit.

T'Challa crashed into the ice formation just as it came into view for Nakia. A cloud of white mist erupted, and then she saw him spiral, left wing shattered. He tumbled into more formations, leaving behind a trail of icy clouds and more shards of glider apparatus.

When she found him, he was freezing and barely conscious. His helmet's visor was broken. Ice filled his nostrils.

Nakia jumped off her cycle and knelt at his side cradling his head.

"Oh, T'Challa," she said. "What in Bast's name were you thinking?"

His eyes fluttered open and he mumbled something. She leaned closer and placed her ear to his barely moving lips.

"Nakia?" he was saying. "Nakia? Why are you here?"

HE DIDN'T NEED convincing to lead her to his hideout, so badly bruised he was. A sharp ache stabbed through his rib cage with every sudden movement. The still-functioning glider suit did most of the navigation work, while Nakia simply rode the cycle as gently as she could to prevent bumps from reactivating his hurting ribs. When the hideout finally came into view—a small but equipped abode, tucked into a crevice in a mountain range like forgotten lint in an old coat pocket—T'Challa felt vulnerable, far too exposed. Knowing Nakia, he could almost hear her thoughts, her wondering how lonely it must've felt to live all alone in the icy armpit of an already lonely planet.

At least inside was state of the art, and a shelter from the elements. She paced the small main area—filled, as expected, with holos and screens—while T'Challa retreated to the small alcove where he slept to change out of his suit, cleaned and bound his wounds, and took some medication. When he returned, barechested and leaning on a walking aid, the concern was written plainly across her face. This version of himself standing before her was a man broken in more ways than one, aged by trauma, grief, disappointment. How could she have known that he waited here for her?

He was a man who needed someone, who needed her. And perhaps not just as a romantic partner but something more. Someone to remind him of who he was, to urge him toward who he could be.

"Thank you for helping me home." The walking aid creaked, straining with the weight of his physique.

This isn't home. He brushed the thought away.

He watched as Nakia stared at the screens that rotated images of ancient Wakandan heroes, N'Yami now among them. Her gaze returned to him, with the same steely assurance N'Yami had had. With the medicine settling into his system, T'Challa finally took notice of the cold, hard Vibranium spear strapped to Nakia's back. *It couldn't be.*

She reached behind, unstrapped the spear slowly, and held it aloft before her.

"I wish to return the Spear of Bashenga," she said, "to its rightful owner."

T'Challa looked at the weapon not with surprise but with a kind of bone-deep sadness. He sighed and turned around slowly, his back to Nakia and the spear.

"We've given up war, Nakia," he said. "Given up fighting for half memories and ghosts. Our champion was slaughtered before our very eyes, and that spear is a grim reminder of all I lost that day."

He swallowed hard.

"It has no rightful owner," he concluded.

Without warning, she flipped the spear into a throwing grip and flung it at T'Challa's back.

He might have grown a few gray hairs in her absence and taken on the demeanor of an old and defeated man in the time since, but his body still clung to memory. He could almost hear N'Yami's voice: *Avatar of Bast, the Black Panther, He Who Put the Knife Where It Belonged.*

T'Challa turned around and caught the Spear of Bashenga.

Just like the first time he'd been reunited with the weapon at Cudjoe, something seemed to pass between man and spear, the recognition of an old friend. T'Challa's grip on the Vibranium tightened and the metal *sang* in response, finally having found its way back to its rightful hand. A truth not even he could deny. A victory.

"Dammit, Nakia," said T'Challa, and he sighed.

AS THEY PREPARED to lie down for the evening, T'Challa held on to the spear and moved with purpose, the pain of his wounds already receding, the spear giving him renewed vigor. It was in this moment, watching him, that Nakia realized she finally felt vindicated. She'd felt guilty for each of the choices she'd made since that meeting in M'Baku's office after the memorial—abandoning the Maroon Rebellion at a difficult time, leaving without telling M'Baku and T'Challa, invoking her imperial past and *posing* as an imperial, all less than desirable actions. But if this was the end result? All that she'd endured was worth it.

"It suits you," she told him. T'Challa was putting on some hot broth for them both.

He grunted. "Perhaps." He rose and stared at the screens. "In another life, it would have. This was not my choice, to settle here. But whether I like it or not, I'm a Maroon. So this is the life M'Baku has led us to. But I have no use for weaponry in this life."

N'Yami's image came into rotation. He held the spear up toward her, in honor.

"In this life, I must accept that which I cannot change." He returned to Nakia. "But this is not about what suits me." He sat with her. "Why are you here, Nakia?"

It was her turn to inhale.

"It's happened finally," she said slowly. "Word has gotten out of our location."

This wasn't the reason she'd come here, of course. This was old news, bound to happen sometime soon. Even before her time away, a steady stream of Nameless, both new escapees from imperial mines and old Maroons who hadn't made it on the shuttles but had fled Cudjoe via other means, had begun to trace the Maroon Rebellion to this rock. Dwindling rations aside, M'Baku opted not to turn them away—a good decision, in Nakia's assessment, because this was the worst possible time to have a disgruntled Maroon floating out there in space.

But during the time she'd been away, that stream had quickly become a flood. One Nameless's success story had inspired countless more to the point where even the Askari began to wonder what was spurring all these escape efforts in the mines. Hadn't the Maroon Rebellion been crushed both in arms and spirit? What was keeping this hope alive?

Not long before her return, a detachment of Askari had followed a band of new escapees to this planet. Luckily for M'Baku and his Maroons, the Askari had been foolish to assume this planet could hold nothing of import to the rebellion. The skirmish had been short, though hard-fought. Better yet, more imperial machinery was salvaged from the fallen craft, boosting Maroon defenses for the first time since the events at Cudjoe.

"We would be foolish to think that detachment would be the last," Nakia concluded.

"Hmm," said T'Challa after. "So we must run again."

"No, T'Challa." She couldn't believe she had to tell him this. "We must *fight* again."

"Fight?" He scoffed. "After *years* of hiding on this frozen rock? After leaving countless men, women, and children to the mines? *Now* M'Baku has found heart?"

Nakia grumbled within. This insistence on animosity with M'Baku was childish, and their inability to put it aside was hurting the Maroons more than this rock was.

"I don't expect you to understand M'Baku, or the weight he carries. You believe, as a warrior does, that the greatest sacrifice is to give your life." She jabbed a finger into his bare shoulder. "You know nothing of the sacrifices of generals, of those who order men to give their lives and then must live with that weight."

He tensed now, but soon the tension dissipated from his shoulders. Yes, she could have worded that more kindly, but it was the truth and he knew it. Perhaps, maybe when he could recover his memories and learn that he, too, once, in another life, had commanded scores upon scores of people to give their lives for Wakanda Prime, he'd remember what that felt like and be more sympathetic to M'Baku.

But for now, only one thing mattered: getting T'Challa back into the fold.

"Let's be honest," she said. "That isn't why you are angry, is it? M'Baku isn't the only one who's running, is he?"

T'Challa rose then, abandoning the rest of the meal before them. The tip of his walking aid clicked and clacked on the floor as he gravitated toward a nearby window.

"You never came to see me." He was peering out, not looking at her. The way he said it, Nakia knew he wasn't talking about her leaving and disappearing for months. He was talking about *the other thing*.

"We both know why, T'Challa."

But did he, really? Did he understand that she simply could not yoke her life to his, moving in whatever direction he deemed fit? She cared for him, yes, but that question at the back of their minds would never leave: *What happens to us when you find a way back to your old life?*

"You only had eyes for her," said Nakia, the only way she could explain it that he would understand.

T'Challa banged his forehead softly on the glass. *Thud, thud, thud.*

"Nakia," he said, "I don't even know who she is."

For now, she thought. *And when you do, what then?*

T'Challa turned around. "Do you know what it means to chase phantoms? Do you know what it is to be haunted?" Brow creased, tone rising, agitated. "The Empire doesn't just steal our past. They steal our futures. How can we move forward when we don't know our names? Who we are? Who we love?"

He click-clacked away from the window. "Even as I have escaped, I am *captured,* held fast by these questions. Who am I? What promises have I made and to whom?" He stopped before Nakia and lay both spear and walking aid aside. "How can I move forward, knowing not what I am leaving behind?" He lifted a hand, placed it softly on her cheek. "I am tired, Nakia." Other hand, on her other cheek. "I am *so very tired* of waiting."

Oh, thought Nakia.

She reached out and placed her palm on his cheek in response, fingers finding his comically large ears, tracing the hard edges of his jaw, feeling the wet softness of his lips. Despite the cloud of anger and despair that hung over him, he was still a very fine specimen of a man. And that was what she often failed to remember: that he was very much that—human—with all the hardness, softness, vulnerability, and fallibility that came with it.

She could cut him some slack. He, too, was just as confused as she was. He knew the weight meant for his shoulders, destined for them even. But there was also the weight of that which he didn't know, no less punishing a weight all in its own right. Was she asking too much of him, to take up this mantle?

Her hands dropped from his cheeks.

No. N'Yami had believed in this—believed in *him*—with every fiber of her being, up until her dying day. She'd entrusted this task to Nakia and she couldn't let feelings, whether good or confused, get in the way. Not when so much was at stake.

She removed T'Challa's hands from her cheeks—gently, lovingly—and clasped them together.

"T'Challa." She said his name with softness, with heart, wrapping it around her tongue like a cocoon. "Never doubt, for one second, that I could love you—that I *want to* love you. But I want to love the *whole* you, filled with all of those lost memories and promises. It's not too late for us, T'Challa. It's *not* too late."

His face settled. He was hearing her. He was reading between the lines. *I want to,* she was saying. *But not now.*

"Nakia." Her name on his lips was equally gentle. "I was ready to fight. No one wanted that more than me. It was not my choice to come here."

"No, it was not," she said. "But it was also not your burden to shepherd our lives. M'Baku never asked for this. He has not always been as wise as I would like. But he has protected us." She was staring at the screen as it rotated past N'Yami's image again.

"With all the losses after her death," Nakia continued, "M'Baku has kept us safe. Allowed us to live to fight another day." She turned around to face him. "T'Challa, that day is now. We can no longer hide. You can no longer hide."

He looked genuinely perplexed. "What do you mean?"

Nakia shook her head pitifully. "All these years, and you still cannot claim it." She picked up the spear from where he'd dropped it nearby. "You used to say you came to find out who you were." She thrust the spear before him again. "But the answer has always been there."

She dropped the spear in his hand. He caught it.

"It just seems so ridiculous that you reject it." Nakia found she was losing her patience. "Instead, you wake up every day warring against phantoms, trying to kill yourself."

He wanted to interject but she put up a hand, turned around, and picked up her overcoat.

"Your little flight through that passageway, it wasn't the first time." She slipped into her coat. "I've watched you for a while, T'Challa. And the Maroons have heard the stories, too. Free dives into icy oceans. Wild predator hunts." She made a disapproving sound at the back of her throat. "I know what you're trying to do. But it won't work. It's not to be."

She slipped her hand into her jacket pocket and reached for the final piece of her puzzle.

Upon her return from Kurao, she'd finally had the time to rummage some more through the belongings N'Yami had left for her. She found something this time, something she'd missed earlier: a holo recording N'Yami had made of herself addressing the Maroons. It had never been broadcast but was now in Nakia's hands.

Nakia had pondered for a while what to do with it. She couldn't give the holo to M'Baku—she could anticipate his response, which would be to destroy it. *No use trying to rile up a broken people with more false promises,* he would say, crunching the recording in his large fists. And he'd be right, there was no reason to offer new promise when they couldn't be sure of delivering.

But it was the very contents of the recording that led Nakia to decide that, though it wouldn't be broadcast to the Maroons, there was someone specific who absolutely had to be privy to the contents of the holo recording. That person was T'Challa.

She pulled it out now, rubbed the holo disc between her fingers. *This is it,* she thought, *my last shot. If the Spear of Bashenga and the words from N'Yami's own lips don't work, nothing else will.*

She held the recording aloft before T'Challa's eyes.

"The hope for you and me is not just in the war against the Empire, but in the war for your soul." She held his palm open and gently placed the holo disc in it. "You have to accept who you are, T'Challa. N'Jadaka already has."

And then she turned and left him with much to ponder.

CHAPTER 25

△▽△▽

NEW MAROON HIDEOUT, NEHANDA'S LATTICE

AFTER NAKIA WAS GONE, T'Challa placed the spear with the rest of his panther gear, then made himself a hot beverage. Staring out the window, warm mug in one hand, walking aid in the other, he tried not to glance over his shoulder at the holo disc Nakia had left behind. It tempted him from the desk, an itch behind his ear that he didn't want to scratch.

He didn't yet know what was on the recording, but he knew that the moment he listened to whatever was on there, it would be over. There would be no going back.

Are you so lost that you will let them reduce you to this?

The words of that old prisoner on Goree, eons ago now, often returned to him in moments of distress. *They have stolen your name,* the man had said, *your culture, your god. Do not let them steal your mind.*

I'm trying, he would respond to himself, to the darkness. *I'm fighting.*

But was he really?

Much of his time since N'Yami's death he'd spent in isolation even before moving to this corner of the ice rock. The captain meant a different thing to every Maroon, and each mourned her separately, in private, in addition to collectively grieving in public. And while most Maroons—Nakia included—saw T'Challa as the stoic hero, what they didn't know was that he was suffering too.

He missed N'Yami, not just for her warmth, but for her font of knowledge, for how she pushed him to uncover new parts of his missing memories. She'd been the deepest well from which he had drawn. With her, he'd finally started to fill the voids that made him, to shine a light on the darkness that caused him to act in the manner he did. Now that she was gone, he could feel the darkness creeping up on him again. He felt like he owed it to her to become someone better, more useful. Someone who could remember. Someone who could eventually go home.

Do not let them steal your mind. The weight of being this *T'Challa*, living up to this name and this person, to be who the Maroons wanted him to be, had become too much to bear. Not that he couldn't be this person—he simply hadn't *chosen* this struggle. It had been thrust upon him, confusing and frustrating; caught up in the weeds of becoming a hero, a savior, he could no longer find his way to being the person he would like to be. A person he couldn't define.

I am lost, he conceded to the darkness. *I must find myself.*

To shed the weight of this name, he decided, he would have to become someone else first. A different T'Challa, separate from the one everyone thought he should be.

It was upon this confusion that the closeness between him and Nakia had sprouted. Once he'd decided he didn't want to be a warrior all the time, that he could be a different person with her— a softer, gentler, kinder soul—he wanted more and more to be that person. The more he was that person, of course, the more he realized he wanted to give this softness to someone else, too: the white-haired woman, whose own softness had kept him alive and sane in the most dire times. This conflict of mind had, over time, overshadowed his quest for a different kind of self. That is, until Nakia decided to leave, pretty much ending that concern.

After her departure, a different kind of conflict colonized his mind: a crisis of identity. He had not, so far, felt any relationship with Bast, the goddess to which he was apparently yoked (and who, to his knowledge, had anointed N'Jadaka her avatar; he wasn't even sure if she could be trusted). He couldn't be avatar to a goddess he'd yet to meet; he couldn't make her his north star. She, too, seemed as rudderless as he was, lacking clear identity.

And then, his two actual north stars—N'Yami and Nakia— gone. Beyond them, he was no longer a part of M'Baku's fold, no longer a warrior for himself or the Maroons. He was no longer invested in memory recovery as N'Yami had encouraged. And he was no longer captured by the allure of being loved, of being wanted, as Nakia's presence had offered.

He was well and truly alone. *I am nothing. I am no one.*

By Nakia's return, this rot had set in too deep. He was resigned to being this *nothing*, this *no one*. But here she was, back again to offer hope, a light at the end of the tunnel, beckoning, urging, saying: *You can be someone again, something again.*

He sipped on his beverage.

Night had fallen. This backwater planet's sky often lit up with an array of lights upon darkness—an aurora that danced above the mountains—the only thing that could be said to be beautiful about this place. But something else was beautiful as well, perhaps something which he'd been reluctant to acknowledge for so long.

The embers of a rebellion, inextinguishable, still burning however low.

And the hope of those embers returning to a roaring fire lay with him.

He sipped, burning his tongue. *We can no longer hide,* Nakia had said. *You can no longer hide.*

I'm not hiding. Or at least, he didn't think he was. He just found it difficult to put his trust in something that had failed him multiple times before. Before M'Baku's current decision to curl up in a fetal position on this planet, it had been N'Yami's unfounded belief in him. And even she couldn't live long enough to see it to fruition. And now it was Nakia, taking up the mantle others had dropped.

Could he trust again? Could he trust *her*?

I want to love you. But I want to love the whole you. It's not too late for us.

Indeed it wasn't. And he did want to love her, too, even though he knew somewhere out there, the white-haired woman waited for him. He wondered, for a moment, if this was the same kind of confusion Bast struggled with: whether to stick with the emperor, the avatar she had anointed, or some rumored legendary warrior from Ancient Wakanda with no clear evidence of existence. How did she reconcile with this? How could he?

Whether he gave his heart to Nakia or the white-haired woman, T'Challa decided, one thing was sure: It would be impossible to give himself over to anyone if he didn't know who he was, if he wasn't *whole* and *complete* and *true*. He couldn't get there by abandoning the fight midway through.

Nakia was right. It wasn't too late, not for him, not for her, and not for the Maroon Rebellion. And whatever he ended up being in this place, *whoever* he ended up being, it was going to exist, whether he liked it or not, at the nexus of where the three most important people in his life here—Nakia, N'Yami, and M'Baku—met.

He put down the mug, picked up the holo disc, and placed it in the projector.

> Captain N'Yami reporting from Sector 9A of Nehanda's Lattice. I bring you good tidings, comrades. We have recovered a great weapon in our fight to restore the Nameless—the M'Kraan Shard. With it, and the technology we will develop from it, we may be able to mount significant attacks on the Empire's key strongholds.
>
> But more important than that, I am now convinced that we have found the champion whom N'Jadaka so fears. He fights with the strength of twenty men and is

haunted by dreams of a woman whom I believe to be the
Hadari Yao—the walker of clouds, the goddess who
preserves the balance of all natural things.

There is no doubt in my mind who this man is—
T'Challa, He Who Put the Knife Where It Belonged.

Unfortunately, while I am convinced of his identity,
it will take some effort to convince the champion
himself. The chronicles say that T'Challa of Wakanda
Prime preferred the warrior's spear to a king's crown.
It is said that he had to grow into what he ultimately
became. And so it is with our king returned.

I pledge myself to aid him in this growth. But I fear
that T'Challa may ultimately have to walk the path
alone.

Captain N'Yami out.

T'Challa was surprised to find his eyes wet when the recording ended. Fists clenched, neck muscles straining. His whole body tense, as if it had been waiting for that message, for that belief to seep through and take it over.

Sometime during the recording, he'd fallen to his knees, head bowed once the holo ended. Now he lifted his head, pinched his eyes and squeezed the tears from them. Then he rose slowly. This time, he didn't pick up his walking aid.

He ambled over to his panther suit. Now, next to it lay the Spear of Bashenga, the weapon of choice for *He Who Put the Knife Where It Belonged*. There it was, the *knife*. All that was left was to find the place where it belonged: the heart of the empire.

But first, he needed to become a different person.

He'd been going about this the wrong way, he decided. He'd been thinking he needed to become a different person for some imagined future; for himself, for Nakia, for N'Yami, for the white-haired woman, for those he'd left behind. But what he really needed, he realized now, was to become a different person for the people *here now*.

If he truly wanted to succeed at striking the heart of the Empire, to *put the knife where it belonged,* he would need the rest of the Maroon Rebellion behind him. For that, he would first have to get behind *them*.

To go home, he was going to have to fight for the home he had now.

IT TOOK T'CHALLA a day to get prepared. He packed up everything that needed packing, set aside this abode for some time in the future, perhaps when he was old and wizened and this galaxy was free and he needed some time in isolation. But deep down, some part of him knew that if he was lucky—if he was successful—he would likely never see this place again.

He put on his mended glider suit, climbed to the top of the scraggly crevice, spread his wings, and jumped.

Nakia had been right about the flying. Gliding in the icy wind like this, coasting into its spiky blasts against his helmet—it was the only thing that filled him with life these days. These flights and other such outdoor events had kept him sane, prevented him from going gently into the warm, dark embrace of despair. And now he was riding the same winds into his future and the future of the Maroon Rebellion.

Flying to the new Maroon base took hours of navigation. It had been quite a while since he'd been here, and M'Baku and company had done extensive work to keep it hidden, obscured by sharp gales and ice storms. But despite the snowy blitz, icy rain clattering against the metal of his armor, he guided his glider into the valley where the base was tucked. Soon his vision cleared and there was the full base.

He half expected to be immediately met with defensive fire, so long had he been away. He braced for an attack but none came.

Instead, he landed gently on the rooftop, right next to Maroons on sentry duty.

They turned as one to regard him.

Once he'd taken off his helmet and revealed himself, none of them said a word. Rather they nodded in silent greeting, then guided him toward an open door.

It was almost as if they expected him, as if they knew he'd been coming.

They left the heavy snow and went down dark hallways. Familiar smells slowly came back to T'Challa—the musty smell of an underground base; the metal and oil of equipment and weaponry; the lingering sweat of Maroons dressed in body armor for hours upon hours. He found himself smiling. Only took him so much time away from other people to remember how much he missed being annoyed by them.

They went into a grand room that immediately looked, to T'Challa, like a command center. Screens, strategy tables, holos. Maroons milled around, cross-chatter consuming the space. And there, in the middle of it all, was M'Baku.

The Maroon captain turned around. His eyes met T'Challa's from across the room.

The chatter in the command center fell to a hush.

T'Challa expected something to the tune of: *Go back to wherever you came from.* He expected: *You think you can just abandon us and return whenever you like?* He expected: *You're a coward, and you don't belong here, among us Maroons.* They were statements T'Challa could see himself making, wouldn't have been surprised if M'Baku said any of these things. He had told himself some of these anyway.

But M'Baku looked much older than the time that had passed, the sides of his hair, above his ears, graying. He seemed to be perpetually squinting now. All of this gave him a calmer, wiser look, a demeanor he seemed to have accepted and even embodied. Because, as soon as he turned around and saw T'Challa, he chuckled and cracked a little grin.

Just then, Nakia walked in. She was in the same suit from her visit, the same face paint, the same hairstyle. It was like she'd delivered her message to him then come straight back here.

Perhaps she had. Perhaps it was why they were expecting him, likely the reason for this muted response. And perhaps she really did know him.

Slowly, T'Challa placed his glider helmet on a nearby desk. Then he placed both arms across his chest in the Wakanda Prime salute, fists balled, honesty and vulnerability and respect in the gesture.

M'Baku nodded slowly. Then he returned the salute. Nakia, next to him, turned to T'Challa and did the same.

One by one, all in the command center crossed their arms over their chests. And though no one said a word, the resounding salutation was as loud as if it had been roared by the panther god Bast herself:

Wakanda forever!

"All right, then," said M'Baku, first to speak. "Let's get back to work."

CHAPTER 26

△▽△▽

THE
PLEASURE-SHIP *OSHUN*

SOMEWHERE IN THE PTAH REGION, deep in the annals of the Benhazin System, a man sat at a card table in the bowels of the pleasure-ship *Oshun*.

He was not a plain-looking man by any means. Well-dressed, well-coiffed, well-spoken, he radiated wealth and importance by every metric and parameter. His ear, wrist, and neck jewelry were consistent with one who occupied the higher echelons of imperial office. His overcoat, a purple and velvet affair, clung to his frame without excess, fitting in the way that it could only have been custom-made. His demeanor and air were that of understated importance, of one who did not need to flaunt who he was in order to get others to recognize it.

Despite all of these things going for him, though, the events of the game table before him . . . not so much.

The card tables consisted of simple trick games: Dealer deals face down per player, places the first trick card, and then each player hopes their following card is simultaneously of the same suit *and* the highest ranking in the deck according to the official rules of the game. Heavy on luck, low on skill, equal probability of winning and losing. Just as the imperial man liked it, the game sufficiently exciting without requiring a huge amount of mental energy.

Around them, fast music boomed and kaleidoscopic lights flashed. Revelers of all species and races danced, gambled, and wooed, quiet and loud in equal measure. The imperial man was the only one bored by this, so often had he frequented such establishments. In fact, he had an economic stake in this ship and many more like it, having visited pleasure-ships of all kinds as a result. Shoulders hunched, elbows over the table, fist in his cheek, he glanced apathetically at the deck of cards.

"Blast it," he said to the dealer.

The dealer dealt the trick, then the follow-up. The imperial man flipped his card without much thought. *Ugh.* Not a follow, and not a high-ranking card. Epic fail.

"Care to go again?" the dealer asked in a monotone, unmoved by his losing streak. This irked the imperial man a bit, though he opted to keep his calm and not expose his true self. He chalked the dealer's lack of commiseration to this likely being something they saw every night, just like he, too, had become bored with such revelry. Or perhaps the dealer was new—his usual table runner was nowhere to be seen tonight. Or maybe it was even a cultural thing. He'd heard that the Ptah were a people with a flatter affect than most.

"No," he replied. "I think I've donated quite enough this evening."

He tossed the rest of his cards, paid up, and left the table. He was considering a drink and headed to the bar when he passed by one of the private lookouts—the solo spots built with a large window and a sublime view of the starry darkness of space—and spotted a woman there.

For once, he was forced to pause. His boredom abated, swiftly replaced by excitement. Heart racing, toes tingling, carnal excitement, the kind that came with not only attraction but the promise of a mystery he was now dedicated to solving.

The woman seated in the lookout wasn't the most beautiful woman he had ever seen—there had been so many, over the years—but there was something unique about her. Not *special* in any sense, but a measured, controlled sensuousness that was hard to miss. Her appearance was not atypical for the attendees of these pleasure-ships: thick, voluminous braids; body-fitting red tube dress with a knowing slit that went much past the knee; all completed with an exquisite choker that glistened with the club lights. She was of some species or race he didn't quite know—definitely wasn't human. But she wore the dispositions of a human woman so well: the impeccable facial makeup, the wrist, nose, and ear jewelry, the facial expressions and mannerisms. It seemed practiced, and therefore slightly odd, but somehow that made her all the more attractive.

The imperial man soon realized she'd noticed him watching her, and therefore stepped up to her. They shared a long and knowing look.

"Is this seat taken?" he asked, pointing to the unoccupied spot in her two-seater.

"It is," she replied with a smile. "By you." Her voice was soft, velveteen, and, yet again, obviously practiced.

The imperial man sat, enamored, enraptured. He knew, by now, that she wasn't one of the regulars on this ship, a number of whom he'd been with and whose mannerisms he knew. The average imperial subject was the same in many ways: tame, restrained, lukewarm. They understood the Empire to exist in a state of balance, one they had a duty to keep aright.

Judging by her slightly stilted performance—edgy, brash, askance—she was likely a new recruit, only just come under imperial rule, yet to learn the ways of the five galaxies.

The fresher, the better. He licked his lips at the thought.

"No luck at cards tonight, eh?" she asked.

He chuckled. "No. But I've decided to try my luck at another game."

She chuckled, an imitation of his. "What's your name?"

This part surprised yet intrigued him. The regulars on this ship would never be so forward. To be fair, most of them had an inkling of who he was and were therefore often demure. This newcomer clearly had no idea. *Excellent.* Just as he liked it.

"What does it matter, my name?" he asked.

She offered a wry smile. "Because when I tell this story, I want to have the name attached."

"Well." He gave a big grin. "All you need to know is that I am an important man in the Ptah Region. And I love stories."

"Important, eh?"

"If not for my, shall we say, *discretion,* the Askari would shut this whole operation down in a minute."

"Wow, the Askari . . ." She seemed genuinely surprised. "You really *are* important."

Oh yes, he thought, and this would be the last good and true thought he'd have for a while.

CHAPTER 27

△▽△▽

THE
MACKANDAL

DEEP IN THE BENHAZIN SYSTEM, home of Planet Bast and the imperial throneworld, the cloaked *Mackandal* floated.

It had been many years since the Maroons had ventured this close to the imperial seat of power. They had never, as a force, set foot on Planet Bast itself or sanctioned any campaigns in the Golden City where the emperor resided. The Maroon captains before N'Yami had been particularly conservative in their approaches, preferring to win smaller battles on the fringes of the Empire and garner support among peoples and species who hadn't yet swallowed imperial promises hook, line, and sinker. N'Yami herself had been one of the more progressive captains, opting to strike closer and closer to the heart of this oppressive behemoth. Stealth raids that targeted important imperial bases. Hijacking of imperial freighters for supplies and tech upgrades. Catch-and-release operations that involved prominent communal figures allied with the Empire. Closer and closer they got to the Empire with each mission, so that it became almost a matter of *when*, not *if*, they would eventually begin operating in the Empire's own backyard.

Today's mission was simply the first of many to come.

I'm just doing what she would've done, M'Baku told himself as he peered into the screen before him and watched the feed that came through.

The feed was the relay from the camera implant worn by a Maroon operative who was currently running an undercover operation on a nearby imperial pleasure-ship, *Oshun,* in whose shadow the *Mackandal* lay in wait, out of sight, ears and sensors attuned for the signal that would prompt their next move and usher in the next phase of the operation.

M'Baku sat in the captain's chair in the command center alongside two of his primary officers: T'Challa, who was now his right-hand man, and Taku, who was running comms. Together, they appraised the situation before them.

The target was a wealthy card gambler who was attending the ship's recreational activities—gambling, solicitation, and the like—most of them illicit by the Empire's own laws. However, the man—young, attractive, well-dressed, obviously wealthy—was well practiced in the participation in these illicit acts. Pleasure-ships like the *Oshun* operated as open secrets within the Empire, allowed to function in the shadows so long as they remained discreet, their proceeds passing back under the table to powerful imperial actors. It helped, of course, that such powerful actors could then themselves partake in these activities so long as they didn't quite reveal who they truly were and didn't speak of these activities outside the ship. Whatever happened on the pleasure-ships stayed on the pleasure-ships.

Which was why this young man was such an excellent target: No matter what happened here tonight, he could not speak of it to his peers or superiors.

The man had now struck up a conversation with a young, attractive woman who seemed to be welcoming his advances. The *Mackandal* trio watched his interactions with this woman as he attempted to woo her with saccharine expressions, which didn't seem to work all the way. So far, he'd maintained his cover as a simple wealthy young man looking for some fun. But soon enough, the blanket of covertness he had worn all night began to slip as, in the hope of impressing her, he began to reveal, here and there, a little bit about himself.

"*Well,*" he was saying, "*all you need to know is that I am an important man in the Ptah Region.*"

"Here we go," said Taku.

"*If not for my, shall we say, discretion, the Askari would shut this whole operation down in a minute.*"

Taku turned to the two men. "I'd say that's a positive ID, M'Baku."

M'Baku nodded. "Agreed." To T'Challa, he said: "Can they see us yet?"

T'Challa looked at the feed from the *Mackandal*'s exterior cameras, whose screens were brimming with images of the curved, luxurious hull of the massive pleasure-ship. So far no defense mechanisms had been activated, not that they had much of them. They weren't called pleasure-ships for nothing: These were craft built specifically with recreation in mind. Most of the mechanisms built into the ship were dedicated to safety and evacuation, particularly with the understanding that it would be hosting a lot of important guests. Keeping the people on the ship safe and alive was of utmost importance. Fighting back against enemies, not so much.

If these activities weren't so illicit, such a ship would typically be accompanied by Askari warships who would do the dirty work of providing security. But of course, the Askari couldn't grant them full immunity, which meant they were vulnerable.

"The new cloak is working perfectly," T'Challa replied.

One of the few things that had long prevented the Maroon Rebellion from operating in the Benhazin System was the lack of improved cloaking technology. What the rebellion had employed for years before the raid on the Shango Array was decent but relatively primitive technology, much of which could be sniffed out by updated imperial sensors and an attentive Askari. But now, thanks to their capture of the M'Kraan Shard before the Cudjoe attack, the Maroon Rebellion had spent time in their new hideout mining the stolen crystal's gifts, and with the fruit of their labor upgraded a significant amount of their technology and weaponry. Among these upgrades was brand-new cloaking technology that, dare he say it, *surpassed* the Intergalactic Empire's.

M'Baku looked to T'Challa. *We haven't just been lying idle,* he found himself wanting to say. *We've been working hard to bounce back better, stronger, mightier.* But he opted not to say that. He'd decided, long ago, that he was not going to gloat when it came to T'Challa and his choice to abandon the Maroons in their time of need. The rebellion had seen enough loss as it was. This was no time to engineer further discord. Whether he liked it or not, T'Challa was useful, perhaps even crucial, to the rebellion's activities.

So instead, M'Baku replied, "Good. Let's give them a warm hello."

THE *WARM HELLO* came in the form of three missiles.

M'Baku ensured Taku aimed for the *Oshun*'s thrusters, hitting the pleasure-ship hard enough that they'd be unable to make a swift escape but not so hard that their systems all failed at once and everyone on board perished in the annals of space. There was still a Maroon operative on board after all.

The *Mackandal* remained barely visible to any on the ship who'd be looking—and there *were* many who, as soon as the walls around them rocked and the floors on which they stood tilted and the glasses in their hands shattered, immediately turned to the windows to catch a glimpse of their possible assailants. They saw little of the still cloaked ship, though, which incited panic, and which, as M'Baku was hoping, led many to think that this might not be an enemy attack, but warning shots fired by Askari who'd finally tracked them down and intended to kill the operation.

One of those who thought this was the young man whom they were tracking—his name was Kofi, by their intel. He shot to his feet like everyone else and peered outside.

"What in Bast . . . ? That sounded like . . ."

Another set of missiles was deployed. A fresh round of blasts rocked the pleasure-ship. Kofi's eyes widened.

"*No . . . it can't be.*"

M'Baku was unsure if he'd clocked now that their attackers were not Askari, but there was little time to contemplate that, because Kofi had begun moving.

"*My dear,*" he was saying to the woman he'd been courting all night. "*It appears we've encountered a problem. Fortunately, I have provisions for such an occurrence.*" He extended an arm. "*Would you do me the honor?*"

The woman glanced at his offered hand, contemplating the risk of going with him before rising to take it.

"*Lead the way,*" she said.

"On the move," said Taku as the two dashed through maze-like hallways onscreen. She pulled up a map of the ship. "Looks like they're heading toward an escape shuttle."

M'Baku gritted his teeth. "Likely with a cloaking mechanism. Dammit." He sighed. "All right, assemble the assault team now. Tell them to head down to the chagas—"

"Sir."

T'Challa, quiet so far, was suddenly standing quite close to M'Baku's chair. M'Baku turned to him, mid-sentence.

"Sir, wait," T'Challa was saying. "If you move now, we lose all subterfuge."

M'Baku had a retort at the tip of the tongue, something about years of experience leading Maroon missions and expertise in the art of subterfuge, but stopped short of voicing it. That was the old M'Baku—combative, adamant, steadfast. But N'Yami's death and the short disappearance of both Nakia and T'Challa had, over time, worn away at those parts of him. This new M'Baku was patient, slower to react, prone to biting down his restless tongue in favor of more amicable and sometimes unusual solutions.

"You have a better idea?" he asked T'Challa.

"I . . . not exactly." T'Challa was tentative, which surprised M'Baku. For a man who always seemed so sure of himself, not once had M'Baku ever witnessed him stutter. Perhaps this was a new T'Challa as well.

"But," T'Challa continued, "I have a . . . feeling. I would advise waiting just a little longer."

There's the T'Challa I know, thought M'Baku. Assured, optimistic, sometimes dangerously so. But there was earnestness in the way he said it, and M'Baku knew it was less the rash old T'Challa speaking and the new, hopeful man.

So, he nodded and returned to watching the feeds.

By now, their subject, with the woman in tow, had arrived at the shuttle bay.

"Hmm, this is very bad," Kofi was saying to the woman. *"But not for us."* They had entered the shuttle, which it turned out was less escape shuttle and more of a medium-sized luxurious travelcraft, fitted with all the trappings of comfort one might need on a journey to the nearest safe destination. There was even a bedroom in this so-called shuttle, decorated in a manner that suggested that even in escape, clients of the pleasure-ship didn't need to forgo their desire for pleasure. They might be leaving the pleasure-ship and its experience behind, but they could keep something for the road.

It became instantly clear—to the watching trio in the *Mackandal,* and to the woman accompanying Kofi—that this was what Kofi himself intended.

"Private shuttle?" the woman was saying, glancing around, taking it all in.

"The Oshun *makes certain arrangements for its high-end clientele,"* Kofi replied, getting into the pilot seat and firing up the engines. *"It really is your lucky day, my dear."*

"Commander," Taku interjected. "He's readying stellar engines. If we're going to send in an assault team, we'd better do it now."

M'Baku looked from his chief intelligence officer to T'Challa, weighing his options.

"How soon until they enter the fold?" he asked.

"Two to three minutes," said Taku. "Then our operative is on Planet Bast—and *alone.*"

M'Baku looked to T'Challa again. His first officer's gaze was fixated on the screen, watching Kofi and his companion as the shuttle geared up to leave.

"Steady, Commander," T'Challa said without averting his eyes as if reading the growing restlessness of M'Baku's mind. "Steady."

M'Baku watched T'Challa for a moment, then turned to Taku: "Tell the assault team to stand by."

As Taku relayed the information, both men kept their gazes on the feeds. The escape shuttle had now completed all readiness for exit. Kofi had settled fully into his role as pilot, and the woman stood beside him as he prepared for launch.

"Where are we going?" she asked, a lack of conviction evident in her tone.

"Planet Bast," said Kofi. *"Emperor N'Jadaka's court."*

The woman nodded slowly, as if finally coming to an understanding of something she'd suspected quite a while ago.

"You did say 'important,'" she said.

"More than you know." Now no longer bound by the covertness of the pleasure-ship, Kofi's tone was boastful. *"We'll be feted and treated as royalty."* He snapped a finger. *"Now, do me a favor, my dear, and—"*

He didn't get to finish the sentence. A blinding light filled the screens, accompanied by a sharp crack. There was a short scream—a whimper, really. And then the feeds returned to normal, light and sound both gone, only the low thrumming of the shuttle engines serving as background noise.

Kofi lay limp in his pilot chair. The woman, a device in hand— the same device that had emitted both light and sound—stood next to him.

"It's like the man said . . ." she said aloud to the room, to the comms, all the way to the trio in the *Mackandal,* as her voice and outfit and hair and clothing slowly changed to reveal Nakia in her battle suit, *". . . my lucky day."*

CHAPTER 28

△▽△▽

THE
MACKANDAL

"MACKANDAL, *THIS IS NAKIA*. *I'm heading home and I come bearing a gift."*

The private shuttle carrying Nakia and the unconscious Kofi had slipped away from the pleasure-ship and was now preparing to dock on the *Mackandal.* M'Baku, finally, was able to lean into the commander's chair and relax.

"We read you, Captain Nakia," Taku responded. "Well done."

Well done, indeed, Captain. When Nakia had returned from her sojourn and recommitted herself to the Maroons, he'd known the question of Maroon leadership would be revisited eventually. Of course, at the time, he had no idea that she'd gone off to retrieve the Spear of Bashenga in order to convince T'Challa to return to the fold and therefore hadn't been so eager to revisit the question so quickly—especially not without raising the dirty question of her prior (and in the wake of her disappearance, current) allegiances. But he'd known Nakia a long time. She didn't simply disappear without cause. So he'd waited, bided his time.

And then she'd brought T'Challa home.

It was easy after that. They'd decided, he and other top Maroon officials, that she was the natural successor to N'Yami in ability, acumen, and spirit. It made sense for her to retain N'Yami's title as captain. But Nakia remained adamant that she didn't want to *be* captain. Now that she'd been out in the galaxy on her own, she'd witnessed the Empire's long hand in Kurao. She wanted to be out there in the thick of things, hitting the Empire where it hurt, not seated behind screens on the *Mackandal*.

So M'Baku acquiesced and, being the most senior commander, took on the role of captain in all but name. The role suited him perfectly, especially once he'd accepted Nakia's suggestion to bring T'Challa in as his first officer. He'd been skeptical at first, but this new T'Challa had turned out to be a significant asset, as had been proven today and many other times before.

With the three of them at the helm, supported by Taku, the Maroon Rebellion was surely destined for great things.

He turned to T'Challa in appreciation.

"Thank you. You were right."

T'Challa crossed his arms over his chest in the Wakanda Prime salute.

AFTERWARD, M'BAKU STOOD in front of a camera and addressed the Maroon Rebellion, the feeds before him broadcasted to every Maroon all over the planet. Beside him stood T'Challa, and with him Taku, who gave M'Baku the thumbs-up to begin his prepared speech.

"Like all empires," he began, "the Empire of Wakanda is counterfeit. It is a confederacy of villains who've elevated criminality to galactic law. The Empire creates nothing. It enlightens no one. Because, as the great Changamire taught, *Empires do not enlighten; they plunder.* In this field, I must admit, the Empire has been a pioneer."

The feeds switched from M'Baku's solemn face to rotating images of various examples of the Empire's misdeeds: attacks on the Rigellans, the Teku-Maza, the Kronans, the Shadow People. Dire scenes of bombing, destruction, torture, and captivity filled the screens.

"The font of the Empire's great power is the Imperial Archive—its vast collection of knowledge, all of it plundered from the memories of the millions they've enslaved. More than the might of N'Jadaka, the archive is the font of imperial power. It is the archive that gave the Empire its culture and technology. From the Rigellans, the Empire acquired its vast knowledge of the stars. From the Teku-Maza, they pilfered literature and song. From the Kronans, they learned the true power of Vibranium—lifeblood of the Empire. From the Shadow People, they stole knowledge of governance and hierarchy."

Then the scenes switched to a feed of Kofi, who'd now been extracted from the escape shuttle docked in the *Mackandal* and transferred to a secure location on the starship. He was, at the moment, strapped to a chair, still limp, eyes taped shut, lips bound securely with a metal gag, limbs held in place. Around his head was fitted a device, which was in turn orbited by a large, whirring multiarmed machine that seemed to be extracting . . . *something* from him.

"You are familiar with our system of keeping the memories we have now—the Maroon Archival Project. You are aware how our shamans have volunteered themselves to keep oral forms as backup. Last time, the Empire caught us unprepared. We aim for things to be different if they come again. But even better, we aim to be proactive, to prevent such a second coming. We aim to strike first."

Spittle dribbled down Kofi's lips, gathering in a pool at his chin. Tears followed suit from both eyes.

"This man we've captured," M'Baku announced, "is the Empire's chief technologist. He has many responsibilities, including maintenance of the archive. We are going to do to him precisely what he has done to so many: mine every inch of his brain for intelligence and then use it to neutralize the Empire's archive."

He gave a moment to let that sink in, imagining the news settling into every Maroon on the continent, before continuing.

"The Empire evolves too fast for us to fight because the archive is *alive*. It does not just hold knowledge. It analyzes and dissects it, searching for patterns, for new ways to conquer and enslave." He balled a fist, put it up where everyone could see. "But we aren't just going to neutralize the archive. We are going to avenge its victims and make them whole."

Here, he glanced at T'Challa, who watched with rapt attention, head held high.

"The Empire didn't simply steal our technologies and culture." M'Baku held T'Challa's eyes. "They stole our *lives*. So let us fight for our memories, comrades. Let us recover our names."

CHAPTER 29

△▽△

PLANET BAST

IN THE DUST-LADEN Askari training arena of the Golden City, six men stood, five surrounding one. They all carried two batons each, all dressed the same: bare upper torsos, wrists and ankles wrapped in strips of cloth, tight training bottoms. All were bald or sported little hair save for the singular man in the center, who wore lengthy locs, tightly held together by a thick band.

The five men advanced, and one by one, with superhuman swiftness and agility, the loc-haired man knocked them down.

He wasn't particularly bigger than his opponents, neither did he sport any visible implants or enhancements. He seemed like the average imperial Wakandan. But no eyes that witnessed the brutality with which he set upon these men—colleagues in arms, even— could leave that arena unchanged and unshaken.

His batons delivered the deadliest blows each time, aiming for the face, joints, groin, limbs. Every attack carried destructive intent and investment in permanent damage. No defense by his opponents was enough—no block, no dodge, no escape. He found them wherever they moved and struck them down, leaving them limp in the dust, motionless in pools and splatters of their own blood.

From the top of the arena, the emperor of the Intergalactic Empire of Wakanda, N'Jadaka, stood and watched. Beside him was

Counselor Achebe. And in front of N'Jadaka, his hands on tiny shoulders, was the emperor's little daughter, Zenzi.

Her eyes were fixed on the brutal battle in the arena below, her gaze never leaving the man with the locs. Enraptured, enamored, mesmerized. Not even the blood splattered all over his arms and dripping into his eyes caused her to turn away. If anything, N'Jadaka thought, they seemed to be contributing to his beauty in her eyes.

N'Jadaka hadn't wanted to bring Zenzi with him to watch the Manifold's training sessions. She wasn't a child interested in much of anything that had to do with the Empire. When she was a few years old, he and his wife, Nareema, had to explain to her what a princess was and what being one meant.

"Your parents are blessed by the gods," was how Nareema put it. "And therefore, so are you."

"So, because we're blessed, I cannot play with the other children?" Zenzi had asked, annoyed. "Not fair."

She was always a precocious child in this way, one of fleeting interests. She'd since grown to understand her role as a royal and channeled her frustration over not being able to scour the galaxies as she would've liked into seeking other ways to satiate that desire for adventure. These had, of course, led her down a few inadvisable roads. Only a few years ago, she'd led an expedition tracking some local reptilian wildlife in protected grounds, spending three days in the forest. There had been a small army of Askari watching over her the whole time, of course, as well as a royal handler. Upon their return, the handler reported to her parents: "It was like we weren't even there. She was completely in her own world."

So, when Zenzi began insisting upon coming along to the training arena, he chalked it up to another one of her fleeting interests. However, he was a bit worried this time. Previous training sessions hadn't been so brutal. The Manifold was only just returning to full strength after facing some of the toughest attacks on the Empire in the most recent years. The suit itself was in constant development, and the man who wore it needed to continue to improve himself.

So, despite the Manifold's performance looking quite satisfactory, N'Jadaka regretted his decision to bring Zenzi along. He wanted her to be aware of the ways of the Empire, sure, but exposure to this much brutality in such large doses didn't seem advisable. Perhaps this was to be the last of such visits.

He distracted himself from the scene with the report Achebe relayed to him.

"The chief technologist has been missing for almost two weeks now, Sire," Achebe was saying. "Neither his family nor friends have heard from him. All very strange."

N'Jadaka scoffed. "No, Achebe. It's not *strange* at all. Our chief technologist, this . . . *Kofi* . . . has a rather sprawling array of interests. My sources tell me that they include a fleet of pleasure-ships that operate without imperial sanction."

Achebe gulped audibly. *As you should,* thought N'Jadaka. If he himself had to be the one with all the intel, the one having to know everything all the time, what did he have a counselor for?

N'Jadaka clicked his tongue. He didn't have time to berate the one senior counselor he had left. There were more pressing affairs.

"Coordinates in the Ptah Region have already been sent to your office. Track down these pleasure-ships and then subject the chief technologist to interrogation."

Achebe bowed his understanding and acceptance. The emperor spoke no further, and the counselor took that as his cue to leave. But just as he half turned away, he paused.

"And the Manifold?" asked Achebe. "It was, after all, the chief technologist who was charged with his upkeep."

N'Jadaka glanced at his counselor. "And?"

"Well," said Achebe, wringing his hands, "his neural readings this morning indicated some rather peculiar anomalies."

N'Jadaka turned back to the scene in the arena. The fighting had stopped. Or rather, *ended*. All five opponents of the Manifold lay motionless, the Manifold soaked in their blood—arms, chest, face, even his hair. His batons bore a new color: crimson.

Zenzi clapped.

"Sire?" Achebe pressed.

"See for yourself, Counselor," said N'Jadaka. "He seems to be performing marvelously."

BACK IN THE PALACE, N'Jadaka, after putting Zenzi to bed for the night, placed a call to Nareema. She'd been away for days now on a caregiving mission, helping a new colony in T'Chaka's Reach adjust to the demands of their new imperial rulers. *The alternative warm, welcoming blanket to the Askari's unforgiving stun baton,* as she liked to put it. They spoke every day, not just about the mission's progress reports, but also about their daughter.

N'Jadaka was telling her about the day's events, and Nareema, like him, was genuinely concerned about Zenzi's new proclivities.

"I'm handling it," he assured her. "Just focus on what you went there to do."

"But how can I focus?" Nareema—lithe, with high cheekbones, piercing eyes, and exquisitely braided hair—looked incredibly radiant even through the video screen, even after a hard day's work. It never failed to baffle him that he'd been so lucky to find someone who complemented him so much, but was also in all ways a better person—wiser, more approachable, more beautiful. *Lucky* did not quite capture how incredibly fortunate he was to have her in his life.

"You can focus by trusting me," he said.

She sighed. "You're sure you can handle it?"

"Oh please, my dear. If I can manage five galaxies, I think I can—"

"Do not underestimate her, Erik."

He liked when she called him by his moniker. Only *she* was allowed to do so.

"I don't underestimate her, Nareema." He poured himself a warm beverage and sipped from the mug. "I know she's precocious. It makes me proud."

"More than precocious," Nareema pressed. "So many questions lately. I don't like it. Please, keep her close."

"Of course. I'm off to do that right now." He lifted a cup to her. "Enjoy your trip, my love."

"I will." She sighed again. "Forgive my worries. You are a great man and a great father." She put a hand to the screen. "Until soon."

N'Jadaka put a palm to his screen. "But not soon enough."

After the call ended, his heart warmed by both beverage and love, N'Jadaka went up to say good night to his daughter. When he entered the room, Zenzi was up, her back to the door. She was watching a soundless feed, projected from her personal wrist wearable, the light of the projection washing over her face. Even from here, without sight of the screen, he knew exactly what she was watching. It was the same recording she watched every night since she'd started going to the training arena with him.

Through the round floor-to-ceiling window of the room, stars twinkled outside, planetary ghosts casting their ethereal lights over Zenzi.

"Good evening, Father," the girl said without turning her head.

"Good evening, beloved." N'Jadaka stepped forward and squatted before her. Sure enough, she was watching just what he'd suspected: recordings of the Manifold's deeds all over the five galaxies, crushing enemies of the Empire without remorse. Blood and death, fire and destruction filled her screen, reflected in her eyes.

"You've been busy, I see."

She didn't reply, completely engrossed in a scene of the Manifold, this time in the full suit, stomping on a rebellious imperial subject.

"How would you like to go to the fortress with me tomorrow?" N'Jadaka asked. "You could even see my work, up close."

Only now did she turn her head, the recording before her paused.

"You'd do that for me, Father?" Her tone was earnest, innocent, a little sad. She knew what he was doing, he could tell—dangling a new opportunity before her yet taking away the one thing she was tethered to. He could see, now, how cruel it would be to simply yank her away from the Manifold. Perhaps a more gradual exit would fare better, easing her out of this appetite for violence rather than severing the roots, a sort of violence in itself. Perhaps a gradual unwrapping of the fingers of this grip, rather than an intense struggle, kicking and screaming?

Perhaps one last visit, then, to the arena? For old times' sake?

"Of course, my dear," N'Jadaka replied, acceding to the un-asked request. "Anything for you, Zenzi."

CHAPTER 30

△▽△▽

PLANET BAST

THE NEXT DAY at the arena began like any other day. The Manifold stepped out, surrounded by a new set of opponent combatants. The blood of the previous day washed away, the batons replaced. The dust of the arena clinging to their feet as they crouched in ready stances.

Zenzi pressed a bead on her wearable and began recording.

She couldn't remember exactly when this desire to watch the Manifold began. She could say it wasn't a desire at all, but something akin to a possession. Suddenly there one day when she couldn't remember having ever had this desire before.

And since then, how this desire consumed her! Every waking moment was filled with a *need* to watch the Manifold, to bear witness to his conquests, to understand every aspect of his actions, his mind, his being. As if she'd somehow become tethered to him—and she *was* tethered—in a way.

Like now, when the opponent combatants moved.

Zenzi's eyes followed them. Something twitched in her eyes, in her heart, in her spirit.

Down in the arena, something in the Manifold's eyes, heart, and spirit twitched in response. And just as quickly as Zenzi thought it, the Manifold swung out his batons and attacked.

PART THREE

△▽△▽

CHAPTER 31

△▽△

THE
MACKANDAL

THE MAROON REBELLION was now in the thick of its offense. Back in their home turf of Nehanda's Lattice, they were in the midst of yet another mission, one that began, just like many others, in the shadow of an imperial ship.

With the new cloaking technology powered by the M'Kraan Shard, they'd so far managed to successfully target various imperial vessels. The current vessel they were tracking was the imperial freighter *Taharqua,* on its way from collecting Vibranium from the galaxy's various mines and delivering it to the imperial throne-world. Its cargo hold was filled with the mineral, and based on the size of the freighter and Maroon leadership's estimates, it held enough Vibranium to serve the rebellion's efforts ten times over.

So, naturally, they were going to take the ship.

But the *Taharqua* was also ten times the size of the *Mackandal.* A direct firefight was out of the question. Nakia, seated in the command center and leading the mission, opted for the next best thing, that in which the Maroon Rebellion was most skilled: infiltration.

"I spot three warm bodies at control," she said into the mouthpiece as she peered at the screens before her. "Be careful."

Over on the other end of comms, there was silence. She knew

that T'Challa had heard her but had opted to keep his discreet position—tucked into lifeless crannies of the ship's innards—just so.

Soon she could hear his breath as he moved. The feed from his panther helmet was shaky, unclear, but the audio was crisp and clean enough that, when he started to get near the Askari guards, she could hear their own conversation loud and clear.

"*Repairs are almost complete, Commander,*" one was saying.

"*Good,*" replied the other. "*We are on a tight schedule for cargo deliveries. So, unless we want to have a session with an imperial interrogator, there can be no delays.*"

It amused and angered Nakia to no end how banally the machinery of oppression operated. Here were underlings of the Empire worried about job performance and punishment for not meeting their targets while literally carrying the product of slave labor—slaves who had no agency, whose work was brutally forced out of them. If the guards could manage a little bit of self-reflection, they could see the irony there. But alas, this was what the Empire did: It short-circuited the mental dexterity of its oppressed and allying populations, held them both hostage in different ways but in equal measure. It was hard to deeply consider the factors of one's existence with a boot on your neck, a gun to your head, a spear tip to your ribs.

The feed shook violently, and a thud jolted Nakia out of her musings. Following the sounds—*thud! crack! slap!*—she deduced that T'Challa had attacked. There was the whine of a weapon, the crackle of burning, the soft hiss of smoke. Then all was quiet again.

Two minutes, she counted. *Better than the last time.*

"Okay, Nakia," came T'Challa's voice over comms. "I'm in."

NAKIA GAVE T'CHALLA the instructions to upload the jamming virus that the Maroon Rebellion used in every imperial ship they encountered. It prevented the vessels' controls from sending out distress signals and the rest of the ships' inhabitants from knowing their control centers had been infiltrated. Typically, the Maroon Rebellion exited the vessels the same way they'd entered: silently. (The inhabitants often wouldn't find out they'd been hijacked until they realized their ship was veering off course and no one had been piloting it, or that some of the systems or actions they'd expected— changes, responses—weren't responding.) By the time the Maroon visit had been discovered, the rebellion operatives were already far, far away.

This time wouldn't be much different.

Once the virus was in, T'Challa began to verify that the raw Vibranium was indeed in the cargo hold.

"Done and . . ." He drifted off. *"Done."*

"Excellent."

"Wait." He sounded apprehensive. *"We have a problem . . ."*

Nakia gave him time to figure out what he was seeing. Soon enough, he was moving. A moment later, he was in the very place he'd been peering into over screens: the cargo hold itself.

"There are two classes of cargo here," he said finally. *"One is Vibranium. The other is something much . . . more."*

His camera was back on, and this time he moved gingerly, avoiding shaking the camera too much and disrupting the feed's stability. He moved closer to the items in question, making a point to turn his head, scanning row to row, top to bottom, so Nakia could see the endless array, stacks upon stacks, of . . .

People.

Slaves. Species of all kinds, across the five galaxies, each laid out in a coffin-like pod, suspended in some kind of cryo-sleep. The anguish expressed on their faces at the time of capture seemed glued in place, many of the sleeping bodies retaining a wide-eyed, teeth-bared expression.

"By the Orishas . . ." Nakia found herself saying, breathlessly. "How many people do they have in there?"

"Hundreds." T'Challa's tone was solemn. *"And you know what's going to happen to them."*

Please don't, thought Nakia. *Don't make me have to do this.*

"*We can't leave them,*" he said, and once he'd said it, Nakia knew there was no going back.

"T'Challa . . ."

"*Don't say it.*"

"We *have* to leave them, T'Challa. We don't have the capacity to take on that kind of weight."

A pause. "*But we need soldiers.*"

"Soldiers, yes. Not refugees."

"*I was one of those refugees.*"

"No, T'Challa. You were . . . an *asset*. We chose to raid that mine because you were there. We'd seen what you could do. We have no such assurances here."

Comms on the other end had gone quiet again. He was listening, contemplating, deciding. She had to talk some sense into him now before he went and did anything rash.

"Remember what we're here for, T'Challa. The raw Vibranium is the first thing we need in our plans to create a conduit to the Imperial Archive, without which we cannot restore the memories of the Nameless. We've expended a significant amount of resources on these missions, including getting our hands on the chief technologist. We can't change the plan now. The Vibranium is the priority."

She could hear the *grrr* in his throat.

"*But what are we fighting for,*" he started, "*if not—*"

"Stop it, T'Challa!" She didn't have the time or patience for this. "This is a *war,* not a philosophy class. Now get that damn can of raw Vibranium disengaged so we can lock on to it, do you hear me? And don't bother coming back without it. Am I clear?"

Silence. Then: "*Perfectly.*"

And she knew, immediately, that everything she'd said had fallen on deaf ears.

"HOW GOES IT, General Nakia?"

She'd regrouped with M'Baku in the hallway outside command

center. If T'Challa was going to do anything stupid, it would be better if all of Maroon leadership was aware of it.

"About as well as you could expect," she replied.

"Let me guess," said M'Baku. "The *king* is writing his own orders again, is he?"

She sighed. M'Baku said this as a sardonic little jab at her growing belief in T'Challa. Once, she'd have scoffed at this word, *king,* like M'Baku did. But that had changed. N'Yami's belief had buttressed her own, and her time with T'Challa had solidified that. So, today, even though he was back to his most obstinate self, she held out hope in him. She *believed* in him, in the possibility of his future leadership—*kingship,* even. They'd have to punish him for these actions, of course. But that was a bridge best crossed later.

"Seems we have to find new ways to be patient with him every day," she said. "He's a great warrior—"

"—and a poor soldier," M'Baku completed, and nodded. He and Nakia stared out the window, into space, and together wondered what T'Challa was up to this time.

CHAPTER 32

ᐃᐁᐁ

THE
TAHARQUA

AWAY WITH THAT, thought T'Challa. *Away with the idea that some of us are expendable for a greater purpose. You should know better, Nakia. You should do better. And if no one has the guts to do better, then I will have to do it myself.*

These thoughts pinged around in his head as he crawled through the dark, empty liminal spaces in the *Taharqua.* He hadn't decided what he was going to do or how he would succeed, but one thing was sure: There was no way that he, once Nameless, would allow the people in that cargo hold to become Nameless, too.

Amid his stealthy prowl of the ship, a cluster of voices came to him down an isolated hallway.

"Get in the machine, mule!" someone screamed, followed by the *bzzt!* sound of a stun baton. The sounds—the command, the stun baton, the *mule* slur—were all so familiar that they brought a visceral reaction to his body. He felt, at once, like he was back in Goree, trapped, subject to the whims and desires of brutal imperial guards.

"Leave him alone!" another voice said, fearful yet bold. "You can't do this to us!"

T'Challa crouched and angled his head around the bend. In the hallway were two Askari, guards in red visors with sharpened teeth and stun batons. Three prisoners—Nameless, or soon to be—were with them. Two children and an elderly man, all dressed in the same plain garb meant for imperial subjects—imperial *property*.

The older child, teenaged from the look of him, curled up on the floor, cringing as the Askari stunned him. The older man held on to the much younger child, shielding him from the unfolding brutality.

"We'll do whatever we want," said one Askari, stunning the teenager again. The boy's body jerked and then slumped.

T'Challa gritted his teeth and, with the images from Goree flashing in his mind's eye, moved.

When asked, later, what exactly had happened in this moment, T'Challa would be unable to say. His mind ran on the desire for revenge alone, limbs powered by little else but rage. He only remembered covering the length of the hallway in a few short seconds and before the Askari looked up, he was upon them.

Wham. Brak. Crash. He was an animal, a madman, tearing, slashing, breaking. Foot to jaw, claws to face, elbow to spine. Shattered a visor in one blow, pieces stabbing the wearer's face. Slammed another into nearby glass. Picked up his stun baton and *bzzt! bzzzzt! bzzzzztttt!* until he lay limp.

Blood curdled on T'Challa's knuckles, congealed underneath his fingernails, dripped down his chest. The Askari guards lay motionless in pools of crimson, limbs pointing in unnatural directions. When his narrow vision cleared, T'Challa realized he was breathing heavily, that there'd been a whine in his head all this time. Both began to abate as he stilled, baton in hand. His vision widened again.

The elderly prisoner stood there, mouth agape. The young child he was protecting blinked rapidly, eyes moving from dead Askari to the mountain of a man that now stood over them.

"By the light of Bast!" said the elder. "It is you! The *Avenger!* The One Who Put the Knife Where It Belongs! The savior!"

T'Challa groaned. He'd heard enough of these titles and platitudes for a lifetime. Couldn't he just be a soldier? One who would fight with everything he had, platitudes or not, if it would eventually lead him home and back to his own name and true title?

"I am a fighter, baba, not a savior." He put down the stun baton and checked on the limp teenager. The boy remained unconscious and had a weak pulse. *Thank Bast,* thought T'Challa. *Still breathing.*

"But one does not disqualify the other, my son." The way the man spoke reminded him of the elderly prisoner on Goree who'd opted to offer him advice. But T'Challa wasn't in the headspace for that kind of talk right now.

"Today it does." He rose, ready to turn away. But the little child behind the elder caught his eye. The boy was crying.

"I don't understand," said the elder. "You have not come to save us? But to *abandon* us? Do you know what they will do to us? To our women? Our children?"

The little boy's tears glistened under the hallway lights.

"You are Nameless," said T'Challa quietly, almost to himself. "Like me."

"No," the elder replied. "We were captured only days ago! Our memories are still with us! But not for long. You see the machines are primed for us."

He was talking about the cryo-sleep pods. Was this how the Empire extracted and erased memories in one go? Were those people's memories being erased *right now*?

"They will strip us of everything, even each other. But you can save us! It is your destiny! Your—"

"Die, mule!" came a scream, and a firearm blast cut the elderly man down mid-speech.

"Nooo!" screamed T'Challa, but it was too late. The old man was struck, smoke sizzling from a black hole in his back.

T'Challa caught him as he fell, and in the same motion, pulled out the Spear of Bashenga, aimed it in the direction of the fallen Askari—the one who'd awoken from near-death just long enough to pick up a discarded firearm to execute one last act of destruction—and flung it.

The spear caught the Askari in the chest, went fully through, and pinned him to the ground. He made no sound as he died.

T'Challa lay the old man on the ground, kneeling beside him. "Baba . . ."

"Oh, child . . ." The man's lungs were rapidly filling with blood as evidenced by the gurgle in his airways. Thick, green ichor colored his teeth and oozed out the sides of his mouth.

"No . . . no . . ." he still managed to say. "Not a child at all. A . . . hero. A . . . king."

Then he passed.

T'Challa, head bowed, let the limp body settle on the ground. He rose, took off his panther helmet, and stood there, paying his respects.

Next to him, the small boy stepped up and bowed his head as well. Tears dripped from his eyes and splattered on the floor.

Without looking, T'Challa passed the boy his panther helmet. The boy, at first, was confused. Then his eyes widened as surprise took over him. He wiped the tears from his face with the back of his hand, then wiped the hand on his clothes before receiving the helmet.

T'Challa waited for him to put it on, try it out. Once he had, he guided the boy to the nearby vent he'd just crawled through to emerge in this hallway. He opened up the grate and ensured that both the younger boy and the still-unconscious teen were inside, safe and protected, before shutting it.

Then T'Challa rose, pulled out his two sidearms, inhaled deeply, and headed into the belly of the ship.

THE *TAHARQUA* WAS a massive behemoth, but T'Challa found every Askari easily. This large a freighter, it was uncommon for there to be big gatherings of people, especially security, who had to be spread out to cover as much ground as possible. This made it easier for him to pick them off in batches, surely and stealthily, before the next group knew what was happening.

Blam. Blam. Blam.

T'Challa fired and fired and fired, unthinking. He went from enclosure to enclosure, chamber to chamber, quarter to quarter. Everywhere he went, he fired, and every warm body in service of the oppressive Empire fell and became cold.

Blam. Blam. Blam.

The old man's words played over and over in his mind.

Blam!

A hero.

Blam! Blam!

A king.

Blam! Blam! Blam!

Soon the ship was clear, top to bottom. Not an imperial soul left alive. Only then did he return to the hallway, put away his smoking firearms, and speak.

"You can come out now."

The little boy, who'd indeed never wandered away, crawled out from the vent. He was still wearing the panther helmet, which was too big for his head, hanging awkwardly below his chin. He was no longer crying and didn't look afraid anymore.

"Did you do it?" he asked, which T'Challa interpreted to mean: *Is it done? Is it over? Are our enemies dead?*

But instead, T'Challa found himself answering another question, one the boy hadn't asked, but which T'Challa had been asking himself the moment he saw those bodies in storage pods.

"No," he said. "Not yet."

He took the boys with him, back to the command center, carrying the still-unconscious teenager over his shoulder and placing him gently on the ground nearby where he could keep an eye on him. Then he turned on navigation systems, prepared the ship's stellar engine, and set the destination.

02.57.96, read the ship's computer, stating the coordinates. *GALACTIC SIGN: NEHANDA'S LATTICE.*

As if on cue, his earpiece, which had so far been radio silent—

thank Bast—suddenly burst into life. Nakia, once again, was on comms.

"T'Challa," she said. *"Why is that vessel's stellar engine charging? You know the plan is for us to now send a zulu to you to collect the Vibranium. What the hell are you doing?"*

How could he tell her that he *finally* understood? That his mission was not just to embrace the name of the Avenger, the warrior-king, the ancient ruler of Wakanda Prime—but to also embrace his ethos of care, of duty, of dedication to salvation? That his path to recovering all he'd lost could never be achieved alone, but in community with others—others who could never be in community with him if they remained Nameless, in captivity of one kind or another? How could he find his own way home if no one else did? How could he be a king, a hero, a savior, if he was always leaving people behind?

No. This time was going to be different. *This time, no one gets left behind.*

So he told her the only thing he could, the only thing she could understand.

"What I am destined to do, Nakia," he said, a protective arm around the little boy beside him. "Putting the knife where it belongs."

CHAPTER 33

△▽△▽

THE
TEKU-MAZA REVOLUTIONARY
GUARD SHIP

AS SOON AS the Teku-Maza battleship *Zhingha* downed stellar engines and settled into mid–Nehanda's Lattice, just outside of the Zanj Region, commander in chief of the Teku-Maza Revolutionary Guard, Jafari, was called to deck. Something big—no, *massive*—was in the area, and it was moving. Nothing from the preliminary scans showed that it had anything to do with the Maroon Rebellion. This seemed to have a significant amount of cargo and likely a significant enough force to guard it. By every metric, this seemed like imperial business.

Jafari, standing at the helm of the Teku-Maza ship, surrounded by pilots and controllers, was flabbergasted. An imperial freighter of this size and importance this far from the throneworld? Carrying cargo—likely Vibranium, or something precious and useful— yet sailing through space uncloaked and unbothered? And doing so in Nehanda's Lattice, the galaxy with the most rebellion activity?

He couldn't believe it.

Or perhaps he could. The Empire was brazen and callous, after all, willing to do whatever it took and go to whatever lengths to see to their aims. Sometimes that included demonstrating to the enemy that they were not afraid of attacks, that they thought themselves too big to be conquered. Sometimes that meant sailing through enemy territory and hoping to draw them out, especially when said enemy had been in hiding for quite a while with minimal key activity since, making them hard to predict.

Perhaps it was a trap.

"Do we hail?" asked his second-in-command. "Or do we hide?"

Jafari was of a mind to hail. When the imperial forces had conquered his homeland of Agwé, they had one goal: to make it clear that no matter who the Teku-Maza were, no matter *where* they were, they were to understand that everything around them was owned and operated by the Empire. The waters of Agwé in which they lived, the resources they mined, the airspace they plied, the very air they breathed—everything was the Empire's. If they wished to continue living, so the Empire's mandate went, they could only do so under one condition: in service of the Empire and its goals.

In that way, Jafari didn't quite think they had any choice. He wasn't a stronghead like the others, like, say, Farouk and his allies. They were all about *rebellion, rebellion, rebellion.* They worshipped the idea and memory of N'Yami, the great Maroon who'd given up all she had to fight for freedom—first for the Teku-Maza and their ancestors, the Ancient Jengu; and then for the Maroon Rebellion itself. Her story was known throughout Agwé and had inspired so many that, ever since that first taste of freedom, every attempt by the Empire to reinstate their authority had been rebuffed by the Teku-Maza Revolutionary Guard with a ferociousness akin to a religious zeal, all buttressed by a devout belief in N'Yami's memory and the liberation it promised.

However, in lieu of devout worship, Jafari was of a more realistic mind. Agwé's resources were dwindling. Continuous fighting was impossible. Farouk and his allies wanted to be warriors, but how many Teku-Maza truly could afford such a life? Was it truly good freedom if one's family was too depleted to enjoy it? Could they truly continue like this?

As leader of the Teku-Maza Revolutionary Guard, he'd decided they needed help. That was what had led him out here in the first place. He couldn't let an encounter with a rogue imperial ship complicate his mission.

"Let's . . . wait and see what they do first," Jafari finally replied. "If we hide, who knows what they'll take that to mean? I suspect their anti-cloaking tech is advanced enough to suss us out anyway. Let's . . . wait and see."

They waited. The imperial freighter—which, by now, they'd figured out was called the *Taharqua*—simply sailed forward, just as unbothered as when they'd picked it up on their radars. Worse, it seemed to be headed in the same direction as their own ship: into the Zanj Region. By simple calculation, Jafari suspected their trajectories would lead to the same location, toward the undisclosed, unnamed ice planet where the Maroon Rebellion was holed up.

Did they really know where it was? Even the Teku-Maza didn't know where for sure, and were out here in the hope that once recognized, the Maroons would welcome them with trust, based on their shared comradeship of N'Yami's leadership.

They waited.

The imperial ship passed by them silently. It took an age, so large it was. Beautiful ship, too. But silent. *Too* silent. So silent, in fact, that once it had passed, Jafari immediately changed his mind and requested a hail.

"Are you sure?" asked his second-in-command.

"Something isn't right," he said. "Hail."

SOMETHING WAS INDEED not right, because it turned out the ship wasn't helmed by imperials. It was like the Ancient Jengu and her ancestors had smiled kindly on Jafari and the Revolutionary Guard, as the ship was inexplicably helmed by a Maroon. And not just *any* Maroon. The famed—and infamous—*king,* the one in whom N'Yami had believed, the one whom the emperor sought, the very one who'd so far been the striking blade at the tip of the Maroon Rebellion's spear.

The one they called T'Challa: *He Who Put the Knife Where It Belonged.*

The *Zhingha* was welcomed to dock without fuss. Jafari went into the *Taharqua* alone, wanting to be sure of the circumstances before putting the rest of his crew in danger. And sure enough, there was T'Challa to welcome him, with—yet again, inexplicably—a young boy in his company. The rest of the ship seemed to be empty save for them both, but as Jafari would later come to learn, it was in fact filled with imperial prisoners.

"I would welcome you with more spectacle," said T'Challa, "if this was actually my ship, and if we met under less grim circumstances."

The circumstances were indeed grim. Only after Jafari took a proper look at the vessel did the evidence of what had truly happened here come to the fore. Blood and matter everywhere, innards separated from their owners. And though it seemed T'Challa had spent most of his time on board moving the bodies and stashing them somewhere unknown—or, even worse, shunting them out of the ship to float in space—their ghosts haunted the place.

He looked at this man now, and decided that no, the rumors of a warrior returned, a man who could be the legendary Black Panther of Ancient Wakanda, arisen to lead them to glory . . . weren't quite right. This man's name might be T'Challa, but he was no leader, no king. This T'Challa, he decided, was a thug, a rogue soldier. And he was *exactly* the person Jafari needed to see this Teku-Maza war through.

"EONS AGO," Jafari began, after he'd introduced himself to T'Challa and they'd sat down to converse, "the Ancient Jengu ruled the seas of Agwé. It was from the Jengu that we Teku-Maza evolved into our current form. We have built a great civilization beneath the waves but we have never forgotten whose whim truly moves those waves."

Jafari had told this story many times before. Most Nameless in the Zanj Region had heard the tale or parts of it in one form or another, especially among Maroons who had a Teku-Maza as their leader. Witnessing T'Challa receive this story for the first time was a welcome experience for Jafari. It was like writing on a fresh slate, a mind upon which he could paint images and inscribe as he wished.

"And then the imperials came." He sighed, aiming for dramatic effect. "We fought them, of course. But as you already know, the Empire is not to be denied. And by way of the wars they waged upon us, our beloved Jengu were hunted to extinction." He shook his head. "You know the Empire, so you know what came next. Our people were enslaved, our memories ripped from us, our culture plundered. Just like you and many others, we became Nameless—a people without memory."

Only here did T'Challa speak up. "And yet you have just told a story of this. From memory."

Jafari smiled. He had the man hooked, as he wished.

"Yes," he said. "Because we were only Nameless for a while. Our memories, luckily for us, are not simply stored in our minds like other species. The Jengu, as our ancestors, are also keepers of our memories, just like your ancestors are. But unlike you, we do not have to reach beyond the realm of the physical to receive our memories from them. Our own ancestors are right here, and our memories with them, in the Jengu's mind. A living archive of who we are, retrievable at any time."

T'Challa sat up. This was getting somewhere.

"How?" he asked.

"Think of our Jengu as possessing a conduit," Jafari explained. "That conduit is the Jengu's *scale*, through which we Teku-Maza offer and receive knowledge. All that is needed for said transfer of knowledge and memory"—he tapped his finger lightly against T'Challa's arm—"is a simple touch."

"A Teku-Maza's touch?"

Jafari shook his head. "*Anyone's* touch. *Anyone* can recover their memories through the Jengu's scale. The scale simply needs to, at the time, simultaneously be in contact with the archive containing said memories. So, *person, conduit, archive.* For us Teku-Maza, the latter two are one and the same—the Jengu. But for everyone else, all they need is the scale and the archive containing their memories, and"—Jafari snapped a finger—"their memories are returned, just like that."

T'Challa looked skeptical. To be fair, it did sound contrived, deeply mystical, and quite impossible. And in a way, it was all those things to a small degree. But it was also true. It was the most truthful thing Jafari had said today.

"What do you want from me?" asked T'Challa. "From us?"

Good, thought Jafari. *The big question.*

"Well, perhaps the real question is what do *you* want?" Jafari said. "What opportunities can this revelation offer you? I know that recovering your memories is a significant aspect of the Maroon Rebellion's cause. It was what N'Yami pursued with all her heart. And I know this holds an outsized importance for you. So perhaps I will start by saying this: I can offer you a Jengu's scale in exchange for your help."

"What kind of help?"

"Everything you Maroons can offer us to help win this war on Agwé. Intel, technology, manpower, particularly the expertise of your best soldiers." Jafari leaned in. "We have heard of your exploits, T'Challa. Anyone will be happy to have you on their side. It's no wonder the emperor keeps sending his forces after you. He must have heard of you, too." He clasped his hands together. "Come to Agwé. Help me secure Agwé and our Jengu. If we succeed, I will personally pluck a scale and hand it to you, and with it, you may begin the journey to recovering everything that has been stripped from you, memories and all."

This brought T'Challa back down to reality. He leaned into his chair, deep in thought. Jafari waited. He was sure, of course, that the final decision would not be T'Challa's. He was willing to make this impassioned speech to the others—Captain Nakia, Commander M'Baku, even First Officer Taku. But still, the warrior was vital. He knew that if he could convince T'Challa, convincing the true decision-makers would be far less of a challenge.

"If the Jengu's scale can truly do what you said," T'Challa finally replied after much musing, "how will you get one? You said all the Jengu had been hunted to extinction by the Empire."

Jafari grinned. "Yes. All except *one*."

CHAPTER 34

△▽△▽

NEW MAROON HIDEOUT, NEHANDA'S LATTICE

THE *TAHARQUA* CAME slowly into port. Nakia made sure to be there with M'Baku and the rest of the Maroon leadership when T'Challa brought it in. It turned out the vessel was too large to settle into their ramshackle, makeshift bay, so they found a nearby frozen lake and landed the beast of a ship on sturdy ice.

They stood in the cold, feet deep in the snow, dressed in a mix of panther suits and chunky overcoats. It had been a while since Nakia had been out in the open this way, that *any* Maroon or their ships had been in the open, so easily spotted from orbit by anyone who knew where and how to look. This was so like T'Challa, wasn't it? To engage in actions that put not just him at risk, but everyone else.

M'Baku, standing beside her, was stone-faced. He hadn't said much since she'd updated him about T'Challa's choices, but she knew, immediately, what his decision was to be. And as much as she cared for T'Challa—as much as she'd desired him to return to the fold and help do these exact things he had done—she found herself unfortunately in support of M'Baku this time. It would seem limp and apathetic for Maroon leadership to simply brush this aside as one of T'Challa's antics. They had little choice here.

The *Taharqua*'s cargo doors opened and T'Challa stepped out into the cold wind. Behind him were rows upon rows of cargo that went on forever. Nakia deduced they'd likely contain both the Vibranium and the prisoners in cryo-sleep, which explained why there weren't a significant amount of people stepping out of those doors.

T'Challa wasn't alone, though. Beside him stood a small boy dressed in thin clothes, shivering as soon as the wind touched his fragile body. Nakia groaned and grabbed a fat overcoat from a nearby Maroon, who switched to the heated comfort of their panther suit.

"Don't do anything until I've spoken to him," she said, then went onto the ice.

T'Challa didn't look one inch remorseful, which was to be expected. She couldn't begrudge him that—he had done the "right" thing after all. She'd thought about what she would've done in the situation and how keen she might've been to accept whatever punishment came her way.

"Hello," said Nakia, kneeling at the foot of the doors. "My name is Nakia, and we, here, are the Maroons. You're safe here." She held up the coat. "Would you like to come out of the cold?"

The boy looked up to T'Challa, who looked down at him and nodded.

"She's a friend," he said. "Go."

The boy went and received the coat joyfully. Nakia pointed him toward the rest of the Maroons.

"Go gently across the ice," she said. "They'll take you somewhere warm and get you a nice cup of hot beverage, okay?"

The boy hopped gently away. Nakia rose and faced T'Challa.

"Big of you," she said, "using a frightened boy as buffer. I suspect you think this will quell our ire for your transgressions."

"Don't lecture me," he said. "Just do what you need to." He put both his arms forward, requesting the shackles of his impending imprisonment. "But at least listen first to what the Teku-Maza have to say."

This took Nakia aback. "The *Teku-Maza*?"

"The head of N'Yami's Revolutionary Guard. His name is Jafari."

She peered behind him, into the cargo hold. "He's *here?*"

"No. On his ship, the *Zhingha.* Out in orbit."

Her eyes widened. "You led him *here?*"

T'Challa scoffed. "Of course not. What do you take me for?" He lowered his arms. "I asked him to wait at a specific location, close enough to reach us by comms but not close enough to track our exact location or trace our signals."

"I see." She observed the *Taharqua* top to bottom. "And he couldn't have followed this ship here?"

"Imperial cloaking tech is unrivaled. You of all people know that."

Light footsteps, behind them. Nakia glanced over her shoulder to see M'Baku coming over the ice with a couple Maroons in tow. Her time had run out.

"Well, it seems I won't be party to those discussions," T'Challa said, eyes narrowing at the advancing group. "But no worries. I did what I needed to do. I brought home the Vibranium. I rescued every Nameless I could." He leaned in toward Nakia. "Now, do your part. Listen. Be open-minded. It might just save us all."

With that, he walked past her and toward the advancing group to meet his fate.

THE COMMANDER IN CHIEF of the Teku-Maza Revolutionary Guard, Jafari, wore a grin Nakia decided didn't fit on his face. To her, it felt practiced, like he focused much more on his presentation than what he was actually trying to convince them about. It made it harder for her to concentrate as she, M'Baku, and Taku sat in the hideout's command center, listening to him speak. So far he'd told the story of how he met T'Challa, and then the same history he'd told to T'Challa of the Teku-Maza's revolutionary efforts, from the Jengu to N'Yami to the current wars. But she found herself drifting off, thinking about T'Challa alone in his prison cell, gritting his teeth for being punished after doing all this *good* on behalf of the rebellion.

"The last living Jengu," Jafari was saying, "hid away in the depths of the planet in the deepest ocean. And when we rebelled, she joined our battle. She is the last of her kind. Her connection to our planet is inviolable."

M'Baku, impatient, was saying: "Yes, yes, and now you need us to help you rescue her, all for the price of . . . a scale?"

"Exactly that!" Jafari said. "And with that scale, you can recover all the memories you need. As long as the Jengu lives, so will her scale."

M'Baku, as usual, was circumspect. He muted Jafari and turned to Nakia.

"T'Challa believed this?" he asked. "He must be more gullible than I thought."

"Well . . ." Here, Nakia felt the need to defend N'Yami instead of T'Challa. "Captain N'Yami did tell me of the Jengu and their prowess. And she formed this Revolutionary Guard, which means the Teku-Maza are our natural allies. To combine our efforts toward the Empire's downfall sounds like a natural course of action."

"And yet . . . ?" M'Baku asked, sensing hesitation.

Nakia sighed. "Say we ignore him and proceed with our current plan to conquer the Imperial Archive. We have more than enough Vibranium, plus a small boost to our numbers once we wake all those Nameless from cryo-sleep. We have all that info from the chief technologist and all that new tech from the M'Kraan Shard." She shifted in her seat. "Say we succeed and gain access to the archive. Now what? How do we restore these memories, put them *back* into the heads of every Nameless?" She shrugged. "We're going to need some sort of *conduit* to do that, and likely on a large scale." She pointed to Jafari. "What that man is telling us, if I understand correctly, is that this is what the Jengu's scale can do."

"Mmm-hmm. But you're not sure if what he says is true."

"Or, let's say I'm not sure if it'll *work*. And I'm not sure that he knows that for sure either."

M'Baku retreated into deep thought. Taku, who'd been silent all this time, said: "If I may." M'Baku nodded, and she continued. "If we're going to proceed with our plans anyway, then perhaps it won't hurt to have a backup plan? The backup being this Jengu's scale, that is. Whatever plans we already have, we can continue with. I suspect that the help they need from us won't require our full squadrons anyway. We can dispatch a small squad of Maroons to help them, get what we want."

M'Baku seemed to like this approach, and Nakia couldn't fault it either. All that was left was to deduce the nature of the help needed.

M'Baku unmuted Jafari.

"Oh, just one Maroon fighter will be fine," said Jafari, leaning to peer around the three. "Where's T'Challa, if I may ask?"

"Imprisoned," said M'Baku.

Jafari frowned at this. "Why?"

"Maroon law," was all M'Baku offered. "Now, you say one Maroon fighter is all you need?"

Jafari shook his head. "No, no. I mean *one specific* Maroon fighter—T'Challa."

The three glanced at one another.

"Ah well, that's too bad," said M'Baku. "T'Challa is banned from going on future missions for a while. I suggest you make do with someone else." He pointed toward Nakia. "Captain Nakia is our finest. Perhaps she can lead a small squad on our behalf."

Jafari was still shaking his head. "No, no, no. The man with the Spear of Bashenga, or nobody else."

Off he went, the screen going dark. The three Maroons looked to one another.

Nakia sighed. "I'll talk to him."

M'Baku shook his head. "That won't suffice. You know this."

Nakia nodded. "Yes, I know. I'll talk to him. Then I'll take a squad and go with him."

CHAPTER 35

△▽△▽

THE
ZHINGHA

THE *ZHINGHA*, NAKIA MUSED, was much less prepared to be a battleship than the *Mackandal* was. That did not stop the atmosphere in the arms and kit chamber from being much more heightened than the *Mackandal*'s. Preparing for battle among Maroons was more often than not a silent endeavor, each mulling over the possibility of death, a sudden end to their long lives given to this cause. On the *Zhingha,* it was a ruckus.

Now that Jafari had succeeded in convincing M'Baku to release T'Challa and send him to Agwé, he and Nakia were finally here after a short intra-galactic hop to join the Teku-Maza Revolutionary Guard in their ongoing battle against . . . well, the Teku-Maza Revolutionary Guard.

They were at war against their own people, who were outside the ship right now, firing.

The *Zhingha* rocked, and the Teku-Maza in the arms and kit chamber cackled.

Nakia wasn't sure if she found most of this amusing or troubling. First of all, the whole mission had been rushed. She had barely gotten time to prepare before being shipped off into a proxy war that didn't quite seem to be directly connected to the Maroon Rebellion's mission. T'Challa hadn't said much to her since his return—he was still upset about the events surrounding the *Tahar-qua* mission. M'Baku himself had not offered her more than what she already knew. So most of the additional information she possessed she'd gleaned from listening to the incessant chatter among the Teku-Maza as they prepared for battle.

"Your cousin," one was saying, "they say she's with the outlaws now."

"That she is," replied the other. "Sold her spirit for scraps, is what."

Nakia found it a bit of a challenge to understand them without her translator, but her time with N'Yami had allowed her to get comfortable with their way of speaking, which carried underneath it a trill, a consequence of amphibian lungs and airways. But whether she heard it or not, their body language did all the talking for her. The jittery excitement of one who was still young, not old enough to have seen the perils of war and become jaded by them. One who had so long wanted to visit their anger about injustice on someone that when the opportunity arrived, they didn't stop to ask if that someone was the right recipient of their ire. Especially if that someone was family.

She looked at T'Challa now as they and the rest of the assigned Maroon squadron put on their amphibian suits. Outside, the ship was surrounded by water. Nakia had never fought an underwater battle before and wondered what it would be like going up against opponents native to this environment. Could she conquer their home advantage? The other Maroons wore expressions that showed they were just as unconvinced as she was. But T'Challa's face, as usual, was set firm, focused only on the plan before them.

The ship rocked again as another set of projectiles exploded against the hull's shields.

Jafari walked into the room then. Nakia had only seen him onscreen and so was surprised to find he was a large, large man, towering over both her and T'Challa and most of the other Maroons and Teku-Maza. He wore the same self-satisfied smile she recognized from the screens but in person bore a boisterous energy that Nakia didn't like. He was supposed to be the one calming the Teku-Maza soldiers down, not keeping them buzzed. But maybe it was a cultural thing, she mused. Maybe they just thought about war differently.

N'Yami trusted him once. Maybe she should trust him, too.

"Greetings, Maroon friends," Jafari said. "I was informed that you were getting ready to launch, but I wanted to personally come in here and speak to you before I return to the command deck." He was suited up, but not in the same suit as them, which led Nakia to believe he wouldn't be participating in the fight himself but administering it from behind a screen. Nakia couldn't imagine her or M'Baku, or even N'Yami, not joining in a fight themselves—Taku could remain on board if they needed help from the ship. But perhaps, again, they did things differently here.

"All other battles have come to a stalemate." He spoke as they plucked their final items, helmet and arms, from the racks and filed out of the room. "But this time, thank N'Yami, we have help."

"Indeed, Commander Jafari," said Nakia. "As long as the terms of the Maroons' help are clear. We must have the Jengu's scale."

This, to her, was the only reason she'd agreed to come. She'd promised T'Challa that she'd help him get his memories back, even if he was refusing to acknowledge said sacrifice on her part. She'd also promised N'Yami that she'd dedicate her service to the Maroon Rebellion to ensure that this happened—not just for T'Challa, but for all Nameless. If all they needed to do was trade a few pieces of tech and manpower for the Jengu's scale, then so be it.

"Of course, General Nakia," said Jafari. "Our war is your war."

He led them out, into the hallways, explaining how the Teku-Maza Revolutionary Guard had driven the imperials—he made sure to mention how they were a common foe between the Maroon Rebellion and the Teku-Maza—from Agwé. Agwé was free for the first time since N'Yami herself had been present on the planet. But now, something had happened: The long arm of the Empire had found them again. Despite its absence, the Empire had found a way to destroy Agwé's revolutionary gains by infecting sections of its own people with the promise of personal riches if they could fulfill one task: Capture and murder the final Jengu.

If the Maroons wanted the Jengu's scale, then they'd have to help him get the great creature back safely.

"It's these very forces we've engaged," Jafari said. "The self-same forces who've kidnapped the Jengu. Our mission is quite simple: Defeat these traitors and liberate the Jengu in one fell swoop." He sighed. "It's shameful, really. The Empire cannot defeat us from without, so it sows dissent within." He held up a finger. "But make no mistake! These men pose as rebels but they're really outlaws. Enemies of the Teku-Maza Revolutionary Guard who would sell us all back into bondage for a few imperial credits."

After his speech, Jafari left them. Nakia found that it was best to get the message that had been burning in her chest across to T'Challa before the doors opened and the heat of battle was visited upon them.

"T'Challa." She ran up to him. "T'Challa, a moment?"

He only grunted his assent.

"Don't make this complicated," Nakia said. "That scale is key to the memories of the Nameless."

Another grunt, then: "I have not said a word."

Of course you haven't, thought Nakia as they boarded the exit platform and strapped on their underwater helmets.

"You don't ever say anything," she said. "You just *do.* And that's the problem. We're still hurting from your stunt on the *Taharqua.* So, we do this simple and easy—get in, get out."

A small explosion rocked the water outside. A blinding flash of light washed over them as they ascended into the airlock and it began to flood.

Nakia could feel T'Challa eyeing her when he said: "Right . . . simple and easy."

The doors opened, and the sounds of war were upon them.

WAR WAS ALWAYS brutal on the mind and body. A cacophony of stimuli and emotions, crashing on a soldier in one huge wave. In Nakia's experience, whether as a Maroon or in her former life as an Askari, there was barely ever time to think an action through, to process the possible implications of a choice. It was all heat, all fire, all lung-bursting attack and *cut, cut, cut through*.

War underwater was the same, with everything multiplied a hundredfold.

Despite the underwater suits, the first thing that struck Nakia was the pressure against her body that the water exerted. A constant blanket pressing all around her so that it was hard to discern what was nothing and what was something. And a lot of some-things were in fact happening around her: missiles shot, rockets launched, ships battling ships, the foot soldiers—*aquatic* soldiers—yet to engage in any combat.

Ahead of her and her squadron, the rebel Teku-Maza soldiers advanced.

They didn't even wear separate colors from her squadron or hoist a separate emblem. From this distance, she could see that in every single way, they were simply just another group of Teku-Maza. She turned to look at T'Challa and the rest of her squadron to see if they had the same thoughts. Were they simply okay cutting down fellow inhabitants of the same planet? People who could have once been their own neighbors?

The faces of her soldiers were set, defiant. Ahead, all they saw was the sameness of the Empire, a mass of people tainted by imperial stink. There was no mercy there, only vengeance.

Perhaps this was what worried Nakia even more, as she realized she and T'Challa and the other Maroons who'd joined them might be at a much larger disadvantage than she'd envisioned. The water pressure wasn't her only concern. The very lack of footing—of something to jump off of, to propel herself from and leap into battle—was a challenge: Half her attack modes and battle skills rested on the existence of solid infrastructure. Being in this battle meant that she and the others would have to rely on weaponry alone, something the rebel Teku-Maza also had. Could T'Challa's skills, much touted by Jafari, be of any use here? In fact, were the Maroons not significantly weaker going up against these opponents?

The rebel Teku-Maza were only a few yards away now, their eyes and teeth visible behind their helmet visors. Only now, when they were this close, did it suddenly occur to Nakia:

Has Jafari set us up? Is the Maroon Rebellion being thrown to the dogs?

Beside her, T'Challa shot forward.

As was typical, he didn't wait for her signal. He was off, plowing into the rebels, who scattered like pollen in the wind. Then he fired at both ships and people. The rest of the squadron, without thinking, shot forward with him and joined in the attack, engaging the rebels.

But then something began to take shape in Nakia's eye. The rebels were only invested in keeping the squadron at bay. They specifically weren't firing back at T'Challa, not even when he took down a nearby ship by returning the ship's missile—aimed for the *Zhingha*—with his own hand. Rather, they gathered in numbers in what was clearly a formation.

A formation around T'Challa.

Oh no.

T'Challa, too, saw it too late, but seemed to interpret the strategy as something other than what it was.

"Ack!" he yelled. "Nakia! I've got too many!"

Exactly, she thought. *Because that was the plan.*

"I'm coming!" she screamed, and propelled herself to him.

The rebel Teku-Maza converged as one, encircling T'Challa like insects encircling prey to take back to their hive. T'Challa, smothered by a ball of Teku-Maza soldiers, a mass of limbs and armor, hand reaching for her as he was pulled away.

She stretched forth her hand to catch him, to pull him out. But then a piercing, sizzling light came from within the ball of limbs, growing brighter and brighter and—

"What are they—"

Nakia didn't finish the question. She caught T'Challa's hand right before there was a snap, like two fingers clicking.

Space fold, she thought, as all the water around her went away, and then it was dark and cold and nowhere.

CHAPTER 36

△▽△▽

TEKU-MAZA REBEL HIDEOUT

T'CHALLA. T'CHALLA.

A voice was calling him from beyond the deepness. A single ray of light in a dark cave. He opened his eyes, lifted his head. No, that was an actual ray of light. And that voice, that was Nakia.

Then all feeling began to return. The cold in his feet, in his elbows. The slimy feel of something binding his hands together, so tightly that they were impossible to separate. The pain of one crooked finger pressed into his palm, stuck there. The constant thumping in his head.

"Ughhhh." He blinked. "My head . . ."

Nakia was there, kneeling over him on the floor. His voice echoed—they were in a vestibule or chamber of some sort. He lifted himself to his elbows. *Where in Bast's name are we?*

"No time for that now." Nakia, as if she had read his mind, was no longer looking at him but at a porthole in the wall from where the light shone. She would be hoping to subtly catch a glimpse of their fellow Maroons, having lost sight of them in the commotion. "We have company."

True to her word, behind the yellow light of the porthole, the silhouette of a round head appeared. Slowly said silhouette stepped forward, and their features became clearer. Teku-Maza; piercing blue eyes, face that showed a bit of age; a fighter or soldier from the way their gaze was set.

Then another shape appeared in front of their faces. Something triangular, sharp. The tip of a spear.

T'Challa's eyes widened. *My spear!*

He pulled at his hands, which he now realized were bound by some sort of mollusk creature. It seemed dormant—alive yet frozen in stasis. It seemed to respond, however, to T'Challa's distress. The harder he attempted to pull his hands apart, the tighter it wound around to bind them together again.

The Teku-Maza only watched from the porthole.

Frustrated, defeated, T'Challa shouted at the figure, "That spear you hold . . . it was made to be wielded by a king. Are you a king?"

The Teku-Maza figure leaned forward, as if making sure they'd heard clearly what had been said. Then slowly, gently, as if responding to a child, replied.

"No. My name is Farouk, and you can consider me a regent. A caretaker for a boy who has yet to learn the weight of such a weapon." The voice—*his* voice—was deep, worn, practiced. One could tell that this man, Farouk, had spoken to many a person in this way.

"Remove these bonds or we'll remove them ourselves," Nakia interjected. "And when we do, that won't be the only thing we remove."

"Threats and bluster," said Farouk. "Precisely what I expected." He shook his head, the way a disappointed parent would at a silly child. "Tell me, mighty Nakia, when did N'Yami's revolution so violently turn against its own?"

Nakia gritted her teeth. "You aren't our own. You've taken the Ancient Jengu. You collaborate with the Empire. You would reenslave the very home of our N'Yami."

Farouk was quiet after this. Too quiet.

"So that's what they told you, is it?" said Farouk with a sigh.

"No." T'Challa wasn't about to let up. "It's what we've seen with our own eyes. We know that N'Yami founded the Revolutionary Guard and you oppose her banner. We know the Ancient Jengu is the symbol of the Teku-Maza resistance, and you have imprisoned her and plan to sell her off to the imperials."

Farouk fell silent again. The quiet, this time, T'Challa recognized to be like the last: one born of confusion, some disappointment, and much, much exasperation.

"You've been deceived, T'Challa," Farouk said gently, softly. "More than I'd even realized." He stretched out an arm, away from the door. "We could argue back and forth for the next hour, nothing I could say would convince you. But if you are, in fact, who N'Yami thought you to be . . ." He sighed. "It's the deeds that matter."

A beep, and the door to the chamber shifted open. At the same time, the mollusk around T'Challa's wrists shrieked softly, shivered, and slid off his wrists.

Farouk was standing there, Spear of Bashenga in hand. He thrust the spear forward and placed it into T'Challa's hand. The Vibranium responded to T'Challa's presence, the power of Wakanda Prime surging through him, awakening his drive. But his mind, his heart, that part of him that still managed to think rationally, remained confused, asking: *What's happening?*

T'Challa didn't wait for the answer. He lunged for Farouk, pinned him to a nearby wall, spear a hair's breadth from his eye.

Farouk remained unmoved, holding T'Challa's gaze, refusing to look away from the possibility of certain death. *Do it,* his eyes seemed to challenge. *Do it if you are who you say you are.*

And looking in those eyes, T'Challa was forced to ask himself: *Who am I?*

He'd been told by others that he was many things: slave, soldier, savior, redeemer, king. He'd had names bestowed upon him, rumors painted onto his body. He'd been told he was brash, unruly, unhinged, but also kind, caring, invested in the freedom and progress of people he called his own. Maybe he was all of these things. Maybe he was none of these things. The truth was that no one really knew who he was, and neither did he.

Perhaps this was an opportunity for him to stop asking the question and start answering it in the way he wanted it to be answered. Become the answer to a different question: *Who do I want to be?*

T'Challa squeezed the spear in his fist. The blade inched closer to Farouk's eye.

"Go ahead," said Farouk. "Do it . . . *King*."

Become the answer.

A weight slowly loosened over his shoulder, slipped away. He let his hand fall, the spear with it.

If they called him a king, it was not enough to simply accept such a title. If they thought him a king, then they expected discernment, wisdom, careful consideration. They saw something in him that it was time to start seeing in himself.

He hadn't put much thought into this mission since the events of the *Taharqua*. And if he did, now, consider that Farouk had captured him unharmed just to speak with him, then freed him and handed him back his spear, perhaps something wasn't quite right about the stories he'd been told about this Teku-Maza rebel force and their alleged collaboration with imperial forces.

"You've felt it from the moment you arrived here on Agwé, haven't you?" Farouk said, reading his eyes. "Something is wrong."

Behind T'Challa, there was another soft shriek, another shiver, and the mollusk encapsulating Nakia's wrists slithered off just as his had.

"Nothing that putting you in this cell won't fix," said Nakia, massaging her wrists, clearly still angry.

Farouk spat a bitter chuckle. "I *freed* you, a token of goodwill, because I believe you truly are N'Yami's children. You owe me an audience, at least."

T'Challa and Nakia looked at each other. It was the first time since the *Zhingha* that they'd looked at each other this way, earnestly, without bitterness. N'Yami's name always did that, invoking this earnestness from them both. She was the one piece of glue that still held this Maroon ship together—him, Nakia, M'Baku. Even when she was gone, she still worked wonders from the beyond. That was the kind of person T'Challa wanted to become, for his words and deeds to bear good fruit.

Nakia, too, seemed to think the same, for she turned to Farouk and said: "Fine. Explain yourself."

YOU HAVE BEEN DECEIVED.

This was how Farouk began his story, and this was the sentence that rang in Nakia's ears until he was finished.

The first half of his tale was no different from the one Jafari had shared the first time he'd brought his proposition to the Maroons. The beats were all the same, almost practiced, a rote oral history passed down: first, the Jengu; then, the Teku-Maza, their descendants; and finally, the imperial arrival, and the hunting of the beloved Jengu into extinction. The Teku-Maza enslaved, their memories ripped from them, a species devolved into nothing more than a simple addition to the vast Nameless in the five galaxies. But one Jengu survived, hidden away, and that was why they were all here.

But there was a tenor to Farouk's story that was different. While Jafari's rendition was one of puffed up pride and braggadocio—one that, at the time, Nakia had attributed to pride in N'Yami's Revolutionary Guard and their accomplishments—Farouk's tone was one of sorrow and lament.

It was the Jengu who told us the old stories, he'd said. *It is the Jengu who holds the last vestiges of what we once were.*

This, Nakia would later come to realize, was the turning point, the moment in which she decided to trust Farouk. This was the collective ache shared by Nameless all over the Empire, something she herself had never had to share but had borne witness to since the day she joined the rebellion. This was the ache she had to witness T'Challa bear every single day. It was recognizable, succinct, sharp. It stabbed and drew blood, and Nakia realized that she could, truly, see Farouk bleeding.

"You are being told that we have kidnapped the Jengu, that we work with the Empire," Farouk said. "You have been misled."

"How so?" Nakia truly wanted to know.

"Follow me, please, and I will show you."

"Follow you *where*?" asked T'Challa.

"You came to see the Jengu, did you not?" Farouk seemed to have a limitless amount of patience. "I will show her to you, but first you must know why she is even here, and why there is even this current rebellion."

FAROUK GUIDED THEM through dark halls, through structures that bore resemblance to caves and caverns. Much of the building they were in seemed to have organic matter as the basis of its architecture. Pillars that twisted and warped like wood but seemed sturdy as metal; decorative flora that moved yet bore the consistency of paper; furniture that looked like it was made from stretched skin. Moving through the spaces was a surreal experience for Nakia, as if she were inside a tree that grew itself into a house. Even the stairs bore soft padding that could be grass or moss or artificial carpet—it was hard to tell.

As they moved, Farouk spoke, paying little attention to their ingenuous appreciation of the place.

"N'Yami had left to join the larger resistance years prior," he said. "And so our first thought was to forge an alliance with you, N'Yami's Maroons. But when our entreaties went unanswered, new measures were considered."

The Cudjoe attack, Nakia thought, glancing at T'Challa. He returned her gaze in understanding.

"Forgive us," she said to Farouk. "We were running for our lives."

"Mmm," he said. "Well, your ally Jafari came up with a novel idea: Sue for peace with the Empire . . . by offering up the Jengu."

They'd been descending stairs, and when Farouk said this, it brought them all to a halt. He stopped as well, as if he'd been expecting their reaction, as if he, too, was still stricken by the very thought of such betrayal.

"*What?*" Nakia found herself saying. "Jafari is a freedom fighter. He still is fighting for freedom—*his* freedom."

Farouk snickered. "Jafari cares only for himself and Agwé. He isn't concerned with the Empire's doings elsewhere. He surely does not care for you."

"But you opposed him," said T'Challa. "*That* is what began this current war."

"Of course I opposed him," Farouk said. "Wouldn't you? He made a deal with the Empire! It's a betrayal of all that N'Yami stood for."

They'd resumed moving and were now suddenly standing at a massive round but blocked entrance. *Jengu's lair, perhaps,* thought Nakia. As she thought that, it came to her notice that all this time, being led out in the open by Farouk, the volume of their conversation had drawn the attention of other Teku-Maza—fighters, workers, ordinary individuals, some with children. As Nakia watched them gather on the fringes, in the darkness, listening in on the conversation, she suddenly realized what this place was: a hideout, just like the Maroons on the ice rock.

Farouk and Jafari might both be rebels on opposite sides of the Teku-Maza resistance to imperial power, but only one of them was in hiding. That, she decided, was telling.

"I suspect Jafari has now gone much further with his promises to the Empire," said Farouk. "So far he's failed to deliver the Jengu, and has thus likely promised something more."

It started to make sense to Nakia now, Jafari's plan.

"Something like . . . *us,*" she said slowly.

And then an explosion cut through her hearing.

△▽△▽

CHAPTER 37

ABOVE PLANET AGWÉ

A SHADOW APPEARED over the *Mackandal*.

Floating above Agwé, the Maroon starship sat quietly, cloaked as usual, awaiting the conclusion of the Teku-Maza civil war on the planet below, after which they would ferry T'Challa and Nakia and the rest of their loan squadron home. But then, out of nowhere came the shadow, a double-winged monstrosity that sailed over the *Mackandal* and smothered it like a tight fist.

M'Baku and Taku, manning the command center, looked up at the same time.

"What the—?" M'Baku started before the rain of fire began.

An imperial cruiser manifested from thin air in the same way the *Mackandal* had done so many times before. Its guns were already out and blazing before the rest of the ship came into view, a vessel seven times the size of the Maroon's largest starship. Every inch of its hull was fitted with weaponry despite it being a cruiser and not a warship. This was just like the Empire: Nothing was spared from participating in its nefarious deeds. Warship or not, every vessel in its service was dedicated to achieving its overall goal of conquest and decimation.

"How did they find us!?" Taku asked over the patter of gunfire on the *Mackandal*'s hull.

"We've been betrayed!" M'Baku shouted back.

As they steered the ship out of range of the guns, out came the imperial cruiser's cannons. They turned slowly but fired all at once, each a deafening boom. Even before they hit the *Mackandal's* hull, M'Baku knew they'd cause heavy damage.

The explosion rocked the *Mackandal* so much that it shifted M'Baku in his seat. Taku had to hold on to her panel for support.

"They're not letting up!" she screamed. "Our shields are holding, but our engine's gone! We're dead in space!"

M'Baku ordered the ship swung around, tracing a circle. They could run, but they had to remain within Agwé airspace. T'Challa and Nakia were pains in his behind, but he couldn't abandon them mid-mission. It wasn't the Maroon way. N'Yami would never approve.

More explosions rattled the *Mackandal*. M'Baku ordered another run around the circle, turning to Taku.

"Still no word?"

She held his gaze. "None."

M'Baku gritted his teeth. "Okay. We need to buy some time. Scramble the zulus."

A few more explosions later, the *Mackandal's* bay opened and out dropped multiple zulus, entering Agwé airspace like floaters in water. As the pilots settled into their courses, dodging the imperial cruiser's guns, returning fire, evading the craft the cruiser had dropped in countermeasure, M'Baku's voice came over all comms.

"Maroons!" He gave the rallying cry. "You know your mission. We must recover the Jengu's scale." Dropping into a softer tone, the commander continued: "More than our lives are at stake. That scale is the key to recovering our names, our memories, everything the Empire took from us." And then, back to the growl, the warrior's voice: "Until then, your name is death. Teach it to your enemy."

Scores of zulus surged forward as one, the cry of their commander ringing in their ears, and then the war over Agwé was in full force.

△▽△▽

IN THE COMMAND CENTER of the imperial cruiser, Counselor Achebe sat behind a row of Askari pilots, watching the Maroon starship and craft scramble outside. Since the death of his counselor partner and comrade, Demba, at the hands of N'Jadaka himself, Achebe had slowly found himself taking over Demba's role of leading the imperial offense against the Maroons. And now, here he was, in pole position to see to his goals once and for all. The ship, their commanders, their promised savior and hero—all in one place. It was like being blessed by Bast herself.

If all went well today, this might be the last time he'd have to stand here in service of this matter.

"Counterattack commenced, General Achebe," said one of the pilots.

Achebe smiled contentedly. "Good. Clear them out."

He didn't need them to take out all the Maroon zulus or bomb the Maroon ship into oblivion. What he truly needed was to command the airspace over Agwé, from where they could see to retrieving the Jengu in a manner that ensured everything went smoothly. Only then would the next phase of the attack commence.

"We can have no interference once the anchor is in place," he said to the Askari.

"Yes, General," the lead Askari replied. "Our assets below have infiltrated the Jengu lair and should be—" The man paused, listening to something in his ear. His expression turned sour.

"General," said the Askari, "we're receiving a priority transmission from the emperor."

Achebe frowned. "The emperor? *Our* emperor, N'Jadaka himself?"

"The emperor himself, General."

Well, thought Achebe. *That's strange.* N'Jadaka never communicated during a mission. He only always received updates after, directly from Achebe himself. If he was calling on them now, in the middle of a mission . . .

Achebe shot to his feet. Something was wrong.

"Put it through," he ordered the Askari and walked into an adjoining chamber, switching to private comms.

The emperor's visage appeared over holo, head only. *Oh, not audio only,* Achebe realized. Worse, the emperor was wearing his panther helmet, which he only wore when he was about to have a public audience. Or worse, when he was going to war.

Achebe prayed it wasn't the latter.

"My liege," he greeted. "I was just preparing a report on our—"

"Save your sniveling, Achebe." The emperor's tone was that of something twisted to its fraying ends, preparing to snap. "I did not call on you for your flattery."

Achebe fell to one knee. This sounded like it would be more of the latter, then.

"There is a trickery about," N'Jadaka said. "High treason. A thousand tortures upon the betrayer!" An anxiety Achebe had not heard in a long time had crept into the emperor's voice. He was *furious.*

"My liege . . . ?" Achebe didn't know what else to say. Even asking the wrong question in this situation could get him killed. He remembered Demba with a shiver.

"My daughter, Achebe." The emperor sounded like he could cry. "The rebels have taken my daughter!"

CHAPTER 38

△▽△▽

TEKU-MAZA REBEL HIDEOUT

THE MANIFOLD WAS BACK.

T'Challa could tell even without seeing the source of the explosion. He knew, because his body remembered it all from that day at Cudjoe—the thundering vibrations, the smell of hot metal and dust, the hair on his arms standing erect. The Vibranium whine of the Manifold's suit still played in his head, the high-pitched ringing of his space fold portals as he opened them and swallowed people and weaponry both.

Oh, he was back all right. And this time, T'Challa was ready.

"Put us back out there," he said to Farouk immediately. "We'll hold them off."

"ARE YOU NUTS?" Nakia was whispering as they prepared in the situation room Farouk had just led them into. "He's *thrice* more powerful than he was at Cudjoe!"

And I'm thrice more powerful than I was at Cudjoe, he wanted to respond, but said instead, "Cudjoe was a surprise, an ambush. We know more now. We can be more tactful in tackling him." He pointed to the rest of the Teku-Maza in the room, all tapping away at visuals, screaming into mouthpieces, relaying orders. "Look at these people. Do we want them to become Nameless, too? Do we want the last living Jengu to die? Because that's what will happen if we don't go out there and face him."

Nakia sighed. He could tell she knew he had a point. She also knew that he wasn't sharing the real reason why he had to get out there: If the last living Jengu was killed and/or captured by the Empire, then *he* would never get his memories back. *He* would return to being Nameless, perhaps forever. *He* would die without ever knowing the name of the white-haired woman from his dreams.

He would rather be crushed by the Manifold than let that happen.

"Okay," said Nakia, and both returned to listening to Farouk.

On the visuals before Farouk, a map of the ongoing battle was spread out, with the scale of the advancing imperial army projected. *Larger than I thought,* T'Challa realized. And ahead of that advancing army of underwater vessels, small craft, and Askari infantry, a new player had appeared on the field. The cameras zoomed closer, and soon the orange lights of the Manifold's Vibranium suit came into view.

T'Challa gritted his teeth. "*That's* the key. Take him off the field, and we have a chance."

"His target is the Jengu, no doubt," said Farouk. "But according to our reports, the Manifold has to know *where* he's going in order to teleport there. And since he didn't teleport directly into the Jengu's lair, he must not yet know its exact location."

After the explosion and before they'd arrived here, Farouk had put a fresh battalion of Teku-Maza soldiers on guard at the entrance to the lair. T'Challa wondered, now, if he would have been better served just crossing that stonewalled entrance and proceeding to retrieve the Jengu's scale. That way, regardless of the outcome of this war, the Maroons would have something to work with. Even if *he* didn't make it, other Nameless could recover their own memories.

But then he thought, *No.* That would mean abandoning the Teku-Maza to the imperial forces. How could the Maroons be free if others weren't? No one would be free until everyone was.

So, it was with that in mind that he jogged alongside Nakia and a new Teku-Maza squadron to the nearest arms and kit chamber.

"SIR!" CAME THE MESSAGE over comms as soon as T'Challa put on his helmet. *"The* Mackandal *is up against masai fighters and an imperial cruiser. They can't hold out much longer!"*

Nakia turned to him, eyes wide, at the same time he glanced at her. They shared the same concern in that moment—their comrades could be in pieces in the next few moments. M'Baku, Taku, the entire crew. Could they survive another leadership death?

Another explosion rocked the hideout.

"Farouk," Nakia said into her helmet before T'Challa could speak. "We can't deal with that right now. We have to win *here* if there's to be any hope for them out there."

A brief silence, then Farouk came back. "Okay. Get me a clean shot at the Manifold, and we will."

Nakia turned to T'Challa, nodded. He nodded back.

OUTSIDE, THE IMPERIAL ASKARI, led by the Manifold, pummeled the hideout's exterior with guns. A second battalion, consisting mostly of a sect known as the Between—Vibranium cyborgs bearing the consciousness of imperials—hoisted laser cannons and supported with booming fire. The hideouts' shields were holding on so far, but with sustained fire at this level, they couldn't last forever.

So, Nakia devised a plan.

A piece of old mining tech Farouk had mentioned in the arms and kit chamber turned out to be of use. It was a shield projector, a large device offering a sphere of protection around those who remained within the confines of its projection, which wasn't very large. The good news was that it worked differently in either direction: Those within the shield could fire out or extend matter beyond the shield, but anything attempting to *enter* the sphere was repelled.

There *was* bad news, though. The sphere could only fit eight or so people, including the projector's carrier, Nakia. This meant there could be only seven attackers, T'Challa included. That was less than half the squadron.

It'll have to do, he thought as they emerged from the hideout.

Immediately, they were peppered by ongoing imperial fire. But the sphere was surprisingly functional, deflecting even laser cannon fire. And to test its multidirectional nature, T'Challa lifted the Spear of Bashenga, aimed it at the nearest Between with a laser cannon, and threw.

Out of the sphere of protection went the spear, cutting through fire and smoke and water. It went through the Between, front to back, shattering its Vibranium armor along the way.

And then, surprisingly—or perhaps, *unsurprisingly*—the spear, having completed its task, flew back into the sphere, undeflected. T'Challa caught it, equal parts puzzled and impressed.

"Great Jengu," one of the Teku-Maza soldiers whispered. "It really is *him*."

"*Teku-Maza!*" screamed Farouk into all their ears. "*Give it to them!*"

Out went the fire from Teku-Maza cannons of their own, cutting through Askari and Between both. As they fired, the Teku-Maza soldiers shrieked, some unintelligibly, some with phrases T'Challa could understand.

For N'Yami! For Agwé!

T'Challa turned his focus, then, to the Manifold, the whine of the imperial's suit, even though still far away, now louder in his ears. The Manifold was doing a successful job of displacing fire with his space fold portals and redirecting them back at the sphere. Attacking him was pointless, a waste of ammunition.

But the soldiers around him fell. And once the extra protec-

tion had whittled away, he stood alone, isolated in the waters of
Agwé.

"Farouk!" Nakia screamed into comms. "This is about the
clearest shot you're going to get! Do it now!"

From comms came Farouk's voice: "*Understood.*" Then under
his breath: "*Activate proximity charges.*"

There was a pause, and then a hiss behind them. Out of nowhere emerged scores of missiles, sailing past their sphere, all
headed at once for the Manifold.

This is the plan? thought T'Challa. Didn't Farouk know? The
Manifold couldn't be hit at all. He'd simply portal them all away.

And the Manifold was doing exactly that, displacing all the
missiles. But something else was happening. They weren't seam-
lessly portaling. Whenever each missile approached a space fold
portal, it detonated.

Ah, thought T'Challa. *Smart man, Farouk.*

Soon, there were enough explosions that the Manifold was
blinded, engulfed in fire and smoke and unable to portal all that
descended upon him. And that small moment of hesitation was all
it took.

Two proximity charges struck the Manifold: head and shoulder. The imperial tumbled backward into Agwé's waters, then lay
still, floating.

The whine of the Vibranium in T'Challa's head went quiet.

"*Manifold down!*" screamed Farouk into their ears. "*Now, finish it. Send these slavers back to Benhazin in pieces!*"

The sphere shield flickered, running out of juice. T'Challa knew
what this meant—long distance fighting was over. They were still
outnumbered, but now that the strongest imperial weapon had
been taken off the board, it was time to unleash Agwé's.

Him.

"Come out, every battalion!" T'Challa screamed into comms.
"Today, we fight, for Agwé!"

The shield flickered one last time, disappeared, and T'Challa
shot forward into the war.

△▽△▽

"TEKU-MAZA, *this is Farouk. Lay down your weapons."*

The broadcast seemed to be coming from a place far away, a voice that wasn't here, inside T'Challa's helmet. Whenever he was fighting, all sound drifted away. Only the solidness of what was before him was real. Something he could touch, pummel into. He never heard the snaps, the squelches, the bullets and weapons that missed him, the blood that splattered across his own body.

But this—this cut through the loud silence and stopped him in his tracks. He caught his returning spear, and as the three Between soldiers before him drifted away, oozing green ichor, he paused and leaned closer into the quiet, away from the pressure of water all around him, trying to be sure he'd heard right.

"Teku-Maza, I repeat, lay down your weapons."

That was definitely Farouk's voice. *What in Bast's name is going on?*

Next to T'Challa, Nakia looked just as puzzled. She'd just been trying to explain to him that after finishing up here, they were going to head to the *Mackandal* to aid in their efforts.

"Are you hearing this?" she asked, flabbergasted.

And then the Vibranium whine arose in T'Challa's head again. He swung around, and there, in the faraway darkness, were the orange lights of the Manifold shining bright.

A ruse, T'Challa realized. *It was all a ruse.*

"Do it now!" Farouk pressed. *"The future of our people depends on it."*

T'Challa almost chuckled at the genius of the plan. For the Manifold to pretend to be defeated, for the Between cyborgs to draw Teku-Maza fire and take up T'Challa's time. And while they'd been fighting a phantom threat, the real imperial force must have snuck inside Agwé into the rebel hideout and taken Farouk and the Jengu hostage.

The Manifold sailed over to him and Nakia and the rebels now, accompanied by a handful of Between and Askari that had hidden away.

"You heard the man." The Manifold's voice was metallic, grinding. "Surrender the spear."

T'Challa, reluctantly, placed his Spear of Bashenga in the Manifold's hand. Nakia did the same with her cannon, and the rebels followed suit.

"This is bad," Nakia said. "Really bad."

T'Challa agreed. And it would almost be also funny if his hands weren't now being bound, and he wasn't now being captured and imprisoned for the second time today.

CHAPTER 39

△▽△▽

ABOVE PLANET AGWÉ

ONLY MOMENTS EARLIER in the imperial cruiser, Achebe had made a decision.

"The *Mackandal* is down, General," the Askari controller pilot said to him. "Atmospheric supremacy achieved."

Achebe nodded. "And the Manifold?"

"Waiting on us, sir. But our anchor is ready."

"Mmm." Achebe shut his eyes, inhaled and exhaled deeply. "Then it's time. Bring the Manifold back online and let's end this."

As the imperial soldier whirred back into life, surprising the Teku-Maza warriors, something else was happening. The "anchor"—what had been their code name for the stealth unit they'd sent to infiltrate the rebel hideout while everyone else was occupied by the battle outside—had dropped. A dozen or so Askari and a small number of Between had finally arrived at the site of the Jengu's lair, which the Manifold had been unable to teleport directly into for lack of a specific location. A short skirmish and a few dead Between later, the Teku-Maza rebels on fight duty had been rounded up, leading to the eventual capture of their leader, a feisty Teku-Maza warrior named Farouk.

From there, it was easy to get everyone else to stand down.

Now, the rest of the Teku-Maza rebels—fighters and nonfighters both—had been captured and ferried back up here, into the hold of the imperial cruiser. But it wasn't just Teku-Maza. The Maroons who had shown up to join them were also there, and among those Maroons were two very important people: the heir-apparent captain, Nakia, and the escaped former prisoner, the man touted to be the reincarnation of the great T'Challa, the Avenger, Avatar of Bast, He Who Put the Knife Where It Belonged.

Achebe shuddered with delight and trepidation at the thought of meeting him.

He'd heard much about this man since his joining the rebellion. The stories of the one who was soldier and savior, king and servant to his people. When Achebe had joined N'Jadaka's service, it was with the understanding that the emperor had Bast's blessing and had become her avatar. But then N'Jadaka had gotten involved with whatever that symbiote was, growing more and more powerful, losing favor with Bast in the process. Achebe couldn't say N'Jadaka was the kind of man about whom people were writing songs of praise anymore. But this T'Challa, well, he was loved. And Achebe wanted to see what it took for that to happen.

The Askari controller was back, talking to him again. "General, the Manifold is bringing our Teku-Maza contact, Jafari, and the rebel leaders to the bridge."

Achebe leaned back into his chair. "Good. We will deal with this rebellion at last."

The bridge door opened. The first person to walk in was Jafari, clad in his usual regal red attire. Before he was even through the doorway, he began talking.

"There!" he said. "I've delivered your precious avatar and the Jengu is now in your clutches." He made a clicking sound in the back of his throat. "I trust I shall be adequately compensated."

Achebe regarded the man for a moment, then looked behind him at the prisoners being led onto the bridge by the Manifold, still in his full suit. Three people were next to him: a Teku-Maza, whom Achebe assumed to be Farouk, and two humans—a woman, whom he assumed to be Nakia, and a man, whom he realized was T'Challa.

To be fair, he looked, in this moment, like nothing. Or, not *nothing*, but definitely not as grand as the stories suggested. He was pretty ordinary, built just like any other soldier. They were still in their underwater suits, sans helmets. There simply didn't seem to be anything special about him or the Maroons in general.

Fascinating, Achebe thought, that these were the people giving the Empire so much of a headache. He would laugh if the situation wasn't so dire.

He returned to Jafari, who was still grinning.

"Do not overstate your service," said Achebe. "It was the Manifold who assured our victory." He angled himself in his chair, propped himself up with one hand. "And as for your compensation, consider yourself paid in full, dog."

And then he pulled out a gun and shot Jafari in the chest.

As the man fell, the Askari looked on, confused, unsure. He could see the questions written all over their faces. *What just happened? Also, was Achebe allowed to do that?* He could see the doubt creeping up, rising to the surface, ready to burst out and manifest as something unpalatable. Something that would make for tough handling in the cramped space of this bridge.

So he did what he'd prepared to do. He pulled out the secret remote tucked into the sleeve of his attire and pushed the detonate button.

One by one, all the Askari on the bridge went *boom*! Tiny explosive devices, installed into their armor, connected to each of their neck implants, erupted. Blood splattered over nearby dashboards. Bodies fell to the floor in syncopated thumps, crashed into devices, writhed in pain. All was soon quiet again on the bridge.

The prisoners were wide-eyed, mouths agape. The Manifold had neither moved nor lifted a finger to aid the dying soldiers.

"What are you doing?" asked Nakia, aghast.

Achebe rose slowly, went to the dashboard, and pushed aside a dead Askari whose blood was still spilling over the board. He flicked open a restricted chamber and keyed in his authorization code.

"What you clearly could not do," he said to Nakia. "Saving your sorry rebellion."

He thumbed the self-destruct button. As the ship announced its own self-destruct sequence, Achebe turned to the Manifold.

"Eden," he said to the man beyond the Vibranium, calling him by his non-imperial name, "it's time."

WEEKS AGO, Zenzi had come to him.

He'd known immediately that something was wrong. With the girl, but also in general—with the Empire, with N'Jadaka, with the Manifold, with the way things had been happening on Planet Bast for a while. So that evening, when Zenzi appeared, cloaked in folds of cloth and whispering, acting like something a hundred times her age, he knew, then, that he wasn't speaking to Zenzi the girl, but to someone—or something—far older.

When Zenzi had asked him to betray the Empire, to aid the Maroon Rebellion, to find a way to bring T'Challa and Nakia back from the war and to the *Mackandal* in one piece, he knew he was receiving instructions from someone greater than he was, and he was in no position to ask questions.

The Manifold, he'd asked, and Zenzi had said: *Do not worry about Eden.*

It was the first time Achebe had heard the man's true name, and that was when he knew who he was dealing with. When Zenzi asked to watch the Manifold train in the arena, N'Jadaka had acceded, never knowing that it would be the start of his demise. Achebe had watched the emperor and realized that he had truly been so blinded by power, by Bast's abandonment, that he couldn't see the shifts happening under his own nose, under his own roof. It didn't help that Nareema was away, of course. *She* would've noticed.

When he learns I have boarded the rebel ship, Zenzi had said before she left, *he will contact you. He will be stricken. Take that as your sign. Begin then.*

Now, as the Manifold opened a space fold portal on the bridge of the imperial cruiser, all five of them—him, the Manifold, T'Challa, Nakia, and Farouk—walked through to join the *Mackandal* on the other side.

THE BRIDGE OF the *Mackandal* was unnaturally full when T'Challa emerged from the space fold. Or perhaps he was seeing things, considering he was still reeling from the events on the bridge of the imperial cruiser.

What was that? The emperor's counselor murdering Jafari and his own bridge crew? Self-destructing the imperial cruiser? The Manifold now on the side of the rebels?

What in Bast's name was happening?

"M'Baku," said T'Challa as he stumbled onto the bridge, spotting the Maroon leader standing next to Taku, their eyes fixated on something. He wanted to ask what was going on, but found that M'Baku was just as transfixed by the same thing that everyone else was.

What are they staring at—

The explosion from the imperial cruiser's self-destruction cut him off as he was consumed by blinding orange light. The blast rocked the ship so hard that most people on the bridge fell, including T'Challa himself.

As the orange light dimmed, T'Challa, on his knees, gritted his teeth.

"What in Bast's name . . ." he growled.

"You disappoint me, T'Challa." A voice punctured the silent bridge.

T'Challa rose. Seated in the captain's chair—the place it turned out everyone was staring at—was a young girl. Some imperial's child from the look of her clothing, her hair, her comportment. But something wasn't quite right with her. She was superbly poised—

too poised—for such a young girl. Perhaps she was of royal blood, a princess. But no, that wasn't just it. She was something far, far greater. She had to be. Because . . .

How does she know my name?

She turned to him then, as if reading his mind. Her eyes lit up, deep pools of yellow light, and her voice grew larger, exponential, taking on a celestial edge.

"*You* above all," she said, brimming with light, "should know never to take my name in vain."

PART FOUR

△▽△▽

CHAPTER 40

⏃⏆⏉

AGWÉ

AT THE DOOR to the Jengu's lair, six Askari stood. Since securing the lair, they had been waiting for some time with no word from the imperial cruiser. For some reason, they could no longer reach their comrades on the ship above the planet. That made them antsy.

"General Achebe, are you reading us?" the lead Askari tried for the umpteenth time. "We've secured the Jengu, and the Teku-Maza have all surrendered. The heretic and his disciples were sent up to the flagship moments ago, but we've lost contact."

No response, only static. The Askari groaned.

"General Achebe? Are you reading us, sir?"

Then, out of nowhere, a miracle: a crackle on the other end.

"Yes, Lieutenant" came the response. *"Indeed I am."*

"Excellent, sir! I was worried that—"

"Ah, but it's not your job to worry, is it?"

The Askari looked to his comrades, who were all perplexed by the general's languid nature. Surely he'd be more concerned that the flagship was unreachable? But the Askari gave an expected response.

"No, sir. It is not."

"Your job is to do as you are told by your superiors. And right now, I have one here who is superior to even me." Achebe

paused and then said, *"The heir to the emperor himself: Princess Zenzi."*

The men's eyes widened. The *princess* was aboard the imperial cruiser? *In person?* How? Rumor had gotten around that she'd been pilfered by the rebels somehow. Had she been recaptured? When? So many questions.

"General, I thought—"

"What did Achebe just tell you, dog?"

The voice that came through comms didn't at all sound like a young princess. It was the voice of someone with command, with title, with *power.* Someone who knew what they could achieve simply by speaking it into existence.

"What is your job?" the princess asked.

The Askari men looked to one another, then back at their lieutenant. The man gulped.

"T-to take orders, Princess."

"Exactly. And here are my orders to you and your men." A pause for breath. *"Kill yourselves, all of you."*

When the order arrived, the Askari lieutenant almost laughed. His first thought: *Surely, she can't be serious? Surely, this is a joke?* He could see the same incredulity written across his men's faces. Of course she was the princess, heir to the Empire in which they served, and of course they were always bound to do as they were told. But to *kill themselves*? He snorted, away from his mouthpiece.

But then came the second command, a voice like thunder, like worlds, like stars and universes. A voice older than time, a voice that carried with it undeniable compulsion, inviolable and sacrosanct.

"Do it, now!"

The command surged through comms, through their earpieces, into their brains, their minds, their spirits, their souls. It touched the epicenter of their beings in a manner that made it impossible to resist—no matter how hard they, now trapped in prisons of their own minds, fought to do so. It made a nest in their chests and convictions and sprouted seeds, so that all at once, all six men knew what they must do.

"Yes, Princess," they answered in a chorus. "At once."

M'BAKU WATCHED WITH dismay all that was happening on his ship. He was as much a believer in the goddess Bast and her power and benevolence as any other person, Maroon or otherwise. He was happy to accede to whatever plans she had for them as a people. They prayed to her, after all, for support and succor.

But *this*—this was not succor. This was something malicious, vindictive. It made sense to him, now, that she had anointed N'Jadaka her avatar. Was she any different in this manner, killing indiscriminately without provocation? And as much as he didn't believe in the prophecies of a savior from Ancient Wakanda, he was now prompted to ask the question: Was this why she'd held out for so long on selecting a new avatar?

"*All* dead?" Farouk was on his comm, conversing with his planet-side rebels in the hideout. "Suicide, you say? But the Jengu's secure?" He nodded toward everyone else to assure them that the Jengu was indeed secure, then returned to speaking to his people. "No, no, no—never mind whatever made them do that. Consider it, say, a gift from our great protector, Bast." He cast a sideways glance at the goddess, wearing the body of Zenzi, then leaned back into his earpiece. "Just . . . focus on commencing repairs. And stand by for further orders."

He cut off the comms, then returned to Zenzi—or, as it was in this case, Bast.

"So, it's true," said Farouk. "The goddess walks among us! But I still don't understand. Why *now*? And why with the help of these imperials?" He swiveled around, pointing a long finger at the Manifold. "Why is *he* here?"

Bast, who was back to embodying the most normal version of Zenzi that she could, narrowed her eyes ever so slightly. The movement was so subtle as to be imperceptible to the average onlooker.

However, since the moment this little girl stepped on board his ship, M'Baku had known what seemed insignificant was in fact quite a monumental shift for a deity such as her. She might as well, with a small frown, have decided that Farouk was going to perish for questioning her choices.

"Do not question the weapons a goddess may choose to wield," she said, pointing to the Manifold. "His *name* is *Eden*. And while I can forgive your ignorance, Farouk"—and here, she turned to T'Challa—"my *avatar* should know exactly why he is here."

T'Challa, who had so far been taking this all in as quietly as M'Baku had, lifted his head. There was a perplexity in his eyes that seemed to ask: *Avatar?*

M'Baku, just as surprised—*So she had chosen a new avatar!*—surmised T'Challa had not been informed of this arrangement. That sounded like Bast, to keep them all in the dark. Even her choice, this prisoner from Goree, was an astonishment. But that was the way of the gods, wasn't it? To chart a path forward after sowing confusion with their own choices, then claim victory?

But within T'Challa's perplexity, M'Baku could also see recognition in his expression. Somewhere in the spaces between the rumored tales, he must have finally come to terms with the possibility. He couldn't name himself avatar, obviously, but there must have been a part of him that waited upon a brush with Bast, an event that would certify this nebulous idea, make it real and true and whole.

And if M'Baku was being honest, he, too, had been waiting for such an event. So far, he'd trusted in Nakia and N'Yami because he believed in them, but not necessarily in *their beliefs* about T'Challa, or even in Bast. He needed a sign of his own.

Well, here was the goddess herself, and here was that sign, spoken from her very own mouth.

T'Challa was still yet to speak, watching Bast coolly. M'Baku surmised that the reason was similar to that which also plagued him: This might be the goddess of everything that was good and

Wakandan, but she was also making decisions much too rapidly for the comfort of anyone here. Someone who actually knew how things worked had to take back the reins. Preferably someone who wasn't as taken in with this whole business of *gods* and *kings* and *saviors* as others were.

M'Baku stepped forward.

"Avatar or not," he said, addressing Bast, "T'Challa is a *soldier* of the Maroons. Under *my* command. I will need a moment to confer with him and the rest of *my* crew."

"I am afraid there isn't—" Achebe started.

"Fine, then." Nakia, out of nowhere, cut in. So far, she, too, had been silent. But something was happening now because she moved fast. Before anyone could react, she pulled a firearm from a nearby soldier's hip.

"For the killer of N'Yami," she said, lifting the gun, "the Maroons have only one word: *die*."

Then she shot the Manifold.

KING. SAVIOR. AVATAR. AVENGER. *He Who Put the Knife Where It Belonged.*

These names bounced around T'Challa's head when Bast spoke to him. Others kept talking, but T'Challa found it hard to concentrate, to hear what they were saying. All he kept hearing were these titles, bestowed upon him without request, without concern for who he *wanted* to be. And now here was Bast, bestowing one more upon him, yet another that he couldn't refuse.

He looked around. No one seemed to notice his discontent, the churning mass of emotions in his chest. M'Baku was addressing Bast, Taku stood raptly beside him, and Farouk regarded all three. Achebe, next to Bast, seemed only to be interested in her requests and concerns, not even bothering to look their way. It seemed like the world for which T'Challa was fighting was moving too fast, getting away from him, and he was struggling to catch up.

And then he looked at Nakia and, for the first time since entering the bridge, saw someone else who bore an expression he could understand.

Her face was set, her gaze strong, palpitating with anger. There was only death in her eyes. On the other end of that gaze was a single person: the Manifold.

Or was it Eden now?

T'Challa stared with her at the now rebranded, now supposedly exonerated imperial soldier. Sometime between the imperial cruiser's explosion and Bast's theatrics with the planet-side Askari, the Manifold had desuited. Now there was just a young man standing there—a *boy*, really, if T'Challa was to be honest. He wore loced hair and was visually appealing in the way that a beautiful, sublime predator could be. He still looked ever the imperial soldier, but with all the sharp edges smoothed over, all the death and destruction and decimation he could bring—that he *had* brought—shaved away under the banner of this new coalition. No, this man standing before them couldn't be the Manifold. This truly *was* Eden, a whole other person.

But Nakia, it seemed, was having trouble accepting that. And as T'Challa stared with her at the young Eden, he realized why he was struggling to accept this new title Bast was bestowing upon him.

Maybe he didn't want to be a king, a caregiver, a nurturer of his people. What he truly wanted was to be *free*, and maybe that freedom, as he defined it, meant he could give in to his uglier tendencies. Maybe he wanted to be human and whole, with all the errors and mistakes, pleasant and unpleasant parts both. Maybe he truly didn't want to simply be a vessel for a deity—an *avatar* as she called it.

Maybe, like Nakia beside him, he wanted to allow himself to give in to those tendencies when they came upon him.

T'Challa returned his gaze to her, and she looked at him, realizing he'd clocked what was happening. He nodded at her, to assure her: *I know what you're thinking. I know what you're feeling. I am with you.*

Nakia nodded back. She moved; T'Challa moved with her.

"NAKIA, STOP!" SAID EDEN. "You're making a mistake!"

The man that was once the Manifold dropped to a knee, taking fire. Suit or no suit, he was still able to generate his space folds. And generate them he did, swallowing every discharge from Nakia's firearm, depositing them Bast knew where.

"Stop!" he kept saying. "You're making a mistake!"

Perhaps it was these admonitions that angered T'Challa even more. Who was this imperial mass murderer to tell *them* what was wrong or right? Did he think that because he'd received Bast's favor he could stand here without reprisal when he'd single-handedly rid the Maroon Rebellion of its greatest leader ever?

T'Challa launched for Eden, breaking his concentration. Both tumbled to the floor of the bridge.

"Did you think we'd *forgotten*?" T'Challa pulled out his spear. The ancient Vibranium throbbed in his hands, its power ready to be let loose. "Did you think you would escape our *wrath*?"

He stood above Eden, who refused to fight back. Instead, he held up his hands in surrender.

T'Challa lifted the Spear of Bashenga, ready to strike.

"No, *my king*!"

And just like the moment the spear had entered his hand—just like when N'Yami had first told him who he was; just like the first time he'd remembered seeing the white-haired woman—these words struck the chord of a distant memory within T'Challa. Something beyond the reach of his perception came alight. A powerful resonance.

I know you. From before.

But T'Challa didn't have time to finish this thought because there was a wash of orange light around him, and he was once again surging and sailing and falling through that black nothing-ness he detested so much.

M'BAKU WASN'T IMPRESSED. "What did you do with them?"

Eden—the Manifold—turned to him. "Nothing. I sent them to where Bast wants them. The Jengu's lair. We shall meet them there."

M'Baku didn't believe a word this imperial said. In fact, he was beginning to regret this little coalition and was now considering revoking his consent. Despite the fact that T'Challa and Nakia had attacked without obvious provocation, it was their right to seek revenge against the Manifold. *He* once sought revenge against the Manifold, but at least that decision was his own. He wasn't being denied his rightful rage and teleported away to some corner of Agwé.

"We shall have time to settle our accounts," Eden said. "But not now. And not like this."

"Indeed," said Bast, who'd so far been sitting quietly. "And with their tempers somewhat cooled."

Spoken like someone who truly doesn't know Nakia and T'Challa, M'Baku thought, but grunted a response. These imperi-als kept making decisions on his ship without his input. If they tried that again . . .

A hand dropped on his shoulder. It was Taku.

"We should hear the goddess out," she said coolly.

Fine. M'Baku rose and faced Bast. He was tired of the lies, the betrayals, the roundabout paths. He needed straightforward an-swers.

"Tell me now, Goddess," he said. "What do you want?"

She smiled. "What any god wants. Your total submission."

M'Baku frowned. Did she not already have that? Across the five galaxies, Maroons and imperials both held fast to belief in her, in the prophecies they believed came from the Orisha Gate. Per-haps she was speaking about *him;* perhaps she'd sensed that he couldn't care less what others believed, or in whom. The only be-lief he had was in what lay in front of his eyes. It was the only reason he was listening to her.

"If you knew your own interests, mortal, you would offer it," she continued. "Do you know what's coming?" She cackled. "You think it is merely N'Jadaka the Fearsome, N'Jadaka the Terror of Worlds. You think him merely a tyrant, yet another despot." She shook her head. "No. You are dealing with something much greater, an even higher power."

Higher like a god? M'Baku found himself asking. As if Bast were listening to his thoughts, she replied: "Yes, M'Baku. You are dealing with a *god*."

CHAPTER 41

△▽△▽

THE
JENGU'S LAIR

THE MANIFOLD OPENED up a portal, and all five of them—Bast, Achebe, Eden, Farouk, and M'Baku—walked into it and emerged in an underground cavern.

It was a vast, hollow, connected subterranean system carved into the depths of the rebel hideout. The walls and ceilings sported naturally formed stalactites, stalagmites, and columns, all eons old from the look of them. Every nook and surface dripped with mollusks, all sliding slowly away as the group approached. Between the insects buzzing about, the uneven and slippery ground, and the significant shift in humidity between the ship and here, it was not where M'Baku wanted to be or dreamed he'd be when he awoke this morning. Besides the bioluminescent organisms clinging to little pools of moisture, giving this place an ethereal and otherworldly glow, there was little in this excursion to be excited about.

Bast cared nothing about these discomforts and spoke at length. First, she explained in great detail—with all the divergence and verbosity that gods are wont to employ—of how N'Jadaka had come into the Orisha Gate and drained a significant chunk of her powers by poisoning her divine form with the Klyntar symbiote. The symbiote, which still occupied her divine form, was busy transmitting power to N'Jadaka, leaving her mostly useless. She possessed just enough presence of mind to reach out, latch on to the trail of power that the symbiote left behind, and follow it back through the portals to Planet Bast, into N'Jadaka's household. And it was there that she found one untouched by power, by greed, by every vice that the emperor himself had embraced.

And so she began her path to revenge by taking the first of many things precious to him: his heir.

"When he stole my power," she said, "he thought me done. But there are many N'Jadakas, and there is only one Bast! He will learn this lesson if it's the last thing I do!"

"We're not child killers," M'Baku said.

"Neither am I," Bast shot back. "The girl will be fine—better than fine when I'm done. But the point is that I've regained just enough of my power, enough to restore Eden to his former self. And with some help, I can restore my avatar as well."

M'Baku looked ahead to where Nakia and T'Challa were sitting next to the entrance to the Jengu's lair, awaiting the arriving party. Signs of the recent events and skirmishes remained: Blood of varying colors and odors in all compositions intermixed with discarded, defunct weaponry. Bullet holes littered the place. In a way, M'Baku thought this felt more like a natural home for these two, fighters who never knew when to stop, destruction tethered to their very beings.

But still, they were *his* people. He would do anything to protect them. Even T'Challa.

As soon as they arrived, the two stood up, Nakia ready to have another go at Eden, and T'Challa still seething beside her. But M'Baku stepped between them immediately.

"Calm down!" he said. "Listen to what we have to say."

After much glaring, T'Challa and Nakia stood down. M'Baku caught them up as quickly as he could on everything Bast had told him—about N'Jadaka, Zenzi, her plans to restore T'Challa's powers and even his memories. But there was one last truth to reveal, one that only a former Nameless could tell, and there was only one among them who'd been restored.

M'Baku turned to Eden. "Perhaps you'd like to explain?"

Eden breathed deeply, faced T'Challa, and began.

"It's . . . it's worse than you can know or imagine. Remembering everything like this. All the things you'd done, under the haze of worship, of seeking the emperor's favor."

"Is it worse than you murdering N'Yami?" T'Challa asked sarcastically.

"Yes, King T'Challa," Eden answered with earnestness. "Much worse."

T'CHALLA HATED THAT this young man called him *king*. But ever since that first time, when he'd opened his mouth and said this word, something arose in his chest, in his brain, in his memories, and T'Challa now found it difficult to look away.

"He *murdered* N'Yami," Nakia had said as they'd sat there, waiting. "He sent us here!"

Indeed he did, T'Challa had thought. *Indeed he did.*

But here he was now, listening to Eden again, who was talking about the way living in the Empire poisoned one's mind. *Total freedom from wants, from desire,* he said. *All life one great party. All you needed to do was one thing: obey.*

Nakia, who'd become increasingly feisty during their long wait, began to listen as well, enraptured. Something had shifted in her with the mention of life under imperial rule. T'Challa had never asked her for details about her time as an imperial and she'd not been forthcoming. But he could see, now, that she was touched by Eden's experiences, perhaps because they had been hers, too.

"And then, to be yanked out of that so suddenly, to be brought to light after reveling in darkness." He shivered at the memory. "It's like finding breath after drowning underwater for so long."

T'Challa, too, had felt he'd been drowning; he wouldn't mind some of that breath at all. But he was more keen to hear what exactly it was that Eden had remembered.

"This place, this world," said Eden. "This *Wakanda*—it's not the only one."

Wakanda Prime. T'Challa had heard enough about it from N'Yami that this information wasn't new to him. It was myth, belief, a parallel existence—who knew what it really was? But now, to hear it from someone who'd *been* there. This was different.

"There is a Wakanda different from this empire, one that dreams not of conquest, but of *peace.* Nevertheless, it is that Wakanda that birthed this empire. Explorers from that place were sent here, and it was they who settled and formed the first of the Empire's five galaxies."

Now, this part was new to T'Challa, so he had to ask, "Sent by who?"

Eden turned to him then. "By you, King T'Challa."

The world stopped. All was still and silent, T'Challa trapped in a nothingness of his own. *By me? Me?* How was he in two places at once—here and there—but unable to reach one from the other? How did he become enslaved by his own self—by the descendants of the very same people he'd sent here? How was he not even *old?*

In his head, the white-haired woman crooned: *Come back to me.*

He looked to his comrades. M'Baku, Eden, Farouk, and Achebe all looked just as shell-shocked. Even Nakia, who had been pushing him to accept this possibility, seemed surprised. Like him, she'd perhaps never expected the physical truth of it to be standing in front of her. M'Baku, who'd always had his doubts—and probably still had them now—looked flabbergasted.

Come back to me.

T'Challa squeezed his eyes shut, trying to piece together images, to locate the memories that would help him make sense of this. He found nothing but darkness, emptiness, nothing other than the singular image that had haunted him since the day he awoke with his memories gone.

Come back to me.

"You don't remember," Eden said, recognizing T'Challa's anguish. "How could you? After what they did to us. After what they *took.*" He stared into T'Challa's eyes. "But I know it's still in there, in you. I know you have the visions, the dreams of what was. Lost, *stolen* dreams."

It made sense now. Waking up in that cell with other prisoners—it had never made sense to him for that to be the start of his journey. His journey had begun elsewhere, in Wakanda Prime it seemed. And somehow it had brought him here, but not to this planet, to this Nameless existence. He had been someone before, even here, in the Intergalactic Empire.

He had been someone before becoming a Maroon, before fighting for Maroon causes, and he was going to find out who that someone was.

But he wasn't going to abandon the Maroons in their time of need. There were people here who needed his help, who needed to recover their memories just as much as he needed to recover his. And if his memories could serve as a pathway to help them recover theirs—that would be a noble act.

"You don't ever have to forgive me for what I did," Eden said. "I wouldn't ask you for that. Condemn me if you must. But not like this. Not on a lie."

T'Challa sighed. As much as he hated to admit it, Eden was right. This was a lie—a big lie that had made them all victims. As much as he wanted to exact vengeance for N'Yami and everyone else, he wanted to help point that vengeance in the right direction, and that direction was at the heart of the Empire.

In the end, there was only one thing left to do: hear Bast's plan and see how it could help them do exactly this.

So he turned to Bast, and said: "Tell us your grand vision."

BAST'S PLAN WAS SIMPLE: restore her avatar's memories.

"I know, right now, you can only imagine two Wakandas," she said. "The Wakanda of the other world, elsewhere, and the Wakanda of here, today. But what if I told you there have been other Wakandas, that there *are* other Wakandas?"

It sounded like a bold-faced lie to T'Challa. But what did he know about truth at this point? He had no memory to base anything on. And this was the goddess speaking to him, the person to whom he had allegedly been bonded in a life other than this one. Who was he to dispute her words?

"Within that other Wakanda," she continued, "there is a *special* place. A Wakanda *before* Wakanda. We call it the Djalia."

"What does that mean?" asked T'Challa.

"A plane bearing all of Wakandan memory."

All eyes in the chamber widened as one.

"Yes, that's right," said Bast. "A plane of ancestral memory, if you will. An archive of the memories of all bona-fide Wakandans since time immemorial. A spiritual plane only accessible to the avatar of Bast and, thankfully, out of the reach of power-hungry conquerors like N'Jadaka. Only my avatar, through my power, can ascend to this spiritual plane. And in this plane, you will have access to all Wakandan memory, even that which has been stolen." She turned to T'Challa. "Even your own."

The impossibility of it struck T'Challa. Access to the impressions of a line of Wakandan ancestors across time? Something like that, it could consume a person. Could one's body, even the avatar's, hold the weight of all such memory, the intoxication of it? Would they not be poisoned?

"And what about the rest of our soldiers?" he found himself asking. "What of *their* memories? What will they say when it's only me who's restored?"

"Exactly!" M'Baku chimed in. "Besides, us Maroons already have a plan after months of deliberation. The Jengu's scale. The Vibranium. It's all right here for us now. If we can just get to the Imperial Archive—"

"No," spat Bast. "Your plan is folly! The emperor *knows* now that you're coming. Did you think you could simply kidnap a chief architect and no one would know?" She scoffed. "Luckily, I've come to rescue you from your own madness."

M'Baku was about to offer a retort when Achebe put a hand on his arm.

"She's right," he said. "It's a trap."

M'Baku retreated gruffly. T'Challa understood his ire but realized Achebe was right: It made no sense to risk all of the Maroon forces in a battle against the Empire when they could simply make good use of fewer tools, all of which they had right here, right now: Bast, T'Challa, and the last living Jengu.

The goddess, the avatar, and the conduit.

"It won't be only you," Nakia whispered to T'Challa. Tears brimmed in her eyes—he couldn't tell if they were of joy or sadness. "You're simply the *start* of the restoration, not the ending."

"I don't trust you, child," said M'Baku, turning to Bast. "But fine, tell us what T'Challa needs to do."

The goddess eyed him, then opted not to respond. To T'Challa, she said: "When you are restored and have received your own memories, *then* you may beseech the keepers of the Djalia to help restore your people. Everyone, one by one, back to who they always were. Only *then* may the fight begin."

"And how will you get him into the Djalia?" M'Baku pressed.

In response, Bast shut her eyes. As soon as she did, the rock marking the entry to the Jengu's abode stirred. Everyone stepped back as dust and debris fell.

Then Bast opened her eyes, and the rock split in half and opened like an eye, one half parting from the other. On the other side, behind a transparent membrane made of a hardened, resin-like material that kept the water on the opposite side from spilling into the cavern, was the last living Ancient Jengu.

She was seven times the size of the largest person there, a mass of tentacles and a jaw that stretched past the length of two people. She was a fish—all torpedo-shaped, fusiform body, covered in scales—that was not a fish at all: In lieu of dorsal, pelvic, or tail fins, she sported tentacles of all kinds. On any other day, she had a visage not so different from Farouk or Jafari or N'Yami, and T'Challa could see it now—how she and her forebears became the forerunners of the Teku-Maza.

One glowing, inquisitive eye in the front of the Jengu's head peeked through the membrane and regarded the group before her. Once she'd deduced them to be allies, she opened the other glowing, inquisitive eye. Two palms—five-fingered, skeletal, elongated, with fingernails as large as whole human hands and as sharp as any Wakandan spear—came forth and pressed against the membrane. The Jengu leaned closer, took Bast and T'Challa into her sights, and let out a moan of approval that sent an army of bubbles crashing into the membrane.

Her call reverberated throughout the cavern, echoing far into the hollows. The mollusks chittered in response, the insects buzzed about with much fervor. Farouk, behind them, dropped to his knees, in supplication or gratification or relief, one couldn't tell. But one thing was sure: This land, this planet, belonged to the Jengu and her forebears, and everything that lived and moved in it went through her.

And if all went right, so would T'Challa and the future of the Maroons.

T'Challa let Bast take his hand and lead him forward, approaching the Jengu. He was afraid but didn't let fear cloud his judgment. This was what he had to do. If he was to be free—if *everyone* was to be free—this was his task to bear.

"I don't know about this," he heard Nakia whisper to Farouk and M'Baku behind him.

I don't know about this, either, T'Challa thought. But that was okay. It would not have been his preferred option, but as it turned out, everything hinged on this. It all boiled down, in the end, to memory.

The Jengu placed its massive, five-fingered palm on the membrane. Bast reciprocated, placing her own palm up on their side. She looked to T'Challa and nodded, urging him to do the same.

T'Challa inhaled, put his palm on the membrane, and ascended into the Djalia.

CHAPTER 42

△▽△▽

THE
PLANE OF WAKANDAN MEMORY

ASCENSION WAS A RUSH, a yank, like being flung out of one's body, upward. T'Challa felt his face being pulled off of his skull, his nose and jaws and mouth hanging open, wind rushing through them. He screamed but had no voice. It was like passing through a spiritual space fold—there was no corporeality, no feeling in his fingers and toes. His mind was here, but his body was not.

And through this mind ran a multitude of images, so fast that he couldn't see any of them long enough to understand. A few lasted just long enough for him to make them out, to remember:

Kings, queens, warriors of Wakanda.

Many panthers, many foes. Many N'Jadakas.
A man called Ulysses . . . Klaw? A woman called . . . Shuri?

A queen mother . . . ?

T'Challa opened his eyes. *Ramonda.*

The woman sitting next to him was white-haired, but she was not his white-haired woman. She was much older, more regal, straight-backed as she sat meditating. Her hair was braided impeccably and tied up behind her in a mass. She was staring forward, ahead, not paying him any mind.

Before them—and around them—was an ancient, dust-laden desert that spread out in all directions for ages and ages. Surrounding their small corner of this world were mountains, tall and stately, carved by astute hands into building-shaped things that cast long, soft shadows. The sky was a fiery orange, but there was no sun. It was stupendously bright, though T'Challa found he didn't need to squint.

It was a place filled with mundanity, yet it defied all definition, all imagination. It was the Plane of Wakandan Memory.

And in this place, T'Challa remembered.

"MOTHER," HE SAID, when he spoke finally, "I remember."

The woman beside him didn't register movement when she said: "Yes, child. I know." There was no breath from her lips, no perceptible shift from the body that spoke. She was an apparition, T'Challa realized, recognizing the sheen that covered her. It was akin to speaking to a holo, except she was not a projection. She was real, and she was *here*. A memory come to life.

"You remember," she said, "because the Djalia never forgets."

"And how could we, my son?" another voice said from behind them. T'Challa, startled, turned around.

A man stood behind them. He wore a headdress, a lengthy cape, and carried a staff of office. *Royalty,* T'Challa mused, though he could not quite remember who this man was—he must've been before his time.

"To forget you would be to forget ourselves," the man said. "And there is weight in that incarnation. As the duke of Adowa, I bore it for my people."

"Then you know there is no singular *me*," said T'Challa, now understanding who he was, how he came to be. "There never was, there never will be. I may be a king, but I am also a nation incarnate."

"Indeed," said the duke. "Indeed, indeed, indeed."

Queen Ramonda rose now, turned to T'Challa, and placed a hand on his cheek. If felt full of light, soft and warm.

"This troubles you, my son?" she asked. "Being incarnate?"

T'Challa nodded. "I have lived, for long, in the shadows of my ancestors." The titles, from the world before, Wakanda Prime, came to him afresh: *T'Chaka's heir. Ramonda's son. N'Yami's blood.* These were the *real* people from whom the intergalactic Wakandans had taken their names. And these were *his* people, in whose shadows he'd lived—as an intergalactic Maroon, but also as king in Wakanda Prime.

The duke was standing at a nearby mountain opening, pointing into the darkness within. A doorway. The sheen around him lit up the framed edges.

"It begins here, doesn't it?" he said. "With your mother?"

T'Challa followed him into the darkness, and suddenly they were no longer standing in the Djalia. They were in a laboratory, something that seemed like it was from eons ago. The technology, for one, was a far cry from what the Intergalactic Empire had now. Even the Maroons sported much better tech and architecture than this. But it was a solid laboratory nonetheless, with the right hardware, storage, mapping, the likes. There was notably no holo tech. This was *way* back.

At the controls stood a young woman, dressed like a royal. Her hair was braided and held up similarly to the Queen Ramonda he'd just met, except hers was much more stylish and she was dark haired. She smiled at the controls, not paying attention to the two visitors who'd just walked into her lab.

By Bast, thought T'Challa. *She was beautiful.*

Much had been said about his mother, T'Challa remembered now, told to him in bits by one person or the other, family or friends or those who'd worked with her. From these he had cobbled together an idea of who his mother was—kind, patient, caring, warm—but had never quite gotten to know her himself. She'd died as he was born, and all he'd ever seen of her were images and recordings.

Standing here, though, looking upon her, something choked in his throat, and he said her name: *N'Yami. Mother.*

"I did not know her," he said aloud to the duke.

"Yes," said the duke. "Alas. But you knew her work."

Indeed he did. Now that he remembered, he remembered *everything*.

"She loved the stars," he said, running his fingers over a model rocket in the lab. "It was her dream to go journeying among them." He picked up the model, surprised that he could, and surprised that N'Yami didn't notice. Perhaps it made sense: This wasn't quite the memory in itself, after all, but a reassembly of one. The Djalia, as a whole, was a re-creation, a copy of the actual memories. An archive of what once was.

"It was not just *our* stars that she loved, my king," said the duke. "But those far beyond our galaxy. Wherever the universe stretched, she wanted to go."

He realized, now, why the N'Yami of the Teku-Maza had taken his mother's name. They were alike in that respect: kind, patient, tough, intelligent, imaginative. Now he wished he could've spent more time with the Teku-Maza woman. Perhaps that would've given him more insight into his own mother.

"She was wondrous," T'Challa found himself saying. "A brilliant woman with her own fantastic dreams." He put down the model rocket. "But all of those dreams were dashed . . . because of me."

"Dashed?" asked the duke. "Or is it that those dreams lived on, as all our dreams live on in our children?"

They were no longer standing in the lab but were now in a throne room of sorts that also doubled as a control center. Standing at the panel were two people—a young woman, dressed in full Wakanda Prime royal regalia—headdress, jewelry, tassels, facial markings. Beside her stood a young man in a panther suit, sans helmet. They were in the middle of an argument, which T'Challa couldn't hear because they were too far away.

Then the man turned around. It was T'Challa.

△▽△▽

"I KNOW YOU don't agree, sister," said T'Challa. "And I understand why. But they will never stop, Shuri."

Shuri folded her hands, turned up her lips.

"This time, it was Ulysses Klaw and that experimental metal, Reverbium," he pressed. "Before that, it was the Desturi." The group, clinging so tightly to Wakandan tradition that they turned it to terror, was a thorn that continued to plague the Crown.

"Yes, yes," said Shuri. "You keep saying it: *Vibranium—our greatest strength, our greatest weakness*. But, T'Challa, after the Desturi, you diversified Wakanda's wealth. Wakanda's future no longer hinges on the Great Mound." She sighed. "We no longer have to *know* what the Mena Ngai is or where it comes from. That was N'Yami's obsession. Perhaps it is time to let it rest with her."

T'Challa shook his head. "If only it were that simple. The Great Mound is just the beginning, sister. *We* can live without the gift of Vibranium. But we cannot live with it in our enemies' hands!"

THE DUKE HAD been replaced.

He was no longer the man dressed in royal regalia but was now a maiden of slight frame and much humbler comportment. Her headwrap was modest, as was her jewelry. She didn't regard T'Challa with the same historian air as the duke had, but with one of guidance and nurturance, like the first image of Queen Ramonda had.

T'Challa racked his newfound memories, trying to pinpoint who she was. Recognition arrived slowly.

Queen Sologon of Wakanda. Foremother. Ancestor.

"I know what you are thinking," she said. "That you were right to have those instincts, to push back against your sister. And perhaps you were. N'Yami, after all, had the same instincts."

She took T'Challa's shoulder and guided him forward. They

had been yanked out of the throne room and into the clouds, sailing together, stars twinkling above and around them.

"The mothers of the nation always know, Damisa-Sarki," said Sologon. "And your mother, she was no idle explorer. She *knew* there was more out there."

Damisa-Sarki. Another name for me, T'Challa remembered, *and other kings who have come before.* It was the Wakandan word, he remembered now, for *panther.*

"The stars she sought," said T'Challa, "she was looking for the source of the gift, wasn't she? She was thinking like I did, that Wakanda's enemies would someday look, too? Tell me I'm right, Queen Sologon. Tell me she thought the same."

Sologon nodded slowly. "Indeed. So many empires have fallen, have crumbled under the egos of men." She shook her head. "But not Wakanda. Not under you, Damisa-Sarki. Because you have indeed heeded your mother's warnings. And you did invest in seeing her mission through."

The clouds before them were beginning to part, revealing a scene below. T'Challa and Sologon sailed forward together and touched down softly into the scene.

THE ALPHA DETACHMENT was ready. Wakanda's first ever interstellar space crew, carrying the dreams of the nation, its history and future, on their shoulders.

Before them stood their king and chief panther, T'Challa, offering instructions and a final speech of farewell.

"We can't be sure exactly what's out there and what isn't," he said. "But our cosmic dating shows the Vibranium meteor that became the Great Mound originating from here, in the Vega System."

He was pointing to a nearby system, few enough light-years away from Earth that the flight could make it there and back before they had gained a few Earth years.

"Long-distance scans show no large-scale deposits. But the dating is sound." He sighed, long and hard. "My fellow Wakandans, you are our hope now. We need you."

NOT LONG AFTER the Alpha detachment left, all trace of them disappeared. Communications were lost midway through the Milky Way system. Months after, and still nothing.

T'Challa, every night, tossed and turned, unable to sleep, as he thought about his people floating through space, unmoored, untethered. He'd sent them to their deaths and now even their bodies couldn't be brought home. What would he tell their families? What would be his excuse?

Why did you not go with them? they would ask. *Why did you leave them to die?*

A hand reached over in bed and touched T'Challa's shoulder, turning him over to face the bearer.

It was the white-haired woman. His partner, his confidant, his support system.

Her name was Ororo. Ororo Munroe. Ororo Iqadi T'Challa. Queen of Wakanda.

"It should have been me out there, Ororo," he was saying to her. "I don't know what happened to them, but if I'd gone with them, I could have saved them. I could have gotten them back home."

Ororo adjusted her head to nestle softly in the pillow. "What are you doing, T'Challa?"

"Protecting my country."

"Hmmm." She placed a hand on his cheek, massaged it with a thumb. "Are you sure that is all you're doing? Are you sure you're not *running*?"

This shook T'Challa. He retreated into his pillow, cowering. What exactly could he be running from? Even he knew the question had merit but struggled to pinpoint what the true source of his fears was.

That he was not *great enough* and that he would never be? That he would never live up to the names and titles of his forebears? That he would forever remain the king who could not achieve the dreams of his mother, Wakanda's greatest visionary? That he would forever remain the king who'd sent a detachment of Wakandans to die in space?

Was this to be his legacy? Was he going to run away from this possibility, chasing and chasing after this missing Alpha flight until he found them? Was he never going to return until he did so?

"Listen," Ororo was saying, trying to read his expressions. "Promise me you'll come back home. Promise you'll come back to me."

Her arms and words enclosed him in a warm cocoon. T'Challa tucked his head into her embrace and whispered back his promise.

HE TOOK ONLY one person with him: a young man called Eden Fesi.

He was a man from another place, a warrior from beyond Wakanda who'd once been believed to be dead until his near lifeless body ended up in Wakanda. There he was restored to full health by the healing powers of the Heart-Shaped Herb and the technological powers of the nation. Thereafter, he swore his allegiance to T'Challa and the nation, joining in battle against anti-Wakandan forces locally and globally, from revolts within the nation to attacks from foreign entities. His teleportation skills were of significant use, as he could simply teleport T'Challa and his forces to specific locations behind enemy lines.

T'Challa took him because he was the only one who was skilled in combat, could fly a long-distance craft, and could teleport them out of trouble. He refused to take anyone else—he didn't want to put more Wakandans in danger. Eden agreed to go for the same reason that he had sworn himself to aiding T'Challa—because the nation had saved his life, and he owed it to them.

They took the Royal Talon Fighter and followed the exact

pathway as the Alpha flight. The details of the trip were hazy, but T'Challa remembered it being long and lonely, just him and Eden and the inky blackness of space. They sang songs and told stories to keep themselves sane, but otherwise remained on course. When T'Challa slept, all he dreamed of were Ororo's words: *Come back to me.*

And in his sleep, he whispered back: *I will.*

One day, the readings went awry. Everything looked fine—the ship was fine, the pathway was fine, everything was great. But there was an anomaly in the waves, and it didn't take long for them to look out and see what it was.

"Is that—" Eden, sitting in the pilot seat, leaned forward to look out the window with his own eyes. "What is *that*?"

It looked like a hole. Or, more correctly, a *portal*. Something to pass through, like a gate. A *galactic gate.*

"You think they went through it?" asked Eden.

It was right in the middle of their course. To go around it would mean leaving the pathway entirely. They were Wakandans, they were brave. To T'Challa's thinking, there was only one thing they would do.

And that was the *exact* same thing he was going to do.

"Through," he said to Eden.

His companion looked up, into his face. "Are you sure about that?" He looked back to the screens. "This doesn't look good. Maybe we bail?"

"Through," T'Challa repeated, adamant. "No matter where it leads."

"WELCOME, TRAVELER."

The galaxy was inky black, all streaks and stars and nothingness. It suffocated, coddled, drowned. It was dread personified, a darkness that plagued and gave no assurances. And it was through this darkness that T'Challa heard that voice.

He tried to open his eyes, but all he could see was Ororo's face in the darkness, saying: *Come back to me.*

"Greetings," came the voice again. "Voyager."

He forced open his eyes, and this time, painful white light shot through. And it wasn't just pain in his eyes, but in his bones, in his teeth. He tried to turn, see the source of the voice, but his joints wouldn't work. He was propped up in a semi-sitting, semi-lying position in a reclined bed.

A *hospital* bed, he realized.

Slowly, it all came back to him. Shooting through the galactic gate, stellar engines turned on. Being sucked into a dark tunnel, pulled at a speed too fast to comprehend, time and space bending beyond what their minds could take. They screamed, he and Eden, their brains feeling like they would explode. The ship groaned, all systems shutting down, some shorting, some exploding. Then, they were falling, falling, falling.

He didn't remember the moment when they crashed. His mind had already left his body by then.

Immediately, he wondered: *Where is Eden? Is he still alive?* He didn't even ask the more important question, which was: *Where is this? Where am I?*

"Greetings, voyager," the voice from before repeated, and then its owner came into view.

He was a young man, well-built—like a warrior. Broad-faced, broad-jawed, good-looking. He was every bit a Wakandan, from the clothes to the hairstyle to the cultural affects, all with a royal flair and stately visage. He was smiling, warm and welcoming.

But something was strange about this, because absolutely nothing about this felt Wakandan. It felt like a parody of it, a copy, a foreign assemblage. And T'Challa found his hunch proven when the man before him said:

"As emperor of Wakanda, it is my pleasure to welcome you to my home."

CHAPTER 43

△▽△▽

THE
JENGU'S LAIR

T'CHALLA EMERGED SOLEMNLY from the Djalia, still clutching Bast's hand. The goddess in the little girl's body squeezed his palm before letting go. He felt his feet touch solid ground, the feeling of floating dissipating. On the other side of the membrane, the Jengu, unperturbed, removed its palm from the surface.

Senses returned in a rush, and with them a flurry of feet. T'Challa turned around to find that those he'd left in the Jengu's lair were still there. Nakia, Eden, Achebe, Farouk, M'Baku—all had wide eyes and open mouths.

"That was . . ." Farouk started, trailing off.

"We don't know what that was," said Achebe.

"No," said Nakia, eyes shining with tears. "We *know* what that was." She stood, straight backed. "A king restored. Nameless no longer."

T'Challa looked to M'Baku, often the skeptic, and was surprised to find even his eyes brimming.

"Yes," M'Baku said. "*King.*"

"King T'Challa," Eden echoed. "True avatar of the goddess Bast."

T'Challa knew, now, why this title rang true in his bones, why its cadence was so familiar—because it *was* true. He *was* the king of Wakanda, or as these people called it, Ancient Wakanda.

And unlike everyone here, who bore a name borrowed from the Wakanda that he called home, T'Challa was indeed his true name: son of T'Chaka, husband to Ororo, protector of his people.

He had to find a way back, now more than ever. But he wouldn't repeat the same mistake. This time, before he left, he would ensure that those who remained here would be safe, especially if it was possible he could never return. The Intergalactic Empire could never be a threat again—not to the people of these five galaxies, and not to the people of his own faraway galaxy.

"N'Jadaka will be coming," said the goddess Bast, pointing to herself. "She is his daughter, after all. He will not relent."

"Let him come," said Eden. "The Empire has its king, we have ours."

"Not so fast," said Bast. "First, you must clarify what you want." To the group, she said: "You wish to restore memories? Well, here. You have the Jengu. One by one, you bring every Maroon to the Jengu. Let them touch this membrane, find out who they truly are, just as your king has done."

"Then what?" asked M'Baku. "We can't fight the Empire with memories."

"Oh, but you can," said Bast. "They will have no power over you! Only once you have reclaimed your memories can you attack them with abandon—the M'Kraan Shard, am I correct? Only then can it truly *sting*. Destroy all their archives, their ships, their technologies. Kill the infrastructure, kill the Empire."

"And then?" asked Nakia.

"And then you keep stinging until the Empire is dead."

"That . . . feels too simple," said Farouk, turning to T'Challa. "Is it this simple?"

Of course it wasn't that simple, but T'Challa understood what Bast was saying. Survival was a fickle and insufficient thing to fight for all on its own. What was to keep one fighting if one truly didn't know themselves? Give a person their history, their memories, echoes of the people they love and the things they lived for, and one could make a rebel out of *anyone*.

"It requires a leap of faith, of course," Bast said. "And alacrity. You must do this before the emperor finds this place. Because he *will* find this place." She turned to T'Challa. "Rest assured, my avatar will be with you all the way. Will you not?"

T'Challa nodded. After witnessing so much in the Djalia, he found that out here, words failed him. But his resolve, that was filled to the brim, and would remain so for as long as these memories existed.

"But remember," Bast continued, "his end goal is not the Empire, is it? His end goal is to go home."

All eyes turned to look at T'Challa. Under their gazes, guilt weighed on him. But it was true: As much as he'd help them fight this Empire, he would also begin working on a way to get home. And sure, he could see in their gazes that they were going to help him, but he could also see that they were just as sad about the prospect of him leaving as he was.

Nakia refused to catch his eyes when he directed his gaze toward her. He returned to the group.

"The first step is done," he announced, his tone taking on a royal air. "We will regroup and recover. We will reunite our people with their memories, even if we have to do so one by one. We will send this good message of recovery across the galaxies, to all captured in the Empire's choke hold. We will recruit, we will fortify—we will do all in our power to meet the Empire's power wherever it is. And, Bast willing, we will conquer. I, T'Challa, King of Wakanda and Avatar of Bast, Damisa-Sarki, the One Who Put the Knife Where It Belonged, have said it, and so shall it be."

Silence gripped the group. Then Eden stepped forward.

"My king!" He crossed his arms in the Wakandan salute. "Wakanda forever!"

Nakia, stepping forward, repeated the salute. "Wakanda forever."

M'Baku, Farouk, and Achebe stepped forward and saluted. "Wakanda forever!"

T'Challa glanced at Bast, who gave him an approving nod. He stepped forward, threw his arms across his chest, and saluted his people in return.

"Wakanda forever!"

BACK ON PLANET BAST, the Black Panther of the Intergalactic Empire of Wakanda sat in the throne room, battle ready in his full suit. About him roiled the power of the Klyntar symbiote, slashing and screeching at nothing, supercharged by the power of the gods they had swallowed and kept trapped. Trapped, just like the emperor himself felt.

His goddess had betrayed him. His most senior counselor had betrayed him. The boy he'd kept in his care, treated like a son, had betrayed him. They'd joined up with that heretic, T'Challa, and that forsaken underground rebellion, to bring about his demise. They'd blown up his imperial freighters and wiped out his forces on Agwé.

As if that wasn't enough, they'd kidnapped his daughter, the one precious thing he had in this life.

His symbiote lashed out wildly, knocking over random artifacts in the throne room. Oh, how he wanted to blow them all to pieces! Get on a ship of his own, zip out there, and fire the biggest warhead he had. But they had gambled well, unfortunately, keeping Zenzi on the ship to ensure that he couldn't do exactly that. So instead, he was forced to wait for their demands before deciding on a plan of action.

Never, as emperor, had he been made to wait. Not even by the gods. But here he was, waiting.

It was how he knew, now, that he had been wrong. Wrong to treat Eden like a son, to treat T'Challa like a simple heretic, sentencing him to Goree instead of death by execution. He should have executed both once they'd arrived on this planet. Or, perhaps, once he'd gained all the information he needed to become the most powerful emperor across the galaxies. He should've been more brutal, should've never let T'Challa disappear only to rise again, never given him the opportunity to collude with members of his own house. He had been soft, and therefore had been punished.

Never again.

The symbiote lashed out, wilder and wilder. N'Jadaka didn't care that T'Challa had regained his memories, had been restored as avatar of Bast. He had the power of a god and the power of a symbiote on his side. He had five galaxies. He would *crush* them.

But first: to get his daughter back. Then, to ensure T'Challa never found his way home, to the Wakanda that birthed him, to put an end, forever, to the One Who Put the Knife Where It Belonged.

△▽△▽

THE PLANE OF WAKANDAN MEMORY

COME BACK TO ME.

Many, many light-years away from the five galaxies of the Intergalactic Empire, a white-haired woman stands at a floor-to-ceiling window, staring out to space. The sky above is not the inky black of galaxies, and the land before her is not the rock and dirt and ice of abandoned planets. It is lush, productive land, cultivated with care and a depth of resources. The city within which she stands is built to be the best, on par with the furthest of technological advancements. The architecture, infrastructure, the very essence of the place and people, is at its height. It is a shining nation on a hill, a beacon of hope and futures. It is the land of the free, the home of the brave, the epitome of all that is good and blessed.

They don't call it *Wakanda Prime* for no reason.

You must know by now, traveler, that she is Ororo, queen of Wakanda Prime. She wonders if her husband will ever be back, if he is still alive; and that if he is, and will return, if he will be the same man he was when he left (and she is right to wonder, because he will *never* be the same again). What she does not know, as she stands here in wait, is that the biggest battle the galaxies have ever seen is about to begin, and the Black Panther will be at the center of it.

Centuries of light-years away from where she stands, across the galactic gate, her husband, T'Challa, the Black Panther and king of Wakanda Prime, is holding hands with me, the goddess Bast, in the form of the daughter of an intergalactic emperor. We are locked in a telepathic triangle with the last living giant of an ancient amphibian species. And within that telepathic triangle, T'Challa has found his way into the Plane of Wakandan Memory, this very same place in which I now narrate these events to you, dear traveler. And it is in this plane that he has finally remembered, and will finally understand how to find his way back, and how to defeat the Intergalactic Empire that has formed from the unfortunate events of his Alpha flight.

But time moves differently in these disparate parts, and so in the short moment that Ororo stands there, T'Challa, in the half-second he spends traversing this Wakandan plane, will remember the first years after his arrival in the intergalactic throneworld of Planet Bast.

He never saw Eden again. After T'Challa had finally recuperated, the emperor—who had named himself N'Jadaka, after the infamous Wakandan warrior—finally showed T'Challa where he was—the Intergalactic Empire of Wakanda, founded two thousand intergalactic years ago, by the very same Alpha flight mission from Wakanda Prime.

It was glorious! The dream of his mother fulfilled—all the Wakandan science, ethics, an entire way of life, all touching whole star systems. It was Wakanda *unbound, amplified, augmented, evolved.* And perhaps that was the problem.

Under these same ethics, the ones the ancestors—the original Alpha flight—had set up, the Empire and the emperor had *enslaved* whole galaxies, *cleansed* them of their original inhabitants and their cultures in order to instill this so-called Wakandan ethic. Invested so much in seeking Vibranium, at the cost of thousands and millions of lives. Building on the stories and adventures of the heroes of Wakanda Prime, transforming them into myth, and using that to develop their bellicose Empire.

T'Challa saw all this and felt a bone-deep sadness. He knew immediately that this was not what his mother would've wanted, this ethic of self-defense converted into an ethic of *conquest*. Two thousand years of *intergalactic crime* was not what he'd dreamed of when he sent out the Alpha flight.

He tried first to gather allies to help convince N'Jadaka, securing the trust of the emperor's court members. But when all else failed, he opted for the truth: revealing to the emperor his origins, explaining Wakanda Prime and the desires of the nation, and of the avatar of Bast. And perhaps that was the failure, his honesty—because N'Jadaka dreamed, too, of becoming my avatar.

Once N'Jadaka finally gained access to me, through T'Challa, he struck.

T'Challa lost it all then. But now, as he holds hands with me and the Jengu, and holds hands with his ancestors in the Plane of Wakandan Memory, he is finding his way back in mind and spirit. Soon, eventually, he will find his way back to Wakanda Prime.

Ororo is right to stand there and wish.

"Come back to me, T'Challa," she whispers into space, and her words carry across galaxies.

ACKNOWLEDGMENTS

—My agent, TAMARA KAWAR: for holding down the fort and keeping me honest in this writing biz, especially when it feels, always, like I'm reeling. Further thanks to all the good folks at DeFiore & Company.

—GABRIELLA MUÑOZ, editor extraordinaire at the Random House Worlds team. Rarely have I met an editor who's such an enthusiastic reader. Keep shining (and keep vibing for N'Jadaka).

—ELIZABETH SCHAFER and the entire editorial team at Random House Worlds: always a pleasure working with you folks! The PR team (David Moench and Ada Maduka) and production (particularly copy editor Clarence A. Haynes): Thank you for your invaluable work.

—THE MARVEL TEAM: Sarah Singer, Jeffery Youngquist, Jeremy West, Sven Larsen, and Wil Moss. Thanks for serving as an invaluable well of *Black Panther* knowledge, and keeping this often-too-excited author from straying too far from canon.

—TA-NEHISI COATES: for writing this comic; for standing on business in this work and the full body of your work, practice, and principles. May you continue to be a shining light in dark times.

—DANIEL ACUÑA: for crafting the exquisite, excellent art that brought this story to life in the comic.

—CHADWICK BOSEMAN: for being a kind, gracious, intelligent human dedicated to the work you did; for being unashamedly and unapologetically Black; for playing the world's most visible Black superhero export with a regal grace that showed your own investment in the cultural moment and legacy of the Black Panther. Rest in Power, King.

—To every Black reader out there, always craving one more story in which we can see ourselves: Bring it! *What?* We right here. We're not going anywhere.

ABOUT THE AUTHOR

△▽△▽

SUYI DAVIES OKUNGBOWA is an award-winning author of fantasy, science fiction, and general speculative work. He has published various novels, the latest of which are *Warrior of the Wind* and *Son of the Storm*—both of The Nameless Republic epic fantasy trilogy—and the science fiction book *Lost Ark Dreaming*. His debut novel, *David Mogo, Godhunter,* won the 2020 Nommo Award for Best Novel. His shorter works have appeared in various periodicals and anthologies and have been nominated for various awards. He earned his MFA in creative writing from the University of Arizona, and lives in Ontario, where he is a professor of creative writing at the University of Ottawa. You can find him online @suyidavies everywhere, or via his newsletter, SuyiAfterFive.com.